Daniel Wilson

# Chatterton

A Biographical Study

Daniel Wilson

**Chatterton**
*A Biographical Study*

ISBN/EAN: 9783337010072

Printed in Europe, USA, Canada, Australia, Japan

Cover: Foto ©Raphael Reischuk / pixelio.de

More available books at **www.hansebooks.com**

# CHATTERTON:

## A BIOGRAPHICAL STUDY.

BY DANIEL WILSON, LL.D.

PROFESSOR OF HISTORY AND ENGLISH IN UNIVERSITY COLLEGE, TORONTO.

"And we at sober eve would round thee throng,
Hanging, enraptured, on thy stately song;
And greet with smiles the young-eyed Poesy,
All deftly mask'd, as hoar Antiquity."
                                        COLERIDGE.

London:

MACMILLAN AND CO.

1869.

IN LOVING TOKEN

OF ENDURING FRIENDSHIP AND IN ADMIRATION OF HIS GENIUS

THIS VOLUME

**Is Dedicated**

TO

# SIR GEORGE HARVEY, KT., F. R. S. E.

PRESIDENT OF THE ROYAL SCOTTISH ACADEMY,

BY HIS OLD FRIEND

## THE AUTHOR.

# CONTENTS.

## CHAPTER VII.



## CHAPTER VIII.



## CHAPTER IX.



## CHAPTER X.



## CHAPTER XI.



## CHAPTER XII.



## CHAPTER XIII.



## CHAPTER XIV.



## CHAPTER XV.

# PREFACE.

"Nobody," says Johnson, "can write the life of a man, but one who has eat and drunk, and lived in social intercourse with him." The time, therefore, is past for writing a true life of Chatterton; for on the 24th of August, 1870, a century will have elapsed since his brief career ended in despair. But it is not too late, but rather, perhaps, a fitting time, for an appeal against the judgment pronounced on him by interested or vindictive contemporaries. Did I not believe that the boy-poet has been misjudged, and that the biographies hitherto written of him are not only imperfect but untrue, I should not now produce this study of a life which has long been to myself a subject of interest.

The first editions of Chatterton's works were not only very defective, but their editors proceeded on the assumption that he was not the author. The earliest edition with any pretension to completeness is that of Southey and Cottle; but to all appearance the former contributed little more than the preface. Writing to his co-editor in August 1802, Southey says: "Well done, good and faithful editor. I suspect that it is fortunate for the edition of Chatterton that its care has devolved upon you." He had previously said of Dr. Gregory's life of the poet: "It is a bad work. Coleridge should write a new one; or, if he declines it, let it devolve on me." Nevertheless the co-editor had to prefix this condemned work to their collection of the poet's writings. If generous kindliness of heart could have sufficed for all editorial *zine*, *Middlesex Journal*, and other periodicals; while valuable, though undigested materials collected at an early date, by Mr. George Cumberland, from the poet's contemporaries and personal friends, are printed in an appendix, in all their original disarray.

Professor Masson's "Chatterton: a Story of the Year 1770," is a very different production. Graphic and vigorous, though slight: it transmutes Dix's raw materials into a life-like picture of the boy, surrounded by the life of his time; and shows that had its author devoted himself to a careful biography, instead of a magazine article, there would have been little need for repeating the story of a life, the interest of which can never die. But while his appreciation of the poet's genius is adequate, and his estimation of his writings discriminating and just: he has, I conceive, accepted too readily the verdict of interested and prejudiced contemporaries on the personal character of the boy.

This critical judgment of Professor Masson might have been expected to prepare the way for a juster estimation of the poet. But he was followed almost immediately by Dr. Maitland, with his "Chatterton: an Essay," in which all the calumny of former traducers is reiterated with keener intensity than ever: "An owl mangling a poor dead nightingale," as Coleridge said of the earlier stupidities of Dean Milles.

The personal character of the poet has thus been reproduced once more in so offensive an aspect as to repel the ordinary reader from poems, already rendered sufficiently unattractive by their uncouth disguise. If this be indeed the true portrait, there is no help for it. But, with the exception of Sir Herbert Croft's strange medley of "Love and Madness," published within a few years after Chatterton's death, and containing more graphic glimpses of the boy than all subsequent writers have supplied: the aim of most of those to whom we owe any direct information, has been to prove that he was not the poet, but only the more or less culpable resetter and defacer of stolen literary treasures. Viewed through so distorting a medium, those most honestly inclined could scarcely avoid misrepresentation; and later biographers, when favourably disposed, have expended their zeal in asserting his right to the merit of his own works; while they assume, at best, an apologetic tone in dealing with aspersions based mainly on the injustice they have refuted.

Reviewed in this light, I have found much in the old materials capable of being turned to new account; and to these research in various directions has enabled me to make some few additions. For access to the Chatterton MSS. still preserved in Bristol, and to other materials bearing on the poet's life and times; as well as for aid in all questions of local topography: I have been largely indebted to the courtesy of John Taylor, Esq., of the Bristol Library; by whom also my attention was first directed to the will of Derrick, as the suggestive source of that of Chatterton.

In interpreting the biographical significance of the "Will" as well as of the Walpole "Vindication," and other documents familiar to previous biographers, it will be seen that I have arrived at conclusions differing from those generally maintained hitherto, and more in accordance with what I conceive to be their true bearing on the poet's life. "Nothing extenuate," was the rule with Chatterton's earliest editors and biographers; but they generally forgot the further precept: "nor set down aught in malice;" and assuredly the latest of these, in his "Chatterton: an Essay," has extenuated nothing that seemed calculated to deepen the shadows of the repulsive portraiture he aimed at. While dealing tenderly, I have sought to deal truthfully with the failings as well as the virtues of the boy: bearing always in remembrance, what it seems to me has too frequently been lost sight of, that he was but a boy;—a boy, and yet a poet of rare power. These results of careful study and research are now submitted to the reader, not without the hope that a like spirit may animate him in the perusal of the following appeal for a reconsideration of the verdict on a life, wayward and erring :

> " Swift as a shadow, short as any dream,
>   Brief as the lightning in the collied night ; "

a record, at best, of " bright things come to confusion ; " yet also of a life replete with genius, and not devoid of genuine traits of personal worth.

UNIVERSITY COLLEGE, TORONTO,
    *Oct.* 14*th*, 1869.

# INTRODUCTION.

> " Saw all the scroll of Fate unravelled ;
> And when the fate-marked babe acome to syghte,
> I saw hym eager gaspynge after lyghte."
> *The Storie of William Canynge.*





THE reader is invited in the following chapters to study the life of a posthumous child, the son of a poor widow, educated at a charity school, and buried in a pauper's grave when he was but seventeen.



Virtuous men have shrunk from disentangling the ravelled skein of the boy's life : for his modern satires are formed on the models of Churchill, the clerical satirist of an age which had Wilkes for its hero ; and his masterpieces are obscured, almost to repulsiveness, by an affectation of antiquity.  Good men long refused his monument admission to consecrated ground : for he died an unbeliever, and by his own hand.  Nevertheless his little fragment of a life is replete with instruction as well as warning ; and as for a monument, he built his own, and asserts his claim to no mean rank among the second generation of the poets of the eighteenth century.



If all who lived in some of the years of Chatterton's brief lifetime are included, he had for contemporaries : Young, Collins, Akenside, Gray, Smollett, and Mason ; Goldsmith, Johnson, Burns, and Cowper.  Some of them were authors before he was born, and continued their labours long after his death.  If the reader—not wholly forgetful of what he himself was at seventeen,—turn to the lives of the best of those contemporaries, and see

what Hazlitt has to say of Smollett ; Boswell of Johnson ;
Forster of Goldsmith ; Southey or Grimshaw of Cowper ;
Cunningham, Chambers, or other biographers, of Burns ;
up to their eighteenth year : he will be better able to
estimate a career which then came to its close.   For he
will be able to answer for himself these questions : What
life did they lead? what faith did the best of them
hold? what work had the most gifted of them done, at
seventeen ?



At every step it is needful to recall this fact of boyhood, apart from every other adverse element of orphanage, poverty, and misguidance.   For the study is that of
a child, a boy, a youth, running counter to all the tastes
and habits of his age ; acting in defiance of ordinary
influences ; at every stage doing a man's work : often
unwisely, perversely, unaccountably ; but still doing the
work of a man, and baffling the astute selfishness of
men, while yet a child.



Viewed in its most unfavourable aspects, such an
intellectual phenomenon may well attract our study, as a
strange example of precocity, approximating almost to
genius acting by instinct : like those manifestations of
irrational vital action, which puzzle us by their resemblance to the highest intelligence.   But the brief existence here retraced has also its phases of sorrowful, and
even tragic interest, on which we now look back as on
a precious inheritance which that eighteenth century
wasted and flung aside.

# CHATTERTON.

## CHAPTER I.

### THE CHATTERTONS.



AMONG the memorials of early wealth and piety in the ancient city and seaport of Bristol, the church of St. Mary Redcliffe attracts an interest far beyond its walls from the novel and enduring associations which have gathered around it in modern times. The office of sexton of St. Mary's had been transmitted for nearly two centuries in the same family; while other members of it had laboured in the maintenance and repair of the venerable fabric. In the parish registers for 1661, and subsequent years, the name of Thomas Chatterton, freemason, repeatedly appears in connexion with payments for work done. A younger Thomas, probably his son, succeeds him on the same register in 1678 and following years, till 1723, when he is replaced by William Chatterton; while an entry on April 25th of that year—" paid Widow Chatterton her salary from Lady-day to the latter end of Easter week, 3*s.* 6*d.*"—shows that some humble situation was found for the widow of the former.[1]



John Chatterton, the last of the name who inherited the office of sexton, "a worthy but singular man," died

[1] Pryce's Canynges' Family, pp. 276, 277.

B

in 1748, after fulfilling its duties for twenty-three years; and appears to have been succeeded, after some brief interval, by his son-in-law, Richard Phillips. Some confusion pervades the references to the connexion of the poet who has conferred celebrity on the name, with this old line of sextons. Thomas Chatterton, his father, is confounded by early biographers and critics with the last



sexton. Dr. Gregory calls him the nephew of the latter; while Mr. Dix, though probably meaning to repeat the statement, has left it so ambiguous, that Mr. George Pryce in following him, in his "Canynges' Family and their Times," makes the sexton uncle of the poet himself. A document printed on a subsequent page serves, at least, to show that this cannot be right.[1] In 1772, William, son of John Chatterton, the sexton, petitions the parish vestry for that appointment, in anticipation of his "brother-in-law, Richard Phillips," the poet's favourite uncle, obtaining that of parish clerk. I presume Mrs. Phillips to have been his father's sister; in which case the old sexton must have been the poet's grandfather; while she herself was the last of the Chattertons to occupy the hereditary sextonship. When, long subsequent to the poet's death, Mr. George Cumberland pursued his inquiries regarding him, he found the widow of Richard Phillips in the office, and a Mr. Perrin, of Colston's Parade, acting as her deputy.



Such a hereditary tenure of the humbler offices of the Church was not without precedent in ancient times; and the register of the muniment room of Redcliffe Church preserved materials for the history of its old line of sextons, till its coffers were invaded and their contents dispersed. Yet even now curious traces of its hereditary

[1] *Vide* Pryce, pp. 277, 299. Dix's words are—"Chatterton's father never was sexton of Redcliffe Church; his uncle, John Chatterton, having been the last of the family who held that office." P. 2. An anecdote communicated to Mr. Cottle by "a gentleman of Bristol who, when a boy, was present," though confounding the sexton and the poet's father, is presumably reliable in referring to the former as an old man. (*Vide* Southey's Ed. Chatterton's Works, vol. iii. p. 496.)

sextonship might reward the diligence of a Bristol antiquary: if only in its contrast to the imaginary descent
from Sire de Chasteautonne, of the house of Rollo, the
first Duke of Normandy, and Eveligina of Ghent; of
which the materials, executed with all suitable heraldic
blazonry by Chatterton's own hand, are preserved in the
British Museum.

The poet's father is the first of the Chattertons who
aspired beyond the humble rank of his fathers, and
attained to a position requiring some education, as
well as natural ability. After filling for a time a subordinate office in a classical school, he received the
appointment of sub-chaunter of Bristol Cathedral, and
the mastership of the Pyle Street Free School, on the
north side of Redcliffe Church, where, in 1752, his
son was born. The genius which the boy manifested,
almost from infancy, was of so rare and exceptional a
nature, that little importance can attach to any traces
of its hereditary development. Nevertheless, a just
interest pertains even to the slightest indications of
inherited genius, apart from the extrinsic influences
which Chatterton unquestionably derived through his
father.

In the muniment room of St. Mary's Church, on
Redcliffe Hill, Bristol, towards the middle of the
eighteenth century, lay accumulated from times when
the Wars of the Roses were current news of the day,
ancient parchments, deeds, and writings of diverse
kinds, secured for the most part in quaint oaken chests
or coffers, which have acquired an interest for all men
since the name of Chatterton won a place in English
letters. The hereditary race of sextons had doubtless
come to regard the church and all its accessories as their
own peculiar domain; and so, when a Chatterton became
master of the neighbouring Free School, he turned its
ancient parchments to account for his primers and copy-
books. Nor were the Chattertons without a direct
interest in those old documents; for among them, as
his daughter states, were family records of the race of

the sextons, carrying them back to the year 1630, if not earlier. "My father," writes Mrs. Newton, the poet's sister, "received the parchments in the year 1750. He discovered by some writings he found among them that persons of the name of Chadderdon were sextons of St. Mary Redclift parish, 120 years before. He therefore supposed that it was the same family; as his father had affirmed that the family had held that office, to use his own phrase, time out of mind."[1]



This inheritor of the family honours of the Chattertons manifested, as we have seen, a capacity for some higher vocation than the sextonship. He was, moreover, seemingly of an aspiring disposition. One of his pupils, Miss James (afterwards Mrs. Edkins), speaks of him as a man of talent, but negligent in his domestic relations; and adds: "All the family were proud."[2] He is described by more than one of his contemporaries as one possessed of somewhat varied abilities. He was fond of reading; in the constant habit of borrowing as well as lending books;[3] one "whose accomplishments were much above his station, and who was not totally destitute of a taste for poetry;"[4] a musical composer, and even a writer of verse.[5] But the only known composition ascribed to him is a catch for three voices, which celebrates above all other joys those of the Pine-apple: a Bristol tavern kept by one Golden, a bookbinder, where the convivial club for which the catch was composed was wont to assemble.



The impression left on the mind of Mr. Chatterton's pupil was not such as to justify regret at the orphanage of his gifted son. She described him, indeed, as a man of talent, but an unkind husband, of dissipated habits, and fond of low society; "a very brutal fellow, with a mouth so wide that he could put his clenched fist into it." The description, however, is probably exaggerated;

---

[1] Works of Chatterton, Southey's Ed. vol. iii. p. 525.
[2] Dix's Life, App. p. 310.
[3] Letter of E. Gardner, Works, iii. p. 523.
[4] Warton's Hist. of Eng. Poetry, vol. ii. p. 341.
[5] Works, iii. p. 495.

as Mrs. Edkins employs the same strong language when speaking of Mr. Lambert, to whom his son was subsequently bound apprentice : describing the irritated attorney as throwing his apprentice's MS. poems at him "with great brutality." A more favourable idea is conveyed in the description of one of his chief associates, a member of the Pine-apple Club. "My father," writes Mr. Edward Gardner, "was the very intimate acquaintance of old Mr. Chatterton, and was Mrs. Newton's godfather by proxy. The two old gentlemen were in constant habits of lending books to each other, for both were fond of reading. . . . Old C. was not a little inclined to a belief in magic, and was deeply read in Cornelius Agrippa. He was one of the singers in the cathedral, and a complete master of the theory and practice of music:"—to all appearance a clever, versatile, dissipated lover of song and good fellowship, for whom domestic life had no charms ; but of whom, also, all that is known reveals glimpses both of genius and an unwonted range of pursuits not greatly dissimilar to those of the son.[1] Among other rare tastes characteristic of both, he appears to have had a great love for antiquities. He had formed a collection of several hundred Roman coins, dug up in the neighbourhood of Bristol, which were subsequently acquired by Sir J. Smith of Ashton Court ; and his son, Sir John Hugh Smith, communicated to the historian of Bristol the circumstances of their discovery, as detailed in conversations with the elder Chatterton.[2]

The convivial habits ascribed to him were common enough in his age ; but his abilities and favourite pursuits appear to have been far above his associates, and accompanied by some eccentricities suggestive of inherited peculiarities of his posthumous child. An old female relative said of him : " He talked little, was very absent

---

[1] Mr. Gardner wrote in 1802, fifty years after the elder Chatterton's death. Associating him, therefore, with his recollection of his own father in later life, he speaks of " the two old gentlemen ;" whereas he died a young man.

[2] Barrett's History and Antiquities of the City of Bristol, note, p. 19.

in company, and used very often to walk by the river side, talking to himself, and flourishing his arms about."[1] Though far from loveable as husband or father, he was undoubtedly, in all intellectual characteristics, one who had a right to aspire to higher duties than those of the hereditary sextonship.

*The poet's mother. .*

The wife of the sub-chaunter, and mother of the poet, appears, on the whole, as a meek, long-suffering woman, of no shining abilities, but tenderly attached to her children. Though her daughter Mary was already in her second year, she was only entering on womanhood when left a widow, to learn the hardest lessons of adversity. It has hitherto escaped notice that she must have been married when a mere girl, and was just of age at the birth of her son. This is apparent from the inscriptions on the family tombstone in Redcliffe churchyard. She cannot have been more than eighteen, while her husband was double that age, at the time of their marriage.[2] She is described by Miss Day, afterwards Mrs. Stockwell,—one of her pupils, who resided for years under her roof,—as "kind and motherly;" though liable to sudden

*Flashes of temper.*

flashes of temper, "sharp but soon over;" or, as Molly Hayfield, an old servant of Mrs. Newton characterised her, "attery," a word used in the north of Scotland as

---

[1] Rev. Sir Herbert Croft's "Love and Madness." (Ed. 1786, p. 167.) This strange volume consists of a series of sentimental letters, professedly addressed by Mr. Hackman, a clergyman, formerly an officer in the 66th Regiment, to Miss Ray, an actress; to whom, though in every way unfit, he had made proposals of marriage. On being refused, he resolved to shoot himself in her presence; but, instead of carrying out his intention, he shot her on the 7th April, 1779, when leaving Covent Garden Theatre. The volume also includes replies ascribed to her. Hackman raves about Goethe's "Werther," love and suicide; and *à-propos* to this Chatterton is dragged in, along with a variety of French and English madmen and suicides. The association is offensive; but the idea stimulated the author to research, at a time when it was still possible to recover facts invaluable for the poet's biography.

[2] "Thos. Chatterton, schoolmaster, died 7th Aug. 1752, æt. 39. Sarah Chatterton, widow of the above, died 25th Dec. 1791, æt. 60. Mary Newton [the poet's sister], died 23d Feb. 1804, æt. 53."

equivalent to fretful. The young widow had cares enough to make her so. But the gentler elements evidently predominated ; and she is spoken of by her niece, Mrs. Stephens, as one of the best of women.[1]

Thomas Chatterton, the cathedral sub-chaunter, died on the 7th of August, 1752, leaving his widow and daughter seemingly without any provision for their maintenance, or for that of the old grandmother—widow, as I presume, of the last hereditary sexton of the name,—who resided under their roof. But the young widow established a girls' school; took in sewing and ornamental needlework ; and appears in an honest though humble way to have provided for her family. To this an important addition was soon to be made ; for on the 20th of November, 1752—upwards of three months after her husband's death,—a son was born ; and, on the first day of the new year, he was baptized at St. Mary's Redcliffe, by his father's name of Thomas.

Brief and strange was the career of the child thus sorrowfully ushered into the world. But that it was a remarkable one is apparent, when, now at the close of a century after that career abruptly terminated in seeming failure, the memory of the poor Bristol boy claims a larger share in the world's estimation than most other things pertaining to the ancient city of his birth. Thomas Chatterton was born, there can be little doubt, in a humble dwelling at the back of Pyle Street School-house, erected only three years before by a Bristol citizen as the residence of the master ; but which the widow had to quit soon after for her later residence and dame-school, opposite the Upper Gate, on Redcliffe Hill. The boy returned, in his fifth year, to Pyle Street School, as a pupil of Mr. Stephen Love.[2] But his faculties lay beyond reach of the routine system in vogue there ; and the

Chap. I.

Death of the sub-chaunter.

The poet's birthplace.

His first teacher.

---

[1] Notes of Mr. G. Cumberland, collected for Cromek. App. Dix's Life, pp. 299, 305, 307.

[2] The immediate successor of the elder Chatterton, as master of Pyle Street School, was Mr. Edmund Chard. He was succeeded, in 1757, by Mr. Love.

impatient teacher remanded him to his mother as an incorrigible dunce. Wayward, as it seems, almost from his cradle, and from the first manifesting few of the common tastes or sympathies of children, Chatterton was regarded for a time as deficient in intellect. But it is impossible to trace out the first indications of his peculiar characteristics, without a keen sense of regret that the child had no one near him more capable of appreciating his wonderful natural faculties, than the kind but simple mother, to whom his strange moods and tastes were only a perplexing riddle.



Mr. R. H. Cromek, a London engraver, with literary aspirations of his own, and considerable zeal as a collector, employed himself in the early part of the present century in accumulating information concerning Chatterton, which he did not live to reduce to form. But to him we are indebted for the valuable though undigested notes of Mr. George Cumberland, printed as an Appendix to Mr. Dix's life of the poet; and especially for the information derived from Mrs. Edkins. She appears to have resided with Mrs. Chatterton, assisting her as a sempstress, and thus enjoyed the most favourable opportunities for studying the disposition and habits of the boy. She was present at his birth, and was wont to speak of him tenderly as her foster-child. "Many," says she, "were the uneasinesses that his singularities cost his mother; and until he was six years and a half old, they thought he was an absolute fool."[1] But this hasty conclusion seems to have been mainly based on his distaste for the rudimentary studies of a child's



schooling. One of his sister's earliest remembrances of him was his "thirst for preeminence. Before he was five years old he would always preside over his playmates as their master, and they his hired servants." His foster-mother also states: he was so ingenious when a child, that if anything got out of order he was always set to mend it, and generally succeeded, to the admiration of his mother; when older, his ingenuity in the mechanic arts

[1] Dix's Life, App. p. 314.

was surprising, and he used to observe that a man might do anything he chose.   His mother, however, considered him in general as stupid, because, when quite a child, he would sit alone crying for hours, nobody knew what for.   Once when he was in one of his silent moods, she said, " When will this stupidity cease?" and Mrs. Edkins added to rouse him, "I wish your father was alive, he would manage you ; " at which, starting, he replied, " I wish he was ! " uttering a deep sigh, and spoke no more for a long time.[1]

These fits of abstraction characterised him to the last. " At seven years old he was tenderly sensible of every one's distresses, and would frequently sit musing in a seeming stupor ; at length the tears would steal, one by one, down his cheeks : for which his mother, thinking to rouse him, sometimes gave him a gentle slap, and told him he was foolish ; and when asked what he cried for, he would say, 'Sister beat me, that's all :'" evading thereby an explanation of the reveries which already occupied his mind.[2]

These strange musings, which ere long were the precursors of his poetical activity, were incomprehensible to those among whom he moved, and only excited suspicion, or doubt of his sanity.   His mother said, " he had cost her many uneasy hours, from the apprehension she entertained of his going mad ; as he was accustomed to remain fixed for above an hour at a time quite motionless, and then he would snatch up a pen and write incessantly."[3]   What he did write, after such prolonged reveries, does not seem to have excited any curiosity.

The influence of this misapprehension and lack of all appreciative sympathy, could not fail to affect the boy's character.   A reserve which was natural, was quickened by this means into habitual secretiveness ; and not a little of the love of mystery which gave so peculiar an aspect to his chief literary achievements at a

---

[1] Dix's Life, App. p. 310.          [2] Ibid. p. 314.
[3] Mrs. Stockwell, Dix, App. p. 300.

later period, may be traced to his being reared, not only in infancy, but at school, and even during his brief apprenticeship, in companionship with those who could not comprehend the aspirations of the boy, or interpret the thoughtful fits of musing of the child, who seemed to them so "dull in learning, not knowing many letters at four years old."[1] It is easy now to perceive that there was no lack of intellect. The reasoning and reflective powers were already at work; though arbitrary alphabetic signs, which appealed only to the memory, and not to the understanding, had no attractions for him. From the first dawn of reason, he appears to have manifested a will and tastes essentially original; and even in the very sentence in which his sister records his tardy mastering of the alphabet, she adds the characteristic trait that he "always objected to read in a small book."



Such manifestations of his peculiar idiosyncrasy were only a puzzle and a grief to the simple woman on whom the early training of the boy devolved. But a happy accident furnished the key to his seemingly dormant intellect. The decorations of an old musical folio of his father's, which his mother was tearing up for waste paper, attracted his notice, and, as she graphically expressed it, he fell in love with its illuminated capitals. The first step in education was thus achieved; the next was equally characteristic. He was taught to read from an old blackletter Bible, selected probably for its size; so that he only turned in later years from medieval illuminations and antique typography, to the unfamiliar aspect of contemporary literature.



The mother's apprehensions about her strange child were thus gradually dissipated. "At seven he visibly improved, to her joy and surprise, and at eight years of age he was so eager for books, that he read from the moment he waked, which was early, until he went to bed, if they would let him." He was, at the same time, domestic in his tastes, and seemingly also frank and companionable, notwithstanding his occasional relapses

[1] Mrs. Newton's Letter, Croft, p. 161.

into reveries, which have been called moody fits. In their extreme form they more nearly approached to a trance. He had a bright eye, a keen satirical sense of humour, and a bold independent bearing; so that his uncle, Richard Phillips, early took a liking to the boy for his spirit.[1] His social qualities were indeed altogether remarkable in one so reticent. He was fond of female society even from a child; had his little favourite, Miss Sukey Webb; and when, after a whole day's absence, no other inducement could tempt him from the deserted lumber room overlooking the garden, which he early converted into a study, his foster-mother would get him to the tea-table by telling him she was going to visit his favourite.

His mother's anxiety was thenceforth occasioned by his intense devotion to study. He was now as grateful for instruction as he had formerly seemed indisposed for it. In the pursuit of knowledge he would neglect both food and sleep. At times he became so absorbed in his studies as to lose consciousness of all that was going on around him; and after being repeatedly addressed, would start and ask what they were talking about.

To such a child, the want of an intelligent father's oversight, or intercourse with some one able to sympathise in his desire for knowledge, and invite his confidence by responding to his curious inquisitiveness, was an irreparable loss. It is easy to see how, in its absence, the habit of secretiveness should grow upon him. He derived in some degree, from both father and mother, a passionate, impulsive nature, which was placed under slight restraint in childhood. According to his mother's description, he was sharp-tempered, but it was soon over. Yet he showed from the first a rare self-control in reference to food and drink, and always regarded tea as his favourite beverage. He also manifested a sensitive, kindly disposition; subject indeed to occasional outbursts of passion; but generous according to his means, always

[1] Mrs. Jane Phillips, Dix's App. p. 302.

*The child-poet's study.*

affectionate, and with peculiarly winning ways when he had an object to gain.

His delight was to lock himself up in his little attic, with his books, papers, and drawing materials. He appears to have had an intuitive taste for drawing, as for so much else that was strange for his years; and there also, before long, he is found with his parchments, " great piece of ochre in a brown pan, pounce bags full of charcoal dust, which he had from a Miss Sanger, a neighbour; also a bottle of black-lead powder, which they once took to clean the stove with, and made him very angry." So at length his mother carried off the key, lest he should hurt his health in this dusty old garret, from whence, after long abstinence, he was wont to emerge, begrimed with the traces of his antiquarian handicraft. Thus excluded from his favourite haunt, " he would come to Mrs. Edkins and kiss her cheek, and coax her to get it for him, using the most persuasive expressions to effect his end."[1]

*Precocious intellectual vigour.*

An intellect of rare power was thus prematurely manifesting itself, and groping in all available directions, with no other guidance for its development than such as a simple loving mother could supply. With anxious wonder she puzzled over the strange ways of the boy; perplexed by her own incapacity, and watching his wayward doings, much as we may fancy the foster-hen when her brood of ducklings takes to the water, in spite of her despairing remonstrances. Doubtless the poor widow exerted herself to procure for him access to the best instruction within her reach; and so we find him, in his eighth year, elected on the foundation of Colston's Charity, situated at St. Austin's Back, on the site of the dissolved house of Friars' Carmelites: the Bluecoat School of Bristol.

[1] Mrs. Edkins, Dix's Life, App. p. 313.

# CHAPTER II.

## ST. MARY REDCLIFFE.

CHATTERTON was seven years and eight months old, when, on the 3d of August, 1760, he was admitted to Colston's Hospital. To the superficial observer he still appeared a dull boy, turning his attention reluctantly to the ordinary routine of instruction. But long before this his mind had been developing under influences altogether peculiar; and before we follow him to the Bluecoat School, where he was subjected for the next seven years to the discipline and restraints of its cloistral rules, it is necessary to understand what those influences were.

The direct line of the old sextons of St. Mary Redcliffe came to an end with the death of John Chatterton, in 1748. But the office did not pass out of the family; and the new sexton, Richard Phillips, regarded his nephew with special favour from early childhood. The house to which Mrs. Chatterton removed was one opposite the Upper Gate, on Redcliffe Hill. There the boy's home-life was passed, in the immediate vicinity of the church with which his ancestry had been connected for centuries; and the favour with which he was regarded by his uncle, the sexton, may be accepted as good evidence of many an hour of his childhood and early youth spent in the spacious precincts of the old church; or wandering through its aisles in wondering admiration of the graceful columns, as they pass, by shaft and groining, to the lofty clerestory and embossed roof.

St. Mary Redcliffe is justly regarded as one of the finest specimens of parochial church architecture in





*Home-life on Redcliffe Hill.*

*St. Mary Redcliffe.*

England; and its elevated site on the "cliff" greatly adds to the effect of a building which has excited the admiration of successive generations. William of Worcester, Camden, Fuller, and many another worthy of later centuries, have lavished their praises on its stately tower, richly groined and many-windowed avenues of nave, choir, transepts, and Lady Chapel. But when the child-poet yielded to its æsthetic influences, the taste for such memorials of ancient piety was at its lowest ebb; though ere long the first glimmerings of that renewed appreciation of medieval art were discernible, which has culminated in our own day in a revival of much else more fitly pertaining to the same "good old times." But the imaginative boy anticipated this medieval passion, and lived apart in an olden world of ideal perfection. "This wonder of mansyons," he exclaims, in one of his early utterances from behind the antique mask which he so speedily assumed, "was ybuildenne bie the nowe Mastre Canynge, of whych need no oder to bie said botte see ytte and bee astonyed. Ytte was desyned bie Johne a Shaillinger, a Bristowe manne borne; who yn the sayde chyrche wyll shewe hys Reede for aye: each one pyllare stondynge as a letterre in hys blase."

This idea of fame reaching far into the coming time was strong within him even as a child; and it grew and took its strange shape as he made himself familiar with the ancient dwellers in Redcliffe Church: pondering over the beautiful altar-tomb of William Canynge and his wife Joan, with its laudatory epitaph in prose and verse, the addition of a later age; or studying the quaint sculpture of the nameless occupant of an adjoining tomb, where the reputed purse-bearer of the old merchant and church-builder lies, with an angel supporting his head, and at his feet his dog with a huge bone in its paws. Near by a plain slab, decorated only with a large knife and strainer, records in antique characters a prayer for the soul of one faithful servitor, supposed to have been his cook; another slab, with incised cross, is dedicated to his reputed brewer; while on an adjoining altar-tomb reposes a nameless ecclesiastic commonly regarded as the same "riche merchant of Bristowe," in his later character as Dean of Westbury.

Thus on every hand the boy found that old generation reposing there in dignified contrast to the men of his own day. Nor was he wholly limited to Canynge and his times. Under the great window of the north transept lies the effigy of a mailed knight, cross-legged after the fashion of an old crusader: supposed to represent Robert de Berkeley, Lord of Bedminster and Redcliffe, whose armorial bearings, along with those of the Beauchamps, Montacutes, and other benefactors of the church, are sculptured on bosses in the north aisle of the nave. Other benefactors are commemorated in like heraldic fashion, in sculpture or painted glass; and in earlier times the windows were rich with the blazonry of the Cradocks, Sturtons, Says, Fitzwarrens, Rivers, and others, who claimed a share in the exequies and requiems for founders and benefactors. Everywhere walls and floor were enriched, as they still are, with graven brasses of ancient knights and dames, chief justices, and civic dignitaries, of the times of the Roses; judges and magnates of the Tudors and Stuarts; and on one of the pillars, the armour and banners of Admiral Sir William Penn, father of the more celebrated founder and legislator of Pennsylvania.

Such were the chosen associates of Chatterton's boyhood, in whose company many a pleasant hour was dreamt away, until that old past, with its knights, priests, and merchant princes, became for him the world of realities in which alone he willingly dwelt.

> "So the foundations of his mind were laid.
> In such communion, not from terror free,
> While yet a child, and long before his time,
> Had he perceived the presence and the power
> Of greatness; and deep feelings had impressed
> Great objects on his mind, with portraiture
> And colour so distinct, that on his mind
> They lay like substances, and almost seemed
> To haunt the bodily sense."

It is not to be doubted that the strange, stolid-looking child, whose marvellous powers even a mother's eye was slow to discern ; and who, in his eighth year, took his unheeded place among the boys of Colston's Charity : was already living in phantasy, nurturing associations which thenceforth became a part of his being. Ælla, Lord of Bristowe Castel ; Sir Simon Burton, the original founder of Redcliffe Church ; Sir Charles Baldwyne, a famous Lancastrian knight ; with the Canynges and their imaginary friends, became substantial realities to him : and soon the circle was enlarged by the addition of Thomas Rowley, the impersonation of his own ideal as the Bristowe poet of Canynge's time.



The daughter of Richard Phillips, recalling the memory of her little cousin, Chatterton, as her schoolmate at the Pyle Street Free School, described him to Mr. George Cumberland as a cheerful child, having a face round as an apple, rosy dimpled cheeks, flaxen hair, and blue, or more correctly, bright grey eyes. He had a little pouch under his petticoat, in which to carry his fruit and cakes ; and reappears to our imagination as a bright, attractive child. So far, indeed, as I can discern from all the evidence recoverable in reference to him, the terms moody, sullen, dogged, and the like, have been far too indiscriminately employed by his biographers. He was indeed prone from childhood to fits of abstraction ; but his natural disposition appears to have been kindly and social ; he loved a jest ; and, as a good old lady, who had herself been the butt of his practical jokes, said of him, " He was a sad wag of a boy."[1]



But an earnest seriousness appears to have marked Chatterton in all his associations with the ancient church of St. Mary Redcliffe. His cousin Phillips recalling him again, in his eleventh year, when he wore the quaint garb of the Bluecoat School, described him as habitually mounting the steps of the church, and repeating poetry to those whom he preferred among his playfellows.[2]   A

[1] Gent. Mag. N.S. x. p. 603.
[2] Mrs. Stephens, Dix, App. p. 304.

picture in her father's possession—the work, as she believed, of Chatterton's own pencil,—represented him in the same dress, cap in hand, with his mother leading him towards a tomb: not improbably Canynge's altar-tomb, in Redcliffe Church. Around its precincts, or in the fine old church itself, all his leisure hours were spent; and soon the hold it acquired on his fancy manifested itself in the jealousy with which he resented any irreverent encroachment on its sanctity. He was eleven years of age when several satirical pieces, in prose and verse, appeared in *Farley's Bristol Journal*, two of which specially invite attention as illustrations of the veneration thus early manifested.

Mr. Joseph Thomas, churchwarden of St. Mary Redcliffe in 1763, appears to have busied himself after the fashion of æsthetic churchwardens of the eighteenth century. The cemetery around the ancient church, crowded with the memorials of many generations. offended the eye of its new curator, and he resolved to restore it to a tasteful propriety. The grave-mounds were levelled; old familiar monuments disappeared; and, among other good works, it is apparently due to him that the ancient structure, described by William of Worcester, in 1480, as a most beautiful cross of curious workmanship, no longer graces the churchyard on Redcliffe Hill.

It was not till 1789, more than a quarter of a century after the memorable churchwardenship of Mr. Joseph Thomas, that Barrett's long-promised History of Bristol appeared. The historian merely states that an elegant cross, from which sermons used to be preached, formerly stood in the centre of Redcliffe churchyard, but it is now destroyed.[1] But the history of another procedure in the year of the churchwarden's rule on Redcliffe Hill probably throws some light on his motive for its demolition. The ancient city cross, or Bristol High Cross as it was called, after various disasters, restorations, and changes of site, had found a suitable resting-place in the

[1] Barrett's History and Antiquities of Bristol, 4to. p. 588.



Chap. II.<br>Picture of the boy.

The æsthetic church-warden.

Doom of the ancient city cross.

CHAP. II.

*An irreve-
rent age.*

centre of the College Green.   But " even here, in time,"
says the city historian, "the cross lost that reverence and
regard that had been hitherto paid it throughout all ages;
for in the year 1763 it was at length found out that this
beautiful structure, by intersecting one of the walks,
intercepted ladies and gentlemen from walking eight or
ten abreast."[1]   So the Dean and Chapter, on whose
ground it stood, gave their sanction to its demolition.
The spirit of veneration developed in the boy is thus all
the more remarkable in its contrast to every idea and
teaching of the age in which he lived.   The deed and
its chief perpetrators are thus recalled at a later date, in
his metrical Journal, written shortly before he left Bristol,
where he celebrates

> "The lazy Dean,
> Who sold the ancient cross to Hoare
> For one church dinner, nothing more."

*St. Mary
Redcliffe
cross
demolished.*

The example was not lost on the churchwarden of St.
Mary Redcliffe.   There also spacious avenues, since
planted with all the formality of a Dutch garden, were
encumbered with the cross which delighted the eye of
William of Worcester three centuries before; and so it
too was swept away.   A mania for such demolitions
possessed that eighteenth century.   The doom of the
old cross of Edinburgh had been pronounced a few years
before, according to a local satirist, Clandero, "for the
horrid crime of being an incumbrance to the street."
Scott long after recorded, in his "Marmion," his malison

*The parish
Vandal
pilloried.*

on its destroyer's head.   More promptly the Bristol
charity boy took pen in hand—not altogether for the
first time,—and thus pilloried the parish Vandal :—

> " The night was cold, the wind was high,
> And stars bespangled all the sky;
> Churchwarden Joe had laid him down,
> And slept secure on bed of down ;
> But still the pleasing hope of gain,
> That never left his active brain,

---

[1] Barrett's History and Antiquities of Bristol, 4to. p. 475.

> Exposed the churchyard to his view,
> That seat of treasure wholly new.
> 'Pull down that cross,' he quickly cried,
> The mason instantly complied :
> When lo·! behold the golden prize
> Appears ; joy sparkles in his eyes.
> The door now creaks, the window shakes,
> With sudden fear he starts and wakes,"—

CHAP. II.

*The golden prize.*

and finds himself face to face with the ghastly phantom of his own conscience, accusing him of selfish hypocrisy, and of making a gain of godliness. As the production of a boy only emerging from childhood, this slight *jeu d'esprit* is chiefly noticeable for the veneration for the monuments of antiquity in which it had its origin, revealing thereby sympathies as dissimilar to those natural to boyhood, as they were to the taste inculcated by that eighteenth century. In this respect it contrasts with " Apostate Will," another juvenile satire, which embodies borrowed sentiments of· worldly experience, and the current prejudices of his day.

*Fulford the grave-digger.*

What "golden prize" Churchwarden Joe dreamt of as the reward of his vandalism—unless the beautiful old cross was the reputed shrine of some sacred treasure,—is not now apparent. But tradition reports him as a brick-maker, to whom the ancient cemetery presented the lucrative aspect of a clay-field. When accordingly he proceeded to reduce the mouldering heaps of centuries to one uniform level, there appeared in *Felix Farley's Journal* for Jan. 7th, 1764, a letter, under the *nom de plume* of " Fulford the grave-digger," the earliest of Chatterton's literary disguises. Sir Baldwin Fulford, a zealous Lancastrian executed at Bristol in the reign of Edward IV. and the hero ere long of the " Bristowe Tragedie," no doubt suggested the name ; but the ideal impersonation was his own grandfather, the last of the direct line of hereditary sextons. The old grave-digger protests that he has enjoyed his place so long, he has dug the graves of half the parish, and could tell to an inch where they lie; but, he says, " My head master, a great projector, has taken it into his head to level the

CHAP. II.

churchyard, and by digging and throwing about his clay there, and defacing the stones, makes such a confusion among the dead, that no man living will be able to find where to lay them properly;" and, after stating that "even the poor love to bury with their kindred," he adds an ironical offer to rent the old spot, when the green turf is all removed ; and, for decency's sake, to make a potato patch of it, which will prevent the naked appearance, besides helping him to a profitable job, as well as his master ![1]

*Felix Farley's new correspondent.*

*Felix Farley's Journal*, the weekly Bristol newspaper, appears to have placed little restriction on anonymous correspondence ; and hence the boy was able to assume whatever guise his fancy suggested.  At how early a date the idea was formed of figuring behind the mask of "Thomas Rowley, parish priest of St. John's in the city of Bristowe," and resuscitating the time when the bountiful Canynge ruled in Bristowe's civic chair, is now matter of conjecture.  It was, no doubt, a work of gradual development.  First there was the dreamy realization of that remote past when the church of Our Ladye was rising anew from its foundations on Redcliffe Hill; and the knights and dames, princely mayors, architects and priests, who slumber there in stone, were the living actors.  But besides these, there were actual records and parchments, engrossed by the hands of those very artists and builders of the fifteenth century: all already familiar to him almost from his cradle.  The poetical romance which was to win for him an enduring place in English literature was already taking shape in his young mind; while he thus tasted the first pleasures of literary disguise.

*St. Mary's Treasury House.*

Over the north porch of St. Mary Redcliffe—rebuilt on the site of an earlier structure, and traditionally affirmed to have been completed at the cost of William Canynge, merchant, and mayor of Bristol in the reigns of Henry VI. and Edward IV.,—there is a chamber, designated in

---

[1] This piece was first pointed out, and assigned to the author of the "Bristowe Tragedie," by Mr. W. Tyson, of Bristol. (*Vide* Dix, pp. 30, 326.)

ancient deeds the Treasury House, in which lay, deposited in six or seven oaken chests, the charters and title-deeds of the church, including documents of a still earlier date than the present noble edifice. Among those was one large, iron-bound coffer secured with six locks, designated in a deed of the fifteenth century, " William Canynge's chest in the treasury-house of the church of the Blessed Mary of Redcliffe."[1] Such receptacles for the safe-keeping of the holy vessels, vestments, charters, and service-books, are still common in old churches, and are frequently ornamented with iron scroll-work, or wrought in carved panelling according to the style of the contemporary architecture. But Master Canynge's coffer was long guarded with peculiar jealousy, as in the days when it held the treasures of the old merchant. Two of its six keys were entrusted to the vicar and procurator of the church, two to the mayor, and one to each of the churchwardens: whereby it is no marvel that by and by they could nowhere be found. An impatient vestry wanted access to certain deeds; and so, about the year 1730[2] the locks, not only of Mr. Canynge's coffer, but of all the chests, were forced, the deeds relating to the church property removed, and the remaining papers and parchments exposed to neglect, because the vestry attorney could not read them, and they seemed valueless as title-deeds of any church estates.[3]

The actual worth of the ancient documents to the ignorant custodians to whom they were now abandoned, was simply the material on which they were engrossed. The muniment room was accessible to the sexton and

---

[1] Barrett's History, p. 576.

[2] Dr. Gregory says (Life, p. xxiv.) "about the year 1727." Mr. Barrett gives the date 1748, in a letter to Dr. Ducarel of Doctors' Commons, in 1772 (Gent. Mag. vol. lvi. p. 460). But the old Vicar, Mr. Gibb, whose school Bibles were covered with the parchments, was succeeded by Mr. Thomas Broughton in 1744. The date should probably be 1735. In the following year the first of the old documents, hereafter referred to, was produced at a meeting of the Society of Antiquaries.

[3] Barrett, Gent. Mag. vol. lvi. p. 460.

his family, and its contents were turned to account as mere waste paper. Some of the old documents were even employed to wipe the church candlesticks, and many more were carried off for equally vile uses.[1] But the most unscrupulous plunderer was the old sexton's heir, Thomas Chatterton, father of the poet, who found he could turn them to account in various ways in the parish Free School. From time to time, accordingly, bundles of the parchments were removed ; until at length, summoning to his aid a posse of the schoolboys, he carried off a large basketful, and deposited the spoils in a cupboard of the school-room for common use.

Primers and copy-books were thenceforth furnished with wrappers that would now be worth more than any volume they could cover. Twenty Bibles presented to the boys by the Rev. John Gibb, Vicar of St. Mary Redcliffe prior to 1744, were covered with the old parchments ; and when the death of the schoolmaster necessitated his widow's removal from Pyle Street, in 1752, there still remained so large a stock that she emptied the school-room cupboard "partly into a large deal box where her husband used to keep his clothes, and into a square box of a smaller size." The ample receptacles indicate the abundance of the antique store, after all the depredations it had suffered at the hands of her husband and his pupils. It is inconceivable, indeed, that the box-loads still remaining were all parchments. The greater part were probably the ordinary parish registers, accounts, &c., usually found in such repositories : but still including curious, and probably valuable deeds.

Old parchments were thus more abundant in the poor widow's house than ordinary paper : " some being turned into thread-papers, some into patterns, some into dolls," and applied to other equally mean uses.[2] In all probability, Chatterton's first efforts with the pencil and pen were scrawled on the margins of deeds in imitation of

---

[1] Letter of Rev. John Chapman, Gent. Mag. vol. lvi. p. 361.
[2] Mr. William Smith, Milles's Rowley, p. 13.

characters engrossed in the time of the Plantagenets, or when Occleve and Lydgate were feebly reechoing Chaucer's rhythm. Thus the child, who acquired his first knowledge of letters from the illuminated capitals of an ancient music-book, and learned their use in the pages of an old black-letter Bible, was familiar from infancy with medieval palæography and the aspect of antique parchments. Mrs. Phillips remembered that when his mother's thread-papers were found to be of such material he said they belonged to Redcliffe Church, and intimated his intention of informing his uncle, the sexton.[1] Bryant, an early champion of the authenticity of the fifteenth-century Rowley and his poems, assigns the discovery of the antique thread-papers to the period of Chatterton's entering the office of Mr. Lambert. But the date rests on the authority of statements chiefly furnished by Mr. William Smith fully fifteen years after that event; and is contradicted by various independent proofs of his familiarity with the spoils of Canynge's coffer before he entered Colston's Hospital: apart from the more con-clusive fact that he produced some of his Rowley MSS. while still a Bluecoat boy.

*Singular training from infancy.*

The antique poems had no doubt made some progress, and the romance begot in the strange reveries of the young dreamer was assuming shape and consistency, before an actual Thomas Rowley, priest and poet of the olden time, was called into being as their assigned author. The Rowley romance had been realized in the purlieus of St. Mary Redcliffe, by the child-poet, in very early years. But, to his simple unimaginative mother, his reveries were suggestive rather of defective intellect than poetic inspiration. Hence he learned to conceal his poetical recreations as reprehensible, if not altogether criminal indulgences. With a strength of filial attach-ment which never failed him, he nevertheless cherished his most familiar thoughts in his own breast : until we have to note among his many singular characteristics, a

*Thomas Rowley, priest and poet.*

---

[1] Mrs. Jane Phillips, Dix, App. p. 303.

secretiveness altogether remarkable from the consistent persistency with which it was manifested from childhood.

Archaic tastes and old-world reveries, withheld from the knowledge of his own mother and sister, were little likely to be disclosed to others at so early an age. His uncle, Richard Phillips, is described by his daughter as " very reserved on all occasions." To him, more probably than to any other, the boy, who won his favour by his spirit and manly ways, and perhaps also by the interest he manifested in the old church and all that pertained to it, may have been more communicative. We can fancy the old sexton smiling kindly at his childish prattle about the ancient mayor, and the knights and dames whose monuments were familiar to both. But the sexton himself was dead before curiosity had been aroused about his young companion; and his silent ways, so suitable to the duties of his office, left few reminiscences for survivors to retail.



Let us now follow the strange child from the favourite scenes of such antique reveries, in which he could call up at will an imaginary world of the past, to the common-place realities of Colston's Bluecoat School.

# CHAPTER III.

## COLSTON'S HOSPITAL.





EDWARD COLSTON, the heir of an ancient line of merchant adventurers who had flourished in Bristol from the time of Edward III., and furnished sheriffs, mayors, and deputy-lieutenants of the city, in the days of the Tudors and Stuarts, is still venerated there as one of the noblest specimens of its old princely merchants : nor altogether lacking some characteristic traits of the Bristol citizen of later times.  Born there in 1636, his biographer specially notes among the guests at his christening, Colonel Taylor, who fell mortally wounded at the storming of Bristol by General Fairfax, in 1645, and the Rev. Richard Standfast, Rector of Christ Church, "a steadfast and earnest champion of the Church," who was ejected and imprisoned by the Parliamentary Committee in the following year.[1] The facts are not without their significance, reminding us that Colston grew up amid the party strifes of the Commonwealth era, when his own father's life was placed in jeopardy, and his fortune impaired by his royalist leanings.  He was in his twenty-first year when the Protector wrote to his "trusty and well-beloved" Arthur Farmer, the Puritan mayor of Bristol, desiring to be informed "from time to time, what occurs touching the malignant party," and warning him that he heard " on all hands that the Cavaliers are designing to put us into blood."  Within less than three years the glorious Restoration turned the tables on the Roundheads, who now became the " malignants ;" and the young merchant



---

[1] Tovey's Memorials of Colston, 2d edition, pp. 2, 3.

retained through life, and left with his philanthropic bequests to his native city, the lasting impress of opinions formed amid the throes of revolution. "He had seen," says his biographer, "the Church in the beauty of holiness, purity, and peace. He had seen dissent in the deformity of fanaticism, intolerance, and discord;" and so, as we shall by and by see, he took care that his Bristol charities should lend no countenance to "Whiggism" or Nonconformity.[1]



Little is known of Colston's early years. When the first definite notices occur, he appears as a resident of London, though retaining a large interest in the commerce of his native city. According to his earlier biographers, Barrett and Chalmers, he spent some time in Spain, laying the foundation for later commercial dealings with that country; and the same authorities trace his great fortune, in part at least, to the bequests of brothers, one of whom is said to have resided at Venice in the capacity of British Consul. To all appearance, however, he was mainly the architect of his own fortune; and this he freely distributed with wise and generous liberality. All his charitable designs were carried out in his own lifetime; and he personally superintended the organization of schools, hospitals, and other philanthropic schemes, both in Bristol and London: relieving and freeing poor debtors, without their knowing their benefactor; succouring suffering seamen and their orphan families; and providing for the education and establishment in life of poor boys. When challenged by his friends for remaining unmarried, he was wont to reply with grave pleasantry that he found a wife in every destitute widow, and children enough in her orphans.



Colston had already built and endowed almshouses for poor sailors and others; provided for the maintenance of four boys, the sons of free burgesses of Bristol, at Queen Elizabeth's Hospital there; and in various other ways contributed to the charities of Bristol: when in 1706

---

[1] Tovey's Colston, p. 85.

he originated the plan for the Bluecoat School, to which, as the scene of Chatterton's school-life, and his sole means of early maintenance and instruction, its benevolent founder mainly owes the memory of his name in later times beyond the walls of his native city. The Society of Merchants was selected as his trustees, and ere long the " Great House on St. Augustine's Back," an ancient civic mansion where Queen Elizabeth had held court in 1581, and Sir Ferdinando Gorges had dwelt in 1642, was purchased and converted into a hospital for the reception and maintenance of one hundred boys, who were to wear the dress familiar to him as one of the governors of Christ's Hospital, London ; and to be " instructed in the principles of religion as laid down in the Church Catechism," by a master of sound orthodoxy, " approved of by the major part of the beneficed clergy of the city, and licensed by the ordinary." Colston's directions for the government of his hospital further provide for the expulsion of any boy whose parents shall prevail on him to go to meeting ; and for appeal against the trustees should they ever connive at Dissenting teaching in matters of religion. In full accordance with this, he confirms the rules and method of teaching for the boys in Temple Street School, another of his charities, as well calculated to " fit them for apprentices, and also qualify them to be staunch sons of the Church, provided such books are procured for them as have no tincture of Whiggism !" [1]

The political and religious elements thus curiously combined, were characteristic of the age. These benevolent designs for the orthodox training of the poor boys of Bristol were still in progress, in 1710, when Queen Anne dissolved the Whig Parliament by which Marlborough was sustained in his protracted campaigns against the generals of Louis XIV. The triumphant High-Church party of Bristol selected Edward Colston as its Tory representative ; and, amid bonfires and ringing of bells, carried their new member through the city, with the

[1] Tovey's Colston, p. 85.

CHAP. III.

*Enduring
elements of
party strife.*

*Colston's
Cathedral
stall.*

*Bluecoat boy
choristers.*

mitre borne before him, in symbol of victory over the hated sectaries.[1] The elements of party strife which thus intermingled even with the charities of Bristol in the eighteenth century, have furnished notable evidence of their vitality in much more recent times; and were not without their influence on the boy, whose share in the benevolent provisions of the old Bristol merchant for the education of future generations confers a novel interest on the High Church, and Whig and Tory feuds of Sacheverel, Sunderland, and Bolingbroke.

The Dean and Chapter of Bristol Cathedral shared in Mr. Colston's liberality, and manifested their estimate of his rare virtues by appropriating to his use a stall in the cathedral choir, specially designated by his dolphin crest and initials. There also his Bluecoat boys attended on Sundays and saints' days, when it was the custom of the good old merchant to await their arrival at the door, and after patting some on the head, and speaking words of encouragement to others, to follow them to his accustomed seat in the choir.[2] In 1762 the Dean and Chapter perpetuated the evidence of their esteem for his memory, by undertaking to select their six choristers from his Bluecoat boys, and to promote such of them as made good proficiency in music, when vacancies occurred. It is not improbable, therefore, that the connexion of his father with the Cathedral may have paved the way for Chatterton's admission to Colston's Hospital. He was elected on the nomination of the Rev. John Gardiner, Vicar of Henbury, through the influence of Mr. Harris,—the same, probably, who as Mayor of Bristol in 1769, figures in his graceless protégé's "Kew Gardens," and other later satires.[3]

---

[1] The Bristol Post Boy, Oct. 31st, 1710. Tovey's Colston, p. 71.

[2] Tovey's Colston, p. 99.

[3] A list of "Boys admitted into Mr. Colston's Hospital on J. G.'s account," from 1746 to 1763, exists, with this note, "Tho. Chadderton, at the request of Mr. Harris." The name, it will be seen, is spelt nearly as in the old Redcliffe parchments. (*Vide* Notes and Queries, vol. xi. p. 281.)

To the widowed mother this was doubtless a source of gratulation. But the Bluecoat School which he now entered was designed only for the most ordinary class of boys, and had little adaptability for one of such rare genius as was now to be subjected to its meagre culture. The boys were boarded, and clad in the half-monkish garb of blue gown, knee-breeches, and yellow stockings, borrowed from Christ's Hospital, London. But the simple curriculum was in striking contrast to the ample provisions of Edward the Sixth's foundation, with its upper and lower schools, its first and deputy Grecians, and University exhibitions, in which Charles Lamb, and another "inspired charity boy," Coleridge, shared to such good purpose. Its benevolent founder aimed at training up his boys as good citizens, after the most approved standard of his age. The master was to be "one that will make it his chief business to instruct the children in the principles of the Christian religion, as they are laid down in the Church Catechism, and who shall, twice a week, explain it to the meanest capacity, by some good exposition." The Church Catechism, indeed, appears to have occupied the foremost place in all Colston's ideas of education, at least for the poor. For Bristol had also its Grammar School, with liberal endowments and Oxford exhibitions, for burgesses' sons; while the teachers of the Bluecoat School were required only to instruct its inmates in the most ordinary elements of a plain English education.

Chatterton was too young to comprehend the great contrast between the advantages enjoyed by the privileged *élèves* of the Grammar School, and those of the institution to which he was now admitted; and he was at first greatly elated at his election, "thinking he should there get all the learning he wanted; but soon he seemed much hurt, as he said: he could not learn so much at school as he could at home."[1] The consciousness of powers and aims far beyond those of his fellows was

[1] Mrs. Edkins, Dix, App. p. 314.

CHAP. III.

*Simple curriculum for the Bluecoat School.*

*Great contrast with the Grammar School.*

Chap. III.

*Thirst
for pre-
eminence.*

even now manifesting itself in the boy.   As a mere child he had shown a thirst for preeminence; claimed to take the lead among his playmates; began to talk to his mother and sister of the good things in store for them when he grew up and was able to repay their kindness; and already indulged in dreams of future fame.   While still very young, a manufacturer of earthenware undertook to present Mrs. Chatterton's children with specimens of his art, and asked the boy what device he would have upon his.   "Paint me," he replied, "an angel, with wings and a trumpet, to trumpet my name over the world."

*Distaste-
fulness of
Colston's
Hospital.*

It is not to be wondered that to such a child, Colston's Hospital should prove distasteful.   Instead of wandering at pleasure about St. Mary Redcliffe, or musing over its monuments till he dreamt of himself as the monk-poet of the days when it was in building, he had to submit to the actual durance of a modern Bluecoat monk.   The absence of all means of retirement must have been no less irksome to him than the inadequacy of the instruction received.   The unvarying routine of a common school education was only relieved by the catechising and church services of Sundays and saints' days.   The school hours were in the morning, from seven till noon; and from one till five in the afternoon.   During the shorter winter days they did not enter the school-room till eight, and left at four.   But throughout the year they were required to be in bed by eight;[1] so that, with the additional time for meals, the moments snatched for such communings with his own thoughts as the young poet craved must have been scanty enough.   This may well account for his sister's remark, that he became gloomy from the time he began to learn.[2]   All his bright anticipations of getting the knowledge he craved had vanished; and he instinctively longed to return to his own little study, and his solitary musings in Redcliffe Church.

*Eagerness
for know-
ledge.*

But no impediments could shut out the eager youth from the acquisition of knowledge.   By his tenth year he

---

[1] *Bristoliensis,* Gent. Mag. vol. xlviii. p. 403.
[2] Mrs. Newton's Letter, Croft, p. 162.

was perusing all the books accessible to him ; and expending the little pocket-money his mother allowed him in hiring others from a lending library. Then, too, brief hours of release from the noisy playground and the unattractive studies of the school recurred at frequent intervals. Each Saturday brought about its precious half-holiday; and, like its great London prototype, the Bristol Bluecoat School held the saints' days of the Anglican Calendar in becoming reverence. On those welcome occasions the boys were emancipated from the hospital bounds from noon till eight in the evening ; and then Chatterton hastened home to the happy solitude of the attic he had appropriated as his study under his mother's roof. Each Saturday, says Mrs. Edkins, he was always at home, returning punctually a few minutes after the clock struck twelve, to get to his little room and shut himself up. There were deposited his own little stock of books, parchments, and all the materials already in use by him in the first efforts of his antique muse. His scheme of a series of poems to be produced under the guise of an ancient poet-monk was already in embryo ; and he would lock himself in his favourite retreat, and frequently remain there without food the whole day: till his mother became alarmed for his health ; and wonder grew into doubt and suspicion at his strange proceedings, the apparatus, the parchments, both plain and written, " and the begrimed figure he always presented when he came down at tea-time, his face exhibiting many stains of black and yellow. All these circumstances began to alarm them ; and," as Mrs. Edkins relates, " when she could get into his room, she would be very inquisitive, and peep about at everything. Once he put his foot on a parchment on the floor to prevent her from taking it up, saying, ' you are too curious and clear-sighted, I wish you would bide out of the room ; it is my room.' To this she replied it was only a general lumber-room, and that she wanted some parchments, some of his old Rowley's, to make thread-papers of ; "—for already he had familiarised those at home with his imaginary monk,—"but he was offended,

CHAP. III.

*Strange
materials of
the boy's
antique art.*

and would not permit her to touch any of them, not even those that were not written on. But at last, with a voice of entreaty, he said, ' Pray don't touch anything here,' and seemed very anxious to get her away." [1]

At other times, it was only by entreaty, or threats to force the door, that he could be induced to unlock it ; and then, as Mrs. Edkins described it, he sat surrounded by the strange materials of his antique art : his ochre, charcoal, pen and pencils, the little square deal table covered with letters, papers, and parchments in utmost confusion, and all round the room a complete litter of parchments. His hands and face betrayed, as usual, the nature of his work. But it has been too hastily assumed that the boy was systematically engaged in the conversion of modern parchments into spurious antiques. His antique poems became, ere long, voluminous enough; but as to the spurious parchments, all he ever produced could have been manufactured in a few days.

*A self-
taught
draughts-
man.*

But he was a self-taught draughtsman ; delighted in realizing to the eye his fancies of the long-vanished architecture of the Bristowe, of Ælla, Canynge, and Rowley : as in the elaborate elevations of the Bristowe Castle of A.D. 1138, gravely reproduced, with accompanying ground-plans, in Barrett's " History," as " engraved from drawings on vellum preserved to this day." Such drawings are spoken of as numerous. His uncle Phillips had some ; Barrett and Catcott obtained others. His relative Mr. Stephens, Mr. Palmer, Mr. Richard Smith and others, had many of his heraldic drawings ; and Mrs. Edkins, in describing to Mr. George Cumberland " the old deeds that came from the muniment room, which were used indiscriminately for any purpose," adds, " there were many of them covered with strange figures of men's heads, &c., on the backs," which she supposes were his drawing. It may be assumed, therefore, that the half-holidays of the Bluecoat boy were more frequently spent in gratifying his artistic and antiquarian tastes—in recreating, in such visible form, his concep-

[1] Mrs. Edkins, Dix, p. 313.

tions of the past—than in manufacturing professed originals of his Rowley poems. Such spurious antiques belong altogether to a later period, after the poems themselves had been produced, and the originals were called for by Barrett and others.

In every step of Chatterton's brief career we meet with surmises and suspicions of his contemporaries, dealt with at a subsequent period as facts. Towards the close of his residence in Colston's Hospital, where we know some of his Rowley poems were written, he was observed to seclude himself more than ever in his little study. When Mrs. Edkins narrated this to Mr. Cumberland long afterwards, she entertained no doubt that he was then assiduously labouring at the Rowley manuscripts. But this was an after-thought. So little did even the mother and other nearest relations comprehend the strange boy, that when he was nearly fourteen years of age they became apprehensive "lest he should be doing something improper, knowing his want of money and ambition to appear like others;" but the only idea they could conjure up to account for his recluse habits was, "that these colours were to colour himself, and that, perhaps, he would join some gipsies one day or other, as he seemed so discontented with his station in life."[1]

Sometimes, however, especially in the earlier period of his residence in the Bluecoat School, he would spend his holidays in his mother's company, writing "on the seat of the schoolroom window, which was high, and to accomplish which he was obliged to stand on a chair. If any of his mother's pupils interrupted him, he would get down from it in a great rage, and strike them to make them quiet. Occasionally his mother would take the children into an upper room when he was thus engaged, that he might not be disturbed."[2] It was not therefore from an unsocial disposition, or any undue secretiveness, but from the natural craving of the young poet for silence in his hours of inspiration that he

[1] Mrs. Edkins, Dix, App. p. 314.    [2] Dix's Life, p. 15.

learned to court the privacy of his little study.  The noise of his mother's pupils would have been no impediment to the manufacture of antique MSS.; but it was sufficient to banish every antique fancy and poetic thought.

*First publ'c appearance as a poet.*

It appears to have been in his eleventh year that Chatterton took to writing verse; and at the same early age he made his first public appearance as a poet. About this period he was presented to the Bishop for confirmation, and the serious impressions then produced on his youthful mind were reflected in some of his earliest verses.  About the same time, apparently, his sister presented him with a pocket-book as a New Year's gift; and at the end of the year she received it back, filled chiefly with poetry.[1]  Writing long afterwards from memory, she assigned her brother's confirmation to his thirteenth year.[2]  But the researches of Mr. W. Tyson, of Bristol, have led to the discovery of one of the poetical productions referred to by Mrs. Newton, in *Felix Farley's Journal*, of the earlier date of January 8, 1763, when he was only ten years of age.[3]  Soon after his confirmation he paraphrased the ninth chapter of Job: "How shall man be just with God?  If he will contend with Him, he cannot answer Him one of a thousand. . . . . For He is not a man, as I am, that I should answer Him, and we should come together in judgment.  Neither is there any days-man betwixt us, that might lay his hand upon us both."  At the same time he also wrote the following little piece, entitled:

*Earliest religious poem.*

### ON THE LAST EPIPHANY; OR, CHRIST'S COMING TO JUDGMENT.

Behold! just coming from above,
The Judge, with majesty and love!
The sky divides and rolls away
To admit Him thro' the realms of day!

---

[1] Gregory's Life, p. 10.   [2] Mrs. Newton's Letter, Croft, p. 162.
[3] Dix, App. p. 320.

> The sun, astonish'd, hides its face ;
> The moon and stars with wonder gaze
> At Jesu's bright superior rays.
> Dread lightnings flash, and thunders roar,
> And shake the earth and briny shore ;
> The trumpet sounds at Heaven's command,
> And pierceth thro' the sea and land ;
> The dead in each now hear the voice ;
> The sinners fear, and saints rejoice ;
> For now the awful hour is come
> When every tenant of the tomb
> Must rise, and take his everlasting doom.

This simple effusion of youthful piety, though a mere echo of the religious teachings of the schoolroom, is of interest from the contrast it presents to the productions of later years. When finished it so pleased its young author that he dropped it into the letter-box of the weekly journal, now famous chiefly through his contributions, and had the delight of seeing his first work in print. No doubt he took his sister into his confidence, and showed her the wonderful production, which left so strong an impression on her mind that her recollections of it fifteen years afterwards led to its later identification. *Sees his first work in print.*

Now, at length, the young poet had discovered his vocation. "He had been gloomy," his sister says, "from the time he began to learn; but we remarked he was more cheerful after he began to write poetry." He became, ere long, a frequent contributor to *Felix Farley's Journal*, and soon learned to enjoy the delights of anonymous journalism with keenest zest. It was in the following December that the unpopular churchwarden of St. Mary Redcliffe became the butt of his satirical muse; and a few months later "Apostate Will," long regarded as Chatterton's first effort in verse, made its appearance. It is a satirical sketch, in the same measure as "The Churchwarden," of a hypocritical renegade, whose attempts to make a gain of godliness had, no doubt, excited popular censure. The piece, though it refers to the *The poet has discovered his vocation.* *The young satirist.*

> "Days of yore, when Wesley's power
> Gathered new strength by every hour,"

and pictures a bankrupt trader turning Methodist preacher for gain, is not designed, like some of his later productions, to ridicule religious belief; but already he manifested one strong bent of his mind, towards satire, under the influence of which, ere long, neither friend nor foe was to be spared.

*Unwearied zeal in his studies.*

Chatterton now gave full play to his intellectual powers. His reading was pursued with unwearied zeal; and the usher reported that he made rapid progress in arithmetic. Between his eleventh and twelfth years, as his sister reports, "he wrote a catalogue of the books he had read, to the number of seventy. History and divinity were the chief subjects;" and these, as his schoolmates informed her, he retired to read at the hours allotted for play.[1] Ere long, also, the elder poets were lovingly studied. Chaucer was his special favourite. The motto to his "Epistle to Mastre Canynge" is taken from Barbour's "Bruce;" his MSS. in the British Museum include an extract from "Piers Ploughman," though else-

*Familiarity with the poets.*

where he ascribes its authorship to Chaucer. His own writings furnish evidence of his familiarity with Shakespeare, Milton, Dryden, Prior, Cowley, and Gray; Pope and Thomson were studied with care; and Churchill became his favourite model as a satirist. It was probably for modern authors such as those that he resorted to the circulating library; while private collections chiefly supplied the rarer folios and quartos of Hall, Hollingshed, Camden, Stowe, Weever, and the like historical, heraldic, and antiquarian works, which furnished delightful occupation for the play-hour. The loss of the record of his early course of reading is greatly to be regretted, from the light it was calculated to throw on some of his

*Readings in divinity.*

peculiar tastes and modes of thought. His readings in divinity, however, find an illustration from one of the allusions in his "Apostate Will."

> "Then lifting his dissembling eyes:
> How blessed is the sect! he cries;

---

[1] Croft, p. 162.

> Nor Bingham, Young, nor Stillingfleet,
> Shall make me from this sect retreat."





But all this while Chatterton appeared to his companions in the Bluecoat School, dull and unimpressible, and alike devoid of inclination or ability for such literary pursuits as received a very unwonted encouragement there. While secretly resenting the inadequacy of the resources within his reach to satisfy his intellectual cravings, and brooding over thick-coming fancies, speedily to find enduring form: his rough schoolmates were already rivals in verse-making, as well as in the sports of the playground, and no doubt thought him little less fitted for the one than the other. Yet in this seemingly uncongenial retreat he found teachers capable of appreciating some of the finer elements of his nature; while, at the same time, it also yielded materials for his vein of satire.



Stephen Chatterton Phillips, the son of the sexton, and consequently cousin of the poet,—who appears himself to have been a Bluecoat boy,—informed Mr. Cumberland that among the papers found after Chatterton's death, were some written by him while still an inmate of Colston's school; but "all he could remember of them was, that a story went about, when he was at the school, of a lad named Bess, called Crazy Bess by the boys, having got Chatterton to write some lines satirizing the usher, who caught him finishing the last line and corrected him severely for it." The object of the satirical assault thus prematurely arrested, was probably Mr. Warner, the head-master, who is only known from having provoked later attacks from the same caustic pen. The first was the mere thoughtless effervescence of youthful spirit; but the feeling of dislike remained after he had exchanged the schoolroom for an attorney's office, and found vent in new satirical assaults. Dr. Gregory relates the exposure of one of these, chiefly owing to its being written on office paper, with consequent corporal penalties.

The loss of those school-boy lampoons is to be regretted, not from any probable merit they possessed as

CHAP. III.
———
*Biographical value of his satires.*

poems, but solely for their autobiographical value. Their caricatures of the unpopular head-master were no doubt overdrawn and irreverent enough ; but they would have helped to account for the lack of sympathy between him and the most remarkable of his pupils. That the fault was not altogether in the boy, is proved by the fact that Mr. Warner was the only master in Colston's Hospital who failed to appreciate his better qualities, and win his regard. Mr. Haynes, the second master, is indeed quoted by Bryant as reporting of him that "he was not a boy of extraordinary parts, nor did he make any display of abilities during the time he was at school ;"[1] but this blindness to his intellectual gifts did not prevent Chatterton winning his good-will ; and Dr. Gregory informs us that he found in him a friend who conceived for him a strong affection.

*The poetical usher, Phillips.*

But Chatterton's true teacher, so far as the training of others had any share in the development of his genius, appears to have been the junior master, or usher, Thomas Phillips, to whose example and influence his first contributions to *Felix Farley's Bristol Journal* were probably due. Thistlethwaite, another of Phillips' pupils, in writing to Dean Milles, speaks of him as one who, "notwithstanding the disadvantages of a very confined education, possessed a taste for history and poetry," and was himself a frequent contributor to the periodicals of the day.

*Chatterton's early companions.*

In reviewing the account furnished by Thistlethwaite to the Dean of Exeter, of his introduction to Chatterton, through the intervention of Phillips, and their subsequent intercourse, some suggestive hints are furnished in reference to various claimants to early companionship with the boy. For the most part it becomes obvious that they were incapable of appreciating the true worth of their strange, silent, studious companion. "The most perfect masters of human nature in Bristol" did indeed distinguish him, as he tells us in his Will, by the title of "The Mad Genius ;" but even that equivocal recognition of his

[1] Bryant's Observations, p. 560.

gifts was of a considerably later date. We have accounts from those who shared with him the bounty of Colston's Hospital ; from acquaintances of his own age during his later apprenticeship ; and from those who claim to have befriended and patronised him : but all tinged with the same depreciatory tone. The letters of Thistlethwaite, Cary, Smith, and Rudhall, and the narratives of Catcott, Barrett, and other seniors, alike betray the feeling that the boy " was no such great things after all !" But when learned antiquaries, deans, baronets, and professors, began to ply them with inquiries about their past intercourse with him, their self-importance was gratified, and informants became minute and precise about facts and dates, which have since been too implicitly accepted as authentic.

CHAP. III.<br>Disparaging accounts furnished by his companions.

Mr. James Thistlethwaite had better opportunities of knowing Chatterton's early career than he was willing to confess. Bound apprentice to Mr. Grant, bookseller and stationer, near St. Leonard's Gate, Bristol, in 1765, he subsequently went to London, and became a student of law. It was not, therefore, to be expected that he should be anxious to publish to the world that he and Chatterton had worn the Bluecoat garb together, and were under the same obligations to Colston's charity. He was about fourteen months older than Chatterton, a pupil of Phillips, and one who, stimulated by his example, became one of the poets of the school. According to his own more guarded way of stating the case, in the summer of 1763, being then in his twelfth year, he contracted an intimacy with Phillips, and by this means, towards the latter end of the year, formed a connexion with his pupil, Chatterton.[1]

Thistle-thwaite a Bluecoat boy.

Translated into a literal version, the probability is that, towards the close of 1763, the younger Bluecoat boy was promoted to a higher form, and thus came into companionable contact with Thistlethwaite, at the same time that he was brought under the influence of the assistant master, Thomas Phillips. The poetical achievements of

Chatterton makes his acquaintance.

[1] Letter to Dr. Milles, Dean of Exeter.

Chap. III.

*A spirit of
poetical
emulation
excited.*

the usher had already excited a keen spirit of emulation amongst the elder boys in the school. "The love of fame animated their bosoms, and a variety of competitors appeared to dispute the laurel with him." When we think of the ordinary character of the pupils in institutions of this class, the master capable of producing these results from such unpromising materials rises correspondingly in our estimation. Dr. Gregory, indeed, speaks of his taste for poetry having "excited a similar flame in several young men who," he adds, "made no mean figure in the periodical literature of that day; in Chatterton, Thistlethwaite, Cary, Fowler, and others."[1] But if we judge of the names thus associated with Chatterton's by the one best known to us, Thistlethwaite's letter shows that in them the potter had to work on but common clay.[2]

*Account
g.v.n to
Dean
Milles.*

Describing to Dean Milles, nearly twenty years afterwards, Chatterton's communicating his professed acquisition of certain ancient MSS.—the first of the Rowley poems, which were now (in 1764) sorely puzzling Phillips to decipher their antique caligraphy,—Thistlethwaite adds: "For my own part, having little or no taste for such studies, I repined not at the disappointment. Phillips, on the contrary, was to all appearance mortified, indeed much more so than at that time I thought the object deserved, expressing his sorrow at the want of success, and repeatedly declaring his intention of resuming the attempt at a future period." He then adds, "In the year 1765 I was put apprentice to a stationer at Bristol, at which period my acquaintance and correspondence with Chatterton and Phillips seem to have undergone a temporary dissolution." This incidental reference to his own apprenticeship supplies evidence of the most reliable kind on the all-important question of the earliest date when

---

[1] Gregory's Life of Chatterton, p. 7, note.

[2] Fowler's verse is repeatedly alluded to in Chatterton's satires in terms of contempt. *Vide* "*Journal:*" "As heavy as Fowlerian song;" "*Whore of Babylon:*" "What Fowler, happy genius, titles verse;" and the "*Epistle to Rev. Mr. Catcott.*"

Chatterton produced any of his Rowley poems. The letters of his sister to Sir Herbert Croft and Mr. Cottle appeal to us for acceptance by the guilelessness of their apologetic tenderness; but their dates must be tested by other evidence. Mr. George Catcott, another authority, wrote under the influence of a preconceived theory; amended his dates in his letters to the *Gentleman's Magazine* in the same dogmatic fashion in which we shall find him responding to Dr. Johnson's personal inquiries;[1] and indulged in an illogical pertinacity little calculated to carry conviction to any mind. But the year of Thistlethwaite's apprenticeship, in which he left Colston's Hospital, and severed his connexion with Phillips and Chatterton, was too marked a date to admit of error; and therefore fixes beyond dispute the important fact that the orphan charity boy, with only such common English education as the Bluecoat School afforded, had already, in his twelfth year,[2] conceived the idea of a series of antique poems, ascribed to the imaginary Thomas Rowley, a monk of the fifteenth century, which were to puzzle learned critics, deans, titled dilettanti, and a whole century of able editors.

Bearing in remembrance what Thistlethwaite chose to withhold from Dean Milles, that he was himself at the date referred to an inmate of Colston's school, his account is as follows:—"Going down Horse Street, near the school, one day during the summer of 1764, I accidentally met with Chatterton. Entering into conversation with him,



---

[1] Gent. Mag. vol. xlviii. p. 347. "He (Mr. Warton) says Chatterton was seventeen years old when he first produced the poems to me. He was but just turned fifteen. He gave me the poems in the beginning of the year 1768. He had the tonsure on his head, being just come from Mr. Colston's charity school." In a subsequent letter (Ibid. p. 403) he alters the date to the end of the year; "but," he says, "in my opinion it is of little moment as to the precise time in which we became acquainted, as it will not add a single minute to his life, and of course not the least degree of credibility to the supposition of his being the author of the poems attributed to Rowley."

[2] Chatterton was not twelve years of age till November 1764.

he informed me that he was in possession of certain old MSS. which had been deposited in a chest in Redcliffe Church, and that he had lent some or one of them to Phillips. Within a day or two after this, I saw Phillips, and repeated to him the information I had received from Chatterton. Phillips produced a MS. on parchment or vellum, which I am confident was '*Elinoure and Juga*,' a kind of pastoral eclogue, afterwards published in the *Town and Country Magazine*."

Different manuscript copies exist of some of Chatterton's larger antique poems, showing that they were carefully elaborated, and underwent repeated revisions ere he recognised them as complete; but this eclogue, or rather ballad, is only known as it appeared in the *Town and Country Magazine* for May 1769, under the title "Elinoure and Juga : written three hundred years ago by T. Rowley, secular priest."

Two tearful maidens, the nut-brown Elinoure and fair Juga, sit by the banks of the river Rudborne, near St. Albans, bewailing the perils of their absent knights, both of whom prove to have fallen, fighting for the White Rose, in the old wars of York and Lancaster. The language and orthography are of the affected Chaucerian character which formed the disguise of all the Rowley poems; but it is curious to catch in its stanzas echoes of the polished quatrains of Gray's " Elegy," then in the first blush of its popularity. Slightly modernised, two of its stanzas thus present the maidens interchanging their plaints :—

JUGA.

" Sisters in sorrow, on this daisied bank,
  Where melancholy broods, we will lament ;
Bewet with morning dew and even dank ;
  Like levind oaks in each the other bent ;
  Or like forletten halls of merriment,
Whose ghastly mitches hold the train of fright,
Where lethal ravens bark, and owlets wake the night.

ELINOURE.

No more the miskynette shall wake the morn,
  The minstrel dance, good cheer, and morris play ;

CHAP. III.

> No more the ambling palfry and the horn
>     Shall from the lessel rouse the fox away ;
>     I'll seek the forest all the live-long day ;
>     All night among the graved church-glebe will go,
>     And to the passing sprites lecture my tale of woe."

*Archaic
language
and spelling.*

The stanzas as given here are modernised in spelling ; and if in addition to this the small sprinkling of obsolete or coined words were replaced by their modern equivalents in the footnotes—e.g. *forletten*, forsaken ; *mitches*, ruins ; *lessel*, forest, or bush,—the whole would be restored to the language of the eighteenth century. Here and there, indeed, the line would require modification where the modern equivalent in the footnote differs in accent or number of syllables ; and not infrequently a rich alliteration would be lost : as in the replacement of *levynde* by blasted ; *chyrche-glebe*, by churchyard ; *forletten* by forsaken ; and *miskynette* by its interpretation of a small bagpipe. A single couplet will suffice to illustrate the obscurity—so inimical to every chance of popularity,—which Chatterton purposely bestowed on his antique poems by the affectation of ancient orthography.

> "Lyche levynde okes in eche the odher bente,
>     Or lyke forletten halles of merriemente."

*Impressive
incident of
local
history.*

The execution of Sir Baldwin Fulford, at Bristol, in 1461, in the reign of Edward IV., as a Lancastrian plotter against the life of Warwick the King-maker, was one of the incidents of local history belonging to the era of Canynge, which made a lasting impression on Chatterton's mind, and accounts for the choice of his earliest theme, where the nut-brown maid thus plains to the fair Juga :

> " To fyghte for Yorke mie love ys dyght in stele ;
>     O mai ne sanguen steine the whyte rose peyncte."

Here then we have evidence that the boy-poet was already preening the Muse's wing for those strong though devious flights, in which his genius manifested its amplest powers. The " Elinoure and Juga " is simple and tender. It is in reality a little dramatic lyric, or ballad-poem, of

*Thistle-
thwaite
claims to be
the poet's
confidant.*

seven stanzas, such as might fitly be the first offspring of a youthful muse ; but wonderful as the product of a boy at the age to which its origin is assigned.

James Thistlethwaite, to whom we owe the important fact of the date of this early production, was Chatterton's senior by little more than a year. He appears from his letter to Dean Milles to have been a matter-of-fact youth, thrown by accident into companionship with the young poet, but wholly incapable of sympathy with the tastes and aspirations of the schoolmate whom he represents as choosing him for his literary confidant. In reality, however, it was to their master, Thomas Phillips, and not to Thistlethwaite, that the manuscript poem was produced, in antique guise of language and spelling, " the lines written in the manner of prose, and without any regard to punctuation."

*Inadequate
record of
Phillips.*

Dr. Gregory expresses a well-founded regret at the want of any adequate record of this, the only teacher whose mental and moral influences are recognisable in Chatterton's career. He was, I imagine, still young, probably not greatly the senior of his oldest pupils ; of a gentle, kindly, sociable nature, and a vigorous, manly presence, well calculated to win the admiration of his youthful companions. His connexion with Colston's Hospital appears to have ceased soon after Chatterton left it ; as he is referred to in one of the elegies of his gifted pupil, in which those characteristics are perpetuated, as residing at Fairford at the time of his death. The earliest of these elegies is dated October 1769 ; and this, with a longer poem in which Chatterton mourns the death of his loved teacher and friend, are the only records of him besides Thistlethwaite's brief notice. The latter extends to thirty-four stanzas, of very unequal merit, but which might have been compressed, by the rejection of those of inferior character, into a poem worthy to rank alongside the fine creations of his antique muse. In the opening lines he exclaims :

> " Is Phillips dead, and is my friend no more ?
> Gone like the sand divested from the shore."

CHAP. III.

*Elegy on Phillips.*

He then proceeds in strains of extravagant eulogy, to dwell on the virtues of his friend, and his own irreparable loss ; but from these the following may be selected as conveying some idea of the special attractions which left so deep an impression on the mind of Chatterton, long after he had left the Bluecoat School :—

" Peace deck'd in all the softness of the dove,
    Over thy passions spread her silver plume ;
The rosy veil of harmony and love
    Hung on thy soul in one eternal bloom.

Peace, gentlest, softest of the virtues, spread
    Her silver pinions, wet with dewy tears,
Upon her best distinguished poet's head,
    And taught his lyre the music of the spheres.

Temperance, with health and beauty in her train,
    And massy-muscled strength, in graceful pride,
Pointed at scarlet luxury and pain,
    And did at every frugal feast preside."

The virtues recorded in the last stanza preeminently distinguished Chatterton himself, and may have been confirmed and strengthened by Phillips' influence and example.   Other verses betray unmistakeable echoes of the same popular elegy which has been already recognised as his model in part of his first antique ballad ; as in the following :—

*Imitation of Gray's elegy.*

" Here, stretched upon this Heaven-ascending hill,
    I'll wait the horrors of the coming night,
I'll imitate the gently-plaintive rill,
    And by the glare of lambent vapours write.

Wet with the dew the yellow hawthorns bow ;
    The rustic whistles through the echoing cave ;
Far o'er the lea the breathing cattle low,
    And the full Avon lifts the darkened wave.

Now as the mantle of the evening swells,
    Upon my mind I feel a thickening gloom ;
Ah ! could I charm by necromantic spells
    The soul of Phillips from the deathly tomb !

Then would we wander thro' this darkened vale,
    In converse such as heavenly spirits use ;
And, borne upon the pinions of the gale,
    Hymn the Creator, and exert the Muse."

Through the second of the above stanzas Chatterton drew his pen as "too flowery for grief." The same critical taste might have been applied to other stanzas with advantage. It is diffuse and unequal; but the tender recollections of his master and friend are reiterated with all the earnestness of genuine admiration and regret. He dwells on his genius, his unsullied purity, his appreciation of nature under all the changing aspects of the seasons, his honour and unvarying cheerfulness; and as he draws towards a close, exclaims:

> "Now rest, my Muse! but only rest to weep
> A friend made dear by every sacred tie;
> Unknown to me be comfort, peace, or sleep:
> Phillips is dead; 'tis pleasure then to die."



Those stanzas, the work of a later date, when Chatterton was in his seventeenth year, show that his intercourse with his favourite master survived his departure from school, and was only broken by death. Phillips was in many respects such a friend as he then specially needed. The relations in which they had stood to each other as teacher and pupil would make Chatterton look up to him with confidence when their intercourse ceased to be constrained. He, if any one, was fitted to draw his young companion forth from the strange seclusion begot, in no slight degree, by the circumstances of his childhood. In his younger years especially he appears to have been peculiarly open to all kindly influences; and in his teacher he found the congenial sympathy for which he



craved. Could we now trace the various steps in their intercourse, from the first partial confidences of the schoolboy to the franker intercourse of later date, when for a brief period they met on equal terms, it would probably appear that Phillips did more than all others with whom he was brought in contact to develop whatever was great or good in him. The elegy shows that they had their pleasant evening walks together, when they held high converse, worthy of true poets, and yielded willingly to all the devout emotions of that suggestive hour.

Phillips was, no doubt, a man of literary tastes. As to his actual merits as a poet they may have been small enough. Thistlethwaite evidently regarded him as one whose preeminent genius was proved by the triumphs achieved over himself and other youthful poets of the Bluecoat School. The kindly relations established between him and them prove him, at any rate, to have possessed in an eminent degree that sympathetic ardour, so invaluable in a teacher, which enkindled in the group of charity boys among whom his lot was cast a spirit of poetic emulation, little to be looked for in such a class of pupils. But when we learn that in all his contests with them, "Phillips still, to the mortification of his opponents, came off victorious and unhurt,"[1] it would seem that he found gratification in such triumphs ; and we are less tempted to think of him, with Chatterton, as :

"Phillips ! great master of the boundless lyre,"

than as a genial counterpart of Goldsmith's village schoolmaster, content with such preeminence within his own narrow domain. On him Chatterton essayed his first serious attempt to pass off his own verse as the production of a poet of the fifteenth century. The boldness of this poetical masquerading was, under all the circumstances, fully equal to the later attempts on the credulity of Barrett, or even Walpole himself. How far a sincere confidence was subsequently established between them can only be surmised ; but in him the boy found a congenial sympathiser, eager to solve the mystery of the supposed antique parchment, yet not less ready to enter into the aspiring hopes of the young poet. As to Thistlethwaite he is a fair type of old and young in the common circle of Chatterton's acquaintance. To his purblind vision the boy, who was his junior at an age when the difference of a year or two constitutes an important element in the relations of schoolmates,

[1] Letter of Thistlethwaite to Dean Milles.

appeared as simply contenting himself with the sports and pastimes more immediately adapted to his age, and apparently possessing neither inclination, nor indeed ability, for literary pursuits ! The confidence extended to such a companion was not likely to include any hint of the real authorship of the romantic ballad of the White Rose.

*Healthful influences of Colston's Hospital.*

But, notwithstanding the utter inadequacy of Colston's Hospital to satisfy the cravings of the remarkable boy who wore its garb, and partook of the best training it had to offer, it is obvious that its influences were, on the whole, of a healthful nature ; and, above all, the moral culture to which its founder attached such just value appears to have been sound. However evanescent may have been the first religious impressions, which found expression in his Epiphany verses and other juvenile poems, including a lost paraphrase of some portions of Isaiah : all that we know of his youth indicates sound moral feeling. "He was a lover of truth," says his sister, "from the earliest dawn of reason, and nothing would move him so much as being belied. When in the school, we were informed by the usher, his master de- pended on his veracity on all occasions."[1]  His foster- mother describes him, at seven years of age, as "tenderly

*Tender sen- sibility to distress.*

sensible of every one's distresses." At twelve the same sensibility remained unblunted.  "He could not bear to hear of any one suffering ;" and would part with his last halfpence, and submit to the privation of coveted objects he was about to purchase, in order to relieve the beggars who frequented the drawbridge, over which his usual road from school lay. If he had no money, Mrs. Edkins adds, he would request a penny from her for the object of his compassion, telling her "he loved her for it as much as if she had given it to himself."[2]  At a later date she describes him as a good son and brother, preferring his home to every other resort ; and there

---

[1] Mrs. Newton's Letter, Croft, p. 162.
[2] Mrs. Edkins to G. Cumberland, Esq., Dix, App. p. 315.

attracting the love of all who knew him.[1]   For, curiously enough : though silent, reserved, and spending from choice much of his time alone ; he was, nevertheless, of a social disposition, and at a very early age displayed a singular power of winning the sympathy both of old and young.

---

[1] Mrs. Edkins to G. Cumberland, Esq., Dix, App. p. 309.

CHAP. III.<br><br>*Social disposition.*

# CHAPTER IV.

## THE DE BERGHAM PEDIGREE.



WHEN the " Great House " was selected by Colston as the hospital in which his Bluecoat boys should be lodged, it stood amid gardens and orchards, with the open greensward in front reaching to the river's brink. Though the mason's handiwork had encroached on garden and grass-plot by the time Chatterton became an inmate there, it was still a pleasant neighbourhood, to which well-to-do citizens resorted ; and in one of the mansions close by, the Bristol surgeon and antiquary, Mr. William Barrett, resided, with his well-stocked library and other attractions, the value of which were somehow or other discovered and made available by the Bluecoat boy. They trafficked ere long in old parchments, in borrowed books, and in talk on many subjects strange enough to most inmates of a charity school. The surgeon could not fail to see in him something out of the ordinary run of Bluecoat boys ; took special note of his bright, intelligent eye ; and used often to send for him that he might enjoy his eager discussion of some disputed point. In this way Chatterton escaped at times from the hospital and his juvenile associates there, returning with some borrowed volume over which to pore while they were sporting in the playground.

On Saturdays and other half-holidays his road home lay by the drawbridge over the river Frome, a tributary of the Avon, on which the hospital stood, and so by the old bridge to the Somersetshire side of the Avon, and on to Redcliffe Hill. For the most part we know that he made straight for home with as little delay as possible; and then, after a loving welcome from mother and sister, was speedily ensconced in his favourite attic, amid his parchments and drawing materials. But little as the cloistral life of Colston's Hospital seemed calculated to prepare its inmates for free intercourse with the outer world of Bristol, Chatterton appears to have made acquaintance with some of its notabilities at a very early period, and turned them to account. The hospital system of training was framed in part with a view to counteract the evil tendencies which its founder imagined to be inseparable from nonconformity; but to this were added other features, which might seem as though they were directly inherited from the old Friars Carmelites who had been the precursors of the Bluecoat boys. Not only did the boy-monks wear the blue-gown, but they appear to have perpetuated something symbolical of the old friars' shaven crown. " Mr. Capel," says Bryant, " told me that he saw Chatterton the very day that he came from Colston's, with the tonsure on his head, and in the habit of the place;" and Mr. George Catcott, whose shop he passed every time he crossed the bridge, when telling of his receipt of Rowley manuscripts from the boy, says: " He gave me the poems in the beginning of the year 1768. He had then the tonsure on his head, being just come from Mr. Colston's charity school." [1]

Probably in the Bristol of a century ago, as in London even now, the quaint garb of the Bluecoat boy was a passport that facilitated ingress to many resorts not otherwise accessible. But the peculiar tastes and habits of Chatterton must have singled him out ere long, and attracted special notice from some, whose attentions he soon turned to account. There appears to have been a strange fascination about the boy; and when it pleased him it almost seemed as though he could make friends at will.

Writing to his mother soon after his arrival in London, he tells her of a stranger he encountered in Drury Lane

[1] Gent. Mag. vol. xlviii. p. 348.

Theatre, under circumstances which made an introduction
desirable ; and so he says : " I contracted an immediate
acquaintance with him, which you know is no hard task
to me."  The same aptitude for winning the good-will
of others was noticeable from childhood.  He seems to
have taken his place among his seniors, as it were, with
a consciousness of equality that made him at his ease
among the best of them.



Mr. George Catcott, who notes for us the tonsured head
of the young poet ; and who we shall find ere long the
zealous collector of the reputed writings of the good
priest Rowley : had for partner in his trade as pewterer,
Mr. Henry Burgum, a Bristol worthy, with whom Chatterton had some curious dealings.  Mr. Burgum had
come from Gloucestershire to Bristol at an early age, in
a very humble capacity ; obtained help apparently from
one or other of the charities established there by its
philanthropic old merchant, Edward Colston ; and so
was apprenticed to the trade in which he is now found.



He had risen by his own exertions, and appears to have
been a self-taught man, with not a little of the vanity
which is apt to accompany such acquirements.  We glean
from later notices of him, in the " Kew Gardens " and
others of Chatterton's satires, that his language was ungrammatical, and his habit of profane swearing notorious.[1]
He is described by Mr. Richard Smith, Mr. Catcott's
nephew, as " a presumptuous, vulgar fellow, who boasted
of his ancestry."[2]  As, however, he adds that he robbed
his partner of 3,000*l.*, his all,—which is another mode
of stating that the pewtering business failed ;—we may
presume that Mr. Burgum is shown at his worst.  So far
as we can now recover any glimpse of his true character,
it will be found not to be without some redeeming
traits.

Among other characteristic memorials of the benevolent old merchant and High Church M.P. of Bristol

---

[1] *Vide* Chatterton's " Will," " Epistle to Rev. Mr. Catcott," and
" Kew Gardens."

[2] Gent. Mag. N.S. vol. x. p. 604.

in the latter days of Queen Anne, various associations have been organized to celebrate the " Colston anniversary," and emulate his example. First in order among these charitable associations is " The Colston Society," founded in 1729; and which, as Mr. Tovey tells us, has ever been heartily promoted by "many distinguished characters devoted to the constitution in Church and State."[1] Let us hope that, in dispensing their charities, this did not prevent their occasionally relieving a starving dissenter. " The Dolphin Society," named after Colston's well-known crest, followed : " established," according to the same local authority, " by the Tories in 1749." Next came " The Anchor Society," in 1768 : a year famous for Wilkes's Middlesex election, his expulsion from Parliament, and universal political ferment in consequence ; and its memorialist selects as preeminent among the distinguished members of the new charity " Henry Cruger, so highly famed in the electioneering annals of Bristol." This curious admixture of charity and politics is well deserving of note, if we would understand the strange social life into which Chatterton passed on emerging from the cloisters of the Bluecoat School. Without some comprehension of its character, it is impossible to do justice to the youth in his later aspect as local satirist and politician.

But whilst sound Church and State benevolence was thus active, democracy put forth its claim to a share in the good work ; and so, in 1758, " The Grateful Society " was founded : differing from the others, according to Mr. Tovey, " in not blending the elements of party feeling with the pure spirit of charity in which it originated." Sundry citizens who had been educated or otherwise helped in life by Colston's generous provisions, resolved to show their gratitude by establishing a Bristol benevolent society, in which for once politics should have no share ; and amongst its early office-bearers appears the name of Henry Burgum as president in 1766. The poor Gloucestershire boy had owed his start in life,

_______________
[1] Tovey's Colston, pp. 156—160.

CHAP. IV.

*The Colston anniversary.*

*The Dolphin and Anchor Societies.*

*The Grateful Society.*

and probably most of the education he possessed, to Mr. Colston's charities; and it is a pleasant trait in his character to find him prominent among those who were not ashamed, in later life, to acknowledge their obligations to their benefactor.

*Mr. Burgum's aspirations.*

Very possibly the plebeian tradesman, though aspiring enough in his own way, did not sympathise with the benevolent High Church Tories of the "Anchor" and "Dolphin;" but happily no rival "tincture of Whiggism" was called in to mar the simplicity of this best of all the Colston anniversary charities. Mr. Burgum's ambition rather incited him to the patronage of art and letters. Chatterton introduces in his "Kew Gardens" this satirical allusion to one of his blunders as a connoisseur:

> "If Burgum bought a Bacon for a Strange,
> The man has credit, and is great on change."

His reading also extended beyond the current literature of the day, and he is even said to have taught himself Latin and Greek.[1] But if so, repeated allusions in Chatterton's satires serve to indicate that any smattering of classics he had contrived to acquire, only sufficed to expose him to the ridicule of "the lettered throng of Oxonian pedants," headed by the Vicar of St. Mary Redcliffe. But music commanded his special favour.

*His musical taste.*

Dr. Maitland notes his name among the subscribers to a set of quartetts by Kotzwara, the composer of the "Battle of Prague," published at Bath; and to a set of concertos by Norris of Oxford.[2] Mr. Thomas Kerslake of Bristol informs me that thirty years ago he bought a library, the property of a gentleman then far advanced in years, which included two chests about four feet long and twenty inches wide, each containing a concert set of music for about twenty instruments, and in as many volumes, with a partitioned compartment for each. One of the sets was, he believes, Handel's "Messiah;" the other included some of Haydn's pieces. The whole was got up in the most sumptuous and costly style.

---

[1] Croft, p. 183.　　[2] Maitland's Chatterton: an Essay, p. 18.

One of the sets was bound in red morocco, and each volume had the name " Henry Burgum " stamped in gold on the side.  They were believed to be the concert books of a music club which he entertained at his house.  It is obvious, therefore, that Mr. Burgum could be lavish enough when indulging his own favourite tastes.  In that of music Chatterton thoroughly sympathised.  To what extent his practical knowledge of it had been developed we have no record.  But it is not difficult to conceive of mutual grounds of attraction between the Bluecoat boy and the President of " The Grateful Society," apart from such incitements to later intercourse as his library supplied.

The precise date of the most notable transaction in which Chatterton figures in connexion with Mr. Burgum is uncertain.  Mr. Cottle, indeed, speaks of it as occurring when he was about sixteen years of age ; but if a precocity so abnormal may be tested by any ordinary rules, the production now referred to exhibits all the crudeness of one of his earliest antiquarian efforts.  The poetic specimen especially betrays the use of the glossary in its manufacture to an extent in striking contrast with the ease and naturalness of his later Rowley poems. Probably, therefore, Mr. Dix, who derived much of his information from Mr. Cottle more than thirty years later, is right in speaking of " the De Bergham pedigree " as produced while Chatterton was still an inmate of Colston's Hospital.

On a Saturday half-holiday, as we may presume,—at latest in the spring of 1767,—Chatterton paid a visit to the shop of Mr. Burgum, at the west end of Bristol Bridge, then in process of rebuilding, and delighted the pewterer with the announcement that he had discovered among the ancient parchments of Redcliffe Church an heraldic blazon of the De Bergham arms, and had a pedigree at home which proved his descent from some of the noblest families in England.  Mr. Burgum had, no doubt, already betrayed his weakness on the point of family descent, and so furnished the hint which his youthful deceiver turned to such account.  He craved sight of the wondrous pedigree; and within a few days was presented with the De Bergham quarterings blazoned on an old piece of parchment about eight inches square, and a first instalment of the pedigree itself, in Chatterton's own handwriting, copied into a book in which he had already transcribed portions of antique verse with this title: "Poems by Thomas Rowley, Priest of St. John's, in the City of Bristol, containing The Tournament, an Interlude, and a piece by Canynge, called the Gouler's Requiem."



From this pedigree it appeared that Mr. Burgum's ancestor, Simon de Seyncte Lyze, *alias* Senliz, came into England with the Conqueror, married Matilda, daughter of Waltheof, Earl of Northumberland, and in 1075, after the execution of the Earl for high treason, obtained a deed of gift of Bergham Castle, with the title of Earl of Northampton. The document in which this, and much else of the like kind, was set forth, bore this heading in large text: "Account of the family of the De Berghams, from the Norman Conquest to this time; collected from original Records, Tournament Rolls, and the Heralds of March and Garter's Records, by Thomas Chatterton."



The arms alone claimed to be of ancient authority. Nevertheless the sources of the family pedigree are of the most indisputable character. Marginal references abound, with such authorities as the "Roll of Battle Abbey;" "Ex stemma fam. Sir Johan de Leveches," "De Lee," &c.; Stowe, Ashmole, Collins, Dugdale, Rouge Dragon, Garter, Norroy, and, better than all, "Rowley's MSS." Mr. Wilcox, a critical editor, was sorely aggrieved by supposed reference to oral charters, where the marginal note appealed, in a common enough abbreviation, to the originals: *e.g.* "Oral Ch. from Hen. II. to Sir Ino. De Bergham." But, in truth, the references are, in many cases, as apocryphal as the pedigree itself; though not without some interesting traces of the unwonted range of study in which the boy delighted.



The pedigree is also garnished with sundry scraps of heraldic Latin, adapted from Weaver, and other sources not difficult to trace. Notwithstanding Mr. Burgum's reputed scholarship, these infallible evidences of the genuineness of the wondrous document were a mystery to him; and either he or Chatterton must have applied to Mr. Barrett, the learned surgeon and antiquary, as translations in his handwriting form part of the original pedigree. The boy had learned no Latin at Colston's school, and was, indeed, sensitive on his deficiency. In his "Epistle to the Rev. Mr. Catcott," he exclaims:—

> "But my objections may be reckoned weak,
> As nothing but my mother tongue I speak."

And in this and other satires he assails "classic dunces" who "hesitate to speak their native tongue." His companion Mr. William Smith informed Dean Milles that "he had no knowledge either of Greek or Latin, but expressed a design to teach himself Latin;"[1] and there can be no doubt that this design was attempted to be realized. Of Latin scholarship, in any true sense, he had none; but he carried out his intention far enough to be able to master the general import of the Latin passages he appropriated, though his ignorance of the grammar of the language is apparent wherever he had to extend contractions or alter the text. Bryant refers to the numerous Latin quotations in the "Merrie Tricks of Laymyngtonne" as a proof that that interlude was entirely beyond the capacity of the Bristol charity boy. "None of these quotations," he says, "were obvious, and such as a boy could attain to. Nor are they idly and ostentatiously introduced. They are all pertinent and well adapted,"[2] as also, no less so, are those in the De Bergham pedigree; but they turn out to be just the sort of quotations accessible to a student busy with the Latin rudiments. They are borrowed, not without grammatical blunders, from "Cato's Distichs" and "Sentences of Publius Syrius," to be met with in a little volume which in the seventeenth and eighteenth centuries was one of the first put into the hands of the young grammarian.[3]

---

[1] Milles's Rowley, p. 14.    [2] Bryant's Observations, p. 564.
[3] Tyrwhitt's Vindication, p. 209.

But their pertinent adaptation was the work of the self-taught boy.

In this way Chatterton had contrived to fit into the De Bergham pedigree a learned record of one of the pewterer's ancestors, who in the 24th year of the reign of Henry VI. obtained a patent for the use of alchemy, whereby this philosophic metallurgist was to transmute the inferior metals into gold or silver. There was a delicate flattery in this discovery, that working in the baser metals was an honourable art pertaining to the Burgums as a hereditary chartered right. Immediately following this comes another paragraph, no less apt and curious. Thomas de Asheton, the old alchemist, left issue four sons, of whom, according to the De Bergham pedigree, the second was " Edward Asheton, of Chatterton in Com. Lanc. in the right of his wife, the daughter and heir of Radcliffe de Chatterton of Chatterton, the heir-general of many families." The name is sufficiently suggestive to the reader now, though Mr. Burgum doubtless passed it over without thought of its bearing any reference to his humble protégé. RADCLIFFE DE CHATTERTON ! There is a volume of poetical romance crowded into the very name. It is. an epitome of the whole biography of the inspired charity boy.

The delight of the glorified pewterer on the acquisition of his patent of nobility may be imagined. His aspiring partner had already achieved notoriety by more than one notable deed, duly set forth ere long in Chatterton's satirical effusions ; but here was he, without effort of his own, exalted to an equality with the proudest peer of the realm. The first act of the ennobled tradesman was to present the discoverer of his pedigree with five shillings. The sum, though but poor largess from the hands of a De Bergham of Norman lineage, was probably a greater amount than the young herald had ever before possessed ; and its acceptance cost him no scruples, either then or afterwards. It figures at a later date, among other counts in the satirical indictment against Burgum and others, appended to his Will, where he exclaims :—

> "Burgum, I thank thee, thou hast let me see
> That Bristol has impressed her stamp on thee;
> Thy generous spirit emulates the Mayor's;
> Thy generous spirit with thy Bristol pairs.
> Gods! what would Burgum give to get a name,
> And snatch his blundering dialect from shame!
> What would he give to hand his memory down
> To time's remotest boundary? A crown!"

But this was an after-thought, if not a mere piece of satirical exaggeration, when he had exchanged the Blue-coat school for an attorney's office; and experience had given him further insight into the value of money. At the time it was given, Burgum's crown-piece amply rewarded the genealogist, for what I conceive to have been no more, at first, than a roguish experiment on the credulity of the pewterer. That this was the case finds confirmation from another of the boy's heraldic jests. Mr. Richard Smith, a relative both of the Catcotts and Smiths who figure so prominently in connexion with Chatterton, has recorded some interesting reminiscences of him. "Two of my paternal uncles," he says, " were his constant playmates; three of my maternal uncles were very intimate with him; and to this list may be added an aunt and my own father. Every one of these he by turns laughed at, ridiculed, censured, and, with the exception of the female, satirised most unmercifully, and abused most grossly."[1]



Aunt Martha, a venerable spinster, described by her nephew as " one of those pious and wise women ycleped 'old maids,'" appears to have better appreciated the young scapegrace than others who were made the butts of his jests. She told her nephew that " young Chatterton was a sad wag of a boy, and always upon some joke or another." The·old lady incurred his displeasure by taking him to task for some of his misdeeds, whereupon he revenged himself by forwarding to her " a scolding epistle," enclosed in which was her coat of arms, surrounded by a garter, and surmounted, for crest, by what its inheritor describes as a queer-looking flower, tinted

---

[1] Gent. Mag. N.S. vol. x. p. 603.

gules, with a scroll over it, labelled, " The Rose of Virginity ! "

In the same spirit, I doubt not, the first instalment of
the De Bergham pedigree was produced.   But stimulated
by the largess of the ennobled pewterer, and encouraged
by his demands for more, the family tree, which at first
came no nearer his own day than that of Sir John, son of
Alan de Bergham, Kt. of the thirteenth century, was
followed up with a " Continuation of the Account of the
Family of the De Berghams from the Norman Conquest
to this time."   Of this only the second instalment exists,
bringing it down to John, a grandson of William Bergham,
who served under Sir Francis Drake, and who by his
magnificence on the occasion of Queen Elizabeth's accession greatly diminished his fortune.   To compensate for
this the Queen made him keeper of the royal forests in
Gloucestershire, from whence the Berghams emerged in
the eighteenth century in the person of the Bristol pewterer !  The heraldic discoverer had brought the family
tree down to the reign of Charles II., from which period
his own genealogy was clearly traceable.   It required
some caution, therefore, in dealing with the modern ramifications of the Burgums.   It even lay within the bounds
of possibility that Mr. Burgum knew his own grandfather.
But other and still more characteristic guarantees placed
the second instalment of the pedigree beyond suspicion ;
 for not only does Master John de Bergham, a Cistercian
monk of the church of the Blessed Mary of Bristol, a
collateral ancestor of the pewterer, obtain special notice as
" one of the greatest ornaments of the age in which he
lived :" a poet, a translator of the Iliad, and a voluminous
author ; but the dry heraldic document is relieved by one
of the old monk's poetical romances.   John, son of Sir
John de Bergham, says the continuator of the pedigree,
" was a monk of the Cistercian Order in Bristol, as appears by the following testimonial letter :"—and thereupon
follows a commendatory Latin epistle, according to wonted
formulæ, beginning " Universis Sancte Matris Ecclesie
filiis, ad quos præsentes littere pervenerint," &c.   By

this it appears that the Chancellor and Society of Masters of Oxford, piously bearing in mind the scriptural maxim that a lighted candle should not be put under a bushel, and dreading lest, by the envy of calumniators, the brilliant light of their dearest brother, Master John de Bergham, monk, of the church of the Blessed Mary of Bristol, should fail to diffuse its rays far and wide, according to the true merits of his proficiency and worth, had caused these letters to be written, and sealed with the common seal of the University, on the Vigil of All Saints, A.D. 1330. A scrap of antique French is next quoted, as possibly referring to his translation of the Iliad, under the title of " Le Romaunce de Troys."

Having thus led up to the grand act of this "genteel comedy " of the eighteenth century, the commentator naïvely adds :—" To give you an idea of the poetry of the age, take the following piece, wrote by John de Bergham, about 1320." The specimen of the old monk's verse is entitled " The Romaunte of the Cnyghte," but its obscure language and orthography had to be rendered into a modernised paraphrase before Mr. Burgum could comprehend its drift. Its confirmation of the De Bergham genealogy, however, was altogether satisfactory to him, and so he testified his gratification by another gift of five shillings.

The pedigree is described by Dr. Maitland as " a great coat of arms, and a string of rubbish, indescribably ignorant and impudent," preserved, as he conceives, only to the shame of its author ; the memorial of a transaction for which " swindling " appears to him the fittest term.[1] It may console the reader who sympathises in such virtuous indignation, to know that the pedigree did not, after all, prove a bad investment. The copy-books, containing, along with it and its " Romaunte of the Cnyghte," some of the earliest transcripts of the Rowley poems, were ultimately disposed of by the family to Mr. Joseph Cottle, for the sum of five guineas. For its author, however, the results were far from profitable. It

[1] Chatterton : an Essay, p. 19.

CHAP. IV.

*Unprofit-
able results
to the
author.*

was the misfortune of Chatterton to be brought in contact, at a very early age, with vain, credulous men, so
greatly his inferiors in intellect that he was tempted by
their amazing folly to persevere in deceptions which their
credulity had suggested.   Nor can it be doubted that his
success on this occasion, when not more than fourteen
years of age, was calculated to confirm the tendency to
mystery and deception.   If we could ignore the moral
influences on the boy himself, and forget the age, the
privations, and all the disabilities of its perpetrator, the
humour of the hoax would predominate above all else
connected with its history.   But as the production of a
youth, whose whole education had been obtained in a
charity school, though crude enough when tested by
learned heralds and antiquaries, and in its moral effects
on himself injurious beyond all question, it still appears
to me truly wonderful.

*Developing
the humour
of the hoax.*

But it was left for Mr. Burgum and the Rowley com-
mentators to develop all the latent humour of the hoax.
Mr. Cottle learned, on inquiry at the College of Heralds,
that the De Bergham pedigree was formally submitted to
that court of honour by Mr. Burgum, as a document
deriving its chief authority from ancient deeds found in
the muniment-room of Redcliffe Church.   Let the reader
picture, if he can, the disgust of the ennobled pewterer,
on learning that his crown-pieces had been squandered
as the reward of an impudent fabrication.   But the grave
comments perpetrated by learned critics, at long subsequent dates, equal in absurdity the pilgrimage of Mr.
Burgum to Doctors' Commons, to have his pedigree
attested by the College of Heralds.   Mr. Joseph Cottle

*Learned
critics.*

devotes eight pages of small type to "a few cursory
remarks upon it, till the public shall be presented with a
fuller investigation which the subject amply merits;" and
so he proceeds gravely to prove, among other things,
that no such person as Simon de Seycnte Lyze came to
England with the Conqueror : that the De Berghams do
not appear in any heraldic record as entitled to coat
armour : that the Azure, three Hippotames naisant Or ;

Argent, three Fermoulxes sable; Or, between a Fess dancetty sable, two Cat-a-mountains ermine;" and much else of the like kind, including Radcliffe de Chatterton's "Pheon azure, ermine Lyon rampant," &c. &c., are wholly without authority from Garter, Clarencieux, or the Heralds' College![1]

The pomp of heraldry had a fascinating charm for Chatterton ; and the intricacies of its symbolic ramifications evidently furnished a favourite recreation, in which he could live over again that heroic past which he had already made his own. The study was a strange one for the charity boy ; but heraldry had its origin in unlettered ages, and appealed intelligibly to thousands to whom its mottoes were known only traditionally as slogans or *cries de guerre.* In like manner the painted and sculptured blazonry in Redcliffe Church probably attracted his wondering delight, before he had mastered his letters, with the help of the illuminated folio which served as his primer. He was left in no mystery as to his own pedigree, for, sure enough, the parchments of Redcliffe treasury-house preserved the genealogies of its old sextons for at least a hundred and fifty years. But the Radcliffe de Chatterton of the De Bergham pedigree was too pleasant a romance to be summarily dismissed. In his "Last Will and Testament," which Chatterton's biographers have been content to accept as a serious document, he gives directions for inscriptions on four sides of his monument. The first of these, in Norman French, commemorates an imaginary Guateroine Chatterton, of A.D. 1260 ; the second records, in Latin, the names of Alan Chatterton and his wife Alicia, the former of whom is said to have died in 1415 ; while the third is dedicated to the memory of his father, a subchaunter of the cathedral of this city, whose ancestors were residents of St. Mary Redcliffe since the year 1140.

The actual old family name of Chadderdon, recovered by his father from the parchments of Redcliffe muniment-

*The charms of heraldry.*

*A pleasant romance.*

*The old family name.*

CHAP. IV.

[1] Works, vol. ii. p. 455.

room, does not seem to have taken the boy's fancy. Among the MSS. in the British Museum is an elaborate piece of blazonry of nine distinct shields, executed by him as the first materials for an imaginary genealogy of the Chattertons, which was to throw the De Bergham pedigree entirely in the shade. Getting back far beyond Norman William's time, he starts with Sire de Chasteautonne of the House of Rollo, the first Duke of Normandy, and Eveligina of Ghent : a lady perhaps as genuine as the fair Gisella, daughter of Charles the Simple, whom ancient chroniclers assign to Rollo with the dower of Normandy.

If we could discard the elements of youth and all the disadvantages under which the orphan child laboured, it would not be difficult to find a parallel for the ingenious romancer. The charity-boy reappears in fancy, in his quaint Bluecoat garb, poring over his imaginary pedigree with an earnestness akin to that with which Sir Walter Scott contemplated the plans of his Tweed-side mansion, and dreamt of a long array of Scotts of Abbotsford who were to carry down the honours of his line to remote centuries. For the time it was a reality to both. Then came a change in the humour of the dreamer; and, just as Scott could appreciate the absurdity of his own over-ridden hobby, and picture its most grotesque phases in his Baron of Bradwardine, or his Laird of Monkbarns : so the boy-poet and antiquary discerned the humorous side of his self-deceiving fancies, and sported with the weakness of Mr. Burgum ; or wrote to his relative, Mr. Stephens, the Salisbury breeches-maker, "whose good sense disdains flattery :"—"When you quarter your arms in the mullet, say, 'Or a Fess vert, by the name of Chatterton.' I trace your family from FitzStephen, Earl of Ammerle in 1095, son of Od, Earl of Bloys, and Lord of Holderness." The breeches-maker, it seems probable, had already been in correspondence with him on the quarterings of the family shield.

In a different vein he wrote to Ralph Bigland, Esq. Somerset Herald : " Hearing you are composing a book of heraldry,. I trouble you with this. Most of our heralds assert piles should never be borne in even numbers. I have seen several old seals with four, six, and eight; and in the cathedral here is a coat of the Berkeleys with four." Then follows a list of apocryphal coats-of-arms "in and about Bristol;" for he was palming off heraldic fictions on the very custodier of arms in the Court of Honour. But both this letter and the communication to Mr. Stephens of Salisbury belong to the later period of his apprenticeship in an attorney's office, when he had formed the acquaintance of Thomas Palmer, an heraldic engraver, from whom he received instruction in drawing and colouring coats-of-arms. It was a favourite practice with him to inform his friends what their arms were; and meeting his instructor one day, he said, " I'll tell you the meaning of your name. Persons used to go to the Holy Land, and return from thence with palm branches, and so were called Palmers;" and he added, the arms of the Palmers were three palm branches, and the crest a leopard, or tiger, with a palm branch in its mouth.

It was with Chatterton's heraldry, as with his antique prose and verse: a vein of earnestness is inextricably blended with what, in other respects, appears as palpable fraud. We are reminded of the boy and the visionary dreamer, in the midst of his most elaborate fictions, till it becomes a puzzle to determine how much of self-deception and of actual belief were blended with the humour of the jest.

F

# CHAPTER V.





THE history of Chatterton's heraldic dealings with Mr. Burgum exhibits him in one of the least defensible transactions of his boyhood. It shows him, however, while still an inmate of Colston's Hospital, establishing relations with some of those who figure subsequently as his professed patrons. The most noticeable among them turned him to account for their own purposes, and received from him in gift, or for such trifling sums as could be offered to one in his position, parchments which they believed to be valuable ancient documents filched from the repositories of Redcliffe Church. He saw, ere long, through their meanness, and yielding to his satirical vein, lampooned them in a way that some of them never forgave. It became necessary, by and by, to vilify Chatterton, in defence of patrons he had shown in their true light. This spirit animates the correspondence in the *Gentleman's Magazine* many years after his death, and has permanently affected his reputation. His Bristol contemporaries resented every recognition of his genius as an endorsement of all the indiscretions and follies of the juvenile satirist, who caricatured civic and ecclesiastical dignitaries alike, too often with profane levity.

Among those who figure, both in friendly relationship to Chatterton, and as the butts of his unsparing satire, Messrs. Catcott and Burgum occupy a prominent place. They had each an ambition for fame, which showed itself repeatedly in very novel ways ; coveted the distinction of patrons of letters, and achieved considerable notoriety among the citizens of Bristol in their day. This, no doubt, attracted the notice of Chatterton, who had a keen sense of humour; and is not unlikely to have prompted his choice of one of the partners as a confidant in the reputed discovery of his Rowley antiques.

The bold experiment by which the impudent young satirist put the credulity of Mr. Burgum to so severe a test, helps to illustrate the character of both. The vain, arrogant, but kindly tradesman had taken a fancy to the Bluecoat boy, who humoured his follies, and interested him by his saucy wit, as well as by his thirst for knowledge. He had had his own struggles in younger days, which helped to make him somewhat niggardly; had had to pick up for himself such culture as he possessed: and so could sympathise with some, at least, of Chatterton's difficulties. So he lent him books, including possibly his Latin grammar and dictionary; contributed occasionally to the slender pocket-money expended by him,

> "When wildly squandering everything he got
> On books, and learning, and the Lord knows what ;"[1]

hinted mysteriously at ancestral honours of his own ; and treated the boy to Latin quotations and other scraps of learning, such as men of his calibre delight to expend on wondering juniors.

Chatterton speedily gauged the weakness of his Mentor, and estimated his generosity as well as his learning and family honours at their true worth. Nevertheless Mr. Burgum appears to have been one of the first beyond the walls of Colston's Hospital to appreciate his character as something extraordinary ; and in one of the latest and profanest of his satires, the " Kew Gardens," he does his old friend rough justice after the following fashion. Contrasting the homely, vulgar tradesman with the Rev. Thomas Broughton, Vicar of St. Mary Redcliffe, author

---

[1] Chatterton's " Will."

of "An Historical Dictionary of all Religions, from the Creation of the World to this Present Time ;" and, it may be added, the only object connected with Redcliffe Church which failed to win his regard : he exclaims :—

> " Burgum wants learning ; see the lettered throng
> Banter his English in a Latin song.
> If in his jests a discord should appear,
> A dull lampoon is innocently dear ;
> Ye sage, Broughtonian, self-sufficient fools,
> Is this the boasted justice of your schools ?
> Burgum has parts ; parts which would set aside
> The laboured acquisitions of your pride ;
> Uncultivated now his genius lies,
> Instruction sees his latent talents rise ;
> His gold is bullion, yours debased with brass,
> Impressed with Folly's head to make it pass.
> But Burgum swears so loud, so indiscreet,
> His thunders echo through the listening street ;
> Ye rigid Christians, formally severe,
> Blind to his charities, his oaths you hear ;
> Observe his virtues : calumny must own
> A noble soul is in his actions shown ;
> Though dark this bright original you paint,
> I'd rather be a Burgum than a saint." [1]



Such was the final estimate formed by Chatterton of the friend he had hoaxed so cruelly.  It shows sagacity and acute discrimination of character, in judging of the patron to whose vanity we are indebted, not only for a knowledge of juvenile heraldic studies and much other miscellaneous reading, but for proof of the still earlier production of Rowley poems.  The young herald, to whom Mr. Burgum's crown-piece was so welcome a gift, had no pence to spare when the pedigree was in requisi-tion ; and so he appropriated for its first instalment the copy-book into which he had already transcribed "The

---

[1] The same passage occurs, with some variations, in the "Epistle to the Rev. Mr. Catcott."  The reading in the latter of "Ye classic dunces," instead of "Ye sage, Broughtonian, self-sufficient fools," seems to point to the Vicar of St. Mary Redcliffe as one of the pedants whose parade of learning, and ridicule of the self-taught tradesman, offended Chatterton's sense of justice, and provoked his satire.

Tournament," the earliest of his antique dramatic inter-ludes ascribed to Rowley's pen; and the "Gouler's," or Miser's Requiem, the supposed production of his patron, William Canynge. The latter fairly illustrates the cha-racter of the modern antiques already in progress, with their echoes of Chaucerian and other verse, as in the lines :—

> "Soone as the morne dyd dyghte the roddie sunne,
>    A shade of theves eche streake of lyghte dyd seeme ;
> Whann ynn the heavn full half hys course was runn,
>    Eche stirryng nayghbour dyd mie harte afleme."

Here the reader is at once reminded of the Prologue to the "Canterbury Tales :"—

> "Whan  .  .  .  .  .  the yonge soune
>    Hath in the Ram his halfé course yroune."

The "Tournament" no less clearly betrays the hand of the author of the "De Bergham Pedigree," if indeed it did not suggest that production. It opens with the entry of a herald, who announces himself as "Son of Honnoure, [di]spenser of her joys ;" and among the knights who bear themselves gallantly in the Tourney, "Syrr Johan de Berghamme" plays a distinguished part. In all pro-bability the adoption of this name for one of his knights, with the view of gratifying the friendly tradesman, suggested the hoax of the Norman pedigree, with its marvellous array of nobles, poets, and alchemists, ac-cepted with such undoubting faith.

It was difficult for such a boy to deal justly with patrons of this stamp ; and none of them was treated with more injustice than the kindly though parsimonious and con-ceited pewterer. He was duped, satirized, and laughed at by his impudent protégé. And yet the boy, too, is to be felt for. He appears, as it were, two beings : the moody, self-communing poet, living in a past of his own creation ; and the clever, pert, saucy youngster, looking with profane contempt on civic and church dignitaries, elderly citizens, and all who in any way seemed to claim superiority. He was already conscious of intellectual

CHAP. V.

*The poor
charity boy.*

powers of the highest order, and was, nevertheless, treated on all hands, not merely as a boy, but as the poor charity boy: the social as well as the intellectual inferior of even the humblest tradesman who had a book to lend, or a word of advice to spare for him. Life, which is ever a mystery to the young soul, was doubly mysterious to one thus strangely gifted : with a capacity for thought and perception without its equal in the Bristol, if indeed in the England, of his day; but with no more of world's experience than Adam himself when he began life : a man who had never been a child.

*Early
development
of the satiric
vein.*

Hence the early development of the satiric vein in Chatterton. There is an age when most young men are prone to over-estimate themselves, and to gratify this self-esteem by exaggerating the faults or follies of their seniors. But when he began his career as a satirist he was but a child, though such a child as was never before immured within the walls of a charity school. In his ninth year he was laying private and circulating libraries under contribution for books such as it would be difficult to induce most boys of his age to read under any coercion. Before another year was over he had become a recognised contributor to the poet's corner of the *Bristol Weekly Journal;* was known to his school-mates for the satirical powers of his pen ; and incited to turn them to account in the common quarrels of the school.

*The future
historian of
Bristol.*

At St. Austin's Back, in the immediate vicinity of Colston's Hospital, was, as we have seen, the house of Mr. William Barrett, F.S.A., surgeon, the great local antiquary and future historian of Bristol.[1] There, in some unknown but very conceivable way, Chatterton attracted his notice. He was industriously accumulating materials for his proposed history of Bristol ; and the boy, with his intuitive love for some of its most interesting historical memorials, was busy with the old Redcliffe parchments, copying their ornamental initials, poring over their antique caligraphy, and noting here and there

---

[1] *Vide* Letter dated from St. Austin's Back, Gent. Mag. vol. lvi. p. 461.

names already familiar to him, as belonging to the days of the good merchant and church-builder, William Canynge. Old deeds were among the things then most in request by Mr. Barrett, and old parchments, with their genuine or spurious records, were to be had from the boy in return for the mere loan of a volume, or the most trifling gift in money. We need not therefore hunt very curiously for other reasons for his attention to the Bluecoat boy. He, above all others, seemed the most likely to discover his rare gifts; and evidently caught glimpses of his genius, had he possessed any capacity for appreciating them. None of all the earlier reminiscences of Chatterton bring him more strikingly before us, or awaken keener regrets at the want of some one capable of estimating his worth, than that which Sir Herbert Croft learned from Barrett himself, who, as he tells us, "used often to send for him from the charity-school, which is close to his house, and differ from him in opinion, on purpose to make him earnest, and to see how wonderfully his eye would strike fire, kindle, and blaze up."[1]

According to Dr. Gregory, Chatterton was first brought under the notice of the antiquarian surgeon by Mr. Catcott; but in stating this, he assigns the introduction to the later period of his apprenticeship. This is contradicted by various other proofs besides the very distinct evidence of Barrett himself. Mrs. Edkins states that when he was twelve years of age, his desire was to study medicine, and "he wished to be bound to Barrett," but the surgeon objected. She adds that "she doubts if he was kind to him."[2] The De Bergham pedigree also, which is ascribed to the same early period, bears, in the translations of its Latin paragraphs in Mr. Barrett's handwriting, evidence that he was consulted on that juvenile production; and also places beyond doubt that the great Bristol antiquary threw not the slightest discredit on the genuineness of the crude production.

Of all the patrons of Chatterton, Barrett invites our

[1] Croft, p. 272.     [2] Dix, App. p. 315.



*Old parchments in request.*

*First introduction to Barrett.*

CHAP. V.

*His influ-
ence on
Chatterton.*

*The Bristol
antiquary.*

*Unfailing
supply of
antiques.*

special attention in estimating rightly the failure of a life so full of promise at its dawn. He knew the boy best, turned him to most account, and did the least for him.[1] He was apparently at the head of his profession, and estimated himself accordingly. In Chatterton's " Exhibition " he is introduced presiding over a professional conclave ; and a couplet from that unpublished satire may help the fancy to some definite idea of the man. A windy orator's meaningless talk had drawn to an end, when

> " Barrett arose, and, with a thundering air,
> Stretched out his arm, and dignified the chair."

I picture him to myself, with the aid of his quarto volume of " History and Antiquities," as a dull, shallow, pompous man, of a type by no means rare among the antiquarian brotherhood. Vain, self-important, and credulous, he condescendingly patronised the youth whose hoard of antique parchments he was appropriating as materials on which his own fame was to rest. For poetry, in any genuine sense, he had no taste ; though, if sufficiently old and unreadable, it might not be without a charm of its own. It was to Mr. George Catcott, as a general rule, that Chatterton produced his antique poems. But for Mr. Barrett he had a never-failing supply of ancient records, and notices of old castles, churches, crosses, &c. enough to turn the head of any antiquary. When detailing to his learned correspondent, Dr. Ducarel, in 1772, the results of an unsuccessful search for records of the imaginary Rowley, Barrett exclaims exultingly : " No one surely ever had such good fortune as myself in procuring manuscripts and ancient deeds to help me in investigating the history and antiquities of this city."[2] But Chatterton did produce to him a portion of one of his longest poems, under circumstances happily recorded

---

[1] *Vide* Southey's indignant exposure of Barrett, Catcott, and Croft, in his letter to the *Monthly Magazine.* (Gent. Mag. vol. lxx. part i. p. 160.)

[2] Gent. Mag. vol. lvi. p. 544.

for us with some degree of detail. This poem, as set forth in its title, was the "Battle of Hastings, wrote by Turgot the Monk, a Saxon, in the tenth century, and translated by Thomas Rowlie, parish preeste of St. John's, in the city of Bristol, in the year 1465." It extended to fifty-six ten-line heroic stanzas, of alternate rhymes, closing with a couplet. Four lines of another imperfect stanza were added, with this note: "The remainder of the poem I have not been happy enough to meet with."

In spite of its orthography and occasional archaic diction, the language and sentiment of this poem are as modern as its rhythm, and presented no impediment to the appreciation of its vigour and beauty. A single stanza of this first part, slightly modernized in spelling, will sufficiently illustrate this :—

> "And now the battail closed on everych side,
>     And face to face appeared the Knights full brave ;
> They lifted up their bills with mycle pride,
>     And many wounds unto the Normans gave.
> So have I seen two weirs at once give ground,
>     White-foaming high, to roaring combat run ;
> In roaring din and heaven-breaking sound
>     Burst waves on waves, and spangle in the sun ;
>         And when their might in bursting waves is fled,
>         Like cowards steal along their oozy bed."

The piece thus submitted to the judgment of Mr. Barrett is a well-sustained, vigorous poem, marvellous indeed as the work of a boy. The only thing the antiquary took notice of was that the manuscript was in Chatterton's own handwriting. He accordingly pressed him to produce at least some portion of the original. Thus importuned, he at length admitted it was his own composition, and had been written by him for a friend. Still pressed by Barrett,—who was as credulous in the matter of spurious antiques, as he was blind to the rare genius thus appealing to him for recognition,—Chatterton, after a considerable interval, produced the second part of the same poem, extending to fifty-two stanzas ; and a further addition of twenty stanzas was subsequently made,

CHAP. V.

*The "Battle of Hastings."*

*Modern language and sentiment.*

*Demand for the original.*

in consequence of renewed solicitations.  Properly speaking, the new portions are rather another poem, of higher merit, both in form and thought, than a continuation of the first ; and therefore have great value as marking the rapid development of the young poet's mastery of his art.  Instead of the alternate rhymes, and uniform heroic lines, the new stanza approaches in character to the Spenserian ; and the poem opens with this fine apostrophe to Truth, which reads like an indignant rebuke to its recipient, who so persistently repelled the truthful confidence of its author :—



"O Truth ! immortal daughter of the skies,
　　Too little known to writers of these days,
　Teach me, fair saint, thy passing worth to prize ;
　　To blame a friend, and give a foeman praise.
　　The fickle moon, bedeckt with silver rays,
　Leading a train of stars of feeble light,
　　With look adign, the world below surveys,
　The world that wotted not it could be night ;
　　With armour dight, with human gore ydyed,
She sees King Harold stand, fair England's curse and pride."



The language and sentiment have, for the most part, equally little trace of Canynge's age.  Here and there an obsolete or coined word helps, with the affected spelling, to obscure the modernness of the poem ; and sufficed to satisfy the antiquary, to whom its poetical merits constituted no attraction, and who rejected the truth in reference to its history from the very lips of its author.  A longer passage will illustrate its versification, and show its great vigour and beauty.  Harold having driven from his presence the messenger of the Norman duke, prepares for the fight ; and thus the narrative proceeds :—



"A standard made of silk and jewels rare,
　　Wherein all colours wrought about in bighs.
　An armed knight was seen death-doing there,
　　Under, this motte : He conquers or he dies.
　　This standard rich, endazzling mortal eyes,
　Was borne near Harold at the Kenters' head ;
　Who charged his brothers for the great emprise

That straight the host for battle should be spread ;
  To every earl and knight the word is given,
And cries a guerre and slughornes shake the vaulted heaven.

As when the earth, torn by convulsions dire,
  In realms of darkness hid from human sight:
The warring force of water, air, and fire,
  Burst from the regions of eternal night,
  Through the dark caverns seek the realms of light ;
Some lofty mountain, by its fury torn,
  Dreadfully moves, and causes great afright ;
Now here, now there, majestic nods the bourne,
  And awful shakes, moved by the Almighty force,
Whole woods and forests nod, and rivers change their course.

So did the men of war at once advance,
  Linked man to man, enseemed one body light ;
Above a wood, yformed of bill and lance
  That nodded in the air most strange to sight.
  Hard as the iron were the men of might ;
No need of slughorns to enrouse their mind ;
  Each shooting spear yreaden for the fight,
More fierce than falling rocks, more swift than wind ;
  With solemn step, by echo made more dire,
One single body all, they marched, their eyen on fire.

And now the grey-eyed morn, with violets drest,
  Shaking the dewdrops on the flowery meads,
Fled with her rosy radiance to the west ;
  Forth from the eastern gate the fiery steeds
  Of the bright sun awaiting spirits leads.
The sun in fiery pomp enthroned on high,
  Swifter than thought along his journey gledes,
And scatters night's remains from out the sky ;
  He saw the armies make for bloody fray,
And stop'd his driving steeds, and hid his lightsome ray."



Those second and third parts the boy produced in consequence of Mr. Barrett's repeated solicitations "for the conclusion of the poem ;" which, when first presented to him as an antique, he had been told could not be found. Assuredly they did not then exist, but were the work of that "considerable interval of time" which elapsed between the production of the several parts; though now they were presented as copies of an original by the monk-poet of Bristol in the days of Edward IV.;

CHAP. V.

*Responsi-
bility for the
deception.*

for in no other character would Barrett receive them. On whom then rests the responsibility of the deception? On the boy who in vain claimed the authorship of his own poem; or on the purblind antiquary who could look into the poet's eyes, enkindling and flashing with the fire of genius, and go away self-duped by his own monstrous unbelief? The rhythm it will be seen is, at furthest, of the Elizabethan age. In reality the stanza was more probably borrowed from Thomson than Spenser. As to the language, the most of it is as modern as the sentiment. The neuter form of the pronoun *it*, for example, which was unknown to Spenser, and does not once occur in the Authorized Version of the English Bible, is used as in Chatterton's own day; and as for the obsolete words, there are only three or four at most that need explanation: *adigne*, noble, dignified; *bighes*, jewels; *yrcaden*, made ready; and *gledes*, for glides: so used, like many of Spenser's forms, for the rhyme.

*Age of
author
when the
poem was
produced.*

At what precise age the various parts of this remarkable poem were produced we have no record; for the only person who could have supplied the information had his own reasons for regarding all such information as wholly foreign to any question connected with the Rowley poems. Bryant tells us, "Mr. Barrett, a gentleman of reading and judgment, who was perfectly well acquainted with the extent of Chatterton's powers, has repeatedly told me they were by no means shining."[1] To a gentleman of such judgment, persisting, in spite of Chatterton's own statements, in the belief that his antique poems were mere transcripts of fifteenth-century parchments, the age of their copyist was a matter of insignificance. But if maturity of workmanship can be allowed any weight in judging of the productions of a youth of such unparalleled precocity, it may be presumed that the second and third parts belong to the later period of his apprenticeship. It is, however, but a question of months after all; for the whole interval between his quitting the Bluecoat School, and his departure from

[1] Bryant's Observations, p. 560.

Bristol, was only two years and nine months.  But whatever be their date, their history illustrates the dealings of the Bristol antiquary with the young poet.  There is no evidence that he received any pecuniary return from his patron, and it is abundantly obvious that he was denied all other reward.

The obstinate stupidity with which every acknowledgment made by Chatterton of his authorship of the Rowley Poems was repelled, must be borne in remembrance in justification of his later reticence.  Only as professed antiques would the supreme literary authorities of Bristol receive them ; and especially was this the case with its prospective historian.  As an original poet, the boy was slighted, suspected, discredited ; but as a provider of materials for the forthcoming civic history, he could not labour too sedulously alike in prose and verse.

Chatterton early saw through the weaknesses of a character that seems to have been both cold and selfish ; and in the second year of his apprenticeship, he thus sketched the antiquary under a convenient pseudonym :

> "Pulvis, whose knowledge centres in degrees,
>   Is never happy but when taking fees ;
>   Blest with a bushy wig and solemn grace,
>   Catcott admires him for a fossil face.
>   When first his farce of countenance began,
>   Ere the soft down had marked him almost man,
>   A solemn dulness occupied his eyes,
>   And the fond mother thought him wondrous wise ;
>   But little had she read in nature's book
>   That fools assume a philosophic look.
>   O Education, ever in the wrong,
>   To thee the curses of mankind belong ;
>   Thou first great author of our future state,
>   Chief source of our religion, passions, fate ;
>   On every atom of the Doctor's frame
>   Nature has stampt the pedant with his name ;
>   But thou hast made him—ever wast thou blind,—
>   A licensed butcher of the human kind."[1]

But the young satirist was not unmindful of his obligations to Barrett's library, nor ungrateful for his advice :

[1] Happiness.

and, though he thus sketched him in a poem written at
Mr. Catcott's dictation; when dealing with both their
names, in the metrical addition to his "Will," written
immediately before he quitted Bristol in 1770, he writes
of the former:—

> "To Barrett next, he has my thanks sincere
> For all the little knowledge I had here."

*Collections for a civic history.*

The patron whom he thus celebrated was beset with
the ambition to produce one of those dry, unreadable
folios, of which most of our chief cities were made the
theme during the latter part of the eighteenth century.
Chatterton was a child when "collections for the design
were being sought for with great assiduity, and no small
expense."[1]  Its "copper-plates" were in process of engraving, after a fashion familiar to the eighteenth century
topographer: with stiff elevations and impossible per-
spectives, in which any capacity for the appreciation of
medieval art is so obviously wanting, that it is hard to
guess from their feeble generalizations what is the actual
style or age of the buildings represented.  When at length

*Date of its publication.*

the "History of Bristol" issued from the press, in 1789,
with its folio plates folded into the reduced dimensions
of a quarto, the boy Chatterton—to whom it owes all
that confers on it any genuine human interest,—had lain
nearly twenty years in his grave.  It had been heralded
by many a flattering note of promise ; and doubtless its
author awaited its advent with all the eagerness of a
long expected triumph.  Alas for human expectations !
he would appear, more truly than the poet Keats, to
have "let himself be snuffed out by an article ! "

*Comprehen-sive plan of the work.*

The work, planned after the comprehensive fashion
of medieval chronicles, or of Knickerbocker's famous
"History of New York," opens with this imposing
exordium : "The Great Jehovah, who hath made of
one blood all nations to dwell upon the earth, and
determined the bounds of their habitation, assigned to

---

[1] Barrett's History, preface.

man at first this one employ, with labour to till the
ground in which he was placed.  Thus we find patriarchs
and people engaged in agriculture only and the pastoral
life, till increasing they went off in tribes to seek more
distant habitations ; " and so it proceeds, in accordance
with monkish precedent, till Britain and Julius Cæsar
are reached.  The antiquary reposed undoubting faith in
Rowley while this history was in progress ; but the very
existence of any such medieval poet and chronicler was
in question before its publication ; and hence the manuscript appears to have undergone some partial revision,
so as to evade responsibility for the genuineness of the
Rowley contributions, which were nevertheless the foundation and buttress of its whole historical superstructure.
For his own part he evidently did not know what to
make of them.  He corrects Camden, for example, with
the help of Rowley's version of Turgot's "Saxonnes Latyn,"
which " must be acknowledged to be of great weight ;"[1]
quotes the coins of Mr. Canynge's cabinet, as described
" by Thomas Rowlie about 1460, in his own writing, still
extant ;"[2] and then, in his preface and elsewhere, disclaims all responsibility : refers to the " late learned Dean
Milles' elegant edition of Rowley's Poems with notes,"
containing " everything that tends to develop this intricate
and obscure affair ;" and so leaves " the judicious reader "
to form his own opinion, with the soothing hint that
possibly " the truth may be found not to be with one,
but betwixt the two contending parties."[3]

Such was the most judicious of antiquaries and intelligent man of letters which Bristol could furnish as the
patron and adviser of one of the rarest geniuses of that
eighteenth century.  His history winds up with " Annales
Bristolliæ," extending from A.D. 50 to the year 1789, and
the mayoralty of Levi Ames, to whom it is dedicated.
" In this mayoralty, March 5th, 1789, a general joy was
diffused throughout the city, on account of the king's
happy recovery, and being able to resume the reins of
government ;" and so the annals of Bristol draw merrily

---

[1] Barrett's History, p. 31.      [2] Ibid. p. 37.      [3] Ibid. p. 46.

to a close, with "bell-ringing, firing cannons all day from Brandon Hill, a general illumination at night, with transparent emblematical devices, and every demonstration of joy that could be displayed." Soon after this jubilant celebration, the History itself issued from the press ; and on the 4th of November following, Horace Walpole wrote to Miss Hannah More of Bristol : " I am sorry, very sorry for what you tell me of poor Barrett's fate ; though he did write worse than Shakespeare, it is great pity he was told so, as it killed him ! "[1]



The fate of the historian, which really dates nineteen years after Chatterton's death, is characteristic of the weakness and vanity of this his chief patron : who appropriated for a monument to his own fame, works wrought by the cunning hand of his despised protégé, and reaped in this fashion his merited reward. The story told by Dr. Gregory of the first introduction of Chatterton to Mr. Barrett, "whose friendship and patronage," he adds, " by these means our young literary adventurer was fortunate enough to secure," when detached from the circumstantial evidence which evidently misdates it, is as follows : " Mr. Catcott, a gentleman of an inquisitive turn, and fond of reading," walking with a friend in Redcliffe Church, was informed by him of several ancient pieces of poetry which had been found there, and were now in the possession of a young person of his acquaintance. His extreme youth is indicated subsequently by the state-



ment that " Mr. Catcott declared, when he first knew Chatterton he was ignorant even of grammar."[2] It would not be difficult to point out, in the latest productions of the poet, grammatical shortcomings. In his antiques, indeed, it almost seems as if he affected the conjunction of a singular verb with a plural nominative. But Mr. Catcott's remark evidently points to a period when his education was in progress, and therefore when he was still an inmate of the Bluecoat School, where all the

[1] Letters of Horace Walpole, E. of Orford. Cunningham, vol. ix. p. 230.
[2] Gregory's Life, p. 55.

grammar he ever learned was acquired. Mr. Catcott sought an interview with the youth, and soon after "obtained from him, very readily, without any reward, the 'Bristowe Tragedy,' 'Rowley's Epitaph upon Mr. Canynge's Ancestor,' with some other smaller pieces. In a few days he brought some more, among which was the 'Yellow Roll.'"[1] This was the ingenious fiction of a collection of antiquities, manuscripts, coins, &c., accumulated, with all the zeal of a modern antiquary, by the old Mayor of Bristol in the times of the Roses. Nothing could be more opportune. Mr. Barrett's friends were on the look-out for materials for his projected history of the city; and so this "Yellow Roll," and other like treasures of Mr. Catcott's collection, "of which some were copies and some originals," were forthwith communicated to the historian. The loss of the "original MS." of the "Yellow Roll"—lent by Mr. Barrett to a friend, and carried off, it is said, to India,—is needlessly mourned over by more than one Rowleyan believer; for the ingenious romance duly figures in the "History of Bristol" under its quaint title of "England's glorye revyved in Maystre Canynge, beynge some Accounte of hys Cabynet of Auntyaunte Monumentes."

Mr. George Catcott divides with Mr. Barrett the honour of patronising "our young literary adventurer." He was the younger son of the Rev. Alexander Catcott, master of the City Grammar School; and no doubt enjoyed fair educational advantages, which left their impress on his character, notwithstanding the too obvious lack of natural abilities to turn them to any good account. The writer of a satirical article in the *Town and Country Magazine* for 1771, describes him as having "a large collection of books, of which he frequently boasts that none are less than a hundred years old, which indeed seems the principal reason for his having any; for as Pope says, 'his shelves admit not any modern book!' His favourite author is King Charles I. whose works he has nearly by heart. He very seldom goes without them

[1] Gregory's Life, p. 29.



G

in his pocket." His venerable tomes were doubtless the chief attraction to the young protégé he had undertaken to patronise. As for himself, his capacity for making any intelligent use of them is illustrated by the statement of his satirist, that he was always of the opinion of the last author he had read ; and so was liable to very abrupt changes of views, when a succession of writers chanced to differ. He appears to have been a bustling, consequential, little man ; and as the dignity of human nature and the greatness of the art of man were topics on which he delighted to expatiate, he obtained the sobriquet of giant Great Heart ![1]



The prominence which Mr. Catcott's name acquired in connexion with the Rowley poems led strangers to regard him as one of Bristol's most scholarly citizens. But even his nephew and eulogist, Mr. Richard Smith, when depicting his character in its most favourable aspects, says : "The fame of Rowley had been reflected on his ' Midwife,' as my uncle was nicknamed, and it was supposed he must be 'a most learned Theban,' which was a great mistake, for he had small Latin and no Greek. In fact he was nothing more than a simple, plain, single-hearted, honest man."[2] How far this description answers to the man, we have other means



of judging ; for he achieved no little notoriety in his day, in diverse ways, besides that of being the accredited usherer of Rowley into the modern world. Among the triumphs by which he contributed to the local fame of Mr. Burgum and himself, two highly characteristic ones have been celebrated by Chatterton's satiric pen. Their place of business as pewterers, at Bristol Bridge, was in the parish of St. Nicholas, within the bounds of the

---

[1] Town and Country Mag. June 1771, p. 316, where Catcott and his brother, the Vicar of Temple Church, are described under the name of Catskin. The paper is a continuation of Chatterton's series of "A Hunter of Oddities," apparently by one of his literary set ; if, indeed, it be not one of Chatterton's own unrequited contributions to Hamilton.

[2] Gent. Mag. N.S. vol. x. p. 605.

ancient city walls. Towards the middle of the eighteenth century, the passage over the bridge, and through the arch of St. Nicholas Gate, up the High Street, had become so inadequate for the increasing traffic, that both bridge and gate were at length condemned: involving in their demolition the destruction of the beautiful chancel of St. Nicholas Church, which stood over the ancient gateway. The age was marked by an unusual zeal in the indiscriminate removal of such structures; and advantage was taken of the partial mutilation of the church—a venerable building, partly of the twelfth century,—to replace the whole by one of those commonplace, semi-classic edifices, so characteristic of the period.

In 1767, the year in which Chatterton exchanged the Bluecoat School for an attorney's office, the new bridge was so far advanced that on Thursday, the 5th of June, the last stone was laid in the centre arch. On the following morning the ambitious pewterer mounted his horse, and by means of a few planks laid between the piers of the unfinished structure, rode across the Avon, that he might have the glory of affirming ever after, he was the first to effect the passage of the new bridge: the public opening of which ere long was, as we shall see, a memorable event in Chatterton's literary history. Fully two years elapsed before the new church of St. Nicholas was also completed, when Mr. Catcott outdid his former triumph, by ascending the steeple by a rope, at the risk of his neck, and depositing beneath the top stone an inscription graven on pewter, recording the foolhardy achievement.

It is to the interval between those two notable deeds that Dr. Gregory assigns the first introduction to Catcott; but a variety of independent proofs point to his earlier knowledge of the boy. It might, indeed, be inferred from the older date of Mr. Burgum's intercourse with him, that his partner would not have been long left in ignorance of his protégé. But it may be doubted if the two were given to much interchange of confidence beyond the range of their joint trading interests. Mr. Burgum,

CHAP. V.<br>St. Nicholas Gate and Bridge doomed.<br><br>First passage of the new bridge.<br><br>Catcott's first knowledge of Chatterton.

the homely tradesman, whose English was of a very ungrammatical character, whatever his Latin may have been : in all probability delayed the disclosure of his ancestral honours until that submission of them to the College of Heralds which ended so unsatisfactorily.  Mr. Catcott, on the contrary,—son of the Reverend and learned master of the Grammar School, and brother of the Vicar of Temple Church ;—a man of some pretensions to culture and refinement, was in no way disposed to follow the lead of such a partner in his patronage of letters.



But whatever may have been the exact date of Mr. George Catcott's introduction to Chatterton,—and on this point he is confused and contradictory,[1]—the circumstances attending it are full of interest.  According to his own account, at latest when the poet was only fifteen years of age, he received from him in free-gift the " Bristowe Tragedie ; or, the Dethe of Syr Charles Bawdin ;" the " Epitaph on Robert Canynge," and other smaller pieces ; and, according to his nephew's account, the "Songe to Ælla, Lorde of the Castel of Bristowe, ynne daies of Yore ;" the elaborate dramatic interlude of " Ælla," extending to upwards of twelve hundred lines ; and the " Battle of Hastings," an imperfect copy, extending only to five hundred and fifty lines : the first draft apparently of the poem, which Chatterton acknowledged to Mr. Barrett to be his own composition.



The " Bristowe Tragedie," when published in 1772, was ascribed by Horace Walpole to the author of the " Reliques of Ancient English Poetry."  Writing to the poet Mason, he says : " Somebody, I fancy Dr. Percy, has produced a dismal, dull ballad, called ' The Execution of Sir Charles Bawdin,' and given it for one of the Bristol poems, called Rowley's ;" which only serves to show how incapable the critic was of entering into the true merits of the poem.[2]  Assuredly no modern critic will endorse his opinion of this fine ballad.  It opens with this simple but poetic picturing of the dawn :—

[1] Gent. Mag. vol. xlviii. pp. 347, 403.
[2] Walpole's Letters, vol. v. p. 389.

> "The feathered songster, chanticlere,
>   Had wound his bugle horn,
> And told the early villager
>   The coming of the morn.
>
> King Edward saw the ruddy streaks
>   Of light eclipse the grey;
> And heard the raven's croaking throat
>   Proclaim the fated day."

The subject of this ballad is the death of Sir Baldwin Fulford, a zealous Lancastrian, executed at Bristol in 1461, the first year of Edward IV. It extends to ninety-eight stanzas, and sketches with homely pathos, after the prolix fashion of the later ballad minstrels, this tragic episode of the Rowley romance. Maister Canynge, the Mayor, on receiving instructions to have all things in readiness for the execution, kneels before the king and thus intercedes :—

*Subject of the ballad.*

> "My noble liege! good Canynge said,
>   Leave justice to our God;
> And lay the iron rule aside;
>   Be thine the olive rod.
>
> Were God to search our hearts and reins,
>   The best were sinners great;
> Christ's Vicar only knows no sin
>   In all this mortal state.
>
> Let mercy rule thine infant reign,
>   'Twill fast thy crown full sure;
> From race to race thy family,
>   All sovereigns, shall endure.
>
> ********
>
> My noble liege! The truly brave
>   Will valorous actions prize:
> Respect a brave and noble mind,
>   Although in enemies."

The intercession of the good Mayor is without effect. The king swears

*The Mayor's intercession.*

> "By Mary, and all saints in heaven,
>   This sun shall be his last;"

on which Sir Baldwin consorts himself in a lofty tone of

Christian fortitude and resignation, of which a single stanza, with the orthography of the original, will suffice as a sample of both :—

> " Before I sawe the lyghtsome sunne,
>     Thys was appointed mee ;
>   Shall mortal manne repyne or grudge
>     Whatt Godde ordeynes to bee ?"

*Imitation of the antique ballad.*

This is no doubt one of the earliest of Chatterton's longer pieces, and in our more critical age could deceive no one as a veritable antique, still less as a poem of the fourth Edward's reign. But as an imitation of the old ballad, and as a genuine specimen of the homely epic muse, it is wonderful as the production of a boy. But to Catcott's uncritical eye, ode, epic, dramatic interlude, or ballad, were equally acceptable as works of the imaginary priest of the fifteenth century ; and only when the death of their author had awakened some adequate interest in the poems, and excited controversy as to their authorship, did he attempt to recall the dates of their production to him.

*Unreliable reminiscences.*

The recollections of Mr. Catcott, as of most of Chatterton's Bristol friends, have to be sifted with suspicious care. It was not till the outer world of scholars and critics began to discern the merits of the Rowley poems, and to inquire about the strange youth to whom their recovery was ascribed, that his former acquaintances recognised any merit in him. For the most part they scornfully repudiated the idea of Chatterton's authorship ; and among such, Catcott remained an obstinate Rowleyan to the last : evidently thinking that to himself, rather than to Chatterton, the world owed the recovery of the long-lost literary treasures.

*Researches of Rev. J. Chapman.*

The Rev. John Chapman, rector of Weston, near Bath, in a letter to Dr. Ducarel, in 1772, communicates the results of successive visits to Bristol, to ascertain the character of "the Ancient Poems in MS. which were lately found" there. After describing the huckstering fashion in which Catcott offered some of them for sale, and deploring the prospect of others being "thrust head and shoulders into a history of Bristol, for no other end but to help the sale of a heavy work," he thus gives his impressions of Mr. George Catcott : "You must know that this Catcott is a pewterer, and though very fond of scribbling, especially since he has got Rowley's works, is extremely ignorant and illiterate. He is, however, very vain, and fancies himself as great a genius as the great Rowley himself."[1] We need not wonder that the statements of such a patron of letters have, for the most part, a very indirect bearing on the young poet who selected him as the custodian of his antique verse.

The sagacity of the boy is discerned in the choice. No safer confidant could have been found for the purpose of an author whose greatest dread latterly was lest he should be prematurely credited with the production of his own works. To Mr. George Catcott especially it seemed far more conceivable that he himself should write such poems, than that they were the work of the poor charity boy he had befriended. His nephew inherited the volume into which he had copied the correspondence carried on by him with Johnson, Goldsmith, Garrick, Tyrwhitt, Bryant, Warton, Lord Charlemont, Lord Dacre, Sir Herbert Croft, Dean Milles, Bishop Percy, the poet Mason, and many more : in all which his main object was to divert the erring believers in Chatterton's genius, to the imaginary priest of the fifteenth century as the only genuine object of faith. The zeal of the pewterer had a very practical bearing. Goldsmith, who felt all the sympathy of true genius for the boy, whose fate as an author he had himself narrowly escaped, longed to become possessor of his manuscripts, and offered Mr. Catcott his note in payment. But the shrewd tradesman replied with a proper estimate of the credit of poets in his native city, that he feared "a poet's note-of-hand is not very current upon our exchange of Bristol."[2] His zeal had throughout a very practical bearing. "I sold the copy of Rowley's poems as originals of undoubted antiquity," he says ;[3] and he evidently entertained a reason-

CHAP. V.<br>Impressions of Catcott.

Sagacious choice of a confidant.

Goldsmith's interest in the poems.

---

[1] Gent. Mag. vol. lvi. p. 547.     [2] Europ. Mag. vol. xxi. p. 88.
[3] Gent. Mag. vol. xlviii. p. 347.

*Dr. Johnson's interview with Catcott.*

able apprehension of being called upon to refund the money should their modern origin be substantiated.

Boswell has preserved a lively account of the interview of Catcott with Dr. Johnson, when the latter visited Bristol in 1776. "On Monday, April 29th," writes Boswell, "he and I made an excursion to Bristol, where I was entertained with seeing him inquire, upon the spot, into the authenticity of Rowley's poetry. George Catcott, the pewterer, attended us at our inn, and with a triumphant air of lively simplicity, called out, 'I'll make Dr. Johnson a convert.' Dr. Johnson, at his desire, read aloud some of Chatterton's fabricated verses, while Catcott stood at the back of his chair, moving himself like a pendulum, and beating time with his feet, and now and then looking into Dr. Johnson's face, wondering that he was not yet convinced. Honest Catcott seemed to pay no attention whatever to any objections, but insisted, as an end of all controversy, that we should go with him to the tower of St. Mary Redcliffe, and view with our own eyes the ancient chest in which the manuscripts were found. To this Dr. Johnson good-naturedly agreed; and, though troubled with a shortness of breathing, laboured up a long flight of steps, till we came to the place where the wondrous chest stood. 'There,' said Catcott, with a bouncing, confident credulity, 'there is the very chest itself.' After this ocular demonstration there was no more to be said."

*Recollections of the poet's conversations.*

Such was the most enlightened patron that Chatterton could find in his native Bristol, to whom to confide the disguised treasures of his own creation. According to the account furnished by Mr. Catcott, during conversations he had with him, "he heard him mention the names of most of the poems since printed, as being in his possession. He afterwards grew more suspicious and reserved, and it was but rarely, and with difficulty, that any more originals could be obtained from him. He confessed to Mr. Catcott that he had destroyed several; and some which he owned to have been in his possession were never afterwards seen."[1]

[1] Bryant's Observations, p. 517.

Catcott ultimately became possessor of the greater portion of the professed copies of the Rowley poems, and also of some of his prose pieces, in part, at least, as free gifts.[1] To his zeal accordingly we owe the preservation of many of them. But the spirit in which this was done was that of the mere trader, and not of the patron of letters, and therefore amply justifies the tone of Chatterton's lampoons. Soon after the death of the poet, he completed the collection by giving five guineas to the poor widow for all the papers remaining of those her son left with her on setting out for London. The correspondence of Mr. Chapman and Dr. Ducarel shows him, ere long, jealously producing select scraps as specimens of his wares. Before the end of 1771 he is reported to have refused two hundred pounds for the poems, but it is thought would be content with half that sum.[2] A little later he is found offering part of the collection for fifty pounds;[3] and finally he disposes of the whole to Messrs. Payne and Son of London at that price, without thought of the widowed mother, who was in great indigence.

Catcott was made the theme of some of Chatterton's most caustic satires, still preserved with the marginal annotations of their victim, showing that his inordinate vanity discerned in them only laudatory records of his achievements, and fresh avenues to fame. But in all ways his reward was ample. If he supplied occasional contributions to the scanty pocket-money of the boy, they were investments which yielded an abundant return; and if notoriety could gratify him, he had it in its most

[1] Tyrwhitt, preface to Rowley Poems, p. ix.

[2] Gent. Mag. vol. lvi. p. 361.

[3] Ibid. p. 346. There appears to have been some sort of joint property between Catcott and Barrett in certain of the pieces which interfered with Catcott's sale of the whole. Barrett, no doubt, wanted to hold them in reserve for his History, and Catcott grumblingly complied; "though," he says, "Barrett's behaviour to him does not deserve this compliment." (*Vide* Letter of Rev. J. Chapman to Dr. Ducarel, Sept. 12th, 1772.) The Bristol patrons of letters were evidently beginning to quarrel over the spoils.

CHAP. V.

*Acquisition of the Rowley poems.*

*Estimate of the poet's satires.*

CHAP. V.

*A new
subject
suggested.*

attractive forms, as the correspondent of the foremost scholars and critics of his day, and the local authority on all Rowleyan mysteries, till his death in 1802.

Towards the close of the year 1769, famous as that in which Catcott deposited the memorial of his perilous adventure on the summit of St. Nicholas' steeple : according to his own report, when talking one day with Chatterton, the subject of happiness was started, a theme which the boy said had not hitherto occupied his thoughts. How far this is to be literally accepted depends on the date of one of the antique poems ascribed, not to Rowley's, but to Maister Canynge's own pen, "On Happienesse." But this will come under review more fitly hereafter. On the occasion now referred to, Chatterton, on the following day, placed in Mr. Catcott's hands, a piece extending to nearly one hundred and fifty lines of heroic verse, and opening in this fashion :

> "Since happiness was not ordained for man,
> Let's make ourselves as easy as we can."

*Sketches of
Bristol
notabilities.*

This poem has already furnished the characteristic picture of Barrett under the name of Pulvis ; and is noticeable for its satirical sketches of sundry other Bristol notabilities of the day : but especially for that of the aspiring pewterer himself, whose vanity would seem to have found gratification in the following fancied panegyric :—

> "Catcott is very fond of talk and fame ;
> His wish a perpetuity of name ;
> Which to procure, a pewter altar's made,
> To bear his name and signify his trade,
> In pomp burlesqued the rising spire to head,
> To tell futurity a pewterer's dead.
> Incomparable Catcott, still pursue
> The seeming happiness thou hast in view :
> Unfinished chimneys, gaping spires complete,
> Eternal fame on oval dishes beat ;
> Ride four-inch bridges, clouded turrets climb,
> And bravely die, to live in after time.
> Horrid idea ! if on rolls of fame
> The twentieth century only find thy name.
> Unnoticed this, in prose or tagging flower,

> He left his dinner to ascend the tower.
> Then what avails thy anxious spitting pain?
> Thy laugh-provoking labours are in vain.
> On matrimonial pewter set thy hand ;
> Hammer with every power thou canst command ;
> Stamp thy whole self, original as 'tis,
> To propagate thy whimsies, name, and phiz ;
> Then, when the tottering spires or chimneys fall,
> A Catcott shall remain, admired by all."



Some of the allusions, though sufficiently suggestive, are left to the reader's unaided interpretation. When the satire was produced their significance was obvious to every man who looked on the pewterer's dishes, stamped with his favourite device and motto, and needed no explanatory note. It was otherwise with the more important deeds here celebrated. There still exists an interleaved volume of tracts, collected by Mr. Catcott, and enriched with his own comments. Among those this poem of "Happiness" is included, with notes in which the allusions to himself are illustrated with a vain-glorious satisfaction that throws the satire itself into the shade. "Ride four-inch bridges" has its accompanying record of the first crossing of Bristol Bridge, and paying the first toll—of five guineas, it is said,—for the privilege.[1] The more important note reveals what the twentieth century has in store for it, if enduring pewter prove faithful to its trust. A piece of pewter, five inches square, now reposes where it was deposited by the hand of Mr. George Catcott, beneath the top stone of St. Nicholas' spire, with the following inscription deeply graven on its face :—

*Suggestive allusions.*

*Illustrative commentary.*

> "Summum hujusce turris Sancti Nicholai lapidem posuit mensi
> Decembris 1769, Georgius Catcott, philo-architectos,
> Reverendi Alexandri S. Catcott, Filius."

Fully to comprehend Chatterton, and the estimate he formed of the Bristol of his day, it is needful to realize to ourselves the character of those who thus represented to him its intellectual manhood. Inconceivable as it

*Bristol representative men.*

---

[1] J. Evans, Dix's Life, p. 58.

 might seem, it is obvious that the complacent tradesman was wholly unconscious the boy was laughing at his follies.  With such patrons, to whom alone he could submit the works by which he purposed to " live in after time," need we wonder that the young poet turned with a sigh to the good old times of the princely Canynge and his imaginary poet-priest.

# CHAPTER VI.

## BRISTOL FRIENDS.

WHILE Chatterton was still a child, he appears to have CHAP. VI. associated from choice with his seniors; and had circum-stances favoured him, it is probable that his personal friends would, in like manner, have been selected from among those who, by the experience and acquirements of age, were more on an intellectual equality with himself. But at home he had only Mrs. Edkins, Mrs. Phillips, and other gossips of his mother, and so he was thrown entirely on his own resources, or left to such chance school-boy friendships as Colston's Hospital afforded. There accordingly he made the most of the materials within his reach : took Thistlethwaite into his confidence ; made a friend of his bed-fellow Baker; and flung his whole heart into the affection that grew up between him and the young usher, Thomas Phillips. But school-life, with all the advantages and drawbacks pertaining to it, came to an end on the 1st of July, 1767 ; and, after a sojourn of seven years in the Hospital, a new career presented itself to the boy, with its vistas of hope and riper aspirations.

The same day on which Chatterton left the Bluecoat School he was bound apprentice to Mr. John Lambert, a Bristol attorney, to learn the art of a scrivener. The apprentice fee of ten pounds was paid out of the fund left by Mr. Colston for that purpose ; and, as appears from the indentures now preserved in the Bristol Institution, his master engaged to lodge, board, and clothe him; while, by a special agreement, his mother undertook to wash and mend his clothes.

Of the Bristol attorney on whom now devolved the professional training of the gifted boy, little of an authentic character is recoverable. His name does not appear in the official lists of the Bristol charities of his day; nor as a patron of letters, among the subscribers to the famous "History of Bristol," of which so large a portion was to be the work of his own apprentice, during office hours. This much, however, we may confidently surmise in regard to him, that he was a "staunch son of the Church," sound in politics, as well as in faith : for Mr. Colston, writing to his Hospital masters in 1717, conjures them "that they take effectual care, as far as in them lieth, that the boys be bred up in the doctrine of our present established Church of England; and that none of them be afterwards placed out as apprentices to any men that be dissenters from the said communion, as they will be answerable for a breach of their trust at the last and great tribunal before which we must all appear." How far this solemn appeal bore any fruit in the relations now established between Mr. Lambert and his new apprentice, we shall have occasion presently to consider. The Hospital Trustees no doubt conceived they had well and faithfully fulfilled their trust, in transferring their charge to such a master.

So far, it must be owned, Colston's charity had done what it could for the boy. Its meagre curriculum of schooling was, indeed, wholly inadequate to his intellectual cravings. But it gave its best, with such added influences as Phillips could supply; and now, with its aid, he was started on a career which must have seemed well suited to his favourite tastes. Old parchments, law deeds, tenures, and charters, had been his familiar playthings from infancy; so that Mrs. Edkins said of him, she "thought he was a lawyer before his time." He was elated when he received the presentation to Colston's School, because there he imagined there must be books enough to satisfy all his eager longings for knowledge. With no less elation must he have anticipated the emancipation from its routine of dull realities, and their exchange for the attorney's office, where his daily duty would be to handle parchments, engross deeds, and unravel the mysteries of English jurisprudence.

The change from school to the actual business and battle of life is at all times an important one; but it becomes doubly so, when, as in Chatterton's case, it involved the emancipation from rigid constraint, to the freedom which necessarily accompanies office duties and city life. He was now introduced to an entirely new circle of acquaintances, and soon began to interest himself in civic affairs, local politics, and ere long in all the public questions that then agitated the national mind. Mr. Lambert was a Bristol attorney; and when he undertook to board, lodge, and clothe the Bluecoat boy, for seven years, it was with the reasonable expectation that, while teaching him the art and profession of a scrivener, he should receive in return such services as would eke out the very moderate apprentice fee, and remunerate him for his cost and labour. We must not judge too harshly of the attorney if he did deal with a true poet like the peasant who, unwittingly acquiring Apollo's steed, when he only bargained for a farming-drudge, yoked Pegasus to the plough. Each ultimately did justice to the character of the other, according to his capacity of discernment.

To most apprentices transferred from the Bluecoat School to the attorney's home, it would have seemed no great grievance to be required to take his meals with the servants and share a room with the footboy. But Chatterton was " proud,"—proud as the Ayrshire peasant himself. The boy was puzzled by this very element of his character, which sprang from the unconscious recognition of his own preeminent genius. He instinctively resented the association with the illiterate society to which he was remanded; and Mr. Lambert, little dreaming that the charity boy in his office could deem himself

CHAP. VI.
—

*Office and
house hours.*

*Work to
which they
were
a. voted.*

better than the footboy who served him at home : accused him of " a sullen and gloomy temper, which particularly displayed itself among the servants."[1]

Mr. Lambert's office was at some distance from his dwelling. There Chatterton had to attend daily from eight in the morning till eight at night, with the mid-day interval of an hour for dinner. He was not required to be at his master's house till ten ; and the punctuality with which he conformed both to office and house hours is deserving of special notice, in view of other accusations that have been brought against him. He appears to have had the sole charge of the office ; and Mr. Lambert admitted to his sister that, though the footman and other servants had been frequently sent to ascertain if he attended to its duties, they had never found him absent. He had every motive to pass his evenings elsewhere than in his master's kitchen ; but his most frequent resort was his mother's house. His sister says, " he was seldom two evenings together without seeing us ;" and only once, on a Christmas evening spent with a party of friends there, did he exceed the hour fixed for his return.

But while thus regular in office hours, not a few of these were devoted to literary work on which his master looked with as little favour as if his spies had actually found him absent from his post. The hours of attendance seem to have been needlessly long ; for according to his sister's account, " he had little of his master's business to do ; sometimes not two hours in a day, which," she adds, " gave him an opportunity to pursue his genius."[2] When no business requirements occupied his pen, he was instructed to improve himself in professional knowledge, by copying precedents ; and of these one volume of thirty, and another of three hundred and forty closely written folio pages, in Chatterton's writing, are preserved. Besides a library of law books, not wholly unreadable to him, the shelves were enriched

[1] Communicated by Mr. Lambert to a friend. *Vide* Gregory, p. 19.
[2] Mrs. Newton's Letter ; Croft, p. 163.

with an early edition of Camden's " Britannia." By purchase and borrowing, these resources were constantly augmented; and thus he found himself, with coveted solitude and leisure, in a literary atmosphere congenial to his tastes, where study was a legitimate occupation.

Here then we have the young adventurer fairly started, as it seemed, on a professional career; master, to a considerable extent, of his own time, and free to select the companions of his choice. And foremost in his choice must be ranked those silent lettered companions whose society he had coveted even before he entered Colston's School. Books on history, antiquities, and heraldry; on astronomy, natural philosophy, medicine, and surgery; as well as the elder poets, and whatever of general literature or politics came within his reach : were all welcome to his insatiable appetite for knowledge. But besides those, another class of reading reminds us that the good priest Rowley was a frequent visitor at the attorney's office; and laboured systematically there in the creation of the wondrous modern antiques. Mr. Barrett's library furnished him with Skinner's " Etymologicon Linguæ Anglicanæ," and Benson's "Saxon Vocabulary." A copy of Bailey's Dictionary supplemented their Latin with the needful English gloss ; and Mr. Green, a Bristol bookseller, to whom he was indebted for other borrowed volumes, lent him Speght's Chaucer, with its ample glossary. From those and other sources he compiled for his own use a glossary of double references in archaic and modern English, which thenceforward constituted an unfailing resource in his antique poetic labours. On his removal to London, flushed with dreams of triumph in the exciting and profitable field of political warfare, it was neglected or forgotten ; but, so soon as his thoughts reverted to his favourite literary toils, the glossary was again in demand, and is urgently inquired for among the earliest commissions despatched to his mother and sister.

Such were the favourite companions of a solitude which Chatterton guarded from intrusion little less sedulously

CHAP. VI.

*Starting on a professional career.*

*Rowley at the attorney's office.*

*Companions of his solitude.*

H

than that of the lumber-room which had formed his study in his mother's house.   One of his intimate companions of this period, Mr. Thomas Palmer, the heraldic engraver, survived in 1837 to tell Mr. Dix some interesting reminiscences of Chatterton. He was apprenticed to Mr. Anthony Henderson, a jeweller, who rented part of the same building in which Mr. Lambert's office latterly was, and thus the two youths were brought into frequent contact. Mr. Palmer stated that " Chatterton was much alone in his office, and much disliked being disturbed in the day-time ; but he, with some of the other apprentices in the house, were in the habit of spending much of their time of an evening with Chatterton, Mr. Thomas Tipton, and Mr. Thomas Capel in the office." These, with Mr. Thistlethwaite, were wont to consult together on literary subjects, and in preparing articles for the Bristol newspapers and magazines.  Mr. Palmer describes Chatterton as having been " at this time very reserved, and apparently possessed of great pride.  He would sometimes, for days together, go in and out of the house without speaking to any one, and seemingly absorbed in thought.   After such occasions he frequently called some of his associates into his room, and read them some portions of Rowley."[1]   The old priest of Bristowe, his self-created *alter ego*, had become the sole sharer of those lonely hours on which he dreaded the intrusion of the outer world.   The spirit of the boy seemed then to pass at will into that other life ; and the attorney's apprentice of the eighteenth century was replaced by the parish priest of St. John's ; the confessor and confidential friend of William Canynge ;  the Bristowe poet of the times when Richard Nevill, Earl of Warwick, was making and unmaking kings.

But Chatterton had also hours of leisure to spare for the society of his seniors, including among these such literary men as Bristol afforded ; and the companions of his own age, if incapable of sympathy with the aspirations of his poetic mind, appear to have been the most

[1] Dix's Life, pp. 29, 30.

intellectual he could find. Thistlethwaite, Fowler, Cary, Gardner, Lockstone, Capel, and Smith, were all writers of verse and contributors to *Farley's Journal*, the *Town and Country Magazine*, or other periodicals of the day; Alcock was a miniature painter in good repute, and Palmer the best heraldic authority within reach.

Mrs. Newton says of her brother, in his earlier years, " his intimates in the school were but few, and they solid lads; and, except the next neighbour's sons, I know of none acquaintance he had out." It was otherwise with the attorney's apprentice, who lived more in the world of Bristol, and made himself known, ere long, as one of its most noticeable characters. But even then she could still report of him that " he had many cap acquaintances," who already recognised by their greeting one in whom a more than ordinary interest centred; " but few intimate friends." Yet with the few there was no lack of frankness; and had his simple mother and sister been capable of appreciating his labours, they might have had his full confidence. To the former he read the " Bristowe Tragedie;" and when she admired it, he readily acknowledged its authorship. The latter, with little less effort, drew from him the acknowledgment that the poem " On Oure Ladies Chyrche " was his own;[1] and, to learned controversialists, questioning her after his death, she replied that, at home, he was perpetually talking about Rowley's poems; and once, in particular, when their relative, Mr. Stephens, of Salisbury, visited them, the year after he quitted the Bluecoat School, he talked of nothing else.[2]

Could Chatterton, at this critical period, have found a friend capable of faith in his genius, to receive his confidence, and urge him onward in the one course on which it moved unerringly in its sustained and lofty flights, how different might his whole career have been! But the precious seed fell upon stony ground, and only the elements common to him and them were fostered by the meaner natures with whom he associated. This, I think,

CHAP. VI.

*A bevy of poets and artists.*

*Mrs. Newton's report of her brother.*

*Want of an appreciative friend*

---

[1] Mrs. Newton's Letter to Southey; Works, iii. p. 524.
[2] Milles's Preliminary Dissertation, p. 7.

Chap. VI.

*Craving for sympathy.*

*Mr. Barrett's incredulity.*

*Thistle-thwaite, the Blue-coat boy.*

*Renewed acquaintance with Chatterton.*

becomes apparent from the confidence that existed between them. So far from being naturally the deceptive or reticent recluse he has been described, Chatterton appears to have had a keen craving for the sympathy of some kindred soul ; and, for lack of better, to have made the most of such companions as he had.

Mr. Barrett, as we have seen, was told in plainest terms that "The Battle of Hastings" was Chatterton's own work. But he treated the statement simply as an absurd lie : pressing the boy to produce the original fifteenth-century manuscript, from which he persisted in taking for granted it had been copied. It was the same with the companions of the poet's own age. Ever and anon we find him trying their capacity to appreciate or comprehend his Rowleyan mystery ; and then, repelled by their stolid dulness, he retires once more to solitary communings with the creations of his own fancy.

James Thistlethwaite, the Bluecoat boy, has already been referred to at the period when he and Chatterton were companions in Colston's Hospital. As his senior, he left it nearly two years before Chatterton ; and he describes the consequent interruption and resumption of their intercourse, in his letter to the Dean of Exeter. He was apprenticed, as we have seen, to a Bristol stationer, in 1765 ; and some few months after Chatterton had entered the office of Mr. Lambert, in 1767, his former school-mate was sent for some of the attorney's books for the purpose of binding. Thus, accidentally, the acquaintance was renewed, and in their first interview Thistlethwaite learned that his companion "had been venturing in the fields of Parnassus, having produced several trifles, both in prose and verse, which had then lately made their appearance in the public prints." The acquaintance thus resumed ripened, in Thistlethwaite's estimation at least, into intimate friendship ; and he thus sets forth his estimate of the communicativeness of the young poet. "That vanity and an inordinate thirst after praise eminently distinguished Chatterton, all who knew him will readily admit. From a long and intimate acquaintance with him, I venture to assert that, from the date of his first poetical attempt until the final period of his departure from Bristol, he never wrote any piece, however trifling in its nature, and even unworthy of himself, but he first communicated it to every acquaintance he met, indiscriminately: as wishing to derive applause from productions which I am assured, were he now living, he would be heartily ashamed of." It was scarcely to be expected that Thistlethwaite should conceive it possible that Chatterton gauged the capacity of such critics, and limited his confidence by the appreciation they displayed; and so he draws this inference from his premises, that "had Chatterton been the author of the poems imputed to Rowley, so far from secreting such a circumstance, he would have made it his first, his greatest pride; for to suppose him ignorant of the intrinsic beauty of those compositions would be a most unpardonable presumption."

Thistlethwaite was in the habit of stepping into Mr. Lambert's office from time to time to have a chat with his new acquaintance, and with his aid we are able now to discern much that was invisible to his faithless sight. The eager youth was acquiring knowledge in all ways. Without a guide, and dependent on the chance resources of such private libraries and booksellers' shelves as were accessible to him, his studies were desultory enough. But we see him undaunted by impediments, turning the most unlikely means to account, and from all sources striving to acquire for himself, what schools and colleges were offering to thousands heedless of its value. No knowledge was without some attractions for him. "One day he might be found busily employed in the study of heraldry and English antiquities, both of which are numbered amongst the most favourite of his pursuits; the next discovered him deeply engaged, confounded, and perplexed, amidst the subtleties of metaphysical disquisition, or lost and bewildered in the abstruse labyrinth of mathematical researches; and these in an instant again neglected and thrown aside to make room for

astronomy and music, of both which sciences his knowledge was entirely confined to theory.   Even physic was
not without a charm to allure his imagination, and he
would talk of Galen, Hippocrates, and Paracelsus with
all the confidence and familiarity of a modern empiric."

*Uncom-*
*prehended*
*by his*
*companion.*

Such is the account of Thistlethwaite, who, as by his
own confession he had little or no taste for such studies,
fancied all this miscellaneous reading was vague and purposeless.   But he only gave fresh proof thereby of his
inability to comprehend his gifted companion.   Chatterton's studies were, of necessity, unsystematic ; but, so far
as his opportunities permitted, he aimed at a mastery of
the subjects he took in hand.   In medicine, for example,
he not only turned Mr. Barrett's library to account, but
solicited from him instruction in surgery ; and such was
his confidence in the extent of the knowledge he had acquired in a study so foreign to his favourite pursuits, that
we shall find him reverting to it in his final struggles
before he abandoned himself to despair ; and applying
to Mr. Barrett for a testimonial of his acquirements, with
a view to offering himself for the appointment of a surgeon's mate.

*Visits to the*
*attorney's*
*office.*

But in Thistlethwaite's visits to the office he also repeatedly found Chatterton at work on the Rowley poems.
He had long ago, as a Bluecoat boy, been admitted to
the confidence of his companion, so far as to learn of the
reputed discoveries in the ancient coffers of Redcliffe
Church, and judge for himself of the beautiful little
ballad of " Elinoure and Juga."   But he had no taste
for such studies ; and in later days, as indeed to the
last, he held stoutly to the belief in an actual monk
Rowley, of the fifteenth century.   There was no use,
therefore, in Chatterton trying to find a sympathising
confidant in him.   So Thistlethwaite walked in and out
of the office ; at diverse visits, in the year 1768, " found

*Copying*
*Rowley.*

him employed in copying Rowley," from what he had no
doubt were authentic originals ; and as he told the Dean
of Exeter eleven years after the poet's death, " Among
others, I perfectly remember to have read several stanzas

copied from the 'Deathe of Sir Charles Bawdin,' the original also of which then lay before him. The beautiful simplicity, animation, and pathos that so abundantly prevail through the course of that poem, made a lasting impression on my memory. I am, nevertheless, of opinion that the language, as I then saw it, was much more obsolete than it appears in the edition published by Mr. Tyrwhitt: probably occasioned by certain interpolations of Chatterton, ignorantly made, with an intention, as he thought, of improving them."

He then assigns to the same year sundry pieces, including "certain pretended translations from the Saxon and Ancient British," which appeared at a later date in the *Town and Country Magazine*. These, he says, Chatterton readily acknowledged to be the offspring of his own fancy. But, "on the contrary, his declaration, whenever questioned as to the authenticity of the poems attributed to Rowley, was invariably and uniformly in support of their antiquity, and the reputation of their author Rowley; instantly sacrificing thereby all the credit he might, without a possibility of detection, have taken to himself, by assuming a character to which he was conscious he had no legal claim : a circumstance which I am assured could not, in its effect, fail of operating upon a mind like his, prone to vanity, and eager of applause, even to an extreme."

The inconsequential nature of this, and much other reasoning of the same kind, which thus satisfied Thistlethwaite of the vanity of his friend, and therefore of his capacity to execute the inferior but not the truly poetical antiques, is amusing enough. But also it shows the necessity of reconsidering the verdict thus pronounced on one declared to have been notably distinguished for "vanity and an inordinate thirst for praise;" but who gratified this assumed ruling passion by producing to his companions the lampoons and other trifles of the hour; while he withheld from them all knowledge of his part in the immortal works which he was secretly treasuring as his passports to fame.

CHAP. VI.

*Confidence
repelled.*

Chatterton had, indeed, in a moment of rare confidence, yielded to Mr. Barrett's solicitations, and acknowledged one of the finest of the presumed antiques as his own. But Barrett and Thistlethwaite got over the difficulty with equal ease, by the simple assumption that the boy told a lie! "With respect to the first poem of the Battle of Hastings," says Thistlethwaite, "it has been said that Chatterton acknowledged it to be a forgery of his own. But let any unprejudiced person, of common discernment, advert only for a moment to the situation in which Chatterton then stood, and the reason and necessity of such a declaration will be apparent." And then, after referring to "the very contracted state of his finances," and the meanness of Bristol patrons, who received his poems, but made no adequate return, Thistlethwaite goes on to say: "From this circumstance it is easy to account for the answer given to Mr. Barrett on his repeated solicitations for the original, viz. *that he himself wrote that poem for a friend;* thinking, perhaps, that if he parted with the original poem, he might not be properly rewarded for the loss of it."

*Confusion
of ideas.*

The reader "of common discernment" cannot fail to mark the strange confusion of ideas, so characteristic of a century of criticism on these remarkable poems. If Chatterton produces a beautiful poem, and acknowledges himself to be its author, it is not to receive the credit due to him as such. He merely confesses it to be "a forgery of his own!"

*Want of
faith in
Chatterton's
genius.*

But even this is a rare admission of his presumption of authorship. There is a ludicrous uniformity in the disclaimers of Chatterton's companions, alike of sympathy with his tastes, or faith in his genius. Mr. William Smith, according to his nephew's account, "was Chatterton's bosom friend. In fact," he says, "they were birds of a feather," which may well be doubted. But they recognised some community of feeling as contributors to *Farley's Journal* and other periodicals. To him Chatterton addressed his "Defence," a vigorous though unequal maintenance of rationalistic views, written a few months before he left Bristol ; and within a fortnight after reaching London, he transmits this message to him through his friend Cary : "When you have any poetry for publication send it to me, to be left at the Chapter Coffee-house, Paternoster Row, and it shall most certainly appear." He was the correspondent addressed as the "Infallible Doctor," in a medley of ironical superlatives, evidently in reply to some poetical scheme propounded in grandiloquent fashion by his friend, the Actor, "who," as his nephew reports, "wrote verses in torrents daily, to within a few hours of his death ;"[1] and therefore might very fitly be answered in the fashion adopted in this odd epistolary vein :

"INFALLIBLE DOCTOR,

"Let this apologize for long silence. Your request would have been long since granted, but I know not what it is best to compose : a Hendecasyllabum carmen Hexastichon, Ogdastich, Tetrametrum, or Septennarius ;" and after much of the same sort the letter thus winds up : "I am resolved to forsake the Parnassian Mount, and would advise you to do so too, and attain the mystery of composing smegma. Think not I make a mysterismus in mentioning smegma. No ; my mnemosque will let me see—unless I have an amblyopia,—your great services, which shall be always remembered by

"HASMOT ETCHAORNTT."[2]

Mr. William Smith informed Dean Milles that Chatterton read many of Rowley's poems to him while he was an apprentice of Mr. Lambert. Sometimes he read whole treatises, sometimes parts only, and that very often. He did not know that they were all by Rowley, but never heard him mention any other ancient poet, and, it is plain, never troubled himself to ask. He had also very

---

[1] Gent. Mag. N.S. x. p. 605.

[2] This letter was furnished to Mr. Cottle by Catcott, and is printed in the edition of 1803, with the signature "*Flasmot Eychaorit ;*" but it is obviously a mere transposition of the letters of *Thomas Chatterton.* Mr. Cottle has been followed in this and other misreadings of Chatterton's MSS. by subsequent editors ; as in the De Bergham Pedigree, where he gives *Simon de Leyncte Lyze,* instead of *De Syncte Lyze,* alias *Senliz.*

CHAP. VI.

*His friends Cary and Smith.*

*To the infallible doctor.*

*Readings of Rowley's poems.*

often seen him at work at Mr. Lambert's office, transcribing some of the ancient pieces of writing which came, as he assumed, from the Redcliffe muniment-room; and he had read them to him immediately after he had written them out. But Mr. Smith added, he had no taste for such things; was, in fact, bored by them; and wondered how his companion could take up his time with such incomprehensible stuff. He also told the Dean that "Chatterton was fond of walking in the fields, and particularly in Redcliffe meadows; of talking with him about these MSS. and reading them to him. 'You and I,' says he, 'will take a walk in Redcliffe meadow. I have got the cleverest thing for you that ever was. It is worth half-a-crown to have a sight of it only and to hear me read it to you.' He would then produce and read the parchment;" but he never seemed to wish that any one should regard him as the author; and Mr. Smith was quite certain he never dreamt of claiming them as his own.[1]

*Walks in Redcliffe meadows.*

Let the reader fancy the enthusiastic young poet pacing the meadows under Redcliffe Church, and reading the latest of his Rowley poems to this "bosom friend." "I have often talked with him on the subject," says Mr. Richard Smith. "'What, sir!' (he would say,) 'he write Rowley? No! no! no! I knew him well. He was a clever fellow, but he could not write Rowley. There was a mystery about the poems beyond me; but Tom no more wrote them than I did. He could not!'"[2] No wonder that to such friends Chatterton was content to produce some lively *jeu d'esprit*, or trifling lampoon, and seem delighted with the applause of his admiring critics. As for the antiques, he spoke of all as really ancient; some as Rowley's, but whether all of them Smith did not know: "He never seemed desirous that any one should suspect, much less believe, them to be written by him."[3]

*The poet's "bosom friend."*

So it is with all Chatterton's companions. Each echoes the sentiment of the others. Mr. John Rudhall, apprentice to Mr. Francis Greesley, a Bristol apothecary

---

[1] Milles's Rowley, p. 14.    [2] Gent. Mag. N.S. vol. x. p. 605.
[3] Milles's Rowley, p. 14.

in the neighbourhood of Mr. Lambert's office, was taken into his confidence at an early date, as to the authorship of the "Opening of the Old Bridge," which, as we shall presently see, created no little sensation on its appearance in *Farley's Bristol Journal.* Yet for all this, as he tells the Dean of Exeter, "he thinks Chatterton to have been incapable of writing the Battle of Hastings, or any of those poems produced by him under the name of Rowley;" though he did intimate to him that "he was possessed of some valuable literary productions:" but under promise of secrecy so binding that he scrupulously kept the secret for nine years, and only revealed it at last, as he said, on the prospect of procuring a gratuity of ten pounds for Chatterton's mother, from a gentleman who came to Bristol to collect information about the poet; and "he thought so material a benefit to the family would fully justify him for divulging a secret by which no person living could be a sufferer."[1] In other words, this friend— to whom, in some hour of special confidence, Chatterton had hinted, that besides the ephemeral satires, eclogues, and other trifles of his muse, he had poems by him of real and enduring worth,—was still in doubt, nine years after the poet's death, whether he had made secret confession that he was a forger or a thief!

Even Mr. Thomas Cary, who is named by Mrs. Edkins, and seemingly with reason, as Chatterton's most intimate friend; to whom he will be found writing confidentially from London, within a few months of his death, enclosing his "Kew Gardens" and other poems : even he discards the idea of his being " equal to the works of Rowley" as too absurd for any rational being to entertain.[2]

Mr. Cary was a literary tradesman of Bristol, who had been drawn into friendly sympathy with the boy. There must have been considerable disparity in years ; for in writing to Mr. Catcott he speaks of having observed the progress of his genius from infancy. But this did not prevent an intimacy, partaking more of the confidence

Chap. VI.

*Confidence extended to Mr. Rudhall.*

*Intimate relations with Mr. Cary.*

*A literary pipe-maker.*

----

[1] Milles's Rowley, p. 436.
[2] Letter to Mr. G. Catcott, Works, vol. iii. p. 482.

of mutual friendship than is discernible in his intercourse with any other of his seniors. This is probably traceable, in part, to a greater social equality. Mr. Cary was a Bristol pipe-maker, in humble circumstances, seemingly; for Chatterton appears to have been commissioned by him, on reaching London, to inquire what better chance there might be for prosecuting his trade there. In one of the early London letters to his mother, she is directed to tell the literary pipe-maker: "Upon inquiry, I find his trade dwindled into nothing here. A man may very nobly starve by it; but he must have luck indeed who can live by it." He was a contributor to London as well as Bristol periodicals; a man of critical taste in musical matters; and altogether too much of a literary turn, it is to be feared, to give the pipe-making any fair chance.



Chatterton, it may be seen, condescended to his humble friend, patronised him in some degree, and received in return a better appreciation of his capacity than from most of his associates. Cary says of him: "His abilities, for his age, were beyond conception great;" but, he adds, "not equal to the works of Rowley, particularly at the age that he produced them to light." For he had frequently heard the boy make mention of such writings being in his possession, "when he could not have been more than fifteen years of age;" and so he thus naïvely combines his own verdict and the evidence of his fitness to pronounce an opinion on the question: "Not having any taste myself for ancient poetry, I do not recollect his ever having shown them to me; but that he often mentioned them, at an age when (great as his capacity was) I am convinced he was incapable of writing them himself, I am very clear in, and confess it to be astonishing how any person, knowing these circumstances, can entertain even a shadow of a doubt of their being the works of Rowley."



In much of this it is obvious that the young poet was feeling his way. No wonder that his half-confidences, met by such inappreciative, or incredulous responses, went no further. Phillips, his old teacher, was full of interest in the first antique ballad put into his hands; traced the obscure letters on the parchment with his pen; and astonished the unimpressible Thistlethwaite with the earnestness he displayed, so disproportioned, as it seemed to him, to the worth of the object. But with the death of the poetical usher, Chatterton's last sympathising confidant was gone; and every advance he made towards confessing himself to be the true Rowley was repelled with the same ludicrous faith in its impossibility. It was far easier to believe him a "forger," a "liar," and a cheat, than to discern in the poor charity-boy, or attorney's clerk, a poet of rare genius and strange creative power. So he soon learned to produce to them only his local satires and other ephemeral pieces. They were adapted to the capacity of such critics. But his great secret he cherished more closely in his own breast, anticipating the time when he might, at length, find fit audience to acknowledge its worth.

From such associates there was some relief in escaping to the society of those who, by social position and knowledge of the world, had acquired some wisdom to which he was a stranger: so he cultivated the acquaintance of Mr. Barrett and Mr. George Catcott; decoyed Mr. Burgum into confidential talk on genealogies; or made his way into the Temple parsonage, and got into collision with the vicar on his Hutchinsonian system of cosmogony. The hours passed in such society redeemed him, as it were, from the social degradation which he instinctively resented in his daily enforced equality with his master's menials. His spirits rose with the recognition of his worth; and, confident in his own powers, he pictured to his mother and sister a splendid future in which they were to share.

Of those among the citizens of Bristol who thus extended friendly recognition and aid to Chatterton, Mr. Michael Clayfield, though one of the latest in point of time, occupies a place altogether distinct. Barrett and Catcott patronised him, and turned his supposed discoveries to account for their own advantage. Burgum

CHAP. VI.

*Last sympathising confidant.*

*Associates of higher social position.*

*Mr. Michael Clayfield.*

helped him in difficulties, in a kindly, if somewhat niggard fashion; and seems, from the terms in which Chatterton refers to him in his latest satire, to have borne no malice on account of the heraldic hoax. But Clayfield befriended him with intelligent estimation of his worth, and met with a response in striking contrast to the feelings manifested towards his condescending patrons.

*Commencement of their acquaintanceship.*

According to Mrs. Newton's account, it was when her brother was about seventeen, and therefore very shortly before he quitted Bristol, that he became acquainted with Mr. Clayfield, who was a distiller in Castle Street. This is confirmed by the date of one of his elegies on the death of his favourite teacher, addressed to him as one "long renowned the Muses' friend," and, it may be presumed, the friend and patron of Phillips. The copy of this elegy in the British Museum is dated October 30th, 1769, and differs considerably from another version printed in Southey's edition. Its merit as a poem is small, but it was probably the first introduction to Mr. Clayfield, and thus determines the commencement of their brief intercourse. Mrs. Newton speaks of him as lending her brother many books on astronomy. In reply

*Borrowing books.*

to Dr. Glynn's inquiries at a subsequent date, he named Martin's Philosophical Grammar and a volume of his philosophy, as the only books he remembered to have been borrowed by Chatterton. But, whatever may have been the amount of such favours, the brief intercourse between them appears to have been frank and cordial; and to him alone, of all beyond his own family circle, he refers at the last in unqualified terms of earnest gratitude. He appears to have been a man of literary tastes and of a speculative turn of mind, from whom the boy received intelligent advice, and to whose judgment he deferred.

*Doubtful feature of their intercourse.*

The only doubtful feature in their intercourse is suggested by a passage in one of Chatterton's latest satires,[1] in which the sentiments of his new friend are produced in confirmation of his own antagonism to the science and theology of the age. With the political free-thinking of

---

[1] Epistle to Rev. Mr. Catcott.

the same period, when Chatterton marshalled himself under the banner of "Wilkes and Liberty," Mr. Clayfield can scarcely be supposed to have had any sympathy; for the most noticeable fact now recoverable concerning him is that his name figures among the Presidents of the Dolphin Society; established, as Mr. Tovey tell us, "by the Tories of Bristol." But those questions will come under review more fittingly along with others marking the close of Chatterton's Bristol career. Meanwhile, what is known of Mr. Clayfield indicates that in him the boy found a friend to whom he was disposed to extend a confidence necessarily withheld from the associates hitherto furnished to him from Bristol circles.

Chatterton delighted in his company, turned his library to account, and read with him the poets of his own day, such as Pope and Thomson. When, at the close of his Bristol career, he bequeathed with bitter irony his vigour and fire of youth to Mr. George Catcott; his humility to the Rev. Mr. Camplin, senior, "being sensible he is most in need of it;" to Mr. Burgum all his prosody and grammar, with one moiety of his modesty; and to the City of Bristol all his spirit and disinterestedness, as graces unknown there since the days of Canynge : he changes from banter to a tone of earnest gravity, and leaves to Mr. Clayfield the sincerest thanks his gratitude can give.

It is necessary to anticipate, thus far, some of the later incidents of Chatterton's Bristol career, in order to bring into one view the social relations which chiefly influenced him. He evidently longed for congenial society, and knew no fatigue in his own favourite pursuits ; but from these he had to return to the illiterate companionship of the servants' hall. It need not therefore be wondered that, as his sister states, while "his ambition increased daily, his spirits were rather uneven; sometimes so gloomed, that for many days together he would say but very little, and that by constraint." But much of this seeming depression is traceable to the abstraction of a mind withdrawing itself into an antique world of its own creation. In the solitude of the attorney's office, when

CHAP. VI.

*Cure for
despondency.*

*An
unwelcome
intruder.*

left free to consort with the heroes of that olden time, he could emancipate himself, at will, from deepest despondency. Mr. Catcott left him one evening totally depressed, as he imagined; but he returned the next morning in unusual spirits, saying "he had sprung a mine;" and produced his fine Rowleyan poem, the "Parliament of Sprytes."

All intruders during such fits of poetic reverie were unwelcome; but there was one whose visits never failed to exorcise the good priest, or the princely merchant of Bristowe, and recall the dreamer to the rudest realities of life. Mr. Lambert, I fancy to myself, a thin, nervous, prosaic little man; of formal habits, an unenterprising disposition, and suspicious temperament: who had means enough from some other source, official or private, to dispense with the professional income his attorneyship should have yielded. He was a bachelor seemingly, living in some style, with his mother for housekeeper. Chatterton describes him as fretful, irritating, and vexatious in his petty interferences; and so timid as to be "afraid of his own shadow." The old mother's name only once appears, in connexion with the event that led to Chatterton's dismissal. It is obvious that neither she nor her son regarded the gifted inmate of their house with greater interest than they extended to the chance menials whose meals he shared. With no possibility of retirement, either in Mr. Lambert's kitchen or the bedroom he had in common with the footboy, his advantages there were even less than when in Colston's Hospital. But of the attorney's office Chatterton appears, for the most part, to have enjoyed the sole occupancy. There, therefore, after the average two hours of actual office-work had been accomplished, and a reasonable number of folio pages of law precedents copied, much leisure time remained for Rowleyan creations, and the more ordinary contributions to the periodicals of the day.

But this "idleness," as Mr. Lambert called it, was intolerable to him; and, according to Mrs. Edkins' account, "he took every opportunity to vex, cross, and mortify" his apprentice. If, by chance, any of his verses were found on his desk, he instantly tore them in pieces, and scattered the fragments abroad, with the exclamation: "There is your stuff!" The misappropriation of the office paper to such unprofessional uses appears to have been an additional grievance, on which he dwelt when pouring contempt on the boy and his compositions. Mrs. Edkins, who manifested towards him all the love of a foster-mother, was the sympathising confidant of his sorrows; and used frequently to give him money to buy paper. He would tell her, with looks full of trouble, that all his paper was gone; and recount to her how his master had got at his literary stores, and destroyed the whole, because they contained writings on subjects not pertaining to the office. It was even a crime to find this unprofessional paper in his drawer. Mr. Lambert would tax him with its possession; and with great ill-nature in his manner, demand where he got it. On being told that it was honestly acquired, he would tear it up and throw it at him.

When the paper thus destroyed contained manuscript poems, Chatterton was filled with grief. He did not so much regret the destruction of letters written to his friends, for those he could rewrite; but his poetical compositions were lost for ever. The coarse violence of such a master was little calculated to win on the better nature of the boy; while it tended still more to confirm his habits of secretiveness with reference to his poetical labours. Yet the attorney had no graver charge to bring against him than the writing of verse during office hours, after the regular work was done. Mrs. Edkins called on him in company with Mrs. Chatterton, when the latter inquired if her son was a good apprentice; to which Mr. Lambert replied, "There was no keeping boys from idleness;" but he had no other charge against him than that he neglected to read law-books, and wrote "stuff." Mrs. Edkins speaks of his being rude, and even brutal; and that Chatterton complained of his playing the dog in the manger: neither providing work enough to occupy



CHAP. VI.

His sympathising confidant.

Original poems destroyed.

his time, nor permitting him to turn it to useful account for himself. But though Chatterton resented the degradation he was subjected to in his house, and bitterly felt the repeated loss of his poetical compositions, he appears to have recognised with a clear sense of justice, the rights of Lambert as his master; and, so far as appears, never expended on him the shafts of his satiric wit. These, in truth, were but the sportive sallies of the young poet, in retaliation at times for fancied slights or illiberal censures; and should be estimated accordingly. But Lambert's treatment of him embittered his life; and was referred to, if at all, with tears.

# CHAPTER VII.

## THE PASSAGE OF THE BRIDGE.



IN Chatterton's younger days, the river Avon, at Bristol, was crossed by an ancient stone bridge built in the reign of Henry II. and subsequently widened by the addition of flying arches. On one of those, with the help of a pier in mid-stream, a chapel was erected by Edward III. and his queen, Philippa, called the Chapel of the Assumption of the Blessed Virgin Mary, to which various citizens of note contributed liberal endowments. Gradually the lateral arches and piers on either side were crowded with lofty gabled tenements overhanging the Avon, and converting its roadway into a picturesque thoroughfare, not unlike that of old London Bridge.[1] But the approaches were steep and narrow, and further straitened by the ancient gateway already referred to, surmounted by the chancel of St. Michael's Church. Moreover, to the great obstruction of the river, the old builders, as Barrett records, had made its massive piers as if "they were building for eternity;" while the growing commerce of Bristol, the increasing use of carriages, and the crowding of the river with barges and lighters, all combined to enforce the necessity of ampler accommodation for the passage of the Avon.



At length, in 1761, when Chatterton was in his tenth year, the doom of the Old Bridge was pronounced ; and the ancient chapel of Our Lady, with all the quaint

[1] *Vide* Barrett's History, p. 80, for a view of the Old Bridge.

I 2

buildings on either side, were cleared away, preparatory
to its destruction.　This accomplished, a new bridge of
slenderer piers and more ample proportions of roadway,
gradually rose in the room of the venerable Gothic structure, with corresponding improvement in its approaches.
Seven years had been expended on the work ; Mr. George
Catcott had achieved his memorable triumph of riding
over the unfinished structure, and paying the first toll ;
and Chatterton had nearly completed his sixteenth year :
when, in the month of September 1768, the new bridge
was opened for foot passengers, and in November for
carriages.　In the interval between these two important
local events, the editor of the *Bristol Weekly Journal*
received the following note, with its accompanying
narrative of ceremonies observed on the opening of the
ancient structure that had just been swept away :—

*To the Printer of Farley's Bristol Journal.*



"Mr. Printer,

　　"The following Description of the Mayor's first passing
over the Old Bridge, taken from an old manuscript, may not at this
time be unacceptable to the generality of your readers.

"Yours, &c.

"Dunelmus Bristoliensis.

"On Fridaie was the Time fixed for passing the newe Brydge :
Aboute the Time of the Tollynge the tenth Clock, Master Greggorie
Dalbenye, mounted on a Fergreyne Horse, enformed Master Maior
all Thyngs were prepared : when two Beadils want fyrst streyng
fresh stre, next came a Manne dressed up as follows : Hose of
Goatskyn, erinepart outwards, Doublet and Waystcoat also, over
which a white Robe without sleeves, much like an albe, but not so
longe, reeching but to his Lends ; a girdle of Azure over his left
shoulder, rechde also to his Lends on the Ryght, and doubled back
to his Left, bucklyng with a Gouldin Buckel, dangled to his knee ;
thereby representing a Saxon Elderman.　In his hande he bare a
shield, the Maystrie of Gille a Brogton, who paincted the same,
representyng Saincte Warburgh crossynge the Ford.　Then a mickle
strong Manne, in armour, carried a huge anlace ; after whom came
six claryons and Minstrels, who sang the Song of Saincte Warburgh ;
then came Master Maior, mounted on a white Horse, dight with
sable Trappyng, wrought about by the Nunnes of Saincte Kenna,
with gould and silver."　Next followed the "Eldermen and Cittie

Broders" all fitly mounted and caparisoned ; and after them a procession of priests and friars, also singing St. Warburgh's Song.

"In thilk Manner reechyng the Brydge, the Manne with the anlace stode on the fyrst Top of a Mound, yreed in the midst of the Bridge ; then want up the Manne with the sheelde, after him the Minstrels and Clarions ; and then the Preestes and Freeres, all in white Albs, makyng a most goodlie shewe ; the Maior and Eldermen standyng round, theie sang, with the sound of Clarions, the Song of Saincte Baldwyn ; which beyng done, the Manne on the Top threwe with greet Myght his anlace into the see, and the Clarions sounded an auntiant charge and Forloyn : then theie sang againe the Songe of Saincte Warburgh, and proceeded up Chryst's Hill, to the Cross, where a Latin Sermon was preached by Ralph de Blundeville. And with sound of clarion theie agayne went to the Brydge, and there dined, spendyng the rest of the Daie in Sportes and Plaies :• the Freeres of Saincte Augustine doeyng the Plaie of the Knyghtes of Bristowe, making a greete Fire at Night on Kynwulph Hyll."

In spite of its affectations of antique phraseology, the narrative is graphic, and highly picturesque ; nor is there lacking a quiet touch of humour in the Latin sermon preached at the Cross, by Ralph de Blunderville, as Cottle read it.[1] This well-timed article naturally attracted considerable notice, and, above all, did not escape the eye of Mr. Barrett : already busy in the collection of materials for his projected folio. Twenty-one years afterwards, the credulous antiquary, still incapable of arriving at any definite opinion on the Rowley MSS. or their author, referred his readers to Dean Milles's edition of " Rowley's Poems," for " the ceremony and joy said to be displayed on this occasion, with the songs of St. Baldwin and St. Warburgh." For, by and by, the same ingenious research which brought so opportunely to light the " old manuscript" describing the mayor's first

---

[1] Southey and Cottle's version, which has supplied the text of every subsequent copy, except Grant's Cambridge edition, is exceedingly inaccurate, and has furnished the misreading of the " Fryar's" instead of the " Mayor's first passing over the Old Bridge," since universally adopted. I am indebted to John Taylor, Esq. of the Bristol Library, for collating this with the original Journal. The heading is there printed in Roman type and the rest in Italics. Barrett must have secured the original MS., as it is now in the British Museum,—Additional MSS. No. 5766.

passage of the bridge, was able to add the songs sung on that occasion.

But who was this learned *Dunelmus Bristoliensis ?* Mr. Farley knew no more than his readers. The MS. had been handed into his office by a stranger ; and possessed sufficient intrinsic value to need no special authentication. But ere long Chatterton presented himself at the office of the *Bristol Journal* with another contribution, and was called to account for his acquisition of the former piece. His age and appearance altogether precluded the idea of his being the author. The genuineness of the narrative was not, indeed, likely to be challenged in that uncritical age. But he repelled the threats of those who treated him as a child with a haughty refusal to render any account of his discovery. Gentler means were resorted to, apparently with better success ; and then, for the first time, appeared the definite story,—about which critics and antiquaries have laboriously wrangled ever since ;— that this was one of many ancient manuscripts which his father had taken from the old coffer in the muniment-room of Redcliffe Church.

Chatterton had his confidants, however, from the first, and " soon after he had printed the account of the Bridge, told Mr. John Rudhall," a companion of his own age, " that he was the author of it." [1] Subsequently he showed him the process of imitating the old caligraphy, and giving parchments a look of antiquity. *Dunelmus Bristoliensis*, then, was Thomas Chatterton. Under this signature he not only continued his contributions to *Farley's Bristol Journal;* but in the acknowledgments to correspondents in the *London Town and Country Magazine* for November of the same year, appears this editorial note : " D.B. of Bristol's favour will be gladly received." The boy had already enrolled himself among men of letters, and the Rowleyan mystery had had its public inauguration.

If the reader turn from the biographer's pages to those of the historian and antiquary of Bristol, for information

[1] Milles's Rowley, p. 437.

about William Canynge the elder, merchant and Mayor of Bristol in the age of Chaucer, when Edward III. and his grandson Richard reigned ; or for the facts concerning the younger Canynges of the times of the Roses ; of Sir Symon de Byrtoune, Sir Baldwin Fulford, or even of the good priest Rowley: he suddenly finds himself involved in the most ludicrous perplexities. Mr. Barrett was, in earlier days, an undoubted believer in Rowley, and continued to welcome with unquestioning credulity the apt discoveries which were ever rewarding the researches of Chatterton among the old parchments purloined by his father from Redcliffe Church. Did the historian attempt to follow up his first chapter of British and Roman Bristol, with its Roman camps, roads, and coins, by a second, treating in like manner of Saxon and Norman Bristol: his meagre data are forthwith augmented by the discovery of an account by Turgot, a Saxon ecclesiastic, who lived not long after the time assigned by Camden for the origin of the city, "Of auncient coynes found at and near Bristowe, with the hystorie of the fyrst coynynge by the Saxonnes; done from the Saxon ynto Englyshe, by T. Rowlie." From the same veracious pen follows an account of "Mayster Canynge, hys cabinet of auntyaunte monuments;" the same being a wondrous library and antiquarian museum of Bristol in the days of Henry VI. Did Leland fail the historian, painfully assiduous in researches into early ecclesiastical foundations: an old MS. of Rowley fortunately turns up, with valuable notes on St. Baldwyn's Chapelle in Baldwyn's Street; the Chapelle of St. Mary Magdalen, in the time of Earl Goodwyne; Seyncte Austin's Chapelle with its "aunciauntrie and nice carvellynge;" and other equally curious and apocryphal edifices.

So it is throughout the volume. Chatterton had "sprung a mine," as he himself said, on producing one of the Rowleyan creations; and Barrett was eager to profit by its yield. Gildas, William of Worcester, Leland, and Camden, intermingle with Rowleyan contributions of

CHAP. VII.
———
*Historical perplexities.*

*Unfailing supply of materials.*

*Sprung a mine.*

the most miscellaneous kind. How the antiquarian dupe must have gloated over his prizes; while the adept laughed in his sleeve at the airs assumed by his condescending patron! Twenty years later the antiquary was still in a helpless maze. He had interwoven his Rowleyan treasures so inextricably into his history, that neither he nor any one else could separate the golden threads from the worthless tissue, without destroying the whole. He had no faith in the "misguided youth" of whom he writes with unsympathetic callousness at the close of his absurd *mélange* of local antiquities, history, and romance. He could not exactly tell at the last, whether he believed in Rowley or not. The only thing he was certain about was that the charity boy he had patronised, and helped to some scraps from his own stores of professional and antiquarian learning, was wholly incapable of producing the gems of ancient poetry and history with which his pages were enriched. Not



the least curious among the works of Chatterton is this so-called " History and Antiquities of the City of Bristol, compiled from original records and authentic manuscripts, by William Barrett, Surgeon, F.S.A.," published, with its long list of royal, noble, and learned subscribers, nineteen years after what Barrett calls " The horrible catastrophe of T. Chatterton, the producer of Rowley and his poems to the world."



For some of his ingenious prose and poetic fictions, Chatterton received pecuniary remuneration. Let the fact be clearly recognised in all its enormity. The latest believer in an actual Thomas Rowley, priest and poet of the fifteenth century : the learned S. R. Maitland, D.D., F.R.S., F.S.A.,—who closes his " Chatterton Essay " with an entreaty to all archæologists " not to allow the notion of forgery to prevent their keeping a look-out for Old Rowley ;" — states the case in this delicate fashion : " Though we might, just at this outset, shut our eyes, and dream of poetic enthusiasm, they would, as we proceed, be gradually and irresistibly opened to the fact that, whatever other 'value' the clever poetical lad might find in them, the sharp attorney's clerk very soon began to see their 'value' as things which might bring him money or advancement." The author of the "Dunciad," with not a few mysteries and trickeries about its editions, as well as about his "Letters," &c., had made a similar discovery, to good purpose, before him; as did after him another mystery-loving "attorney's clerk," the author of "Waverley." Indeed, the noble Ayrshire peasant had ideas on this subject that never entered into the head of the noble Lord Byron. "I repeat my belief," says the Rev. Dr. Maitland, "that Chatterton had a notion of making his fortune by the help of these MSS. ;" only the learned essayist adds to this very credible belief, another, but most incredible one : that a charity boy, just transferred from the society of Colston's Hospital to that of Mr. Lambert's kitchen ; and so converted at the age of sixteen into "a sharp attorney's clerk," had taste and sagacity enough to appreciate, and to decipher for the benefit of the tradesmen of Bristol, the fifteenth-century MSS. of an unheard-of poet of Chaucer's school. Still more, this untutored charity boy, while asserting persistently their antique authorship, was all the while destroying the original parchments, for the purposeless end of substituting for them bungling and disfigured imitations to be passed off as the originals. The credulity of the unbeliever is proverbial. Possibly, however, another theory may be formed, at once more conceivable, and more consistent with what is known of the boy-poet.

To those who recognise Chatterton as not only the author between his tenth and twelfth years, of various serious and satirical pieces already referred to ; but the "maker" of the Rowleyan Eclogue of "Elinoure and Juga" before the close of the following year: he is one of the most remarkable examples of intellectual precocity on record. With none of the advantages of Pope, it may far more literally be said of Chatterton than of him, "that he lisped in numbers ;" and, not unsuccessfully, dared

> "To stammer where old Chaucer used to sing."

The child, musing in his favourite haunt of Redcliffe Church, moved by strange impulses of poetic insight, with an intellect far beyond that of common men ; but with all the inexperience of childhood : conceived of the merchant prince, William Canynge, as of his ideal patron ; and of himself as the poet-priest, in those " good old times " so different from his own.   The hard struggles of a poor widow force upon her little orphan, at a very early period, the value of money ; yet his foster-mother tells us that, at twelve years of age, so sensitive was he to the sufferings of others, that she has seen him distribute his last half-pence to the beggars that frequented Bristol drawbridge, and go without what he was about to purchase for himself ; just as at a later date he is found spending his first London earnings on gifts for his mother and sister.



Every well-ascertained fact controverts the idea that mercenary motives stimulated Chatterton's muse.   His earlier contributions to *Farley's Journal* and to the *Town and Country Magazine* were anonymous ventures for fame alone.   But the young poet wanted books ; he wanted even paper on which to record the promptings of his muse : and there is nothing to show that his master, Lambert, gave him more than the promised board and lodging in return for office work.   He did indeed clothe him also : an item of ever-increasing importance in the estimation of a proud-spirited youth ; but was the clothing which Mr. Lambert thought good enough for the idle apprentice in his kitchen, such as was



likely to satisfy the young poet, whose " ambition increased daily," after his introduction to Mr. Barrett and other literary seniors ; or when he bethought himself of cultivating female society, " supposing it might soften the austerity of temper study had occasioned," and so " would frequently walk the college green with the young girls that statedly paraded there to show their finery ?"[1]   His companion, Thistlethwaite, when attempting, long afterwards, in his blundering way, to account for Chatterton

_______
[1] Mrs. Newton's Letter to Sir H. Croft.

taking credit for the authorship of "The Battle of Hastings," which he never doubted to be a genuine antique, says : "The very contracted state of his finances, aided by a vain desire of appearing superior to what his circumstances afforded, induced him, from time to time, to dispose of the poems in his possession ;" but he adds that Chatterton was disappointed in the anticipations he had formed of the liberality of his Bristol patrons, and their estimation of the worth of his communications. He was paid, at most, as the mere copying clerk, without reference to the value of the originals ; though, after his death, both Catcott and Barrett dealt with his MSS. as though the copyright had absolutely passed to them. But we have glimpses of other means by which he sought to improve his finances ; and, in particular, Mr. Capel told Bryant of his composing a play for some itinerant players, from which both appear to have drawn the same logical conclusion, "that the real author of 'Ælla' would never have written for strollers," however contracted his finances might have been.[1]

One of the contrasts the poet drew between London and his native city, before he had been a fortnight there, was that he need no longer fear being judged of solely by his dress.   In his second letter to his mother he writes : "Dress, which is in Bristol an eternal fund of scandal, is here only introduced as a subject of taste.   If a man dresses well, he has taste ; if careless, he has his own reasons for so doing, and is prudent.   Need I remind you of the contrast?"   And then he goes on, in the following sentence, to refer to the proverbial poverty of authors.

The young poet wanted money for many legitimate objects familiar to youths of his age, whether poets or not.   So Mr. George Catcott, "a gentleman of an inquisitive turn, and fond of reading," after receiving in free gift various specimens both of modern verse and the modern antiques, was induced—not unreluctantly, let us hope,—to acknowledge the substantial value of others by

[1] Bryant's Observations, p. 525.

CHAP. VII.

*Temptations to dispose of poems.*

*Contrast of Bristol and London.*

*Legitimate necessity for money.*

occasional pecuniary returns.　He had at least transcribed them, whoever might be their author, and for that, at any rate, remuneration was due.　With a touch of humour highly characteristic of the boy, he presented the following bill, on the only occasion on which he is known to have made a direct application for money in any form :—

Mr. G. Catcott to the executors of T. Rowley, Dr.

|                                                   | £ | s. | d. |
|---------------------------------------------------|---|----|----|
| To pleasure recd. in readg. his Historic works . . | 5 | 5  | 0  |
| „　　　„　　　„　　　Poetic works . . . | 5 | 5  | 0  |
|                                                   | £10 | 10 | 0 |

Mr. Barrett and Mr. Burgum also occasionally supplied him with money, in no very extravagant fashion ; and Mr. Clayfield in this, as well as in other ways, so generously aided him as to win his lasting gratitude as "the Muses' friend," and the rightful heir to whatever debt the world might yet own as the poet's due.



On glancing over the collected works of Chatterton, it will be seen that, in addition to some of his modern poems directly addressed to Bristol patrons, the best of the remainder are derived from original manuscripts in their possession.　For these, at least, the boy-poet had as much right to receive a pecuniary return as Pope or Goldsmith ; as Scott, Byron, Wordsworth, or any poet laureate, ancient or modern, for his verse.　But the Rowley poems appear, for the most part, to have been reluctantly produced—as the crude MS. of Goldsmith's "Vicar of Wakefield" was,—when necessity tempted their author to barter portions of his incompleted scheme, while he hoarded the secret of its authorship as sacred to himself alone.　To Thistlethwaite, and others of the same stamp, he seemed prodigal in his indiscriminate disclosure of the most worthless productions of his pen.



Of his imitations of Ossian, and the like crude attempts, such as his "Ethelgar," "Kenrick," "Cerdick," and "Gorthmund," when asked for the originals, he "hesitated not to confess that they existed only in his own imagination. On the contrary, his declaration, whenever questioned as to the authenticity of the poems attributed to Rowley, was uniformly in support of their antiquity; sacrificing thereby all the credit he might, without a possibility of detection, have taken to himself by assuming a character to which," adds Thistlethwaite, "he was conscious he had no legal claim;" and so he arrives at the conclusion that, "had Chatterton been the author of the poems imputed to Rowley, so far from secreting such a circumstance, he would have made it his first, his greatest pride; for to suppose him ignorant of the intrinsic beauty of those compositions would be a most unpardonable presumption."

Without drawing the same inference, it is obvious that the Rowleyan romance was guarded as a treasure for clearer eyes and brighter days that never dawned. With the child-poet, Rowley and himself, I conceive, were one. In the solitude on which he dreaded intrusion, he dwelt apart, another being, in that ideal world of the past. But as the child grew into boyhood, and the boy emerged from Colston's cloisters into the wider world of Bristol, the fiction of his waking dreams took tangible shape, challenged inquiry, and involved him in the dilemma of enforced confidences, or of such fraud as has not been uncommon in the maskings of literature. It has, indeed, its very diverse phases: its innocent fictions, like Moore's "Raphael Hythloday" and his Utopian experiences; and its impudent forgeries, like the "Vortigern and Rowena" of Ireland. Assuredly Chatterton's good priest Rowley approaches far nearer the former than the latter. Yet this critical period was, to him, in its most significant sense, "The passage of the bridge." To a truthful mind, the necessity of maintaining a literary fiction at all hazards is not a healthful condition of things. "The imagination of a boy is healthy, and the mature imagination of a man is healthy; but there is a space of life between, in which the soul is in a ferment, the character undecided, the way of life uncertain, the ambi-



*Maintenance of Rowley's antiquity.*

*Anticipation of brighter days.*

*Diverse literary maskings.*

tion thick-sighted ;"[1] and on this transitional stage—beyond which Chatterton never reached,—he was now entering.  His sister says of him : "He was a lover of truth from the earliest dawn of reason, and nothing would move him so much as being belied."  The usher at Colston's School bore testimony to the fact that "his master depended on his veracity on all occasions."  But the secret of Rowley, with its unaccomplished dreams, was his own, and had to be guarded at whatever sacrifice ; though with very different degrees of reticence, according to the character of the inquirer.



Mrs. Newton tells us : "My brother read to me the poem on 'Our Ladies Church.'  After he had read it several times, I insisted upon it he had made it.  He begged to know what reason I had to think so.  I added, his style was easily discovered in that poem.  He replied, 'I confess I made this, but don't you say anything about it.'  When he read the 'Death of Sir Charles Bawdin' to my mother, she admired it, and asked him if he made it.  He replied, 'I found the argument and versified it.'  I never saw any parchment in my brother's possession but the account of Canning, with several scraps of the 'Tragedy of Elle' on paper, of his writing, that he read to his family, as a specimen of the treasure he had discovered in the parchments ; and he always spoke of the poems to his friends as treasures he had discovered in the parchments."[2]  It is apparent from this that with loving friends, who had faith in the possible identity of Thomas Chatterton and Thomas Rowley, the disguise was even more lightly worn than that of "The Author of Waverley."  But with the Thistlethwaites, Rudhalls, and Smiths; the Catcotts, Burgums, Carys, and Barretts :—all of whom regarded him with the proverbial honour accorded to a prophet among his own people ;—his secret was guarded as too sacred a thing to be unmasked to vulgar scorn.

The history of humble genius abounds with illustrations

[1] Preface to Keats' Endymion.
[2] Mrs. Newton's Letter to Mr. Cottle.

of such spurious apprizings of literary excellence. When, for example, in 1809, Mr. R. H. Cromek made a pilgrimage to Dumfriesshire in search of reliques of Scottish song, he discovered a Dumfries lad, Allan Cunningham, earning eighteen shillings a week as a stone mason ; but with a wonderful knowledge of the poetry of his country, and a taste and extent of reading altogether surprising. But the young mason was also a poet ; produced some of his own verses ; and used in after-life to imitate, with great humour, the condescending air with which the critic received them, as, " Well, very well, for such a rustic as him." Cromek had no taste to spare for modern verse. His ambition was to rival Percy and Scott in the recovery of a lost Nithsdale minstrelsy, which existed only in his own fancy. So the mason-lad undertook the quest; and plied his delighted patron with antique lyrics which he pronounced " divine ! " " Pray what are the names of the poets of Nithsdale and Galloway ? " writes the credulous dilettante to his correspondent, who had to evade an answer, not having invented a Nithsdale " Rowley " as the father of his songs ; and so, at length, the unknown mason's modern antiques,—which, as his own, would have been summarily rejected ;—were published to the world in a handsome volume, with Cromek's name on the title-page ; and the London critics congratulated their *confrère* on the rich harvest he had gathered in the hitherto barren region beyond the Solway. As for the poor mason-lad, incidentally named in the introduction, no one could fancy him capable of anything so good.

Allan Cunningham, though a true poet of his class, claims no such rank in letters as the Bristol boy. Nevertheless the cases are analogous in their illustration of the temptations to such literary disguisings. Burns himself could assume the mask of the antique minstrel, and was fond of passing off some of his best songs as the work of forgotten bards. But that was the mere sport of the masquerader in the pride of his power, not the device of obscure genius to win a hearing and just award. Chatterton's masking began as an innocent dream of the

CHAP. VII.

*Apprizings of literary excellence.*

*Cromek in search of the antique.*

*Temptations to literary disguisings.*

child-poet, and appears to have been cherished by him to the last as an ideal reality. But it inevitably tended to become a deception, with more or less of sheer falsehood, when maintained with the help of spurious manuscripts and fictitious details of the literary treasures purloined from Canynge's coffer. Nevertheless the striking contrast between the transparent veil of fiction which his mother and sister were allowed to look through, and the impenetrable mystery which was opposed to the searching eye of strangers, must not be overlooked in judging of his conduct in· this false position.

*Bristol sophistries seen through.*

. As Chatterton awoke from the dreams of childhood, his keen eye pierced through the sophistries and conventional disguises of that Bristol of the eighteenth century in which his lot was cast ; and he very clearly perceived that to unmask his "Rowley" to its Barretts, Catcotts, Thistlethwaites, and Smiths, was simply to expose himself to insult and contempt. Incapable of appreciating the true poetry of his song to " Ælla, Lorde of the Castel of Brystowe ynn daies of Yore :" they could at least be persuaded that they did, if he disguised it in obsolete language and unreadable orthography, and disowned all claim to the offspring of his muse. But the undeviating persistency with which the secret was maintained, must also be ascribed to his steady adherence to the purpose of completing a literary scheme, of which, in the rude onslaughts of Lambert on his surreptitious office-work ; and still more, perhaps, in his own last despairing destruction of the incompleted design : mere fragments remain even of what he had accomplished. But from those fragments, imperfect as they are, the natural growth of the poetical romance of Rowley can still be traced, and forms an indispensable chapter in the mental and moral history of its author.

*Comprehensive literary scheme.*

# CHAPTER VIII.

## THE ROWLEY ROMANCE.

AMONG the realities which from the first appealed to all controversialists interested in the question of Thomas Rowley *versus* Thomas Chatterton, as rival claimants to the authorship of the Bristol poems, Maistre Canynge's coffer and the six or seven other old chests in the muniment-room of Redcliffe Church occupied a foremost place. Till the forcing of their locks some years before Chatterton's birth, they were the undoubted receptacles of valuable ancient parchments. Long after the removal of the deeds and other legal documents deemed of practical value, their ancient hoards were but slightly diminished. But no store was set on them by their custodians, beyond such common uses as waste parchments and paper could be turned to. So they were pilfered from time to time, and at last carried off in basket loads : the greediest of the depredators being Chatterton's own father. To some remnant of his spoils his posthumous son fell heir ; and for the first time the old documents found an appreciative owner.

What, then, were those old papers and parchments inherited by Chatterton, and made the basis of so wonderful a poetical and romantic structure, but of which scarcely a genuine scrap remains? It is by no means difficult to illustrate, as well as surmise, their general contents. One of the Rowley MSS. in the British Museum is attached to a portion of a genuine deed, of





K

Chap. VIII.

*A specimen deed.*

the date 10 Hen. IV.   It is a quit claim from one Bristol citizen to another, of his right in four suburban tenements ; and is, no doubt, a fair type of the contents of the parish chest : which may be presumed to have included deeds, presentments, assessment rolls, records and discharges of parochial disbursements, and inventories of vestments, church ornaments, &c., such as one actually printed by Walpole.

*True value of such materials.*

Had they been preserved, they would probably long ere this have furnished the materials for one or more such quarto volumes of Church Registers as figure among the publications of Bannatyne, Abbotsford, and other literary clubs.   The " Registrum Cartarum Ecclesie Sancte Egidii de Edinburgh," for example, embodies materials invaluable for any future historian of the Scottish capital.   But though this church had for its Provost, before the end of the fifteenth century, Gawin Douglas, famous among Scottish poets ; and his name duly figures in its cartulary : we look in vain for a fragment of his " Palice of Honoure," his " King Harte," or the vigorous prologues to his metrical rendering of the " Æneid " in the Scottish tongue.

*Chatterton's share of them.*

What number of parchments of any kind fell into Chatterton's hands is uncertain.   But it was probably much less than has been assumed ; for he inherited only the leavings of wasteful and indiscriminate plunderers.   So early as 1736, that is sixteen years before his birth, the first traces of spoliation appear in a communication to the Society of Antiquaries, of a curious memorandum,—found " in the cabinet of the late John Browning, Esq., of Barton, near Bristol ;"—of the gift by Maistre Canynge to Redcliffe Church, of a new Easter sepulchre and scenic accompaniments, for representing the mystery of the Resurrection. At a considerably later date, however, the bulk of the parchments remained intact, in the old muniment-room.

*Visit to the old muniment-room.*

Bryant describes its condition three years before Chatterton's birth, on the authority of Mr. Shiercliffe, a miniature painter of Bristol.   They then lay about in heaps, covered with dust, rumpled, stained, and torn ; some quite loose, and others tied up; and he was invited by the sexton to take some of them if he pleased. A woman acknowledged that she had carried off a lapful, and employed them in cleaning her kitchen furniture.[1] Mr. Morgan, according to the Dean of Exeter, "a curious man and a great lover of antiquities, although no scholar;" but by the account of Mr. Tyrwhitt and others, a Bristol barber: made free havoc of the same ample hoard.[2] Among other reminiscences of Mrs. Edkins, she stated that once, when a pupil of the poet's father, "she saw the old parchments and books so much talked of, and said to Chatterton, the father: '.Why, I remember those papers were in Canynge's house, and the church room;' at which he was angry, and bid her hold her tongue; putting them up directly and out of sight, having that day been showing them to some gentlemen whom she did not know." It is obvious enough, therefore, that if Rowley's Poems had ever formed part of the contents of Canynge's coffer, they must have been destroyed or published to the world, long before the modern Rowley left his cradle.

The dates assigned for the first exposure of the parchments vary from four to twenty-five years before Chatterton's birth.[3] But at the lowest computation, they had been exposed to a dozen years of the most indiscriminate waste, before he can have interfered even as a child to turn them to any account. They had been ransacked by curious antiquaries, to whom the Rowley MSS. would have been a coveted prize; and plundered by those to whom the autograph copy of the "Canterbury Pilgrimage" would have been worth no more than the parchment on which it was written. Mrs. Chatterton and her sempstresses succeeded the elder Chatterton and his schoolboys in the work of destruction. Supposing, therefore, the boy to have rescued the residue at seven or eight years of age, the Rowleyans had to assume that he recovered from such mere gleanings a consecutive series

CHAP. VIII.

*The anti-
quarian
barber.*

*First expo-
sure of the
parchments.*

*Their
plunderers.*

---

[1] Bryant's Observations, pp. 513, 514.
[2] Commentary, p. 16.  [3] *Vide* ante, p. 21.

K 2

of poems, letters, and historical documents enough to fill two ample volumes.

No doubt, however, Chatterton did acquire some of the Redcliffe parchments. What became of them has been accounted for in more than one way, according to the preconceived theories of the writers. " He had taste enough to find out the genuine merit of the writings, and sufficient knowledge of law to be aware he had no claim to them," says an obstinate Rowleyan, writing so recently as 1859, to " Notes and Queries ; " and so he copied the originals, " the poems," and then burned them.[1] In reality they appear to have passed into the hands of one or two collectors, foremost among whom was Mr. William Barrett, the future historian of Bristol, who had already acquired Morgan's spoils, and established friendly relations with Chatterton at an early period. We know that he did both receive in gift and purchase from the boy, spurious antiques which he regarded as of the greatest value, and did not scruple to appropriate in the full belief that they were part of the spoils of Redcliffe muniment-room. Four parchments which Chatterton picked up there, on learning whence his father had brought the others, were stated by Mrs. Chatterton, after his death, to be in Mr. Barrett's possession ; and no doubt the choicest of the old hoard went the same way. The boy could entertain no idea of wrong in disposing of the sole inheritance he derived from his father. Possibly indeed the spurious antiques only made their appearance when the genuine supply failed.

The Bristol historian, after quoting from a deed the description of the " Cysta ferrata cum sex clavibus, vocata Cysta Willielmi Canynges, in domo thesauria ecclesiæ Beatæ Mariæ de Redclive," adds : " This chest furnished Mr. Morgan with many curious parchments relative to Mr. Canynges and the Church of Redclive ; and many very valuable, there is reason to believe, were taken away before, and since dispersed into private hands," including Barrett's own. So notorious indeed was he as the resetter

<hr>

[1] Notes and Queries, Second Series, vol. viii. p. 234.

of Morgan's spoils, that when his historical labours were completed, long after Chatterton's death, he thus figured in one of Thistlethwaite's satires :—

> "Next Barrett came, of History dubb'd the Quack,
> Old Morgan's rotten papers at his back ;
> Press'd by the load, which, with unceasing pains,
> Full twenty years employed his aching brains."

Barrett had begun to collect his materials before Chatterton was born. He refers to Latin deeds in his possession "such alone as would fill a volume ;" and of these he ascribes the acquisition of the greater number to the assiduity of the antiquarian barber. Mr. Haines, another indefatigable collector, also receives his due meed of praise. In truth the historian's correspondence with Dr. Ducarel shows him absolutely burdened with such stores, which might as well have remained under the six locks of Mr. Canynge's coffer for any use he could make of them.

That there had lain in the parish chests of Redcliffe Church for upwards of three centuries, a collection of poems by an unknown Bristol priest, whose writings surpassed those of Lydgate, the laureat of Henry VI., almost as much as true poetry does mere rhyme, would seem too absurd for discussion, had it not already obtained credence for a century. But, no doubt, the parchments contained genuine names of old Bristol citizens and Church dignitaries ; perhaps of nobles and even kings of that fifteenth century. Did they include, even in the most prosaic association, that of Thomas Rowley? Before attempting to answer this, let us endeavour to trace to its source the origin of the romance to which this name was attached.

In 1760 James Macpherson published his "Fragments of Ancient Poetry, collected in the Highlands of Scotland ;" and thereby produced such a sensation, that the Edinburgh Faculty of Advocates raised the requisite funds to enable him to carry out a thorough search for more. Had he travelled on his own resources, he would

CHAP. VIII.

*The Ossian poems.*

*Influence ascribed to them*

*Imitations of other poets.*

*A romance in stone.*

probably have come back empty-handed. But he must needs make some return for the money expended ; and so, in 1762, he published his " Fingal, an Epic Poem, in Six Books," and in 1763, his " Temora, an Epic in Eight Books," with other poems, all professedly translated from the ancient Gaelic, or Erse, into the English language. Great was the excitement that followed. Homer himself was believed to have been outdone ; and to question the authenticity of the " Ossian Poems," as these came to be called, was, in some literary circles, even more dangerous than to challenge in the orthodox coteries of Bristol the Hutchinsonian theory of creation and the deluge.

When Horace Walpole, nine years after the death of Chatterton, entered on a defence of his neglect of the poet and his wonderful antiques, it seemed to the learned dilettante sufficient to say : " I then imagined, and do still, that the success of Ossian's poems had suggested the idea." What satisfied Walpole has been reëchoed ever since. But the success of Ossian's poems was still a thing of the future when Chatterton placed in the usher Phillips' hand, in 1764, his " Elinoure and Juga ;" nor is there the slightest resemblance between any of the Rowley Poems and the Gaelic epics, either in rhythm, form, or mode of thought. The probability is, that when the Bluecoat boy produced his antique pastoral, he had never heard of " Fingal " or " Temora." When their fame did at length reach his ear, he proceeded to imitate them : as at different periods he imitated Gray, Collins, Churchill, Junius, and other contemporaries. But the true Rowley Poems remain unique ; and the name of Ossian has no talismanic power to solve the riddle. To do this with any satisfactory results, we must fall back on the personal history, and the early circumstances under which the child-poet was nurtured, with as few external helps as ever fell to the lot of genius.

In this age of enthusiastic revival of medieval art, it is less difficult than it was in the eighteenth century to conceive of the influence which the noble church on Redcliffe Hill exercised over the mind of Chatterton, even as a child. He could not, like Beckford or Scott, realize for himself an Arabian fable, or an Abbotsford romance, in stone and lime; but he could appropriate the one already created for him, and live over again the process of its realization.

St. Mary Redcliffe forms, accordingly, the centre around which revolve all the quaint, fanciful, and richly poetic phases of the Rowley fiction. The hold it retained on his imagination repeatedly manifests itself even in his latest London correspondence; as in his letter to Cary, in defence of his " Kew Gardens " satire, and its panegyric on Allen, a Bristol organist, whom he had pronounced "divine." "Step into Redcliffe Church," he exclaims, "look at the noble arches, observe the symmetry, the regularity of the whole; how amazing must that idea be which can comprehend at once all that magnificence of architecture. Do not examine one particular beauty, or dwell upon it minutely; take the astonishing whole into your empty pericranium, and then think what the architect of that pile was in building, Allen is in music." When he wrote this he seemed to be absorbed in the excitement of London, and the politics of the day. But the moment his thoughts reverted to Bristol and its church, the old feelings revived. It was the cradle of his inspiration, and the cynosure of all his latest fancies. Within its charmed precincts he passed at will into another life, and his antique dreams became credible and true. In all his guisings and literary masquerades, the same antique realism predominates. He lives in the middle of that fifteenth century in which lived William Canynge as merchant, mayor, church-builder, priest, and dean; and revels in fancy amid the noble doings of this hero of his romantic dream. With this key to the plot, the Rowley manuscripts acquire a consistent unity, imperfect as they are.

The guise in which Chatterton clothed his Rowley Poems, and the fashion in which his works have been edited, have combined to exclude them from general study almost as effectually as if he had written in the

*True source of the Rowley fiction.*

*The cradle of inspiration.*

*Unattractive disgui*

CHAP. VIII.

Saxon of his monk-poet, Turgot.  In reality, his antique prose and verse work out an historical romance of Bristowe in the olden time, exhibiting in the grouping of its characters the graphic fulness of the novelist, and in many of its passages not a little dramatic power as well as tender lyrical sweetness.

*Thomas Rowley, priest of St. John's.*

Thomas Rowley, a native of Somersetshire, and a zealous Yorkist,[1] of the times when the Red and the White Roses were the badges of party strife in England, was priest of St. John's, in the city of Bristol, in the year 1465.  From early years he had borne the most intimate relations with the Canynges' family.  He and William, the second son of John Canynge, a youth of cunning wit,—as we learn from the " Lyfe of W. Canynge," one of the Chatterton MSS.,—improved their lear together, under the care of the Carmelite brothers, in the old priory which once occupied the site of Colston's School.  In fact,

*Bluecoat boys of the olden time.*

they were Bristol Bluecoat boys of the good old times. " Here," says Rowley, " began the kindness of our lives ; our minds and kinds were alike, and we were always together."  William's father loved him not as he did his brother Robert, because, while the latter was a man after his own heart,—greedy of gain and sparing of alms,— William was courteous and· liberal in word and deed. But both father and brother died the same year, leaving William to inherit their great wealth ; and about the same time his old school-mate, Thomas Rowley, took holy orders, and was made his chaplain and confessor. A brief extract from the good priest's account of his

*The ideal patron.*

friend and benefactor will serve to illustrate the quaint graphic style of the narrative :—" Master Roberte, by Master William's desyre, bequeathed me one hundred marks ; I went to thank ·Master William for his mickle courtesie, and to make tender of myselfe to him. ' Fadre,' quod he, ' I have a crotchett in my brayne that will need your aide.'  ' Master William,' said I, ' if you command me I will go to Roome for you.'  ' Not so farr distant,' said he ; ' I ken you for a mickle learned

---

[1] *Vide* notes to Balade of Charitie.

priest; if you will leave the parysh of our Ladie,[1] and travel for mee, it shall be mickle to your profits.' I gave my hands, and he told mee I must goe to all the abbies and pryorys, and gather together auncient drawyngs, if of anie account, at any price. Consented I to the same, and pursuant sett out the Mundaie following for the Minster of our Ladie and Saint Goodwyne, where a drawing of a steeple, contryvd for the belles when runge to swaie out of the syde into the ayre, had I thence. It was done by Syr Symon de Mambrie, who, in the troublesome rayne of Kyng Stephen, devoted himselfe, and was shorne."

In like fashion the good priest continues to collect valuable drawings and manuscripts for Master Canynge, and to partake liberally of his bounty. But the death of his tenderly loved wife, Johanna, in child-bearing, leaves him widowed and childless; and he thenceforth devotes himself to the patronage of art, letters, and all good works. Then did his nobleness show forth to the world. He was five times Mayor of Bristol: for William Canynge is a genuine historical character, whatever be made of his confessor and biographer. As to his nobleness, he was undoubtedly a princely merchant, and one who rightly estimated pious deeds, according to the standard of his day; though Mr. George Price, in his "Canynges Family and their Times," has gone far to show that he merely laid the foundation of the later portion of St. Mary Redcliffe, in his civic capacity as Mayor; and contributed towards its building, along with "others of the worshipfulle towne of Bristol." But it is with the traditional rather than the historical Master Canynge that we have to deal, in whom the veneration of many generations had impersonated all the nobility and refinement of medieval Bristol; so that it was a matter of faith with the men of Chatterton's day, that they rightly ascribed to their old mayor many memorials of ancient munificence in his native city, besides the beautiful church

---

[1] From this it may be inferred that Chatterton originally purposed to represent Rowley as parish priest of St. Mary Redcliffe.

in which he lies interred.  Rowley lived, as he tells us,
in a house on the hill, but often repaired to the great
Rudde House, near to the water, the princely mansion
of his patron.  This was the resort of a choice set of
poets, artists, and *virtuosi* of that old time; such as
Chatterton might possibly have matched in the circle
that gathered round Sir Joshua Reynolds, at the London
Literary Club, in Gerrard Street, Soho; but which he in
vain sighed for in the Bristol of his day.



The Sir William Canynge of the Rowley Romance
is himself a man of letters, an artist, and even at times
a poet: devoted to all liberal tastes, and especially to
architecture; and he gathers around him a group of
kindred spirits.  There is his friend, Carpenter, Bishop
of Worcester, not incapable of penning a stanza at times:
as appears from an inscription affixed to the cover of an
old mass book, which Chatterton was able to recover for
Mr. Barrett with Rowley's aid.[1]  Maystre John a Iscam,
Canon of St. Augustine's Abbey,—himself a poet,—also
bears his part, on more than one occasion, in the dramatic
performances at the Rudde House; and wins the special
commendation of Maistre Canynge, in the character of
"Celmonde," when Rowley acts "Ælla" in his own
"Tragycal Enterlude."  In a letter of Rowley to his
brother-poet, he thus jestingly invites him to become



verse-monger to a niggard patron of the muse: " I haveth
metten wythe a syllie knyghte of twayne hondreth poundes
bie the yeere.  'God's nayles,' quod hee, 'leave oute mie
scarlette and ermyne doublette, I know nete I love better
than vearses.  I woulde bestowe rentalls of golde for rolles
of hem.'  'Naie,' quod I, 'I bec notte a vearse-monger;
goe to the Black Fryer Mynsterre yn Brystowe wheere the
Freeres rhyme to the swote smelle of the gowtes, theere
maie you deale maiehappe.'  'Now, Johan, wylle you
stocke yis Worscypfulle knyghte wythe somme Ballet
oune Nellye and Bellie?  You quotha naie—botte bee
here bie twa daies, we shall have an Entyrlude to plaie
whyche I haveth made, wherein three kynges will smeethe

---

[1] Works, iii. p. 312.

upon the playne.  You moste bee a kynge and mie sillie knyghte and loverde, the whyche, wythe the Jest of Roberte, wylle bee pleasaunte sporte.'"

Sir Thybbot Gorges, a neighbouring knight of ancient family, contributes to the "Tragycal Enterlude" one of the minstrels' songs, as his quota of verse; enacts the character of " Hurra " the Dane, among the Rudde House amateurs; and pledges, in surety of a liberal benefaction towards the rebuilding of Redcliffe Church, certain jewels of great value.  The group is completed by Sir Allan de Vere, Mastre Edwarde Canynge, and others: knights, aldermen, and minstrels; among whom we may specially picture to ourselves John a Dalbenie,—a citizen fond of wordy strife, and prone to mar the pleasant gatherings at the Rudde House by intruding politics into that haunt of the Muses;—who is twitted by the host in this epigrammatic fashion :—

> " Johne makes a jarre boute Lancaster and Yorke ;
> Bee stille gode manne, and learne to mynde thie worke."

The old merchant prince of Bristowe, the centre of this group, formed in the estimation of Dean Milles,—most enthusiastic among the early champions of the ancient Rowley,—a parallel to Mæcenas with his three friends, Virgil, Horace, and Varus.  To him Rowley sends his verses from time to time, ever sure of some liberal acknowledgment in return.  At times the real author expressed under this guise his own estimate of some of those wondrous creations of his muse, given away, or requited by the niggard dole of Catcott or Barrett; for his chief antique productions figure in Rowley's narrative with their becoming reward.  " I sent him," writes the good priest, " my verses touching his church, for which he did send me mickle good things ;" and again : " I gave Master Cannings my Bristow tragedy, for which he gave me in hands twentie pounds, and did praise it more than I did think myself did deserve ; for I can say in troth I was never proud of my verses since I did read Master Chaucer; and now haveing nought to do, and not

wyling to be ydle, I went to the minster of our Ladie and
Saint Goodwin, and there did purchase the Saxon manuscripts, and sett myself diligently to translate and worde
it in English metre, which in one year I performed, and
styled it the Battle of Hastyngs.  Master William did bar-
gyin for one manuscript, and John Pelham, an esquire, of
Ashley, for another.  Master William did praise it muckle
greatly, but advised me to tender it to no man, beying
the menn whose name were therein mentioned would be
offended.  He gave me 20 markes, and I did goe to
Ashley, to Master Pelham, to be payd of him for the other
one I left with him.  But his ladie being of the family of
the Fiscamps, of whom some things are said, he told me
he had burnt it, and would have me burnt too, if I did
not avaunt.  Dureing this dinn his wife did come out, and
made a dinn, to speake by a figure, would have over
sounded the bells of our Ladie of the Cliffe; I was fain
content to get away in a safe skin."



In the humour of the latter sketch it is not improbable
that Chatterton had in view some squire whose ire he had
roused by his modern verse; and whose lady he may
have favoured with a heraldic blazon as appropriate and
unwelcome as Aunt Martha's " Rose of Virginity."  In
the antique romance as a whole, there is no difficulty in
recognising, through its transparent disguise, the modern
Bluecoat boy fondly imagining, in some fancied school
mate among the Bakers and Thistlethwaites of his own
day, the sympathising friend and future patron, whose
wealth was to be generously shared with the poet; while
in the exercise of a liberal taste he rivalled the triumphs
of medieval art, and called into being a happy brother
hood of kindred spirits, with whom the most sacred con
fidences could be exchanged.  Into this prose romance
as into a quaint, antique setting, the Rowley poems take
their place as so many jewels of varying polish and
lustre.



Going back to elder times than those of Canynge, we
are introduced in prefatory fashion, to the first dedication
of the red cliff to sacred uses, as set forth in the tran

script of "a parchment MS. of Rowley's," printed by Barrett, with one of his two-sided footnotes dubiously asseverating the probable genuineness of the old priest and his poems.[1] In A.D. 1285, Edward I. keeps Christmas at Bristol in company with a body of gallant knights, mustered to join in an expedition into Wales, but who devote the holiday to a grand joust, which furnishes the subject of "The Tournament, an Interlude." This must have been written in an ampler form than it now exists, when Chatterton was not more than fifteen years old. Writing in March 1768, to his old schoolmate, Baker, who had wandered to Charleston, South Carolina, after referring to sundry literary matters, including certain verses in honour of Miss Eleanor Hoyland,—a Bristol belle, as I surmise, to whom, with the poet's help, he is paying his addresses,[2]—he says, "The Tournament I have only one canto of, which I send herewith ; the remainder is entirely lost." Chatterton, it must be remembered, is writing to one who, after much lively banter, he assures, in genuine earnestness : "I am, and ever will be, your unalterable friend." He has been telling of the interruption of his poetical labours by his master's return, and is forwarding specimens of his own work, not palming off spurious antiques. Mr. Lambert, it is to be feared, had pounced on the missing portions, and put them beyond author's or critic's reach. But a copy made by Catcott from Chatterton's MS. supplied the text as it now exists, with its lively action and poetic thought obscured by an extreme, and possibly exaggerated affectation of archaic language : for Cottle, on comparing his copies with originals, found that he was in the habit of altering the orthography, so as to give an appearance of greater antiquity.

The scene of the tournament is Redcliffe Hill, in ancient days, before it was chosen as the site of St.

CHAP. VIII.

*Dedication of the red cliffs.*

*The Tourna- ment.*

*Redcliffe Hill.*

---

[1] Barrett's History, p. 568.
[2] The exclusively local allusions addressed to Miss Hoyland in one of his pieces (Works, i. p. 353) manifestly assume her familiarity with Bristol and its citizens.

Mary's Church. There King Edward and his knights assemble, with minstrels, servitors, and a brilliant heraldic display. A herald opens proceedings as the dispenser of honour's joys; and the jousting begins. Among those who enter the lists, Sir Johan de Berghamme, the pewterer's ancestor, appears, overthrows Sir Ludovic de Clynton; but is himself overcome by Sir Simon de Bourtonne. Thereupon an unknown knight enters, before whose lance five of Edward's knights successively fall; on which Sir Simon vows, if successful against this puissant foe, to build a church to our Lady on the spot where he shall fall:—

*Sir Johan de Berghamme.*

> "By thee, Saint Mary, and thy Son, I swear,
>     That in what place yon doughty Knight shall fall
> Beneath the strong push of my stretched-out spear,
>     There shall arise a holy church's wall,
>     The which iu honour I will Mary's call,
> With pillars large, and spire full high and round;
>     And this I faithfully will stand to all,
> If yonder stranger falleth to the ground.
>     Stranger, be boune,[1] I champion you to war;
>     Sound, sound the slughorns to be heard from far."

*Sir Simon de Bourtonne.*

Sir Simon is victorious, and hence the consecration of the mount, and the erection of the church of our Lady on the red cliff. Sir Simon de Bourtonne—in actual civic history Simon de Burton, an opulent merchant, and Mayor of Bristol.—was succeeded in the work of church-building by William Canynge the elder, who, in 1376, "built the body of Redcliffe Church from the cross-aisle downwards," and so completed the original structure.

*Inaccessible knowledge.*

Rowleyans and anti-Rowleyans were long puzzled to account for the acquisition by a poor charity boy of the knowledge of facts or traditions, preserved, as they believed, only in an inaccessible Latin MS. of William of Worcester. The mystery, however, proves to be of easy solution. Among the friends to whom Chatterton wrote after his removal to London was Mr. Henry Kator, a sugar-baker of a literary turn, in whose parlour,—as we

---

[1] *Boune,* ready.

learn from Mr. Dix,—hung an engraving of Redcliffe Church, published by William Halfpenny, in 1746, with an inscription setting forth its founding "by Simon de Burton, merchant;" and further narrating how, "in the year 1446, the steeple of the said church was blown down in a great storm of thunder and lightning, which did mueh damage to the same; but was by Mr. William Canynge, a worthy merchant, who was several times mayor of ye said town, with the assistance of diverse other wealthy inhabitants, at a great expense, now covered, glazed, and repaired;" and so the inscription proceeds with a concise epitome of the good mayor's life and deeds, in full accordance with the Rowley romance. In 1467, he was commanded to marry again: "Whereupon he gave up the world, and took orders of the Bishop of Worcester, and was made a priest, and sung his first mass at our Lady of Redcliffe," and finally, "was buried worshipfully in ye south end of ye middle ile of ye sd church, near his wife."

The Rowley poems and prose are replete with imaginary details of the old merchant prince, his social life, and pious works. "Oure Ladies Chyrche" especially is the theme of repeated versification, in which its praises and those of its reputed builder are lovingly set forth:—

> "Thou seest this mastery of a human hand,
> The pride of Bristowe and the western land;
>   Yet are the builder's virtues much more great,
> Greater than can by Rowley's pen be scann'd.
>   Thou seest the saints and kings in stony state,
> That seem with breath and human souls dispand;
>   As 'pared to us enseem these men of slate,
>   Such is great Canynge's mind when 'pared to God elate."

Another poem, in lively ballad measure, describes the dedication. At early dawn, when "fairies hide in cowslip cups," troops of friars come forth in procession, marching, with holy relics, "around the high unsainted church." Bishop Carpenter appears, holily mitred, while Mastre Canynge is tricked out "like a barbed king;" and so the first mass is sung in the new church; the



*CHAP. VIII.*

*Redcliffe steeple blown down.*

*Our Lady's Church.*

*Dedication by Bishop Carpenter.*

Bishop preaches, followed with another sermon from
Rowley himself; and then all adjourn to a grand feast
and interlude at Mastre Canynge's house.   Of the dramatic interlude this earlier notice is to be found in one
of Master Canynge's letters to Rowley, dated A.D. 1443.
" The chyrche is ybuylden wythynne and wythoute.
Goe to Byshoppe Carpenterre for him to comme wythe
you to dedycate the same.   Inne all haste ymake a smalle
Entyrlude to be plaied at the tyme."   And so, in Barrett's
" History," may be seen duly set forth at length, "and
submitted to the judgement of the reader : "  " An Entyrlude, plaied bie the Carmelyte Freeres at Mastre Canynges
hys greete howse, before Mastre Canynges and Byshoppe
Carpenterre, on dedicatynge the Chyrche of Our Ladie



of Redclefte, hight : ' The Parlyamente of Sprytes,' wroten
bie T. Rowlie and J. Iscam."   In this the spirits of
departed worthies return to earth to do honour to the
pious work.   The sprite of Brythryc, a Saxon who held
Bristol in the days of the Conqueror, when the red cliff was
but a bare rock, cannot believe that the wondrous structure
that disparts the clouds, and kisses the sky with its lofty
spire, can be the work of human hands.   The sprite of
Byrtoune, the first builder, rejoices that his church was
overthrown, since it has made way for the brave structure
which greets his eye ; and so with the other spirits
assembled : closing with Ælla's devout anticipation that,
when the anchangel's trump shall affright the wicked, and
awaken all :

> " Then Canynge rises to eternal rest,
>   And finds he chose on earth a life the best."



" The Storie of William Canynge," a poem of some
length, and of great beauty, formed part of a work in
prose, which probably supplied the accounts of painters,
carvellers, poets, and other eminent natives of ancient
Bristol, printed by Barrett as Chatterton's communications to Horace Walpole.   The poem appears to have
undergone careful revision, as more than one copy exists,
with variations and additions.   It thus opens :—

> " Anent a brooklet as I lay reclined,
>     Listening to hear the water glide along ;
>   Minding how thorough the green meads it twined,
>     Awhilst the caves respons'd its muttering song,
>   At distant-rising Avon to be sped,
>   Amenged[1] with rising hills did show its head.
>
> " Engarlanded with crowns of osier weeds
>     And wreaths of alders of a bercie scent,
>   And sticking out with cloud-agested[2] reeds,
>     The hoary Avon showed dire semblament ;
>   Whilst blatant Severn, from Sabrina cleped,
>   Roars frighted o'er the sandès that she heaped."

The poet then recalls to memory Ælla, Brythric, Fitz-Hardynge, " and twenty moe," whose brave deeds have been witnessed by those floods ; and muses why they have received so little fame : when suddenly there rises from the stream the vision of a lovely maid, in native beauty unadorned, who introduces herself as " Truth that did descend from heaven." She refers to many champions and men of lore, painters, and carvellers, who have gained good name ; but from those she passes to one worthier than them all ; and, endowing the poet with divine insight, she says :

> " Take thou my power, and see, in child and man,
>   What truly nobleness in Canynge ran."

As the toilworn peasant sleeps almost before he has laid his head on his pillow, so the poet is at once entranced ; his spirit is " from earthly bands untied ;" and he thus describes the familiar translation to those elder times, and that more real poetic life, in which the modern Rowley had revelled from his own childhood :—

> " Straight was I carried back to times of yore,
>     Whilst Canynge swathed yet in fleshly bed,
>   And saw all actions which had been before,
>     And all the scroll of fate unravelled ;
>   And when the fate-marked babe acome to sight,
>   I saw him eager gasping after light.

---

[1] *Amenged*, mingled.    [2] *Agested*, heaped up.



CHAP. VIII.
——
*Opening
stanzas.*

*The vision
of Truth.*

*The poet's
trance.*

> "In all his simple gambols and child's play,
>   In every merry-making, fair, or wake,
> I kenn'd a perpled[1] light of wisdom's ray;
>   He eat down learning with the wastle-cake;
> As wise as any of the aldermen,
> He'd wit enow to make a mayor at ten."

*The fate-marked babe.*

This beautiful picture of the childhood of the ideal patron of Rowley is in reality that of the poet himself: "the fate-marked babe," with his wondrous child-genius, and all his romantic dreams realized. The entranced revery was familiar to him. He had been wont to pass in fancy back to times of yore, since first the solemn beauty of the ancient fane in which he wandered at will in early youth took hold on his imagination, and enkindled in him the poetic flame.

*Chatterton's master-piece.*

The "Tragedy of Ælla," Chatterton's master-piece, was recovered from a manuscript in his own handwriting, dated 1769, when he was sixteen years of age. It is professedly the work of an elder poet than Rowley, "modernised" by the old priest for his patron's behoof; and accompanied by introductory epistles and dedication in verse. The work is thus complete according to the poet's design. The tragedy opens on the morning of Ælla's wedding-day. Ere it closes he is summoned to the field; on the morrow defeats the Danes; but,

*Ælla and his bride.*

by the faithlessness of Celmonde, his bride is decoyed away, under pretence of flying to where he lies sorely wounded. Her betrayer falls, with her, into the hands of the Danes; by whom she is generously restored to her lord, only in time to see him expire from the wounds he had given himself on hearing the report of her flight with her supposed paramour. The simplicity, tenderness, and dramatic action of this tragedy cannot fail to strike the reader who will take the trouble to master its archaic disguise. In one of the introductory epistles Rowley

*The elder poets.*

contrasts the polished versification of his age with the rough vigour of the elder poets, whose power lay in fine thoughts, and not in mere numbers. The criticism is

---

[1] *Perpled*, scattered.

in reality Chatterton's protest against the over-refinement of his own day, in which Pope, " as harmony itself, exact," had given such perfection to the form of verse, that his imitators mistook mere rhythm for thought.   He thus addresses his fancied patron :—

> " Say Canynge, what was verse in days of yore?
>     Fine thoughts, and couplets fetively bewryen ;[1]
> Not such as do annoy this age so sore,
> A studied pointel[2] resting at each line.
> Verse may be good, but poesie wants more :
>     A boundless subject, and a song adign ;[3]
> According to the rule I have this wrought ;
> If it please Canynge, I care not a groat."

Leaving, for the present, the consideration of the tragedy itself, with its striking evidences of the varied powers of its author: another of its ingenious preludes adds a curious episode to the Rowley romance of which it forms a part.   John Lydgate, a London priest,—no doubt meant for Dan John, of Bury St. Edmunds,[4]—and personal friend of the Bristowe poet, is assumed to have challenged Rowley to "a bowtyng match" in rhyme ; whereupon the latter replies :—

[1] *Fetively bewryen*, elegantly expressed.          [2] *Pointel*, pen.
[3] *Adign*, nervous, dignified.
[4] The name has hitherto been printed *Ladgate ;* but Mr. Tyrwhitt found it written *Lydgate* in the professed original vellum in Mr. Barrett's possession.   Indeed few of Chatterton's ancient names are imaginary.   He had some old character in view in all his impersonations.   Turgot was no doubt the biographer of St. Margaret, Malcolm Canmore's queen, though somewhat misdated.   The " Stowe" mentioned in Lydgate's answer is a misprint for Stone, a Carmelite friar of Bristol, educated at Cambridge, and famous as a preacher.   Iscamm is Josephus Iscanus, a Latin poet of the thirteenth century ; and Sir Thybbot Gorges one of a genuine Bristol family.   Canying's wife Johanna receives, from Chatterton, as I presume, the surname of Hathwaie : having in mind the Anne Hathaway of Shakespeare.   Even the Simon de Seynté Lyze, or Senliz of his De Bergham pedigree,—misprinted by Cottle and most subsequent editors Leynte Lyze,—had its origin in Bernard de Senlis, uncle and protector of Rollo's son and grandson ; as Syrr Johan de Berghamme's authenticity is vouched for by the existence of his descendant, the pewterer.

L 2

CHAP. VII

*Poetical criticism.*

*A bowtyng match in rhyme.*

CHAP. VIII.

Rowley's assay piece.

"Well then good John, sith it must needs be so
    That thou and I a bowting match must have,
Let it ne breaking of old friendship be,
    This is the only all-a-boon I crave;"

and so he sends back, as his assay piece, his "Songe to Ælla, Lorde of the Castel of Brystowe ynne daies of Yore." We may conceive of the boy, rapt in his antique revery, dealing with the fancied challenge with all the earnestness of genuine rivalry. He was, for the time being, the poet of the days of yore, pitted against the pupil and successor of Chaucer himself; and so, putting forth all his strength, he produced one of his finest lyrical pieces, worthy to challenge comparison with any antique or modern rival :—

Song to Ælla, Lord of Brystowe Castel.

"Oh thou, or what remains of thee,
    Ælla, the darling of futurity,
Let this, my song, bold as thy courage be,
    As everlasting to posterity!

"When Dacia's sons, whose hair of blood-red hue,
Like kingcups bursting with the morning dew,
    Arranged in drear array,
    Upon the lethal day
Spread far and wide on Watchet's shore :
    Then didst thou furious stand,
    And by thy valiant hand
Besprenged all the meads with gore.

    "Drawn by thine anlace[1] fell,
    Down to the depths of hell
      Thousands of Dacians went ;
    Bristowans, men of might,
    Ydared the bloody fight,
      And acted deeds full quaint.

    "Oh thou, where'er—thy bones at rest—
    Thy sprite to haunt delighteth best ;
Whether upon the blood-embruèd plain,
    Or where thou kenst from far
    The dismal cry of war,
Or seest some mountain made of corse of slain ;
    Or seest the hatchèd[2] steed
    Yprancing on the mead,
And neigh to be among the pointed spears ;

[1] *Anlace*, sword.     [2] *Hatchèd*, covered with achievements.

Chap. VIII

> Or in black armour stalk around
> Embattled Bristowe, once thy ground,
> And glow ardúrous[1] on the castle-stairs ;
> Or fiery round the minstre glare :
> Let Bristowe still be made thy care.
> Guard it from foemen and consuming fire ;
> Let Avon's stream encire it round,
> Ne let a flame enharm the ground,
> Till in one flame all the whole world expire."

This episode of a poetical challenge and rejoinder between the Laureate of Henry VI. and the imaginary Rowley is completed by a transcript of commendatory verses, by Lydgate, in which, after glancing at the great poets of elder times, he concludes by saying that now "in these mokie days" Chaucer lives over again in every line that Rowley writes.

When the romancer gets away from the scenes and times of his Bristowe Mæcenas, he still retains the productions of his antique muse in subordinate relation to that central ideal. The "Tragedy of Goddwyn" has its prologue "made bie Maistre William Canynge ;" and the cast of the piece distributes its characters among the select amateurs of the Rudde House theatricals : the author undertaking "Harolde," and Canynge himself "King Edwarde." This tragedy exists only as a fragment, printed from a copy-book in Catcott's possession, into which Chatterton evidently intended to have copied some of his choicest antiques. It is titled "Eclogues and other Poems by Thomas Rowley, with a Glossary and Annotations by Thomas Chatterton ;" but nothing more had been written than three Eclogues, and the first two scenes of "Goddwyn," abruptly ending with an unfinished chorus. The prologue is strong presumptive evidence that this was the transcript of an already completed work. In it Rowley's patron invites attention to the graphic depiction of character, and unity of action, so well contrived that—

> "We better for to do do champion any one."

---

[1] *Ardurous*, burning.

Mr. Catcott's MS. was probably part of the collection of papers purchased by him from the widow, after her son's death. Happily for us, it included the " Ode to Liberty," supposed to be sung by a chorus of Saxons, at the close of a scene in which the King, Edward the Confessor, proclaims his partiality for his Norman followers. This ode surpasses the " Song to Ælla " in sustained imaginative power; and indeed may claim its place among the finest martial lyrics in the language :—

*The Ode to
Liberty.*

" When Freedom, drest in blood-stained vest,
To every knight her war-song sung,
Upon her head wild weeds were spread,
A gory anlace by her hung.
She danced on the heath ;
She heard the voice of Death ;
Pale-eyed Affright, his heart of silver hue,
In vain assailed her bosom to acale.[1]
She heard unflemed[2] the shrieking voice of woe,
And sadness, in the owlet, shake the dale.
She shook her burled[3] spear ;
On high she jeste[4] her shield ;
Her foemen all appear
And flie along the field.
Power with his heafod straught[5] into the skies,
His spear a sunbeam and his shield a star ;
Alike twae brendyng gronfyres[6] rolls his eyes;
Chafts with his iron feet and sounds to war.
She sits upon a rock ;
She bends before his spear ;
She rises from the shock,
Wielding her own in air.
Hard as the thunder doth she drive it on ;
Wit skilly wimpled[7] guides it to his crown ;
His long sharp spear, his spreading shield is gone ;
He falls, and falling rolleth thousands down.
War, gore-faced War, by Envy burl'd arist,
His fiery helm ynodding to the air,
Ten bloody arrows in his straining fist——"

So abruptly ends this magnificent ode, with one of the

---

[1] *Acale*, freeze.    [2] *Unflemed*, undismayed.    [3] *Burled*, pointed.
[4] *Jeste*, raised.         [5] *Heafod straught*, head stretched.
[6] *Brendyng gronfyres*, flaming meteors.    [7] *Wimpled*, covered.

boldest of its impersonations. No grander fragment has been penned since old Barbour burst forth with the fine apostrophe to Freedom, which is the gem of his "Bruce." The personification is wonderful. Pale-eyed Fear—his own icy heart of silver hue—vainly attempting to chill Freedom's breast; Power trampling the earth with iron feet, as he sounds to war: his head reaching to the sky, his eyes glaring like two burning meteors; his spear a sunbeam, and his shield a star; and gore-faced War, armed by Envy, ten bloody arrows in his straining fist! The Rudde Hall and all its imaginary occupants were forgotten for the time, as his subject thus overmastered the archaic dream of the romancer, and he yielded himself to the inspiration of which true poetry is the offspring.

The history of the "Battle of Hastings" has already been given. It is one of the earliest known productions of his antique muse; and the only one which he deliberately produced as his own. It is professedly the work of Turgot, a Saxon monk, of the tenth century; which, as already narrated, Rowley set himself to translate with all diligence, and got into trouble with certain patrons for his pains. The subject follows up that of "Goddwyn;" and opens with a vigour worthy of the theme:

> "O Christ! it is a grief for me to tell
>     How many a noble earl and valorous knight
> In fighting for King Harold nobly fell,
>     All slain in Hastings field in bloody fight.
> O Sea! our teeming donor, had thy flood
>     Had any fructuous entendement,[1]
> Thou wouldst have rose and sank with tides of blood
>     Before King William's knights had hither went;
> Whose coward arrows many erles slain,
> And 'brued the field with blood as season rain."

[1] Occleve, in the prologue to his *De Regimine Principum*, has the lines:

> "My Maister Chaucer, flower of eloquence,
>     Mirrour of fructuous entendement."

CHAP. VIII.

*The men of Bristowe.*


*The "hygra" of the Severn.*



*Repetition of the favourite simile.*

The scene is as remote from the Avon, as the time is distant from that of Canynge ; but this poem has also its Earl Alfwoulde, trustiest of Harold's generals, whom he despatches at the crisis of the strife, with ten picked Kentishmen and "ten Bristowans for the emprise :" and as he pictures the deeds of the men of Bristowe, he thus borrows the illustrations of their prowess from phenomena familiar to the dwellers in the valley of the Severn :—

> "As when the hygra of the Severn roars
> And thunders ugsome on the sands below,
> The cleembe[1] rebounds to Wedeceter's shore,
> And sweeps the black sand round its hoary prow ;
> So bremie[2] Alfwoulde thro' the war did go ;
> His Kenters and Brystowans slew each side,
> Betreinted all along with bloodless foe,
> And seemed to swim along with bloody tide ;
> From place to place, besmeared with blood, they went,
> And round about them swarthless corse besprent."

The same favourite figure of the " hygra," or bore of the Severn, is employed in a previous stanza of this poem ; and, at greater length, in "Ælla."[3]  His eye, indeed, was ever open to all that nature had to show; and when he borrowed, it was at no second hand.  Some of the passages in this early poem may compare with the matured works of our best descriptive poets.  But one of the finest of them has a further interest from the peculiarly personal nature of the illustration which the

---

[1] *Cleembe*, noise.          [2] *Bremie*, furious.
[3] This familiar feature is described in Drayton's "Polyolbion," b. vii. :—

> "Shut up in narrower bounds the Higar wildly raves
> And frights the straggling flocks the neighbouring shores to fly
> Afar as from the main it comes with hideous cry,
> And on the angry front the curled foam doth bring," &c.

The same phenomenon in the Solway figures both in Scott's "Redgauntlet" and in his "Lochinvar," where

> "Love swells like the Solway, and ebbs like its tide."

old poet-priest is represented as employing. The beauty of Adhelm's Saxon bride is set forth to exalt the sacrifice made by him, in quitting her for Harold's service; and in endowing her with all choicest charms, he assigns to her his own grey, sparkling eyes, setting forth their superiority with as much fervour as ever poet sang of the tender hazel or deep blue glancing of beauty's eye.

" White as the chalky cliffs of Britain's isle,
    Red as the highest coloured Gallic wine,
Gay as all nature at the morning smile :
    Those hues with pleasaunce on her lips combine,
    Her lips more red than summer evening skyne,
Or Phœbus rising in a frosty morn;
    Her breast more white than snow in fields that lyen,
Or lily lambs that never have been shorn :
Swelling like bubbles in a boiling well
Or new-burst brooklets gently whispering in the dell.

" Brown as the filbert dropping from the shell,
    Brown as the nappy ale at Hocktide game,
So brown the crooked rings that featly fell
    Over the neck of the all-beauteous dame.
    Grey as the morn before the ruddy flame
Of Phœbus' charriot rolling thro' the sky ;
    Grey as the steel-horn'd goats Conyan made tame :
So grey appear'd her featly sparkling eye ;
    Those eyne that did oft mickle pleased look
On Adhelm, valiant man, the virtues' doomsday book."

Several additional stanzas of apt description equally sustain this fine poetic picturing. But our present object is to trace the unity running through nearly all Chatterton's antique poems, as parts of that romance which he had created for himself, and in which he had dwelt apart from early childhood.

But not in verse alone does the youthful romancer work out his ideal life of the olden time. Rowley's prose supplies no less apt illustrations. Indeed, as we have seen, the "Memoirs of Canynge," and the correspondence of his friends and brother-poets, fit into each other and make the story complete in all its details. Not a letter

CHAP. VIII

*The charms of Adhelm's bride.*

*Beauty of grey eyes.*

*Rowley's prose illustrations.*

CHAP. VIII.

*Correspondence of old poets and dramatists.*

survives to illustrate the correspondence between Shakespeare and his friends or fellow-players. But somehow those of the poets and dramatists of Canynge's time got all garnered under the six locks of his coffer; and Mr. Barrett—with Chatterton's aid—was able to " submit to the judgement and candour" of the readers of his veracious history an unbroken series of letters between the old merchant and those unheard-of poets who, had they only been heard of, must have made their own Avon famous in song before Shakespeare's Avon claimed its pre-eminence among the tributaries of the Severn.

*Opening of Master Canynge's Lodge.*

The old merchant writes to his friend and confessor an account of his masonic lodge opened on the vigil of Epiphany, 1432, with his address on the value of the fine arts in their application to trade, to a chapter composed of seven-and-twenty friars, sixteen gentlemen, and three brother aldermen, in which this sly touch of humour betrays the modern Rowley's hand : " I dyd speek of the use of the Artes to improve the trade. The Freeres did enlarge, the gentlemen attende, and the Councylmen felle asleepe !" But more interesting to us now is this passage in one of Rowley's letters addressed to Canynge

*Richard of Cirencester.*

from Cirencester: "I have founde the papers of Fryar Rycharde. He saieth nothynge of Bristolle albeit he haveth a long storie of Seyncte Vyncente and the Queede. His Celle is most lovelie depycted on the whyte walles wythe black cole, displaieynge the Iters of the Weste." This passage was alone sufficient to confirm the Dean of Exeter's faith in the ancient Rowley. Now it is of itself evidence enough that he was a monk of the eighteenth century. Chatterton was in his fifth year when Dr. Stukeley delighted the learned world of Europe by

*Bertram's " De Situ Britanniæ."*

the publication of the " De Situ Britanniæ " of Richard of Cirencester, a monk of the fourteenth century, from a MS. professedly discovered at Copenhagen by Charles Julius Bertram : usually designated Professor of the English Language at the Royal Marine Academy there ; but who turns out to have been only an undergraduate when he palmed off this impudent hoax on the antiquarian divine.[1] This production, so characteristic of the age, has proved the most mischievous among all the literary frauds of that eighteenth century, misleading Gibbon, Roy, Whittaker, Chalmers, Hoare, and other eminent historians and topographers for a whole century, and finding its fitting authentication in the epistles of the good priest Rowley.

The collection of letters closes with an editorial colophon from Rowley's pen, setting forth the virtues of his revered patron : "As a leorned wyseager he excelled ynne alle thynges. As a poette and peyncter he was greete. Wythe hym I lyved at Westburie sixe yeeres before he died, and bee nowe hasteynge to the grave mieselfe." So ends this ingenious romance, which Chatterton not only wrote but lived. The disguise is so transparent now, that one marvels it could deceive so long. Not only are Thomas Chatterton and Thomas Rowley one : but the more familiarly he is studied, the more obviously the counterparts to the saucy humour of his modern satire gleam out in the creations of his antique muse. His friend Burgum's self-acquired Latin, for example, only served to expose him to the ridicule of Oxford pedants, including Chatterton's own clerical antagonists ; and so we find him exclaiming in his " Epistle to the Rev. Mr. Catcott :"—

> " Burgum wants learning : see the lettered throng
> Banter his English in a Latin song ;
> Oxonian sages hesitate to speak
> Their native language, but declaim in Greek."

Rowley in his " Epistle to Mastre Canynge on Ælla " has much the same sentiment :—

> "Syr John, a Knyghte, who hath a barne of lore,
> Kenns Latyn att fyrst syghte from Frenche or Greke ;
> Pyghtethe hys knowlachynge ten yeres or more,
> To rynge upon the Latynne worde to speke.
> Whoever spekethe Englysch ys despysed ;
> The Englysch hym to please moste fyrste be latynized."

[1] *Vide* Canadian Journal, July 1869.

Whether, then, Chatterton found among the names that caught his eye in the old parchments of Canynge's coffer that of Thomas Rowley, or invented it for himself, does not greatly matter. He is himself the " True Thomas " of the Rowley poems ; and far truer to the noble gifts of " the fate-marked child," when clad in his antique guise, than when " the strong fit of satire was upon him ; " and, in retaliation for some real or fancied slight, he wrote down to the level of the poor Canynges of his own modern Bristol. There can be little doubt, however, that the name adopted by Chatterton was a genuine antique. In the *Gentleman's Magazine* for May, June, and July, 1786, is published a correspondence between Dr. Ducarel of Doctors' Commons and the Rev. John Chapman, Vicar of Weston near Bath, Mr. Mathew Brickdale of Clifton, and Mr. William Barrett, the historian. The subject is the Rowley poems ; but the name of Chatterton receives a mere passing notice. At the date of the correspondence the faith of Barrett in the ancient priest of St. John's, Bristowe, was undoubting ; and his mode of proving the genuineness of the antiques by means of his own "originals," and then the genuineness of their reputed author by an appeal to his handwriting, furnishes as amusing a specimen of reasoning in a circle as could well be imagined.





Writing to Dr. Ducarel, March 7th, 1772, Barrett says : " All the originals, the few that have been preserved, are in my hands. I can prove the age and exact time when most of them were written by the author's own handwriting." [1] A month later he corrects Dr. Ducarel's misconception that Rowley had been Vicar of Redcliffe, and adds : " I have reason to believe he was a religious. I am now examining the archives of the city for his name and family. I think I have so far succeeded as to be able to pronounce him a Bristol man." [2] At length his industry is rewarded in some degree, and he writes on the 20th July, " I have been taking all methods to inquire out the name, family, burial, &c. of Rowley, but have not, I fear,

[1] Gent. Mag. vol. lvi. p. 460.  [2] Ibid. vol. lvi. p. 463.

succeeded; though I have met with an inscription of one Tho. Rowley, who served bailiff when Mr. Canynge was mayor, and sheriff of Bristol soon after. But he was a merchant, and lies buried in St. John's Church, in this City. Query, if he ever took priest's orders as his friend Mr. Canynge did? The date is 1478, four years only after the death of Mr. Canynge."[1]

*Tho. Rowley, bailiff and sheriff.*

It will be observed that Mr. Barrett speaks of "his friend Mr. Canynge," as though he had caught the veritable poet and schoolmate of the old Bristol merchant: having, no doubt, at one time fancied he had, and forgot for the moment that his discovery could not be made to tally. It would indeed have puzzled the "True Thomas" himself to convert this old merchant and sheriff of Bristol into the priest of St. John's; for his sepulchral brass not only records the death of his wife, Margaret, in 1470, but includes a memorial of six sons and six daughters. There was no lack of Rowleys, therefore, in Bristol, in that fifteenth century. Barrett, indeed, says, "One Thomas Rowley was chantry priest at Redcliffe;"[2] but probably his authority was Chatterton. He mentions no other.

*The Rowleys of the fifteenth century.*

Here, however, is a veritable Thomas Rowley, of St. John's, Bristol, bailiff in 1466, when William Canynge was mayor, and one therefore whose name may have repeatedly occurred among the documents in Master Canynge's coffer, even after its official rifling in 1740. The christian name, we may imagine, caught the eye of Chatterton from its correspondence to his own. Its association with St. John's Church, in some deed or benefaction, fixed the incumbency of the imaginary "greete chauntrie preeste;" and thus he gave the "airy nothing a local habitation and a name."

*A veritable antique Rowley.*

Such I imagine to be the history of the Thomas Rowley, on whose genuine existence as priest and poet of the fifteenth century not a few men of high repute have been willing to stake their fame. But whencesoever derived, Thomas Rowley was no mere *nom de plume,* but a genuine reality to Chatterton. He spoke of him

*Basis of the fiction.*

[1] Gent. Mag. vol. lvi. p. 544.    [2] Barrett's History, p. 489.

CHAP. VIII.

*Earnestness of the poet.*

*Contemporary reception of his labours.*

*Spurious products of the century.*

with the persistent consistency of one in whom his faith was as undoubted as in William Canynge, or in St. Mary Redcliffe itself. I picture the boy, in my own mind, busily labouring at his Canynge biography, his letters, his topographical descriptions, his poems, with all the earnestness common enough in intelligent children at some work in which imagination has full play. So coherent at length grew that ancient past to him that a perfect consistency is traceable through all the quaint, strange glimpses which his prose and verse reveal. It was to him no mere ingenious fiction. He could withdraw to it at will; and I can fancy, often felt it to be more real than the dull realities to which he returned from such reveries.

That the matter-of-fact tradesmen of Bristol slighted the boy, and literary Dryasdusts of that eighteenth century turned from him as an impostor, while contending for a genuine fifteenth century author of his verse, accords with the character of the age which begot so many spurious literary antiques. The taste for the Elizabethan poets was reviving. Rowe, Pope, Theobald, Johnson, and others had inaugurated that textual criticism of Shakespeare which has culminated, in our own day, in the famous " Perkins " folio with its marginal antiques. Percy's " Reliques " had appeared in their first very imperfect form while Chatterton was a Bluecoat boy; but Joseph Ritson had not yet taken pen in hand to school the literary world into habits of accurate criticism ; and so not only " Ossians " and " Rowleys," but even Shakespearian " Vortigerns and Rowenas " were possible things. The century was a very respectable one in its achievements in letters, but historical or literary criticism was by no means its forte ; and so learned Deans and Fellows of Colleges, like Milles and Bryant, staked their reputations on the genuineness of the antiques ; and in their efforts to prove it, only showed that they could not have read or understood a genuine fifteenth century MS. had it fallen into their hands.[1] But if the triumph of

[1] *Vide* Sir F. Madden's preface to " William of Palerne."

deceiving scholarly experts had any share in stimulating the labours of the boy, it has been reserved for our more critical age to receive at the hands of one of its most practised bibliographers the exhortation and entreaty to its archæologists, "not to allow the notion of forgery to prevent their keeping a look out for 'Old Rowley,' and just acquainting themselves with the printed portrait (disfigured though it be,) which has come down to us, that they may know him when they meet him!"[1]   It scarcely adds to the marvel, that this same zealous champion of "Old Rowley" scarcely finds the epithets of Chalmers or Walpole vile enough to express his contempt for the real author, both of Rowley and his works.

One of the earliest waifs of Master Canynge's coffer was an inventory of Easter gifts to the church of St. Mary Redcliffe by the old merchant, after he had become an inmate of Westbury College, with a view to the fitting production of the annual miracle-play on that great festival of the Church.   This document sets forth, in quaintest detail, the presentation, on the 3d of July, 1470, to Maistre Nicholas Pyttes, Vicar of Red-cliffe, of a new sepulchre, well gilt, with all requisite furnishings, including "Heaven, made of timber and stained cloths; Hell made of timber and iron work, with thirteen devils; four pair of angels' wings, well painted; and four angels' chevelers," or perukes!   This genuine document from the Redcliffe muniment-room, though communicated to the Society of Antiquaries long before Chatterton was born, and printed by Walpole in his "Anecdotes of Painters," was neither turned to account by poet nor critics.   The anti-Rowleyans might have found in it the test of one of Chatterton's most notable anachronisms, where, in the concluding stanza of Rowley's "Epistle to Master Canynge," written professedly in the very age of religious mysteries and miracle-plays, he thus addresses their notable encourager in the language and

---

[1] "Chatterton: an Essay;" by the Rev. S. R. Maitland, D.D., F.R.S., and F.S.A. p. 110.

*A critical anachron-ism.*

sentiments of the eighteenth, or still more of the seven-teenth century :—

> " Plays made from holy tales I hold unmeet ;
>   Let some great story of a man be sung ;
> When as a man we God and Jesus treat,
>   In my poor mind we do the Godhead wrong.
> But let no words which droorie[1] might not hear
> Be placed in the same.   Adieu until anere.[2] "

So foreign were such ideas to those of the fifteenth cen-tury, that the venerable Dean of Westbury includes, in the inventory of his Easter sepulchre furnishings for St. Mary Redcliffe, "an ymage of God Almighty risying oute of the Sepulchre, with all the ordynance that 'longeth thereto ; item, the Holy Ghost comyng out of Hevyn into the Sepulchre."   Had this curious inventory attracted Chatterton's attention, Maister Nicholas Pyttes, the Vicar, would no doubt have figured among the select group that frequented the Rudde House ; and the miracle-play would have been noticed in the Rowley correspondence, if it did not receive more prominent consideration.   But it was in the true spirit of the poet, and not of the anti-quary, that Chatterton called up that imaginary past. The boy could not escape the influences of his own era, or imbue his mind with the feelings of Lydgate and his times ; but he could give shape to the heroic age of his fancy's creation, and people it with actors of his own imagining : producing thereby poems compared with which the best of Lydgate's are mere rhyme.

*Master Nicholas the Vicar.*

*A triumph of poetic fiction.*

So far the literary masking in which the boy-poet figured in the guise of his "gode prieste Rowley" invites our unqualified admiration as a triumph of poetic fiction replete with the realities of poetic truth.   In following out the maze in which it involved its creator, other and less acceptable aspects meet our view.

[1] *Droorie*, modesty.          [2] *Anere*, another.

# CHAPTER IX.

## THE MODERN CANYNGE.





THE transition from the romantic illusions of the young dreamer and the ingenious fictions wrought out by him as the child-poet, to the deceptions and trickery of the attorney's clerk, is not a pleasant one. The "vision splendid" was already beginning to "fade into the light of common day." The romance of Rowley, if it was to be adhered to, had to be sustained by means far apart from the poet's true vocation. Those who rejected his claim to the authorship of the "Battle of Hastings," or the "Tragedy of Ælla," nevertheless called for the production of the originals. So the process of manufacturing such was begun. Of this we have more than one account from eye-witnesses. Mr. John Rudhall, to whom he acknowledged the authorship of "The Mayor's first passing the Old Bridge," gave Dean Milles a graphic account of his mode of procedure. "He brought to him one day a piece of parchment, about the size of a half-sheet of foolscap paper. Mr. Rudhall did not think that anything was written on it; but he saw Chatterton write several words, if not lines, in a character which he did not understand, totally unlike English; and, as he apprehended, meant to imitate or represent the original, from which his account was printed." He then adds: "When Chatterton had written on the parchment, he held it over the candle to give it the appearance of antiquity, which changed the colour of the ink, and made the parchment appear black, and a little contracted." Among the few genuine documents reclaimed by the authorities of St.



M

Chap. IX.

*First steps in the process.*

*Motives for producing the early copies.*

*Daily privation.*

Mary Redcliffe, after the death of Chatterton, was a book containing some pages of entries relating to church matters, but with the flyleaf at the end covered with imitations of the characters and writing of the fifteenth century, repeated as in a school-boy's first lessons; and showing, no doubt, the first steps in the process of supplying "originals," when these came to be in demand by Barrett and others. But this deception was an after-thought, forced on him by the perverse credulity of his dupes, who, as in the case of the "Battle of Hastings," insisted on being deceived. There can be little doubt, from the invariable secrecy maintained by him relative to the Rowleyan authorship, that had he possessed means and opportunity to carry out his purpose, the Rowley MSS. would have been withheld from all eyes till the romance was flashed on the literary world in its completed amplitude. But, as Mr. Catcott informs us, he produced transcripts of the alleged antiques from time to time "as his necessities obliged him" and these necessities necessarily increased with his hopes and aspirations. To his mother and sister he often spoke in great rapture of the undoubted success of his plans for future life, and in moments of exultation would enjoy the gleams of drawning fame; and, as Mrs. Newton writes: "Confident of advancement, would promise my mother and me should be partakers of his success." But while thus sanguinely painting a brilliant future, the present was beset with daily stint and privation. He was, as ere long he wrote to Horace Walpole, "the son of a poor widow, who supported him with great difficulty,"[1] and his literary labours won him, as yet, little either of profit or fame. It was a favourite saying of his, "If Rowley had been a Londoner instead of a Bristowyan, his fortune would have been made;" or, as he put it to his mother, "he could

---

[1] Dr. Maitland calls this "a deliberate lie;" because he was then boarded and clothed by Mr. Lambert. But even had the clothing been all that he desired, he had no wages; not even money to buy paper; none to bestow on his mother or sister; or to supply the thousand wants of a youth of his age.

have lived by copying his works." Yet, as we shall see, on his reaching London, it was not by means of his Rowley poems that he strove to win his bread as a literary adventurer. The task-work of that period illustrates the versatility of his mind, in its striking contrast to those cherished productions held in reserve for a time that never arrived for him.

The dream of Chatterton's life, I doubt not, was the realization of some modern Mæcenas—the Canynge of his fancy,—by whom his genius was to be recognised, and to whom all his plans and hopes were then to be revealed. But unhappily he had got mentally and morally entangled in the meshes of his own ingenious sophistries, and the method he resorted to for accomplishing his object tended only to discredit him with the patrons of letters. The boy, moreover, had no natural adviser. His simple mother and his sister he regarded with all the affection of which his nature was capable; but he never dreamt of consulting them in the perplexities of his daring ambition. His very isolation and inexperience helped to foster his self-confidence, and encourage him to cope single-handed with the world, of which all his knowledge had been acquired in Colston's Hospital, before his admission to Lambert's office and the uncongenial society of his kitchen. His intellectual powers have probably rarely been surpassed; perhaps they were never equalled at his age. But any Bristol trader could have told him that his plan of baiting for patronage with spurious antiques was sure to fail.

His first effort at winning his way in the literary world was legitimate enough, from his own point of view. Having completed his tragedy of " Ælla " and other Rowleyan poems, he offered them to Dodsley, the London publisher, in this fashion :—

> " *Bristol, December* 21, 1768.

" SIR,—I take this method to acquaint you that I can procure copies of several ancient poems ; and an interlude, perhaps the oldest dramatic work extant ; wrote by one Rowley, a priest in Bristol, who lived in the reigns of Henry the VIth and Edward

M 2

the IVth.  If these pieces will be of service to you, at your command copies shall be sent to you by

"Your most obedient servant,
"D. B.

"Please to direct for D. B. to be left with Mr. Thomas Chatterton,
Redcliffe Hill, Bristol.
"For Mr. J. Dodsley, bookseller, Pall Mall, London."



D. B., or *Dunelmus Bristoliensis*, was not absolutely
unknown at this date to London readers.  The notes
for correspondents in the *Town and Country Magazine*
of the previous month state that " D. B. of Bristol's
favour will be gladly received ;" and there accordingly
Heraldic papers, Ossianic imitations, and at length, in
the following May, the " Elenoure and Juga " of Rowley,
made their appearance.  But whatever attractions the
language and orthography of Speght's Chaucer might
have for a few antiquaries, the flimsiest modern satires
of the Bristol boy were more likely to win immediate
popularity.  As for Mr. Dodsley's anonymous correspondent, it is doubtful if the letter was thought worth



a reply.  Two months elapsed, and then Chatterton wrote
a second letter in his own name, in which the com-
plexities arising from his literary disguise, and the necessity of warding off the inevitable demand for the original
MS., involve him in a clumsy fabrication still less likely
to lead to success.  He endeavours to secure the advance
of a guinea, professedly for the purpose of obtaining
access to the manuscript of the tragedy of " Ælla,"
which "after long and laborious search " he had been
so happy as to obtain a sight of ; but was denied permis-



sion to copy except on such terms.  So far, however, we
are thus in possession of a definite date at which this
tragedy was complete, and ready to be offered to the
world, if only a patron or publisher could be found.  There
was half a truth even in this statement of the letter : " I
am far from having any mercenary views for myself in this
affair ; and, was I able, would print it at my own risque."
A postscript stated that the poem contained about one
thousand lines.  In reality it extends to upwards of twelve

hundred and fifty as finally printed; and of these the speech of Ælla was selected as a specimen, including this passage :—

> "Let coward London see her town on fire,
>     And strive with gold to stay the ruiner's hand;
> Ælla and Bristow haveth thoughts are higher;
>     We fight not for ourselves, but all the land.
>     As Severn's hyger lodgeth banks of sand,
> Pressing it down beneath the running stream,
>     With dreary din enswolters the high strand,
> Bearing the rocks along in fury breme :
>     So will we bear the Dacian army down,
> And through a storm of blood will reach the champion crown."

*A specimen passage.*

This final postscript was added, which doubtless sets forth one of his plans for achieving the long-coveted recognition of the worth of his verse in its assigned character as the product of Rowley. "If it should not suit you, I should be obliged to you if you would calculate the expense of printing it, as I will endeavour to publish it by subscription on my own account."[1]

The scheme failed, in part at least, by reason of the bungling diplomacy of its projector. Had he, holding to his secret, contented himself with forwarding the manuscript to the publisher, success was not impossible; for the poem is the finest of all the creations of Chatterton's antique muse, exhibiting considerable dramatic power, and interspersed with lyrical pieces of varied sweetness. Here, for example, is the " Elynour and Lord Thomas," a minstrel's song, or, more correctly, a ballad, ascribed to the pen of Syr Thybbot Gorges :—

*Bungling diplomacy.*

> "As Elynour by the green lessel[2] was setting,
>     As from the sun's heatè she harried,
> She said, as her white hands white hosen were knitting,
>     What pleasure it is to be married !

*Elynour and Lord Thomas.*

---

[1] These interesting letters turned up accidentally, long afterwards, among forgotten papers in Dodsley's counting-house. They passed into the hands of an autograph collector, and were first published in Britton's work on Redcliffe Church.

[2] *Lessel,* arbour.

*Chap. IX.*

" My husband, Lord Thomas, a forrester bold,
　　As ever clove pin, or the basket,
Does no cherysaunces[1] from Elynour hold,
　　I have it as soon as I ask it.

" When I lived with my father in merry Clowdell,
　　Tho' 'twas at my lief to mind spinning,
I still wanted something, but what ne could tell,
　　My lord father's barbed hall had ne winning.

" Each morning I rise, do I set my maidèns,
　　Some to spin, some to curdel, some bleaching ;
If any, new entered, do ask for my aidens,
　　Then swythen[2] you find me a teaching.

" Lord Walter, my father, he loved me well,
　　And nothing unto me was needing ;
But should I again go to merry Clowdell,
　　In soothen 'twould be without redeyng.[3]

" She said, and Lord Thomas came over the lea,
　　As he the fat deerkins was chaceing ;
She put up her knitting, and to him went she :
　　So we leave them both kindly embracing."

In this simple ballad we may trace the influence of
Percy's " Reliques," in which is printed from the Pepys
collection " Lord Thomas and fair Ellinor ; " but it is a
grave, tragical piece of greater length, and without the
double rhymes, which suit the lively tone of this
" Minstrel's Song."　Another, and finer lyric, the tender
plaint of a dying maiden, is more obviously suggested by
Ophelia's song in " Hamlet."　It is of greater length, but
admits of abridgment :—



" O ! sing unto my roundelay,
　　O ! drop the briny tear with me :
Dance ne moe at halie-day,
　　Like a running river be ;
　　　My love is dead,
　　　Gone to his death-bed
　　All under the willow-tree.

---

[1] *Cherysaunces*, comforts.　　　　[2] *Swythen*, immediately.
[3] *Redeyng*, wisdom.

" Black his hair as the winter night,
   White his neck as the summer snow,
Rudd his face as the morning light ;
   Cold he lies in the grave below.
     My love, &c.

" Sweet his tongue as the throstle's note,
   Quick in dance as thought can be :
Defte his tabour, cudgel stout :
   O, he lies by the willow-tree.
     My love, &c.

*        *        *        *

" See ! the white moon shines on high :
   Whiter is my true love's shroud ;
Whiter than the morning sky,
   Whiter than the evening cloud.
     My love, &c.

*        *        *        *

" With my hands I'll dent the briars
   Round his halie corse to gree ;
Ouphant[1] fairy, light your fires ;
   Here my body still shall be.
     My love, &c.

" Come with acorn-cup and thorn,
   Drain my heartè's blood away ;
Life and all its good I scorn,
   Dance by night, or feast by day.
     My love is dead,
      Gone to his death-bed
   All under the willow-tree.

" Water-witches, crowned with reyts,[2]
   Bear me to your lethal tide ;
I die ! I come ! my true love waits,——
   Thus the damsel spake and died."

In this, and other examples of suggested ideas, there
is no servile imitation. Repeatedly we catch a glimpse
of such suggestions ; but they are like the stray notes of
seemingly familiar airs that cheat the ear in listening to a
new opera. We are reminded, for example, of the prologue of Shakespeare's " Henry V." in the scene of " Celmonde near Watchette," but it is only for a moment :—



---

[1] *Ouphant,* elfin.       [2] *Reyts,* waterflags.

"O, for a spryte all fire ! to tell the day,
　　The day which shall astound the hearer's rede,
　　Making our foemen's envying hearts to bleed,
Ybearing thro' the world our renom'd name for aye.

"Bright sun had in his ruddy robes been dyght ;
　　From the red east he flitted with his train ;
The hours drew away the gate of night ;
　　Her sable tapestry was rent in twain ;
　　The dancing streaks bedeckèd heaven's plain,
And on the dew did smile with shimering eye ;
　　Like gouts of blood which do black armour stain,
Shining upon the burn which standeth bye :
　　The soldiers stood upon the hillis side
Like young enleafed trees which in a forest bide.

"Ælla rose like the tree beset with briars,
　　His tall spear shining as the stars at night,
His eyne enseeming as a lowe of fire.
　　When he encheerèd every man to fight,
　　His gentle words did move each valorous knight ;
It moveth them as hunters lioncelles.
　　In treeble armour is their courage dighte ;
Each warring heart for praise and renome swells ;
　　Like slowly dinning of the crouching stream,
Such did the murmuring sound of the whole army seem."



Descriptive passages such as this, of considerable length, and occasionally of great beauty, are introduced as prologues to the dramatic dialogue. But of all this Dodsley had no opportunity of judging. He received only the speech of "Ælla ;" selected in all probability because it is beset by more than the wonted interfusion of archaic or coined words; and obscured still further by antiquated misspelling. Yet, probably, only on the assumption of "Ælla" being a genuine antique could any publisher have been induced to entertain the idea of its issue. Its author possibly shrank from the labour of copying out the whole, with the certain cost of transmission and the very probable chance of rejection, and so he asked the guarantee



of a guinea in advance. It only served to complete the chances of failure. But who can tell what hard necessity impelled him to crave the modest sum ?

Chatterton had been looking abroad for some appreciative aid, and, failing the publishers, had conceived the idea of a friendly helper among the lovers of letters in the great outer world. Unhappily the mode of winning such favour, which forthwith possessed his mind, was borrowed from the deceptive processes already pursued with Bristol patrons. Mr. Edward Gardner, one of his latest companions, published, in 1798, a volume of " Miscellanies in Prose and Verse," to which he appended some unpublished poems of Chatterton, and a brief sketch of the Rowleyan controversy. In this, after describing a clumsy attempt witnessed by him "to antiquate" parchment by colouring it with ochre, and then rubbing it on the ground, he adds: " I heard him once, also, affirm that it was very easy for a person who had studied antiquity, with the aid of a few books which he could name, to copy the style of the ancient poets so exactly that the most skilful observer should not be able to detect him. No, said he, not Mr. Walpole himself." Mr. Gardner recalled this conversation, be it remembered, twenty-eight years after its utterance. Too much weight, therefore, must not be given to it in all its details, as an accurate report of Chatterton's words. One point, however, the allusion to Walpole, may be accepted as a reliable glimpse of thoughts that were ere long to bear fruit—of the Dead Sea kind.

As his dream of fame and fortune assumed shape and consistency, and visions of the recognition of his worth by some modern Canynge rose before him, Chatterton had already bethought him of Horace Walpole, subsequently fourth Earl of Orford, as the possible Mæcenas of that eighteenth century. Nor, from his distant point of view, was the idea an extravagant one. To the superficial observer, this vain, yet clever dallier with art, virtu, and belles lettres, might indeed seem the very man. This son of the great minister of the first and second Georges, though he did not abjure politics, made art and letters the real business of his life. He affected an extreme liberalism, akin to the Utopian sentiment of the last days of Bourbon kingship in France. The death-warrant of Charles I. hung in his bedroom, labelled

CHAP. IX.

*Looking out for friendly help.*

*Mr. Gardner's reminiscences.*

*Horace Walpole's liberalism.*

"England's Magna Charta;" and in other ways, by choice of pictures and style of decoration, he sported with a speculative republicanism that seemed to assert an equality and common brotherhood for man. Yet all the while he was, in taste and temperament, fastidiously aristocratic. He, too, had his dream of mediæval art, and realized it in costly, if not very tasteful fashion, by converting his cottage at Strawberry Hill, Twickenham, into a pseudo-Gothic Aladdin's palace, which he filled with miniatures, statuettes, antiques, and bijoutry; and also with rare books and MSS. in apt accordance with the modern Rowley's ideal of "Mayster Canynge's Cabynet of auntyaunte monumentis."



Walpole was also a man of letters, a novelist, a dramatist, and even a clever writer of verse. He had been the personal friend of the poet Gray, and printed his odes at the private press of Strawberry Hill. But, above all, he was the reputed author of a mysterious romance, the famous "Castle of Otranto," replete with antique feudalism, though deriving its immediate popularity from its supernatural wonders. This marvellous story made its first appearance in 1764,—when Chatterton was engaged on his "Apostate Will" and other juvenile efforts, in the Bluecoat School,—professedly as a translation by one William Marshall, from an Italian MS. of Onuphrio Muralto, "found in the library of an ancient Catholic family in the north of England, and printed at Naples, in the black letter, in the year 1529." It won its way at once to public favour; and then, in the second edition, its author takes off the mask, and "flatters himself he shall appear excusable for having offered his work to the world under the borrowed personage of a translator."





The "Castle of Otranto" had doubtless been eagerly read by Chatterton, as it has been by thousands of other boys. But for him the mystery of its antique MS. and its reputed modern authorship had peculiar charms, suggestive of possible sympathy with the concocter of another romance of antique feudalism and mediæval art.

Chatterton had written his second letter to Mr. Dodsley

in the middle of February, and before the end of March had either received the publisher's refusal, or construed his silence into the same significance. Necessity pressed hardly on the young poet. He was producing works which now after the lapse of a century command the admiration of the world; yet he could not obtain recognition of their worth. The irksome routine of Lambert's office, with no duties to furnish legitimate occupation for his active mind; the degradation of his kitchen and its associates; and the harsh conduct of the unsympathising attorney: all prompted him, by some means or other, to achieve his emancipation, and win what was his due. So falling back, once more, on the Rowleyan mystery, he addressed himself to the task of introducing the antique poet to his modern Canynge. But if my interpretation of some of the facts of this introduction is correct, it has hitherto been misunderstood by his biographers.

Mr. Barrett prints in his history of Bristol two elaborate antiquarian papers on " The Ryse of Peyncteynge " and " The Historie of Peyncters in Englande, wroten bie T. Rowleie, 1469, for Mastre Canynge." These, he tells us, " are printed from the very originals in Chatterton's handwriting, sent in two letters to Horace Walpole, Esq.;"[1] and this has been accepted without question by every biographer of the poet. The first of those papers opens in this fashion: " Peyncteynge ynn Englande, haveth of ould tyme bin yn use; for saieth the Roman wryters, the Brytonnes dyd depycte themselves, yn sondrie wyse, of the fourmes of the sonne and moone wythe the hearbe woade; albeytte I doubte theie were no skylled carvellers;" and so it proceeds, with this affected quaintness of language, to treat of painting, carving, and stained glass; of Saxon heraldry; and of embroidery in silver, gold, and silks of divers hues; and not only refers to unheard-of poets, but gives a specimen of the verse of John, Abbot of St. Austin's Minster: the first English painter in oils, and greatest poet of the age in which he lived! The whole piece is a stray leaf out of the

_______________
[1] Barrett's History, p. 639.

Rowley romance.   The armoury of Ælla, Lord of Bristowe Castle, furnishes illustrations of heraldic blazonry;
the representation of St. Warburge, in the stained window
of his own minster chancel, supplies the oldest example
of "the couneynge mysterie of steineynge glasse;" and
"Henrie a Thornton, a geason depeyctor of countenances,
peyncted the walles of Master Canynge hys howse; a
moste daintie and feetyve performaunce, nowe yerased."



The curious narratives, whensoever composed, were
in all probability prepared for Walpole's eye; and with
them this brief letter, also furnished by Barrett, from
"the very original to Horace Walpole, Esq."

> "*Bristol, March 25th, Corn Street.*
> "SIR,—Being versed a little in antiquities, I have met with
> several curious manuscripts, among which the following may be of
> service to you in any future edition of your truly entertaining anec-
> dotes of painting.   In correcting the mistakes (if any) in the notes,
> you will greatly oblige your most humble servant,
>
> "THOMAS CHATTERTON."

Of the notes here referred to by the professed tran-
scriber, two specially attract our notice.   In the one
Master Canynge is characterised as: "The founder of
that noble Gothic pile, Saint Mary Redclift Church in



this city; the Mæcenas of his time; one who could happily
blend the poet, the painter, the priest, and the Christian,
perfect in each; a friend to all in distress, an honor to
Bristol, and a glory to the Church."   The reputed author
of the MS. is also depicted, with a special eye, we may
presume, to the virtuoso of Strawberry Hill: "T. Rowlie
was a secular priest of St. John's in this city; his merit
as a biographer, historiographer, is great, as a poet still
greater; some of his pieces would do honour to Pope;
and the person under whose patronage they may appear
to the world will lay the Englishman, the antiquary, and
the poet under an eternal obligation."



The hint of what the romancer had in view is sufficiently obvious to us now.   Here, on one hand, is "the
Mæcenas of his time," the ideal that Walpole, as a
generous encourager of letters, was expected to realize.

On the other.hand is the poor Bristol poet, whose works only awaited such patronage as he could easily bestow, to lay all men under obligation to him.   There is, to my mind, a curious admixture of the simplicity of inexperienced youth with this artful deception.   But Chatterton was only trying his "'prentice hand."   He had sense enough to see that this, at least, would not do.   So the manuscripts and note were thrown aside, and only recovered among Chatterton's own papers, after his death, to be printed in Barrett's uncritical jumble of romance and blundering, to the confusion of the poet's biographers for a whole century.

This point is of importance, and requires to be carefully looked into.   According to Barrett's account, the manuscripts, notes, and accompanying letter, are all "printed from the very originals in Chatterton's handwriting, sent in two letters to Horace Walpole, Esq."— from which any reader was bound to assume that the historian had obtained from Walpole the authentication of these same "very originals."   But no sooner did Barrett's "History and Antiquities of the City of Bristol" issue from the press than Walpole wrote to Miss Hannah More, referring to the two letters it contained, "pretended to be sent to him, but never sent." Still more explicitly he writes to the Countess of Ossory, July 7th, 1792, after Barrett's death : "Poor Barrett, author of the 'History of Bristol,' printed there two letters to me, found among Chatterton's papers, and which the simple man imagined the lad had sent me, but most assuredly never did, as too preposterous even for him to venture after he had found that I began to suspect his forgeries.   For instance, he had ascribed the invention of heraldry to Hengist, and of painted glass to an unknown monk in the reign of King Edmund."[1] He also writes to Miss Hannah More about the same time, in reply to a letter, telling him of Barrett's death : "I rejoice I did not publish a word in contradiction of

[1] Cunningham's Letters of Horace Walpole, Earl of Orford. vol. ix. p. 380.

the letters which he said Chatterton sent to me, as I
was advised to do.  I might have laughed at the poor
man's folly, and then I should have been miserable to
have added a grain to the poor man's mortification." [1]

The declaration, thus specifically reiterated in private,
was by-and-by made public.  Dr. Farmer, of Emmanuel
College, Oxford, made known that " Mr. Walpole had
authorized his friends to declare that he never saw those
letters from Chatterton which Mr. Barrett has printed,
till they appeared in the new history of Bristol." [2]  But
by this time the evidence had got transferred into fresh
hands, and brought about a further complication which
has misled inquiry ever since.  In the February number
of the *Gentleman's Magazine* for 1797 a letter appears
from a correspondent, R. P. of Bath, calling upon Dr.
Glynn to " say whether he has not seen with his own
eyes those very letters written by Chatterton to Lord
Orford, and whether he has not now in his keeping the
same identical letters, as also Lord Orford's answers to



them."  Lord Orford died in his 80th year, on the 2d
March, within a day or two after the appearance of this
letter, which is written on the erroneous assumption that
he had aimed at "possessing the world with the idea that
no correspondence of any kind had ever passed between
his Lordship and Chatterton."  As to the challenge,—
which was left unanswered, we may presume, owing to
the death of Walpole,—Dr. Glynn must have replied that
what the Bath correspondent asserted in this categorical
fashion was perfectly true, the facts being as follows.



Mr. Barrett obtained, after Chatterton's death,—most
probably as part of the lot of manuscripts purchased
by Catcott from his mother,—the documents referred to,
and printed them in his history, not by any means as
forgeries, but with about as definite a declaration in
favour of their being, in the main, copies of genuine
ancient parchments, as he was capable of.  But they

---

[1] Cunningham's Letters of Horace Walpole, Earl of Orford,
vol. ix. p. 230.

[2] Gent. Mag. vol. lxii. part i. p. 398.

were scarcely published when he died, bequeathing his collection of Chatterton papers to Dr. Glynn, Senior Fellow of St. John's College, Cambridge, by whom they were deposited in the British Museum. Hence the confusion. Dr. Glynn's manuscripts are challenged in confirmation of Mr. Barrett's printed documents, and the British Museum MSS. are appealed to in corroboration of both, without its seemingly occurring to any one that the same documents are reproduced by successive custodians. As to Barrett's affirmation that they were printed from the very originals sent to Walpole, the inference was natural enough; but the assertion only amounts to this, that they were printed from manuscripts in Chatterton's handwriting, found among his papers after his death.

Whether Walpole understood it or not, he had no motive to disavow the letters and papers printed by Barrett. His case would have admitted of far easier defence could he have shown that the boy tried to palm on him his " Ryse of Peyncteynge in Englande." What he did send, according to Walpole's own account, far more nearly approximated to a legitimate appeal to his judgment of the Rowley Poems on their own merits. " Bathoe, my bookseller," he states in his vindication, " brought me a pacquet left with him. It contained an ode, or little poem of two or three stanzas, in alternate rhyme, on the death of Richard I. ; and I was told in very few lines, that the possessor could furnish me with accounts of a series of great painters that had flourished at Bristol."[1]  This is explicit enough so far. He was told of accounts of painters, which could be sent. What he did receive was a poem " On the death of Richard I." Possibly this was the little ode of the apocryphal John, inducted Abbot of St. Austin's Minstre, Bristol, A.D. 1186, printed by Barrett, beginning :—

> " Harte of lyone ! shake thie sworde,
> Bare thie mortheynge steinede honde."

---

[1] Gent. Mag. vol. lii. p. 247.

But, though the Lion-hearted King is the subject, it is not in stanzas, and has no reference to his death. Walpole wrote upwards of a dozen years after the events he recalled to remembrance, and did not pretend to minute accuracy. But he evidently did not recognise in the little piece of twelve lines printed by Barrett the poem he had previously seen. Quoting from memory, he refers to a line in the printed poems of Rowley:—

" Now is Cœur de Lion gone "—

" or some such words," which had evidently caught his eye, and recalled the poem sent to him. This must have been Chatterton's second Eclogue, styled "Nygelle," which extends to eight stanzas, beginning :—

" Rycharde of lyons harte to fyghte is gon."



The so-called Eclogue is an invocation by Nygelle on behalf of his father, who has gone forth in Richard's train, to the Holy War. It does not treat of the king's death ; but it deals with the general carnage wrought by him, in a way sufficiently calculated to leave on the mind an impression of death as the theme ; as in the following stanzas :—

" Distraught affray, with locks of blood-red dye,
    Terror emburlèd in the thunder's rage,
Death linkèd to dismay doth ugsome fly,
    Enchafing every champion war to wage.
    Spears bevyle spears ; swords upon swords engage ;
Armour on armour din, shield upon shield ;
    Nor death of thousands can the war asuage,
But falling numbers sable all the field.
Sprytes of the blest, and every saint ydead,
Pour out your pleasaunce on my father's head.

" The foemen fall around ; the cross waves high ;
    Stainèd in gore, the heart of war is seen ;
King Richard thorough everyche troop doth fly,
    And beareth meynte of Turks unto the green ;
    By him the flower of Asia's men is slain ;
The waning moon doth fade before his sun ;
    By him his knights are formed to actions digne,
Doing such marvels, strangers be aston.
Sprytes of the blest, and every saint ydead,
Pour out your pleasaunce on my father's head."

Possibly this Eclogue, in whole or part, rather than the few lines appended to the "Ryse of Peyncteynge in Englande," was the poem actually sent, as better suited to accomplish the object of awaking Walpole's interest in the "many other old poems found at Bristol." A letter accompanied it, giving some account of Abbot John as a painter, and drawing special attention to Rowley and his poems. "Whether," says Walpole, " the transmitter hinted, or I supposed from the subject, that the discovered treasure was of the age of Richard I. I cannot take upon me to assert. Yet that impression was so strong on my mind that, two years after, when Dr. Goldsmith told me they were then allotted to the age of Henry IV. or V., I said with surprise, ' They have shifted the date extremely.' " Walpole's recollections, therefore, must not be dealt with as accurate in every detail; but if any reliance is to be placed on him, it is obvious that what he did receive differed essentially from the papers printed by Barrett. His correspondent was only known to him, as yet, as a gentleman to whom he owed some curious information on matters of literary and antiquarian interest. He replies to him accordingly with all the gracious urbanity of one patrician man of letters to another; gives him a thousand thanks for the very obliging offer of communicating the manuscript, which Barrett represents to have been actually sent; flatters himself, from the politeness already shown, that he will have permission to consult him; and closes with an apology for the simplicity of a direction that possibly betrays ignorance of some gentleman of distinction in his own city.

In the midst of all this only too polite and affable courtesy, there was one paragraph that touched all the keenest hopes of the poet. "Give me leave," writes Walpole, "to ask you where Rowley's Poems are to be found. I should not be sorry to print them, or at least a specimen of them, if they have never been printed." Chatterton did, accordingly, send a second letter with more copious enclosures, not of the "Historie of Peyncters" printed by Barrett, but specimens of the Rowley Poems,

N

CHAP. IX.

*Walpole's recollections.*

*His correspondence with Chatterton.*

*Keen hopes revived.*

*Fragment of a letter.*

which, whether ancient or modern, had genuine merit of their own to appeal to Walpole, Mason, or any critic capable of estimating true poetry at its worth.

A fragment of the letter which accompanied the specimens of Rowley—returned at a later date, on Chatterton's demand,—still exists among the manuscripts in the British Museum. The proud youth destroyed the evidence of his own appeal to Walpole on finding it vain, and only the last line and a half remains, with its intimation of the enclosure of " some further anecdotes and specimens of poetry." But happily for us Walpole published his vindication, from which we learn that—betrayed by his courtesy into a candour that only required the long-coveted friendly response to be converted into an in-genuous confession of his deception,—he threw himself on the generosity of his correspondent. " Chatterton,"

*Chatterton throws himself on Walpole's generosity*

says Walpole, " informed me that he was the son of a poor widow, who supported him with great difficulty; that he was clerk or apprentice to an attorney, but had a taste and turn for more elegant studies; and hinted a wish that I would assist him with my interest in emerging out of so dull a profession, by procuring him some place in which he could pursue his natural bent." He then referred to the great treasures of ancient poetry discovered in his native city, of which he enclosed specimens, including " an absolute modern pastoral in dialogue, thinly sprinkled with old words : "—the " Elinoure and Juga," no doubt, which he immediately afterwards sent to the *Town and Country Magazine.*[1]

*Careful preparation of his letters.*

The correspondence was conducted on Chatterton's part with a care that shows how much he felt to be at stake. Among his manuscripts in the British Museum are copies of subsequent letters of varying structure, the first drafts of those forwarded to Walpole, or, in some cases, written but never sent. They evince a strong desire to put forward the poems on their own merits,

[1] Gent. Mag. vol. lii. p. 247. The second letter to Walpole is dated March 30th, 1769. The " Elinoure and Juga" appeared in the *Town and Country Magazine* of the following May.

though still as genuine antiques.   He says, for example :
" I thought Rowley's Pastoral had a degree of merit that
would be its own defence."   But he had owned himself
a mere youth, the son of a poor widow ; and appealed to
the sympathy of the patrician *littérateur* for aid in attaining a position where his genius might expatiate freely in
its own favourite field of antique song.

The change which this confession and appeal produced
on the tone of Walpole's letters was only too marked,
though natural enough.   He had characterised the first
antique verses as "wonderful for their harmony and
spirit."   He submitted the later ones to the poets Gray
and Mason, "who at once pronounced them forgeries."
At the same time he wrote to a relative, a noble lady at
Bath, and through her learned the truth of Chatterton's
statement as to his humble and dependent circumstances.
This done, he thus narrates the further course he pursued.   "Being satisfied with my intelligence about Chatterton, I wrote him a letter with as much kindness and
tenderness as if I had been his guardian ; for though I
had no doubt of his imposition, such a spirit of poetry
breathed in his coinage as interested me for him ; nor
was it a grave crime in a young bard to have forged false
notes of hand that were to pass current only in the parish
of Parnassus ;"—and so Walpole did what?   "I un-
deceived him," he says, "about my being a person of
any interest, and urged him that, in duty and gratitude to
his mother, who had straitened herself to breed him up
to a profession, he ought to labour in it, that in her old
age he might absolve his filial debt.   I told him that,
when he should have made a fortune, he might unbend
himself with the studies consonant to his inclinations.   I
told him also, that I had communicated his transcripts
to much better judges, and that they were by no means
satisfied with the authenticity of his supposed MSS."[1]
Chatterton replied, in what Walpole characterises as a
peevish letter, reiterating.the genuineness of the antique
poems, and concluding thus : " Though I am but sixteen

[1] Gent. Mag. vol. lii. p. 248.



*Chap. IX.*

*Change in
Walpole's
tone.*

*His own
account of
his doings.*

years of age, I have lived long enough to see that poverty
attends literature.  I am obliged to you, sir, for your
advice, and will go a little beyond it, by destroying all my
useless lumber of literature, and never using my pen again
but in law."

*Failure of the poet's great hope.*

His great hope had failed him.  Possibly the boy was
sincere in the momentary resolution to have done for
ever with the Muse.  A week later he again wrote request-
ing the return of his papers.  Walpole betrays an irritable
resentment in the terms he applies to each successive
letter; and of this he says: "He demanded to have
them returned."  The point is unimportant; but Chatterton's reasonable demand was thus courteously expressed: "I should be obliged to you to return me the
copy I sent you, having no other."  When this letter
reached Walpole, he was preparing to set out, in a day
or two, for Paris; and, according to his own account,
"either forgot his request of the poems, or perhaps not
having time to have them copied, deferred complying till
my return."  It is not very apparent what right he could
claim to make copies of the poems.  Possibly the idea
was an after-thought; for he adds: "I protest I do not
remember which was the case; and yet, though in a
cause of so little importance, I will not utter a syllable of
which I am not positively certain."

*Waking from the dream of a lifetime.*

To Walpole it was, indeed, a matter of the utmost insignificance.  But to Chatterton it involved a harsh waking
from the dream of a lifetime.  To Paris, accordingly,
Walpole went; spent six weeks among the gaieties of
that brilliant capital; and on his return found on his
table the following spirited, but, as it appeared to him,
"singularly impertinent letter":—

"SIR,—I cannot reconcile your behaviour with the notions I
once entertained of you.  I think myself injured, sir; and did you
not know my circumstances, you would not dare to treat me thus.
I have sent twice for a copy of the manuscripts;—no answer from
you.  An explanation or excuse for your silence would oblige

                                          "THOMAS CHATTERTON.
"July 24th" [1769].

Flinging into the fire a half-written reply, replete with

good advice to "the wrong-headed young man," Walpole packed up the poems and letters; sent them to Chatterton's address; and thought no more of him, till, a year and a half later, at the Royal Academy's dinner, he heard his name mentioned by Goldsmith, with enthusiastic references to the treasures of ancient poetry he had brought to light; and then learned that their author had come to London; struggled to maintain himself with his pen; and failing, had perished by his own hand.

Such, concisely, are the facts of Chatterton's appeal and Walpole's response. Here, assuredly, was no modern Canynge for the true Rowley of his day. In his vindication he thus sets forth his "abilities in the character of a Mæcenas. My fortune is private and moderate; my situation more private; my interest, none. I was neither born to wealth, nor to accumulate it. I have indulged a taste for expensive baubles, with little attention to economy. It did not become me to give myself airs of protection; and, though it might not be generous, I have been less fond of the company of authors than of their works."

Vain and selfish as Walpole undoubtedly was; a fastidious trifler, incapable of any very generous impulse: he has been hardly dealt with in the matter of Chatterton. He never saw the boy; and the mode of introduction resorted to might have failed with better men. To have sent to the author of the "Castle of Otranto" the chorus from "Goddwyn," the "Storie of Canynge," or the "Tragedy of Ælla," as professed antiques, resting them on their own merits, would have fairly tested both his generosity and taste. But to obtrude on the virtuoso's special domain with spurious anecdotes of apocryphal artists was calculated to excite reasonable indignation in one who at best held the professional author in contempt. What poems were actually sent we have no means of determining; but enough is known to show that in them at least the appeal to the man of taste was legitimate; for Walpole acknowledged that they breathed such a spirit of poetry as excited his interest. Had the un-

CHAP. IX.

*Walpole thinks no more of him.*

*No modern Canynge found.*

*True estimate of Walpole's conduct.*

*Legitimate appeal to his taste.*

known correspondent proved to be some lettered patrician sporting with the Muses and their patrons in cowl and mask, the "imposture" would probably have seemed venial enough ; and might have ended in an amicable truce, sealed by the printing of the very *corpus delicti* at the Strawberry Hill Press, for the delectation or bewilderment of the whole antiquarian brotherhood.  But what claim could a mere attorney's clerk, however gifted, have on the forbearance or generosity of the noble patron of letters, who shrunk from the contamination of any supposed fellowship, as an author, with such contemporaries as Johnson or Goldsmith ?[1]  So he vindicated himself with supreme complacency, though somewhat inconsistently with previous professions, in this wise : " I should have been blameable to his mother and society if I had seduced an apprentice from his master to marry him to the Nine Muses ; and I should have encouraged a propensity to forgery, which is not the talent most wanting culture in the present age.  All of the house of forgery are relations ; and though it is just to Chatterton's memory to say that his poverty never made him claim kindred with the richest or most enriching branches, yet his ingenuity in counterfeiting styles, and I believe hands, might easily have led him to those more facile imitations of prose : promissory notes."[2]



Fortunate would it have been for Walpole had he, resisting the promptings of wounded vanity, left the

[1] " I have no thirst to know my contemporaries, from the absurd bombast of Dr. Johnson, down to the silly Dr. Goldsmith."— Letters (to Rev. W. Cole), vol. v. p. 458.  " Goldsmith was an idiot, with once or twice a fit of parts," is his remark to Mason.— Ibid. vol. vi. p. 379.  Again he writes Cole, " You know I shun authors, and would never have been one myself, if it obliged me to keep such bad company."

[2] In his private communications Walpole was less tender of the boy's memory.  To Mason he writes, July 24th, 1778 : " You know how gently I treated him.  He was a consummate villain, and had gone enormous lengths before he destroyed himself. . . . He was an instance that a complete genius and a complete rogue can be formed before a man is of age."—Walpole's Letters, vol. vii. p. 102.

blundering misstatements of Barrett's History unchallenged, and trusted to silence for his best vindication. The world at large might have acquitted him ; for he is a fitter object of pity than of blame. He affected to aim at a life of tranquil obscurity; but he was envious of the reputation of others, and greedy of fame. He toiled with unwearying forethought, to concoct a series of gay and sprightly letters, the supposed offspring of unpremeditated, friendly intercourse. Anecdote, court-gossip, wit, piquant scandal, and lively epigram, were laboriously accumulated as the raw material out of which he constructed incomparable impromptus, designed apparently for none othèr than the eye of a friend :—of Mr. Montague, or Lord Hertford, or Sir Horace Mann ; —but in reality finished compositions, baited for the palate of the fashionable world. They are, in truth, greater frauds than either " The Castle of Otranto " or the Rowley romance.

To this literary sybarite ; this laborious trifler, secretly hungering and toiling for praise ; was offered the chance of such fame as the noblest might envy, and he cast it from him with ill-disguised contempt. A boy of sixteen sent him poems : such marvellous " forgeries " that, with one exception, he admits, " I do not believe there ever existed so masterly a genius." He informed him of his youth, his dependent position, and his ambitious aspirations. Walpole owns that though he " had no doubt of his impositions,"—that is, fully believed they were his own compositions,—" such a spirit of poetry breathed in his coinage as interested me for him ;" and so he gave him good advice ; wrote him as tenderly as if he had been his guardian ; and " told him when he should have made a fortune," he might then turn poet if he pleased ! [1]

---

[1] Walpole was given to self-vindications, being vain and touchy. In one of those defences he tells us, when he was about nineteen, his father gave him the patent place of Usher of the Exchequer, then reckoned worth 900*l.* It was by and by shown to be worth 4,200*l.* Another nice sinecure place of Inspector of the Imports

Did ever dallier in the vestibule of "Fame's proud temple" fling away such laurels? With what a tender spirit of appreciative criticism would the reader have turned to the slightest trivialities of his pen; what a rare brilliancy would have centred on his "Historic Doubts;" his "Castle of Otranto;" his "Letters," and "Anecdotes;" even his "Catalogue of Royal and Noble Authors:" had these appeared as the literary pastimes of him who was privileged to rescue from poverty and neglect one of the most remarkable geniuses of his age! But, with callous insensitiveness, he repeatedly asserts the worth of the jewel he flung aside. To Mason —in the midst of coarse vituperation,—he writes of his "almost incredible genius," of "the amazing prodigy of his producing" the antique poems as "a larger miracle" than if the ancient Rowley had anticipated the style of modern poetry; and again, to the Countess of Ossory: "As for Chatterton, he was a gigantic genius, and might have soared I know not whither." Yet, in his public



defence, he draws strange comfort from the conviction "that premature genius is seldom equally great in its meridian;" and with a perverse confusion of ideas, only too characteristic of Chatterton's defamers, he exclaims: "Upon the whole, I cannot agree that Chatterton's premature fate has defrauded the world of anything half so extraordinary as the miracles he wrought in almost childhood. Had he lived longer, ample proofs of his forgeries, which proofs he destroyed in his rage, might have been preserved; and instead of the posthumous glory of puzzling the learned world, his name might now



be only recorded as that of an arch impostor;"—and all this from one who had himself worn the literary mask!

and Exports,—also got before he was of age,—was afterwards exchanged for what he calls "two other little patent places in the Exchequer, called Comptroller of the Pipe and Clerk of the Estreats." These were followed by other sinecures, bequests, and inheritances. Altogether, Walpole had no need to put aside such Muses as he dallied with, till "he should have made a fortune."

> " Great men may jest with saints; 'tis wit in them,
> But in the less foul profanation."

It is obviously in this spirit that Walpole bandies such phrases as imposition, fraud, forgery. He resented the assumption of antiquarian and literary tastes by the poor widow's son as an impertinence. "True Antiquaries," as he said, "would not taste a genius, if they thought it a contemporary;" and especially an unheard-of plebeian. "Oh ye who honour the name of Man," wrote the indignant Coleridge, "rejoice that this Walpole is called a Lord."

It is not to be doubted that Chatterton bitterly felt this defeat of long-cherished hopes. He resented the contumelious rejection of his advances to the wealthy patrician; without recognising in any degree how much of the blame attached to himself. His pride revolted at the change of tone, from the courtesy of an equal to that of a condescending retailer of commonplace advice; and, with even greater ire than was justified by the facts, —could he have known them,—he brooded over the discourtesy with which his unanswered letter and poems had been returned. To Mr. Catcott he affirmed that Walpole despised him from the time he made known to him his indigent circumstances; and he not only meditated, but in some degree carried out his purpose of retaliation.

Recovering his equanimity, he described the correspondence, and its results, in this complacent fashion, to his relative Mr. Stephens of Salisbury: "Having some curious anecdotes of paintings and painters, I sent them to Mr. Walpole, author of the 'Anecdotes of Painting,' 'Historic Doubts,' and other pieces well known in the learned world. His answer I make bold to send you. Hence I began a literary correspondence, which ended as most such do. I differed with him in the age of a MS. He insists on his superior talents, which is no proof of that superiority. We possibly may publicly engage in one of the periodical publications; though I know

CHAP. IX.

*Impertinent plebeian assumption.*

*Chatterton's keen resentment of defeat.*

*Assumption of philosophic equanimity.*

not who will give the onset." The literary duel, here contemplated, never came off; but opportunities were not wanting on which he could become the assailant. He took his revenge while living; he has had it far more effectually since the world has learned, too late, how slight an effort on Walpole's part might have preserved the aspiring boy who appealed to him in vain.

Chatterton never missed his opportunity of having a fling at the man of taste. To the *Middlesex Journal* he contributed, under the signature of "Decimus," ironical criticisms on an imaginary exhibition of sign paintings, suggested by the proceedings of the Royal Academy, then in its infancy. The allusions are chiefly political. But in the second day's exhibition is No. 12, "A piece of modern antiquity by Horace Walpole. This is no other than a striking portrait of the facetious Mrs. Clive. Horace, finding it too large to be introduced in his next edition of *Virtû*, has returned it on the town." A similar satirical allusion, repeated in his "Advice," has been amusingly mistaken for a reference to Lord Clive, and so produced in proof that Chatterton repented of his assaults on Walpole. It serves, on the contrary, to show how much of the point of his ephemeral satires is lost to the modern reader. Maria R——, of Bristol—no doubt that "female Machiavel, Miss Rumsey," repeatedly referred to in his letters,—is reminded, at the beginning of a new year, how rapidly youth and beauty fade; and the poet thus proceeds :—

> " Yet when that bloom and dancing fire
> In silvered reverence shall expire,
> 　Aged, wrinkled, and defaced ;
> To keep one lover's flame alive
> Requires the genius of a Clive,
> 　With Walpole's mental taste ! "

The *Town and Country Magazine* for 1769 supplies the interpretation of what was, no doubt, intelligible enough to all readers then. The celebrated comic actress, Mrs. Clive, withdrew from the stage that year, after a successful career, begun in 1730 : speaking her farewell in an epilogue written for her by Walpole.[1]  The suggestive " Tête-à-Tête " of the December number is illustrated with the portraits of the " Baron Otranto " and the retired actress, under the name of Mrs. Heidel-burgh,—the discarded " Antiquity " by and by found unsuitable for his next edition of *Virtû*.  For at the very time that Walpole was " undeceiving " Chatterton about his being " a person of any interest," he was providing a house for the actress at Strawberry Hill, which he calls in some of his letters " Cliveden."  This, it will be seen, furnishes an explanation more in accordance with the satirist's humour, than the blunder of Lord Orford's later champions, who—crediting him with penitence for wrong done to the Man of Virtu,—fancied Chatterton had likened his Mæcenas to the hero of Plassey, when he was only thinking of Kitty Clive !

Chatterton was not of a temperament to yield readily to such a change of feeling, even had any motive existed to induce it.  He returns to the assault, in his Burletta of " The Woman of Spirit ; " one of the slighter dra-matic productions of his brief London career.  Lady Tempest—who has so far condescended to forget her quality as to marry " such a tautology of nothing " as Mr. Councillor Latitat—scornfully complains that, this very morning, he has " invited all his antiquated friends, Lord Rust, Horatio Trefoil, Colonel Trajedus, Professor Vase, and Counterfeit the Jew, to sit upon a brass half-penny, which being a little worn, they agreed *nem. con.* to be an Otho ! "  Again in " The Polite Advertiser," contributed to the *Town and Country Magazine* of July 1770," by Sir Butterfly Feather," the first item reveals the same pen.  " Whereas a young fellow, whom I have great reason to imagine is either a linen-draper or haber-dasher, has had the assurance to tie himself to an unac-countable long sword, thought by Horatio Otranto, the great Antiquary, to be three inches longer than the ever-

[1] The farewell epilogue was spoken, April 24th, 1769, and is printed in *The Town and Country Magazine* of the same month, p. 218.

Chap. IX.

*Sir Stentor Ranger and the Baron.*

*The antique dog-kennel.*

*An antiquarian prize.*

memorable one of the famous Earl of Salisbury : this is to inform him that, unless he can wear it without fisting it in the clumsy manner he does, it shall be taken from him."

But the keenest assault of Chatterton's trenchant satire occurs in another of his contributions to the *Town and Country Magazine* entitled " The Memoirs of a Sad Dog." Sir Stentor Ranger, the Rake's brother-in-law, a sporting knight who has converted an ancient Abbey into his stable, and turned the Chapel into a dog-kennel, "had many curious visitors, on account of his ancient painted glass windows : among the rest was the redoubted Baron Otranto, who has spent his whole life in conjectures." After dinner, and some talk, at cross purposes, between the sporting knight and his antiquarian guest, they adjourn to the antique dog-kennel. " The Baron found many things worthy his notice in the ruinated chapel ; but the Knight was so full of the praises of his harriers, that the Antiquary had not opportunity to form one conjecture. After looking round the chapel for some moveable piece, of age, on which he might employ his speculative talents, to the eternal honour of his judgment, he pitched upon a stone which had no antiquity at all ; and, transported with his fancied prize, placed it upon his head, and bore it triumphantly to his chamber, desiring the Knight to give him no disturbance the next day, as he intended to devote it to the service of futurity.

" This important piece of stone had, by the huntsman, been sacrilegiously stolen from the neighbouring churchyard, and employed, with others, to stop up a breach in the kennel, through which the adventurous Jowler had squeezed his lank carcase. Nothing can escape the clutches of curiosity. The letters being ill cut, had an appearance of something Gothic ; and the Baron was so far gone in this Quixotism of literature, that at the first glance he determined them to be of the third Runic alphabet of Wormius. The original inscription was : ' James Hicks lieth here, with Hester his wife.' The broken stone is here represented :—

H·I·C·K·S · L · · ·

R·E · · · · · ·

" The Baron having turned over Camden, Dugdale, Leyland, and Weever, at last determined it to be: *Hic jacet corpus Kenelmæ Sancto Legero; requiescat*, &c., &c. What confirmed him in the above reading, and made it impossible for him to be mistaken, was, that a great man of the name of Sancto Legero had been buried in the country about five hundred years ago.

" Elated with the happy discovery, the Baron had an elegant engraving of the curiosity executed, and presented it to the Society of Antiquaries, who look upon it as one of the most important discoveries which have been made since the great Dr. Trefoil found out that the word *kine* came from the Saxon *cowine*."



Walpole undoubtedly winced under the sarcasms of his assailant; though in one of his letters to the Rev. William Cole he disclaims all feeling in reference to the attack " under the title of Baron of Otranto, which is written with humour. I must," he adds, " have been the sensitive plant, if anything in that character had hurt me !" and then, in the very next sentence, he betrays the vindictive sensitive plant that he really was, by exclaiming: " Think of that young rascal's note, summing up his gains and losses by writing for and against Beckford. . . . There was a lad of too nice honour to be guilty of a forgery !"



The fancy that Horace Walpole was to prove the Mæcenas of the poet had thus been dissipated beyond recall. Chatterton had learned a hard lesson of world's experience, which, unhappily, brought with it none of the sweet uses of adversity. One can see in stray allusions to his plans and hopes, that he had been looking earnestly into the uncertain future, revolving many schemes for emancipation, and falling back on his old dream of a Canynge worthy of the true Rowley; and now came this harsh awakening to the truth that the battle of life had to be fought by himself, as by many another less gifted, without the aid of patronage or help from without. His pride remained unsubdued, and his will resolute as ever; but his moral nature had suffered a shock only too painfully traceable in the brief months of his fevered life that remained. It is to this later period, as we shall find, that his bitter personal satires, and his irreverent assaults on everything most sacred, belong.

# CHAPTER X.

## THE SATIRIST.



AMONG those who influenced Chatterton, and extended some friendly aid to the boy towards the close of his career, the Rev. Alexander Catcott, brother of the more notable pewterer, claims special notice. Their father has been already referred to as master of the Grammar School; but he was also the author of a Latin treatise, published in 1738, on the Hutchinsonian philosophy, and its interpretations of the Mosaic Creation. The book, with its mystical tabulæ of planetary diagrams, elucidated with the help of Hebrew and Latin formulæ, is a specimen of darkening counsel by words without knowledge, which even its later editor, Mr. Maxwell, admits to be " confused, extremely coarse, and not always intelligible."[1]  But his son, as was natural, had formed a much higher estimate of the work, and strove to follow in his father's footsteps, with all the advantages that learning and science could supply. He was a man of very different character from his brother; a clergyman and a scholar, with scientific tastes and literary aspirations to which he still owes some remembrance. But when, ere long, he and his *protégé* came into collision, it was not without some of the verisimilitude which gives the sting to satire that Chatterton described him as :—



> " By birth to prejudice and whim allied,
> And heavy with hereditary pride."

[1] The Ancient Principles of the True and Sacred Philosophy, &c. p. 120.

Mr. Catcott was presented to the vicarage of Temple Church, Bristol, the same year in which Chatterton left Colston's Hospital; and one of his minor poems helps us to trace their mutual relations during the poet's last year in Bristol. The Vicar had not been left in ignorance of the treasures his brother was accumulating from the supposed spoils of Redcliffe Church. But his faith in his brother's judgment in such matters, and his estimate of the worth of the most genuine poetical treasures, were on a par. According to a contemporary, "he considered poetry to have an idle, if not an evil tendency; and was so far from regarding the Rowley specimens of antiquity with an eye of pleasure or curiosity, that he condemned his brother for misspending his time in attending to them."[1] He parted with the greater part of his own library, after a time, reserving only books of divinity and the whole Hutchinsonian controversy; but subsequently finding among the reserved volumes a copy of Barclay's "Ship of Fools," he transferred it to the kitchen for use as waste paper.

The direction of the Vicar's tastes lay in all respects far apart from any of Chatterton's favourite pursuits. He is spoken of as one of the best Hebrew scholars of his day. But his chief fame rests on certain theophilo-sophical speculations, in which he strove, with the combined aid of science and theology, to solve the problems of Creation and the Deluge. So early as 1750, he had explored the neighbouring caves of Banwell,[2] and formed an interesting palæontological collection, still preserved in the Bristol City Library. A writer in the *Town and Country Magazine*, after referring to his collection of minerals and fossils, says: "If you pay him a visit, he conducts you into his best parlour, where are deposited the above valuable curiosities. After he has explained the beauty and remarkableness of each class, the place where they were found, as also how they came into his possession, he asks you, with a look of infinite satis-

---

[1] MSS. Bristol City Library.
[2] In Somersetshire, about sixteen miles from Bristol.

faction, whether all those things do not plainly prove a deluge?"[1]

In 1761, when Chatterton was still a child, Mr. Catcott published his "Treatise on the Deluge and Structure of the Earth," and was busy on a new and enlarged edition, which appeared in 1768, when he first came in contact with the poet. According to Warton, Chatterton owed to him an introduction to the old library at Bristol, with its rare and otherwise inaccessible books; and if, while conferring so welcome a service, he had been capable of sympathising with the poet in his favourite pursuits, his moral influence might have proved invaluable. Due care had doubtless been taken by Mr. Colston's trustees to see that Chatterton was apprenticed to a sound Churchman, according to the pattern of that eighteenth century. But while Mr. Lambert exacted the most rigid conformity to house and office hours, he gave himself no further concern about the boy; and when the weather was favourable, his Sundays appear to have been devoted frequently to long country rambles. But early training had familiarized him with the services of the Church; and his satirical criticisms on preaching, reading, and Church music, suffice at least to show that he did not wholly abandon public worship when left to his own choice. But from repeated allusions, in his satires, it is obvious that, in spite of all the fond associations of Redcliffe Church, its preacher and preaching were alike distasteful to him;[2] and the appointment of Mr. Catcott to the vicarage of the adjoining parish in 1767, probably helped, ere long, to induce his withdrawal from it.

[1] Town and Country Magazine, June 1771, p. 316.

[2] Somewhat may be learned of the Rev. Dr. Broughton, from his virtues and preferments, as set forth on his marble tablet in Redcliffe Church. "He was a profound and elegant scholar; and successfully employed his talents to the support of the Protestant establishment,"—successfully in this respect at least, as appears: he was Rector of St. Andrew's, Holborn, and of Stepington, Herts, Prebendary of Salisbury Cathedral, and Vicar of Bedminster, with the Chapelries of Mary Redcliffe, St. Thomas, and Abbot's Leigh annexed. Evidently a buttress and pillar of the Church.

The intercourse between Chatterton and the new Vicar must, for some brief period, have been both friendly and confidential. According to his own account he had access when he pleased to the parson's study;[1] and Mr. Catcott stated that, having had a conversation with him one evening, he traced its very substance in a piece produced some time after as Rowley's.[2] Whether, therefore, the pleasure of holding intercourse with a man of cultivated intellect, the novelty of the Vicar's Mosaic interpretations, or gratitude for personal attentions, first attracted the boy, he evidently yielded himself for a time unreservedly to his influence. Temple Church is on the Somersetshire side of the Avon, at no great distance from Mrs. Chatterton's house. Thither, on a Sunday morning, Chatterton might occasionally be seen wending his way towards the hour of morning service. For a time curiosity was excited, and an interest awakened in the ingenious speculations of the preacher. But the Vicar had to listen ere long, in his study, to arguments challenging his teachings from the pulpit; and so, as numerous allusions in Chatterton's satires show, the disciple came into collision with his teacher.



The whole subject of cosmical and diluvial geology, alike in its theological and scientific aspects, has undergone so great a revolution, that the ablest treatises of the last century are mainly interesting now as literary curiosities. But in 1768, the Bristol Vicar honestly maintained his long-exploded diluvian theories as a part of revelation. He dogmatized; the sharp-witted boy detected the fallacies in his argument; and on his own productions being subjected to critical censure, he sat down and penned a rhyming epistle to his censor, dated December 6th, 1760, beginning thus :—



> "What strange infatuations rule mankind !
> How narrow are our prospects, how confined !
> With universal vanity possessed,
> We fondly think our own ideas best ;
> Our tottering arguments are ever strong ;
> We're always self-sufficient in the wrong."

---

[1] Gent. Mag. N. S. vol. x. p. 604.　　[2] Gregory's Life, p. 127.

In reviewing the productions of Chatterton's satirical muse, it must not be overlooked that the best of them are hasty effusions, expressing the mere feeling of the moment, rather than any settled convictions. The most of them were neither published, nor designed for publication by their author; but circulated in manuscript among his own circle, in versions modified to suit individual tastes. His "Kew Gardens," "Whore of Babylon," and "Exhibition," have many lines in common. Of the first two, indeed, more than half of each differs from the other only in occasional phrases.[1] In such productions he had no thought of fame. They rank with the loose after-dinner gossip or scandal, rather than with the earnest thoughts, of ordinary men; and their preservation has been due to no regard for Chatterton's good name.

In the very freest fashion of this satirical vein, Chatterton penned his "Epistle to Rev. Mr. Catcott." After an introductory review of the pride and dogmatism of philosophic sages in general, and a glance in passing at various minor objects of animadversion, the reverend geologist is thus pictured in the midst of his cabinets of minerals and fossils, demonstrating, with the aid of his philosophical apparatus, the six days' work of creation, and solving every difficulty in the universe to an assembly of "wondering cits" and fair philosophers :—

> "The ladies are quite ravished as he tells
> The short adventures of the pretty shells.
> Miss Biddy sickens to indulge her touch ;
> Madame, more prudent, thinks 'twould seem too much.
> The doors fly open, instantly he draws
> The spary lode, mid wonders of applause ;
> The full-dressed lady sees with envying eye
> The sparkle of her diamond pendants die ;

---

[1] "Kew Gardens" as "for the first time printed entire," by Mr. Dix, consists of 1,092 lines: far from entire in this that asterisks are substituted even for the most notorious names, so as to render much of it meaningless. But of the 1,092 lines nearly 500 consecutively appear in a more perfect condition in "The Whore of Babylon," printed nearly forty years before. Other lines and passages occur in a different order; and only about 100 lines are really new.

> Sage natural philosophers adore
> The fossil whimseys of the numerous store.
> But see ! the purple stream begins to play,
> To show how fountains climb the hilly way.
> Hark· what a murmur echoes thro' the throng !
> Gods !   That the pretty trifle should be wrong !
> Experience in the voice of Reason tells
> Above its surface water never swells.
>
> Where is the priestly soul of Catcott now ?
> See what a triumph sits upon his brow !
> And can the poor applause of things like these,
> Whose souls and sentiments are all disease,
> Raise little triumphs in a man like you,
> Catcott, the foremost of the judging few ?
> So at Llewellin's your great brother sits,
> The laughter of his tributary wits ;
> Ruling the noisy multitude with ease ;  ·
> Empties his pint, and sputters his decrees."



So far, however imprudent the satire might be, it is not only spirited but legitimate enough ; and when we turn to more critical passages, the judgment of modern science would be on the side of the poet.   But unhappily the science was inextricably interwoven with the theology of the divine ; and more earnest disputants have failed to discriminate between the truths of inspiration and the blundering of its interpreters.   After another flash of satirical licence, he thus ironically advises :—



> " Confute with candour, where you can confute ;
> Reason and arrogance but poorly suit.
> Yourself may fall before some abler pen,
> Infallibility is not for men.
> With modest diffidence new schemes indite ;
> Be not too positive, tho' in the right.
> Tho' pointed fingers mark the man of fame,
> And literary grocers chaunt your name ;
> Though in each tailor's bookcase Catcott shi
> With ornamental flowers and gilded lines ;
> Tho' youthful ladies, who by instinct scan
> The natural philosophy of man,
> Can every reason of your work repeat,
> As sands in Africa retain the heat ;
> Yet check your flowing pride——"

And so the critical censor proceeds to deal with the theory of a universal diluvian dissolution and reconstruction of matter; of aërial vortices propelling the planets in their spheres; and the like teachings of long-forgotten Hutchinsonian philosophy.   He then adds:—

*Chap. X.*

*Teachings of Hutchinsonian philosophy.*

> "'Twas the Eternal's fiat, you reply;
> And who will give Eternity the lie?
> I own the awful truth that God made all;
> And by His fiat worlds and systems fall.
> But study Nature: not an atom there
> Will, unassisted by her powers, appear;
> The fiat, without agents, is at best
> For priestcraft, or for ignorance, a vest."

Clayfield is quoted as censuring the theologian, and demonstrating his theory untrue; and then Moses is confounded with his interpreters, and the sacred Scriptures are handled with irreverent scepticism.   We thus obtain a clue to the period when Chatterton first gave expression to sceptical doubts.   The death of his early friend and adviser, Phillips, occurred, there can be little doubt, in the autumn of 1769; and his introduction to Mr. Clayfield followed on that event, to which indeed it appears to have been mainly due.   With the latter he appears to have discussed the speculations of Mr. Catcott, and to have received encouragement in his antagonism to the new philosophy.

*Irreverent scepticism.*

For the licence of his poetical effusions, so far as their personal satire is concerned, considerable allowance must be made in view of the prevailing style of the period.   Chatterton evidently considered it perfectly compatible with a renewal of friendly relations with the victims of his saucy wit: with whom he contended on terms of perfect equality, while in their estimation he appeared only as a presumptuous boy.   He meant no more than a piece of sportive retaliation for some free criticism of the Vicar on his own writings; and so he thus ironically schools his muse into more becoming courses:—

*Style of the period.*

> " Restrain, O Muse, thy unaccomplished lines;
> Fling not thy saucy satire at divines ;—
> This single truth thy brother bards must tell,
> Thou hast one excellence, of railing well.
> But disputations are befitting those
> Who settle Hebrew points, and scold in prose."

*Plea of the satirist.*

In a postscript, dated December 20th, 1769, he thus seriously disavows the maintenance of the extreme opinions set forth in his satire, and invites a renewal of friendly relations. " Mr. Catcott will be pleased to observe that I admire many things in his learned remarks. This poem is an innocent effort of poetical vengeance, as Mr. Catcott has done me the honour to criticise my trifles. I have taken great poetical liberties, and what I dislike in verse probably deserves my approbation in the plain prose of truth." The "Epistle," therefore, was really sent to the Vicar; and until published long after its author's death,—as the postscript shows,—existed only in the copy he received. We cannot indeed imagine he thought it worth preserving. But probably it was handed to his brother, in confirmation of opinions freely expressed as to his graceless protégé, and the less sensitive pewterer added the satire to his literary hoard.

*Thoughtless effusions of his pen.*

Chatterton, it is obvious, had no malicious design. In the latest piece of composition penned by him before leaving Bristol, we shall find him apologizing to the two brothers for such fruits of his "unlucky way of raillery, when the strong fit of satire is upon him." With all the inexperienced rashness of youth, he gave full play to the dangerous weapon he could handle so cleverly; and he fancied his verses would be laughed at and forgotten. It is accordingly within three days after the above postscript was penned, that we find him dating his "Copernican System," the history of which is thus interestingly associated with the Temple Church and the Vicar's

*The Copernican system.*

sermons. Mr. Corser, who claimed to have been one of Chatterton's intimate acquaintances, well remembered meeting him one Sunday morning, towards the close, as

is manifest, of his last year in Bristol, "at the gate of
Temple Church, when the bells were chiming for service.
There being yet some time to spare before the prayers
commenced, Chatterton proposed their taking a walk
together in the churchyard, which was then open to the
public, and laid out like a garden. 'Come,' said he,
'I want to read you something I have just written;' and
when arrived at a secluded spot, he read to Mr. Corser a
treatise on astronomy, and stated that he had not yet
finished it, but that he intended to make it the subject
of a poem."[1]   It appeared, accordingly, in the last number of the *Town and Country Magazine* of 1769, with
the date, "Bristol, Dec. 23d," and his favourite signature,
D. B.[2]

Up to the date of this interview, he had probably
maintained friendly intercourse with the Vicar, and
listened with an interest in no degree diminished by the
doubts they suggested, to his geological speculations, and
the demonstrations of a system of the universe in harmony with his Hutchinsonian theology.   Hence this
interesting link between the labours of the preacher and
the poet.   Following the planets in their order, the earth
is thus described on her zodiacal path :—

> "More distant still, our globe terraqueous turns,
> Nor chills intense, nor fiercly heated burns;
> Around her rolls the lunar orb of light,
> Trailing her silver glories through the night.
> On the Earth's orbit see the various signs :
> Mark where the Sun, our year completing, shines;
> First the bright Ram his languid ray improves;
> Next, glaring watery, through the Bull he moves;
> The amorous Twins admit his genial ray;
> Now burning, through the Crab he takes his way;
> The Lion, flaming, bears the Solar power;
> The Virgin faints beneath the sultry shower;
> Now the just Ballance weights his equal force,
> The slimy Serpent swelters in his course,

---

[1] Dix's Life, p. 63.
[2] Town and Country Magazine 1769, p. 666.

> The sabled Archer clouds his languid face,
> The Goat with tempest urges on his race;
> Now in the Water his faint beams appear,
> And the cold Fishes end the circling year."

*Production of his astronomical poem.*

This poem was already in hand before the " Epistle " was despatched to the Vicar, if not indeed before it was written. For that piece of satirical retaliation bears all the marks of one of those hasty effusions, in which, scorning Bristol's " narrow notions " of prudence, he says of himself :—

> " When raving in the lunacy of ink,
> I catch my pen and publish what I think." [1]

*Traces of more earnest thought.*

But having thus had his critical revenge, his equanimity was restored; he could even recall with approval some of the Vicar's favourite teachings; and, under the influence of more earnest thoughts, honestly close with this couplet :—

> " These are Thy wondrous works, First Source of good,
> Now more admired in being understood."

It evidently did not occur to Chatterton that his audacious retort need cause any estrangement between him and Mr. Catcott. But less sensitive men would have resented such unscrupulous ridicule : and, as Chatterton added, in closing his postscript, " I am indifferent in all things ; I value neither the praise nor the censure of the multitude ;" so, on finding all friendly relations at an end, he resumed the bitter vein, and proceeded to still less " innocent " forms of poetical vengeance. He apparently contemplated an elaborate satire, after the model of Churchill's unsparing assaults on political and personal antagonists ; as both the " Whore of Babylon," and the " Exhibition," are marked as " Book the First ;" and in each he works up old materials, and abruptly terminates an incompleted design.

*Final breach with the Vicar.*

The " Exhibition " no doubt belongs to the latest

---

[1] Kew Gardens.

months of Chatterton's Bristol career. It has never been published; and it would have been well had it perished, with its evidence that youthful purity had been sullied, and the precocious boy was only too conversant with forbidden things. The copy in the Bristol Library bears date May 1st, 1770—a few days after he reached London,—when we find him also copying his " Kew Gardens," in order to transmit it to his friend Cary. It is entitled "The Exhibition; a personal satyr;" and fully merits its claim to personality in its satirical sketches. Amongst others, the Temple Vicar is dealt with in terms still freer than in the Epistle addressed to himself.



> " This truth, this mighty truth,—if truth can shine
> In the smooth polish of a laboured line,—
> Catcott by sad experience testifies ;
> And who shall tell a sabled priest he lies?
> Bred to the juggling of the specious band
> Predestinated to adorn the land,
> The selfish Catcott ripened to a priest,
> And wore the sable livery of the Beast.
> By birth to prejudice and whim allied,
> And heavy with hereditary pride,
> He modelled pleasure by a fossil rule
> And spent his youth to prove himself a fool;
> Buried existence in a lengthened cave,
> And lost in dreams whatever nature gave."

The parson's study was now finally closed on the reprobate. If he held poetry in little esteem before, it was still less likely to win his favour now. A contemporary, writing four years after his death, says, " Mr. George Catcott believes, had his brother survived him, and these (the Rowley Poems) had fallen into his hands before their publication, that he would have destroyed them."[1] With such a Mentor, collision was, sooner or later, inevitable ; but now, unhappily, the whole clerical order became the objects of his indiscriminate raillery, including Bishop Newton, the editor of Milton, and author of a "Dissertation on the Prophecies," against



---

[1] MSS. Bristol Library, dated 30th March, 1783.

*Apprentice-
ship
drawing
to a close.*

whom "The Whore of Babylon" is chiefly directed, in so far as it differs from "Kew Gardens."

Chatterton's apprenticeship to Mr. Lambert was now drawing towards its abrupt close. After a few more months, he was to start on a course of his own choice. Already we see him claiming equality with the most learned among his critics, and asserting his independence by the bold avowal of opinions calculated to place him in antagonism with the wiser and better class of those who had hitherto admitted him to their society. No fitter opportunity therefore will occur for the consideration of his peculiar mental and moral characteristics.

*The judg-
ment of
posterity on
poets.*

Poets have not in general had to complain of the hard judgment of posterity on their personal failings, whatever may have been the measure meted out to them by contemporaries. Much has been forgiven to Dryden and the lesser wits of the Restoration era; to Ottway, Swift, Gay, Smollett, and even to Savage: in the licence of their lives, or of their pens. But to Chatterton, the very harshest judgment of unappreciating and vindictive contemporaries has been reechoed for a century over his grave. True poets, indeed, have sung the dirge of " The sleepless Soul that perished in his pride ;" but still in prose has been reiterated the echoes of his first traducers.

*Injustice
done to
Chatterton.*

He has had every juvenile folly and indiscretion aggravated ; every false surmise reiterated, as though it were an established truth; and acts in his strange literary career, which he shares in common with Walpole, Percy, Surtees, and Scott, have been spoken of in terms that would be resented as harsh, if applied to Bertram or Macpherson, not to mention Ireland. He is referred to, even by Professor Masson, as dogged, sullen, malicious ; while from the pages of Walpole, Chalmers, Warton, and other critics,—culminating in our own day in the scholarly

*Harsh
epithets
applied.*

librarian of a late Archbishop of Canterbury,—we glean such choice epithets as rogue, swindler, unprincipled impostor, liar, and forger ; a consummate villain, an unprincipled libertine, depraved in mind and profligate in morals ; one, in fact, " whose death was of little consequence, since he could not long have escaped hanging !"[1]



Much of this stupid slander is traceable to the wounded vanity of Bristol patrons; and still more, to the vindictive ire of lettered antiquaries who were puzzled or duped by the boy's spurious antiques. The style of literary discussion in the eighteenth century partook of the bitterness of its satire; and irritated controversialists, convicted of credulity and blundering, took their revenge in maligning the author, over whose works they disputed. Neither party had the poet's reputation in view. Indeed, of those who asserted his authorship of the Rowley Poems, the majority fancied that this was tantamount to establishing their worthlessness. Hence opprobrious epithets circulated unchallenged, till such a confusion of ideas prevailed, that when the author of "The Castle of Otranto," with his own experience in such matters, remarked that "all of the house of forgery are relations;" and spoke of Chatterton's "ingenuity in counterfeiting styles" of imaginary poets of the fifteenth century, as an easy step towards the forging of promissory notes: no one ventured to assert broadly that the creator of the imaginary Rowley and his works had, in that at least, done only what merited applause. It might well be said, in the language of our living laureate :—



> " Wild words wander here and there ;
> God's great gift of speech abused
> Makes thy memory confused—
> But let them rave."

Yet even the stupidest slander does not perpetuate itself without some foundation. If literary forgery were the capital offence, the same gallows should have sufficed for Walpole and Chatterton. But it is not to be overlooked that there are passages in Chatterton's modern prose and verse, and allusions in his letters, which repel



---

[1] Miscellanies, p. 18. Walpole's Vindication; Letters to Mason, Cole, &c. Gent. Mag. N. S. vol. x. p. 133, &c. Maitland, pp. 18, 19, 22, &c. Croft, p. 148, &c. &c.

by their irreverence, and at times by their impurity. In this he only too clearly reflects to us the manners and spirit of that eighteenth century; but no one familiar with the literature of that age can accept it as proof of his systematic profligacy, as has been insinuated, rather than attempted to be proved. Apart from all the profounder elements of interest in a life so brief, and marked by such rare precocity, it has its curious phases as a unique psychological study; and as such, the subserviency of the physical to the intellectual and moral nature of the boy must not be overlooked.



With strange inconsistency the believers in a genuine priest Rowley, resuscitated by Chatterton,—who, according to their theory, had the honesty to disclaim all the glory which he might have appropriated to himself,—have concurred in blackening his moral character, even where they acknowledge his intellectual vigour. Chalmers, and writers of his class, represent him as precocious only in vice. The anonymous editor of his " Miscellanies," with a better appreciation of his intellectual merits, asserts that " his profligacy was, at least, as conspicuous as his abilities ;" while the latest of the Rowleyan school of antiquaries,—having a theory of his own to maintain, which required him to prove that Chatterton suffered no privations in Bristol, made considerable sums of money in London, and never was in want,—acquits him of the charge in this ambiguous fashion : " That he was, in one sense of the word, profligate—that is, that he was a habitual and gross liar, and not restrained by any religious or moral principle from saying or writing that which he knew to be false, for the sake of gain,—is too clear; but that he was profligate as the word is used with reference to sensual immorality, at least in such way as should account for pecuniary distress, I do not believe." [1]





In the same spirit, attempts have been made to give an autobiographic character to passages in some of his slightest contributions to the *Town and Country Magazine,* written after a fashion familiar to readers of

[1] Maitland, p. 47.

the *Tatler* and *Spectator:* in the character of "*Astrea Brockage*," a Bristol boarding-school miss, who boasts that she has read every novel published by Lowndes or Noble; and tells the editor: "I know all the real names of your 'Têtes-à-têtes,' and am very well skilled in deciphering an asterism or dash;" in that of *Maria Friendless*, a frail woman; of *Frances*, a widowed countess who has taken a "false step;" of *Tom Selwood*, the heir of an eccentric country gentleman; and of *Harry Wildfire*, who furnishes a sketch of his own career as a well-born rake, under the title of "Memoirs of a Sad Dog." In more than one of those passages,—such as that of "the redoubted Baron of Otranto," and again of Harry Wildfire, himself, setting up for a man of letters,—unquestionably illustrate points of interest in the life of their author. But beyond this it would be gratuitous folly to go.

The novels of Lowndes and Noble were the impure reading provided for youths of both sexes in that eighteenth century, when Horace Walpole was printing at Strawberry Hill a volume of poems by Lady Temple, some of which could not now be produced without exciting disgust by their indelicacy.[1] Fielding's "Tom Jones" and "Joseph Andrews," Smollett's "Roderick Random," and even his "Peregrine Pickle," then held the place in the family library now filled by Thackeray's and Dickens' writings; and Sir Walter Scott has graphically described the shock with which a venerable lady of his acquaintance made the discovery, on turning over the leaves of one of Mrs. Behn's novels, that she, and all the fashionable world of her youth, habitually read without thought of impropriety, what disgusted her at fourscore.

The *Town and Country Magazine* is no unfair specimen of a periodical of that age. The "Têtes-à-têtes" which the boarding-school miss declares to be no mystery to her, were histories of the current scandal of the day, illustrated by portraits of the real or assumed heroes and heroines. Among these we have already seen "The

1 *Vide* Grenville Correspondence, vol. ii. p. 257.

Baron of Otranto" figuring; possibly with little more justice than other victims of Mrs. Clackitt, of whom Snake says, in "The School for Scandal," "I have more than once traced her causing a tête-à-tête in the *Town and Country Magazine,* when the parties, perhaps, had never seen each other's faces in the course of their lives." To this feature, accordingly, Dr. Maitland refers, in illustration of the "infamy of this publication;" and after describing it in very plain language, as "the principal embellishment and attraction of each number," he adds: "This may be sufficient to enable the reader to form an estimate of the magazine," and, by implication, of its young contributor.[1]   Nothing, on the contrary, could be more misleading.



The *Town and Country Magazine* was brought out in the best style of periodicals of its day; had a large circulation; and, I doubt not, lay unchallenged on many a reputable drawing-room table of that eighteenth century.   The volume most interesting to us in relation to Chatterton,—that of 1769,—apart from the one piece of scandal in each number, would not discredit Sylvanus



Urban's reputation.   It begins with an article "On the State of Europe," next comes a biographical notice of "The late Duke of Newcastle," then follows the "Tête-à-tête" for January, with its Sir E——, Mrs. C——, Sir J—— L——, &c., filling two pages; no doubt piquant enough for the Mrs. Candours and Lady Sneerwells of its day, but obscure enough now.   The next article compares the ancient and modern dress of France and England from the time of the Crusades; and so leads to a letter in the March number, from D. B. of Bristol, show-



ing on the authority of a MS. "written three hundred years ago, by one Rowley, a monk," that "Richardus, abbatte of Seyncte Augustynes, dyd wear a mantelle of scarlette," &c.   So the miscellaneous contents proceed. There are reports of trials and other judicial matters; including the famous "Douglas Cause," and the Great Wilkes' question; accounts of geographical discoveries;

[1] Maitland, p. 48.

notices of local curiosities and antiquities ; reviews of current literature, the drama, and politics ; and along with them, very fairly executed engravings of such notabilities as Alderman Wilkes, Lord Mayor Beckford, Lord Chancellor Camden, the Corsican patriot, Paoli ; and an elaborately executed plate of Garrick reciting his Ode in honour of Shakespeare, at the Stratford Jubilee of that year. Among other illustrations, the reader is attracted by certain political caricatures, carefully executed, and by no means devoid of spirit : the "Brentford Sweepstakes," referring to the famous Middlesex election of the time ; the "Battle of Cornhill," another episode in the grand contest of "Wilkes and Liberty ;" and "The Peace Makers" of 1769 : all full of interest to the readers of a century ago. Woodcuts supply minor illustrations. Mathematical problems are solved with their aid. The apocryphal coats of arms of Keyna, Wessex, &c., accompany a Bristol letter of D. B., on Saxon Heraldry ; and a "wooden portrait" of Samuel Derrick, Esq., late master of the ceremonies at Bath, illustrates certain anecdotes of him which, as will be seen, have a very notable significance in reference to Chatterton. The poetry consists of dramatic prologues and epilogues, odes, elegies, &c.,—some of them, such as an Ode to March, another entitled "Midnight," and a Paraphrase of the First Psalm, of a decidedly religious tone ; and all as chaste as in any periodical of the day. "Amusing and instructive questions" follow, with answers much in the style of our own "Notes and Queries ;" and the whole concludes each month with a summary of foreign and domestic intelligence ; births, marriages, deaths ; prices of gold, grain, and stocks.

To this Miscellany Chatterton contributed during this year, 1769, sixteen pieces in prose and verse. If its editor showed himself ready enough to conform to the licence of the age, these contributions all the more strongly confirm the idea that up to this year, in which the poet was rudely awakened from his dream of literary triumph, his mind remained uncontaminated ; and to its

CHAP. X.

*Engraved illustrations.*

*A Bristol letter of D. B.*

*Chatterton's contributions in prose and verse.*

very close, he published nothing but what consisted with the idea of a mind preoccupied with its own ingenious fancies. None of all those fruits of his versatile industry betrays the slightest idea that he was writing for a licentious periodical. They include his "Ethelgar," "Kenrick," "Cerdick," and other prose poems written on the Ossian model; his papers on Saxon Heraldry and the antiquity of Christmas games; and poems in his most diverse styles, including his "Elinoure and Juga:" not one of which would discredit any modern magazine. But the turning-point in Chatterton's mental development was now reached. For a time, at least, the antique muse was forsaken; and amid the ferment of  one of the most scandalous periods of English political strife, the inexperienced boy enlisted on the popular side, in the rivalries of local and national politics. In such a day, with Wilkes for the hero of the "popular party;" Churchill for his model satirist; Junius for his ideal publicist; and the current writing of the periodical press as pattern for the new literary adventurer: Chatterton unquestionably followed the example of his seniors, and talked and wrote as any reader of Walpole or Boswell knows was the common style of that eighteenth century. But it is a strange injustice to charge a youth in his seventeenth year with the faults of his age, and yet refuse him a trial according to its standard.

 Whatever evidence is furnished by modern poems of Chatterton, that he was capable of matching the licentious models of his own day, only makes more striking the purity and elevation of thought of that antique verse, which was the result of deliberate choice and taste in his highest moods of inspiration. Had he so inclined, Chaucer could have supplied as readily to him as to Pope, a "Wife of Bath," or a "January and May;" and the literary ware would have proved greatly more marketable than his "Elinoure and Juga." But Rowley is altogether his own creation; in fact his ideal self. In that antique world he moved among equals of his own choice, and comported himself accordingly. But the moment he joined the men of his own time, the social element predominated, and tempted him to condescend to their tastes.   He writes his " Romaunte of the Cnyghte" in the character of John de Bergham, Cistercian monk of the fourteenth century; but when he modernises it for Mr. Burgum, the pewterer, he foists in a couplet in the loosest modern vein.   It was as though the poet of an elder and purer time had revisited our earth in that degenerate age, and must needs adapt himself to its ways.   And wonderful was the adaptability of the boy.   He assumed the common clay of that Bristol circle amid which his lot was cast, shared in all the passions, jealousies, and frivolities of their little day ; and was keenly sensitive to their approbation.

When Chatterton produced his " Battle of Hastings," or his " Ælla," he craved in vain the sympathy of appreciative faith in his antique muse.   But when he aped the rakish style of verse and talk of his seniors, he received the full meed of their applause.   As in his " Epistle " to Mr. Catcott, he took great licence ; ridiculed in verse what he owned to be worthy of all approbation in the plain prose of truth ; spared himself least of all in his satirical exaggerations ; and has had to endure the full consequences of their literal acceptance. Among other sketches or caricatures of this class, he has left on record this, which some accept as embodying his own portraiture.   The boy of sixteen exclaims :—

> "O prudence ! if, by friends or counsel swayed,
> I had thy saving institutes obeyed,
> And lost to every love but love of self,
> A wretch like Harris, living but in pelf :
> Then, happy in a coach and turtle-feast,
> I might have been an Alderman at least !
> Sage are the arguments by which I'm taught
> To curb the wild excursive flights of thought :
>
> .    .    .    .    .    .
>
> I must confess, rejoins the prudent sage,
> You're really something clever for your age ;



*Adaptability to the tastes of his associates.*

*Winning his seniors' applause.*

*Apostrophe to prudence.*

Your lines have sentiment ; and now and then
A dash of satire stumbles from your pen.
But ah ! that satire is a dangerous thing,
And often wounds the writer with its sting ;
Your infant muse should sport with other toys,
Men will not bear the ridicule of boys;

.     .     .     .     .     .     .

And if you touch their aldermanic pride,
Bid dark reflection tell how Savage died.
Besides the town,—a sober honest town—
Gives virtue her desert, and vice her frown ;
Bids censure brand with infamy your name—
I, even I, must think you are to blame.
Is there a street within this spacious place
That boasts the happiness of one fair face,
Where conversation does not turn on you,
Blaming your wild amours, your morals too?
Oaths, sacred and tremendous oaths you swear,
Oaths that might shock a Lutterell's soul to hear ;
These very oaths, as if a thing of joke,
Made to betray, intended to be broke,
Whilst the too tender and believing maid—
Remember pretty Fanny,—is betrayed." [1]



The irony, that but for his satire the poet might have
been an alderman, is sufficient to show that the picture
must not be regarded as a piece of literal portraiture.
Nevertheless the youth, who thus wrote, had unquestionably forfeited virgin purity in thought, whatever his manner
of life may have been.  He was at an age concerning
which no biographer would pause over its follies, when
manhood had produced fruits worthy of study.  But we
are dealing with a life that knew no later prime, and are
unconsciously tempted to test immaturities incident to

youth by an exceptional standard.  The world has par-
doned maturer follies in Goldsmith and Burns because of
their song ; and in Byron, even in spite of the creations
of his licentious muse.  If, therefore, in the feverish life
of the boy-poet, he too struggled, and struggled in vain,
with " passions strong," it would suffice that his biographer

[1] From the " Whore of Babylon."  The same passage occurs in
a different connexion, and with some slight variations, in the " Kew
Gardens."

draw a sorrowful veil over the strife, and pass on. But his fate in this respect has been as exceptional as in all else.

That Chatterton was precocious in everything, except in the experience of the world, is manifest enough ; but the preoccupation of his mind on his favourite studies was a valuable safeguard against the temptations of city life ; and the strength of his domestic affections is a proof that it did not fail. That he was systematically vicious, is inconsistent with all the testimony of those by whom he was best known ; and his master, who had every motive to publish his faults, acknowledged the undeviating regularity of his return home each evening at the early hour prescribed. Nothing, indeed, could show more clearly the consciousness of innocence in his dealings with the attorney than this proud appeal in his first letter after reaching London. "Call on Mr. Lambert," he writes to his mother, "show him this, or tell him if I deserve a recommendation he would oblige me to give me one ; if I do not, it will be beneath him to take notice of me."

As a son and a brother his conduct was exemplary ; and his one fault as an apprentice was that he preferred spending his unoccupied time on his own literary work, to the dull routine of copying legal precedents. Till his fifteenth year, his sister tells us, "he was remarkably indifferent to females. One day he was remarking to me the tendency severe study had to sour the temper, and declared he had always seen all the sex with equal indifference, but those that nature made dear. He thought of making an acquaintance with a girl in the neighbourhood," Miss Rumsey, as afterwards appears, "supposing it might soften the austerity of temper study had occasioned." Does the reader fully realize the scene and the actors : the boy of fourteen gravely discussing with his sister, not two years his senior, the tendency of severe study to sour the temper ; and considering whether a little love-making with one of her companions might not prove the best antidote ? So, as his sister narrates,

P 2

Chap. X.

*Precocity and inex-perience.*

*Conscious-ness of innocence.*

*Exemplary private conduct.*

*Acquaint-ance with Miss Rumsey.*

"he wrote a poem to her, and they commenced corresponding acquaintance."[1]    From this time he appears to have dallied with the amorous muse.    His lighter verse is frequently in the form of addresses, acrostics, and other poetical tributes to Miss Clarke, Miss Bush, Miss Hoyland, &c. ; and a remark of his sister, when writing to Sir Herbert Croft of his selected fair correspondent, has been interpreted in a manner never dreamt of by her.    She was writing eight years after her brother's death, in a timid, apologetic tone, as of one whose name was only heard of then in connexion with charges of licentiousness, imposture, and forgery ; and so, after acknowledging that he did write to Sir Horace Walpole, or Warpool, as she calls him, she thus proceeds : "Except his correspondence with Miss Rumsey, the girl I before mentioned, I know of no other.    He would frequently walk the College Green with the young girls that statedly paraded there to show their finery ; but I really believe he was no debauchee, though some have reported it."    The reader will remember that the Dean and Chapter had demolished the ancient City Cross only three years before, because it obstructed the walk, and "interrupted gentlemen and ladies from walking eight or ten abreast ;" and amongst such fashionable promenaders the poet might now be seen, trying, as an antidote against the effects of overstudy, a parade with Miss Rumsey, or Miss Bush, dressed for the occasion in her very gayest attire.

In truth, the interchange of *billets doux* with Miss Rumsey was only a juvenile flirtation with a Bristol belle, to whom it no doubt afforded considerable amusement while it lasted.    He was fifteen years and three months old, when he learned to his disgust that she was on the eve of marriage.    "Your celebrated Miss Rumsey," he writes to his friend Baker, "is going to be married to Mr. Fowler, as he himself informs me.    Pretty children ! about to enter into the comfortable yoke of matrimony, to be at their own liberty ; just *apropos* of the old law,— out of the frying-pan into the fire !    For a lover, Heaven

[1] Mrs. Newton's Letter, Croft, p. 162.

mend him! but for a husband, O excellent! What a female Machiavel this Miss Rumsey is!" Chatterton, one sees, like other precocious lads, had fixed on a girl considerably his senior, with whom to flirt, and carry on an interchange of wit and badinage, in which there was just seriousness enough on his part to make him resentful and indignant when he made the discovery that she had all along regarded him as a boy.

But, before another year's experience had been completed, sterner disappointments had disgusted him with the studies which hitherto formed his true passion ; and it is no longer possible to withhold assent from the discriminating verdict of Professor Masson, on the compositions of this period, as " evidently the productions of a clever boy too conscious of forbidden things, and eager (as boys are, till some real experience of the heart has made them earnest and silent,) to assert his questionable manhood among his compeers, by constant and irreverent talk about the sexes."[1]  This accords with the statement of his companion Thistlethwaite, whose evidence is all the more trustworthy from the depreciatory terms in which he speaks of him in all other respects.  Referring to passages to be found among his papers, "gross and unpardonable," and "which, for the regard I bear his memory, I wish he had never written ;" he adds, "I nevertheless believe them to have originated rather from a warmth of imagination, aided by a vain affectation of singularity, than from any natural depravity, or from a heart vitiated by evil example.  The opportunities a long acquaintance with him afforded me, justify me in saying that while he lived in Bristol he was not the debauched character represented.  Temperate in his living, moderate in his pleasures, and regular in his exercises, he was undeserving of the aspersion."[2]

His foster-mother, Mrs. Edkins, tells us "his female intimates were many, and all very respectable ; but a Miss Thatcher was his favourite.  He talked like a lover to

CHAP. X.
—
*A female Machiavel.*

*Effect of disappointments.*

*Thistlethwaite's testimony.*

*His foster-mother's account.*

[1] Masson's Essays, p. 229.
[2] Thistlethwaite's Letter to Dean Milles.

CHAP. X.

*His fair Bristol friends.*

*Miss Suky Webb.*

*True commentary.*

*Quite in love.*

many, but was seriously engaged to none. He liked their company at the tea-table," where, as she adds, he was immoderate in the indulgence in his favourite drink. In one of his early letters from London he sends a string of messages to numerous fair Bristol friends. Miss Rumsey, who it seems is still unmarried, is told if she comes to London to send him her address. "London is not Bristol. We may patrole the town for a day, without raising one whisper or nod of scandal." Miss Baker, Miss Porter, Miss Singer, and his earliest favourite, Miss Suky Webb, are all remembered. "Miss Thatcher may depend upon it that, if I am not in love with her, I am in love with nobody else;" and so he goes on, with Miss Love, Miss Cotton, Miss Broughton, Miss Watkins. "Let my sister send me a journal of all the transactions of the females within the circle of your acquaintance. I promised, before my departure, to write to some hundreds, I believe;" but, he adds, he finds but little time even to write to his own mother.

This letter is the best commentary on the allusion of his sister. It is addressed to his mother: a tender-hearted, virtuous woman, the humble friend of Miss Hannah More; the very last person to whom a pro-'fligate son would send any message for women of doubtful repute. But there is no mystery, for he had nothing to conceal; and the style of free badinage is such as was thought no way indecorous in that eighteenth century. About a fortnight later he writes a long letter to his sister full of London news, but interspersed with similar messages to fair Bristol friends; and then he adds this postscript: "I am this moment pierced through the heart by the black eye of a young lady, driving along in a hackney-coach. I am quite in love. If my love lasts till that time, you shall hear of it in my next." The boy's heart was untouched. "He jests at scars who never felt a wound;" and jests such as to Addison's ears would have sounded no way strange, and which Goldsmith may have bandied in Johnson's hearing without reproof, have been tortured into evidence of such confirmed profligacy as is belied alike by his regular hours, his studious habits, and the wonderful creations of his prolific muse.

In another respect the virtuous moderation and self-control of Chatterton can be spoken of with no apologetic reservations. He was temperate, even to abstemiousness, in food as well as in drink. Tea was his favourite beverage, of which alone he could be said to drink to excess. He usually drank six or seven cups; tarrying at the tea-table until the supply was exhausted, and laughingly telling his godmother, who most frequently presided there: "I'll stick to you to the last!" When bidding farewell to Bristol and all his old friends, he told his sister that, "for all the good tea Mrs. Edkins had given him, he would, if he did well, send her as good a teapot and stand of silver as money could purchase." But, as the latter remarks, strong liquors he avoided, even when induced by importunity; and she never heard of his being intoxicated in his life.

This testimony, which accords with all that is reported of Chatterton both in Bristol and London, ought to have its full weight when judging of the vague accusations brought against him in reference to other vices. The amount of firmness and self-control which it implies in one so young, can only be fully estimated by recalling the social habits of the age, and the known character or circumstances of some of his friends. Mr. Mease was a vintner, and apparently a crony of his friend Cary; Mr. Clayfield was a distiller; and Mr. William Smith a player, and the son of a brewer. Professor Masson, when imagining the incidents of a political rejoicing in Bristol,— on the very day in which we shall find Chatterton indignantly writing to Mr Barrett: "I keep no worse company than myself; I never drink to excess; and have, without vanity, too much sense to be attached to the mercenary retailers of iniquity;"—does not think it disparaging to the memory of its decorous historian and antiquary to picture him and Mr. Catcott finding their way home together about midnight in a very questionable state of sobriety.[1]  As to Mr. George Catcott, his convivial habits are sketched in Chatterton's freest style in the scene already quoted from the "Epistle" to his brother, where the æsthetic tea-parties at the parsonage are contrasted with the club of topers over which the pewterer presides in all his glory.  After a different fashion, he charges his muse, in mock-heroic vein, to vow for Miss Hoyland—in name, no doubt, of her absent admirer, Baker,—a love more tender

> " Than the soft turtle's cooing in the grove ;
> More than the lark delights to mount the sky,
> Then sinking on the green-sward soft to lie ;
> More than the bird of eve at close of day
> To pour in solemn solitude her lay ;
>
> .　　.　　.　　.　　.　　.
>
> More than sage Catcott does his storm of rain,
> Sprung from th' abyss of his excentric brain ;
> Or than his wild-antique and sputtering brother
> Loves in his ale-house chair to drink and pother !"



At Llewellyn's, Matthew Mease's, or elsewhere, Chatterton met such loquacious topers, and had to encounter all the urgency to excess which was then deemed the height of good fellowship.  But the widowed mother, who had passed many a sleepless night in fear of her husband's return from his orgies at the Pineapple Club, had nothing to apprehend for her son.  In this respect, at least, he set an example of self-control rare among the best men of his time, and remarkable in a youth wholly self-trained.  He systematically avoided whatever tended to impede the free play of the mental faculties, and con-



[1] Professor Masson, in his slight, but picturesque and graphic, sketch, supposes the return of the two Bristol worthies from a famous Wilkes dinner at the Crown.  The tankards of ale and bowls of punch are conceivable enough.  But the idea of the antiquary and foremost practitioner in the good old Tory city of Bristol being a Wilkesite surpasses belief.  As for Catcott, he came of a sound " Church and State " stock, and was faithful to the traditional creed.  He held the royal Martyr in such esteem that the " Eikon Basilike" was his favourite study ; and Wilkes, we may be sure, his special abhorrence.

tented himself with bread and water when his mother and sister indulged in the rare luxury of a hot dinner: telling them "he had a work on hand, and must not make himself more stupid than God had made him." But in another respect his abstinence was carried to a dangerous excess. His moody abstractions were but the preoccupation of his mind with some great pregnant thought. Mr. Catcott left him one evening totally depressed; but he returned the next morning in unusual spirits. "He had sprung a mine," he said, and produced his dramatic mystery, "The Parliament of Sprytes," on which he had spent the hours designed for sleep. This incident is characteristic. He seems to have thought nothing of resuming the duties of a new day, without having retired to rest.

When thus occupied on some engrossing theme, he was frequently for days together alone in his study; and even in the family circle would fall into reveries, during which he seemed unconscious of all around him, until at last, after having been repeatedly spoken to with ever-increasing emphasis, he would suddenly start, and ask "What were you talking about?" Solitary Sunday rambles furnished other favourite occasions when he could commune with his own thoughts. Occasionally on his return he would describe his walks, or produce sketches of churches or other objects which had attracted his notice. But in general he was disinclined to admit others to any share in the occupation of those lonely hours, which extended generally till the twilight had faded away, and he returned home by the light of the stars.[1]

He particularly fancied the long moonlight nights; believed, or affected to believe, that he could then exercise his mental powers with peculiar vigour; towards the full of the moon would often sit up all night writing by its light; and recorded, in the family Bible, his birth within two days of the full moon: possibly, as Mr. John Evans surmises, in mere waggish reference to his popular title, in order to suggest the inference that he was "the mad genius" by birthright.[2]

[1] Croft, p. 181.  [2] Dix, App. Note, p. 336.

CHAP. X.

*Bristol and
London
room-mates.*

The footboy of Mr. Lambert could, in all probability, have given very much the same account of the sharer of his attic, as was communicated by his London room-mate of a later date. The sister of the latter, having never before come across any youth of literary tastes or eccentricities, " took him more for a mad boy than anything else, he would have such flights and vagaries." He took his meals with a relative who lodged in the same house ; but she adds, " He never touched meat, and drank only water, and seemed to live on the air." She then completes the picture by adding : " He used to sit up almost all night, reading and writing ; and her brother said he was afraid to lie with him ; for, to be sure, he was a spirit and never slept ; for he never came to bed till it was morning, and then, for what he saw, never closed his eyes." For however brief had been the period thus allowed for repose, his bedfellow always found him awake when he opened his eyes ; and he got up at the early hour, —between five and six,—at which the young plasterer had to resume his work. He had been busy on his compositions in prose or verse ; and almost every morning the floor was covered with minute pieces of paper into which he had torn his first drafts before coming to bed.[1] The same habits characterised him to the last. Night was his favourite time for literary toil ; and when occupied on some engrossing theme, or transported in fancy to times of yore, "the sleepless soul" was wholly forgetful of the claims of the body ; and the labours of a new day were resumed without any interval of repose.

This indifference to sleep was the real excess, dangerous alike to healthful life and to reason. Abnormal as the precocity of Chatterton's intellect was, there is nothing in the history of his singular career to indicate any unusual tendency towards mental disease. Byron's emphatic dictum was : " Chatterton, I think, was mad." But the same easy method of accounting for the eccentricities of genius has been applied to himself. There are, indeed, the rare types of preeminent intellectual power, like

[1] Croft, p. 216.

Chaucer and Shakespear, who appear to have been equal to every occasion, surpassing ordinary men even in wise shrewdness and common sense. Milton moved with statesmanlike dignity, bearing himself calmly amid the strife of a great revolution. Burns and Scott were both marked by a rare sagacity, in spite of the unpractical shortcomings of each; and Wordsworth dwelt in voluntary seclusion among his favourite mountains, the sage of another period of political convulsion. But the theory of insanity may as fitly be applied to Gay, Collins, perhaps to Pope himself; to Goldsmith, Coleridge, Shelley, or to Byron : as to Chatterton.

*Poets of the first order.* — CHAP. X.

He was, indeed, one to be judged of by no ordinary standard. To his mother, his strange ways, and prolonged fits of reverie, had been incomprehensible enough from childhood; nor were such reveries reserved solely for home. Though always accessible, as Dr. Gregory says, and rather disposed to encourage than repel the advances of others, he would at times be moody and silent in company. His fits of absent-mindedness were frequent and long.[1] For days together he would go in and out of Mr. Lambert's office without speaking to any one, and seemingly absorbed in thought;[2] and, according to his relative, Mrs. Ballance, whose London lodging he shared, " he would often look steadfastly in a person's face without speaking, or seeming to see the person, for a quarter of an hour or more, till it was quite frightful."[3]

*Not to be judged of by ordinary standards.*

Yet all this is comprehensible enough without the old Bristol theory of a "mad genius." The boy at fifteen had a mind such as has rarely been equalled in power and vigour in man's maturest years; but it had been left to develop itself without training or guidance. He was already creating a mystery which a whole century of criticism has not sufficed to solve to the satisfaction of all men. In some respects he was a child, dealing with that for which the schooling of man's tardy maturity is

*The old Bristol theory.*

[1] Gregory's Life, p. 80.  [2] Palmer; Dix's Life, p. 30.
[3] Croft, p. 214.

the natural training, and without even the oversight and culture of ordinary childhood.   In other respects he was already the man of more than ordinary cerebral development and intellectual power; but there also, at every step, compelled to provide experience for himself, or grope his way destructively, like a blind Samson, till he involved himself and his incompleted designs in a common ruin.   But before that end is reached, another all-important element—the religious one,—must be reviewed, in connexion with events which give it a painful prominence in association with the later incidents of his strange career.

# CHAPTER XI.

## EMANCIPATION.



THE rule of Mr. Lambert, and the duties of his office, became ever more irksome to Chatterton, in spite of the unquestionable advantages of leisure and solitude which he enjoyed in the attorney's service. The foremost draw-back, in reality, though unappreciated by him, was the want of any legitimate work for the active mind of the boy. He rebelled against the irksome task of copying precedents, of no use that he could see, to himself or any one else. But the ungenial relations of master and clerk made the bondage still more galling to his proud spirit. The servile position he was compelled to assume offended him more than the routine of office work. He had not been a month away from it when he wrote his mother: "Though as an apprentice none had greater liberties, yet the thoughts of servitude killed me. Now I have that for my labour I always reckoned the first of my pleasures, and have still my liberty." He had liberties, but not liberty: a nice distinction. We learn from his letter to his friend Baker, in Charleston, that Mr. Lambert had been absent in London; but, he says, "I must now close my poetical labours, my master being returned." Again, in his second letter to Dodsley he speaks of him as "now out of town." Mr. Capel told Mr. Bryant that he thought he never saw him copying what he took to be the Rowley parchments, "but when his master was gone from home;"[1] and the admission that the footman was sent from time to time to ascertain

[1] Bryant's Observations, p. 524.

CHAP. XI.

*Welcome intervals of freedom.*

if he was in attendance at the office, confirms the probability that such welcome intervals of freedom were of frequent occurrence. Then he could finish his average two hours of legitimate office work, attend to whatever other duties devolved on him; and these done, indulge at will in modern song and satire; or, retiring behind the mask he had so long worn in secret, revel in the creations of his antique muse.

*The suspicious and irritable attorney.*

But such intervals of freedom would only tend to make the situation more irksome, when the suspicious, irritable attorney returned to task him with misspent time, search his drawer, tear up his poems and letters; and even destroy the paper which by its unprofessional character betrayed its destination for such forbidden uses. Of Mr. Lambert little has been recorded beyond the meagre notes of Mrs. Newton and Mrs. Edkins. But all that we do know suggests the idea of a peevish, fretful, unloveable man, who dealt with the boy committed to his charge as a mere hireling, and "took every opportunity to vex, cross, and mortify" him. Chatterton's susceptible nature

*No kindness to respond to.*

promptly responded to kindness; but there is no glimpse of any such appeal in the attorney's dealings with him. When delayed a few minutes after the hour prescribed for returning to his master's house, he would say with a sigh, "Well I must go, I suppose, now, to be reproved;" and when, towards the close, his mother endeavoured to dissuade him from his design of quitting Mr. Lambert's office, and going to London, his reply was: "What am I to do? You see how I am treated!" If Chatterton drew his picture, either in confidential correspondence, or when moved by the strong fit of satire to indiscriminate raillery, it has not been preserved; but it is

*Cordial relations impossible.*

abundantly obvious that no cordial relations could ever have been established between the proud-spirited youth, already conscious of an intellectual supremacy above all his associates, and the master who saw in him only the charity boy serving him for food and clothing. The attorney regarded the poetical aspirations of his apprentice with angry contempt. In his office he vigilantly

watched lest an unoccupied hour should be wasted in
writing "his stuff." In his house the boy was allowed
to grow up as uncared for as any transient menial who
drudged for hire.

While still an inmate of the Bluecoat School we have
seen Chatterton deeply impressed with religious convictions. When confirmed, at an early age, " he made very
sensible, serious remarks on the awfulness of the ceremony,
and his own feelings and convictions during it." Some
of his first efforts at verse confirm the duration of such
impressions. His " Hymn for Christmas Day," written
about eleven,—though remarkable when the age of its
author is considered,—is chiefly interesting from the
evidence it supplies of his religious emotions. On this
account a stanza or two may be quoted here :—

> " Almighty Framer of the skies !
> O let our pure devotion rise
>   Like incense in Thy sight !
> Wrapt in impenetrable shade
> The texture of our souls was made,
>   Till Thy command gave light.
>
> " The Sun of glory gleam'd, the ray
> Refin'd the darkness into day,
>   And bad the vapours fly ;
> Impelled by His eternal love
> He left His palaces above
>   To cheer our gloomy sky.
>
> .    .    .    .
>
> " My soul, exert thy powers, adore,
> Upon devotion's plumage soar
>   To celebrate the day ;
> The God from whom creation sprung
> Shall animate my grateful tongue ;
>   From Him I'll catch the lay !"

Another beautiful hymn, entitled " Resignation," was
copied by Sir Herbert Croft from the original in Mrs.
Chatterton's possession : the boy having probably given
it to his mother as a piece calculated to gratify her by its
sentiment, if not by its poetical merit. It breathes a

spirit of devout resignation, in language of as true poetry as the best creations of his antique muse. Unfortunately no date is attached to it to help us in assigning it to any specific period :—

### RESIGNATION.

"O God, whose thunder shakes the sky ;
　　Whose eye this atom globe surveys :
To Thee, my only rock, I fly,
　　Thy mercy in Thy justice praise.

"The mystic mazes of Thy will,
　　The shadows of celestial light,
Are past the power of human skill ;
　　But what th' Eternal acts is right.

"O teach me in the trying hour,
　　When anguish swells the dewy tear,
To still my sorrows, own Thy power,
　　Thy goodness love, Thy justice fear.

"If in this bosom aught but Thee,
　　Encroaching, sought a boundless sway,
Omniscience could the danger see,
　　And Mercy look the cause away.

"Then why, my soul, dost thou complain?
　　Why, drooping, seek the dark recess?
Shake off the melancholy chain,
　　For God created all to bless.

"But ah ! my breast is human still ;
　　The rising sigh, the falling tear,
My languid vitals' feeble rill,
　　The sickness of my soul declare.

"But yet, with fortitude resigned,
　　I'll thank the inflicter of the blow ;
Forbid the sigh, compose my mind,
　　Nor let the gush of misery flow.

"The gloomy mantle of the night,
　　Which on my sinking spirit steals,
Will vanish at the morning light,
　　Which God, my east, my sun, reveals." .



The Rowleyan pieces, both in prose and verse, partake of the fervour of medieval piety, with all its picturesque adjuncts; calculated it may be, rather to charm the fancy than to influence the conduct. The tone throughout is reverential; and even when the occasion seems to invite to freer licence, the religious spirit still predominates.

From one of the Rowley papers it appears that a wicked heretic, John à Milverton, had, in the days of the good Bishop Carpenter, taken upon him to challenge the doctrine of the Trinity: whereupon William Canynge and Thomas Rowley are commissioned to deal with the matter, which they do by a proclamation, setting forth that " as what is above human comprehension can neither be proved nor disproved by human arguments, it is vain for the wit of man to pretend to unfold the dark·covering of the Ark of the Trinity: lest, like those of old, he be stricken dead, and his reason lost by breathing in an element too fine and subtle for the gross nature;" so, as they " approve not of invalidating arguments by violence and death, provided a man enjoys his opinion alone: the said T. Rowley will, on Sunday, at Saint Mary's Cross, in the glebe of St. Mary Redcliff, deliver a discourse on the Trinity, after the Matin Song; and after Even Song the said John shall be at liberty, without fear of punishment, to answer, and invalidate the arguments of the said T. Rowley." The ideas on toleration thus ascribed to the controversialists of the fifteenth century, are an amusing anachronism, meant, no doubt, for intolerant theologians of the modern Rowley's own day. But the avoidance of any covert sneer at the mysteries of revelation, where the occasion seems so opportune, is very noticeable, in its contrast to the prevailing tone of his modern satires.

The idea of his Rowley romance was conceived, and to a great extent executed by Chatterton, as we have seen, before that latest change which his profane satires disclose. In Colston's School he had not only to attend on the services of the Church; but religious instruction occupied a prominent place in the regular school work. The boys were never allowed to be out on Sunday, the whole of its time being devoted to public and private

Q

religious exercises.[1] The kindly relation in which he appears to have stood to more than one of his teachers favoured the reception of their precepts; and thus the great truths of religion were presented in the most acceptable form to a mind naturally prone to veneration. But, emancipated from the school, all this was at an end. His associates appear to have been selected for some supposed traits of intellectual sympathy with himself;



while he courted the society of seniors able to aid him in mental culture or access to books. It need not surprise us if among the contributors to the periodical literature of the day, who ere long formed his chosen associates, there were some with whom the creed of Bolingbroke, and Hume, found acceptance, as it too speedily did with himself. Such sceptical tendencies were by no means confined to the youths of that day. It is indeed, to the most esteemed of all his seniors, that he refers as his chief ally in his antagonism to the orthodox vicar of the Temple Church.



The death of Chatterton's favourite teacher and friend, Phillips, and his introduction to Mr. Clayfield, appear to have been nearly simultaneous. The influence, therefore, of the former ceased, and the latter began, in his seventeenth year; and all the evidence which his writings supply confirms the idea that anything like a definite adoption of free-thinking views dates within a very few months of his leaving Bristol. In one of his elegies,



dated 5th January 1769, he refers to the death of Mr. John Tandey, father-in-law of Mr. Barrett, as that of "a sincere Christian friend;" and thus speaks of him:—

> " In him the social virtues joined
> 　His judgment sound, his sense refined,
> 　　His actions ever just :
> 　Who can suppress the rising sigh,
> 　To think such saint-like men must die,
> 　And mix with common dust ?"

Another elegy, written in the following November,—the

---

[1] Bristoliensis, Gent. Mag. vol. xlviii. p. 403.

fruit probably of one of his solitary Sunday rambles up the valley of the Avon ;—though in reverent language, betrays perhaps the first traces of a creed that already tended to confound religion with superstition. The poet thus gives vent to feelings of growing despondency, as he contrasts the realism of his own day with his favourite past :—

> " Joyless I seek the solitary shade
>     Where dusky contemplation veils the scene ;
> The dark retreat, of leafless branches made,
>     Where sickening sorrow wets the yellow'd green.

> " The darksome ruins of some sacred cell,
>     Where erst the sons of superstition trod,
> Tottering upon the mossy meadow, tell
>     We better know, but less adore our God.

> " Now as I mournful tread the gloomy nave,[1]
>     Through the wide window, once with mysteries dight,
> The distant forest, and the darkening wave
>     Of the swoln Avon ravishes my sight."

The piece entitled " Happiness ;" " Kew Gardens," of which the first three hundred lines were forwarded to Mr. Edwards, of the *Middlesex Journal*, in March 1770 ; its counterpart, the " Whore of Babylon ;" the " Epistle to the Reverend Mr. Catcott ;" and " The Defence : "— written apparently in reply to censures provoked by the previous pieces,—all belong to the few last months of his residence in Bristol. The history of the first of those satires has a curious interest as the counterpart of a very different production. In this period of despondency and strife, Mr. Catcott suggested to him the subject, which Chatterton said he had never before thought of ; and on the following day he put into his hands that clever, but licentious satire, extending to one hundred and forty-six heroic lines, and told him that it contained his creed of happiness.[2] So far as any creed is embodied in the lines,

---

[1] *Nave :* the word has been printed *cave* hitherto.
[2] Croft, p. 170.

it is that of the deist, in which Reason is set up in antagonism to Revelation, and priestcraft denounced with the indiscriminating levity of the free-thinker. As a mere piece of composition, executed almost impromptu, and on a prescribed theme, it has many vigorous lines, as in the couplet :—

> " Conscience, the soul-chameleon's varying hue,
> Reflects all notions, to no notion true."

Or where Revelation is daringly characterised as :—

> " Reason's dark-lantern, superstition's sun,
> Whose cause mysterious, and effect, are one ;
> From thee ideal bliss we only trace,
> Fair as ambition's dream, or beauty's face."



In the satirist's more legitimate vein, he sketches " Young Yeatman," the Oxonian pedant :—

> " Who damns good English if not latinised ;
> In Aristotle's scale the muse he weighs,
> And damps his little fire with copied lays :
> Versed in the mystic learning of the schools,
> He rings bob-majors by Leibnitzian rules."



" Pulvis " and the " incomparable Catcott " are exhibited in the same poem, in passages already quoted, with all the unscrupulous freedom of the satirist : for the poem, written at the pewterer's dictation, was adapted to the taste of that patron of letters. He " had never thought on the subject " before ; but no sooner was this free impromptu penned, than the poet, in search of what was ever true happiness to him, betook himself to the heroism  of " tymes of yore ;" and ere long Mr. Catcott was surprised to find that the very subject suggested by him had occurred to Maistre William Canynge three hundred years before. The following are the very diverse reflections on Contentment and Happiness, or " Selynesse," as it is rendered in the professed antique, ascribed to Rowley's patron :—

> "May happiness on earthe's bounds be had ?
>     May it adight in human shape be found ?
> Wot ye it was with Eden's bowers bestad,
>     Or quite erased from the scaunce-laid[1] ground,
>     When from the secret founts the waters did abound ?
> Does it affrighted shun the bodied walk,
> Live to itself, and to its echoes talk ?
>
> All hail Content, thou maid of turtle eyne !
>     As thy beholders think, thou art iwreene ;[2]
> To ope the door to happiness is thine,
>     And Christe's glory doth upon thee sheene ;
>     Doer of the foul thing ne hath thee seen ;
> In caves, in woods, in woe, and dole distress,
> Whoe'er hath thee hath gotten happiness."[3]

Such I assume to be the history of this little poem,—printed from Mr. Catcott's copy ;—the earnest protest of the poet's better self against the degradation of his muse. But if so, "the strong fit of satire" was upon him again with the very next provocation ; and the work of the year closes, so far as dates now guide us, with " The Defence," in which Reason is once more exalted to supreme rule :—

> " Reason, to its possessor a sure guide,
>     Reason, a thorn in Revelation's side."

It is not difficult to perceive from the letters, and the lighter articles of Chatterton both in prose and verse, that he manifested not a little of that self-assertion common to self-taught men, but which is frequently no more than the unrestrained habit of speaking out what others think. It was notably characteristic of Hogg, Cobbett, and Hugh Miller. It is not unapparent in Burns himself. With his strong vein of satire, combined with such arrogant self-assertion, the boy was prone to assail the decorous conventionalities of seniors whom he saw through and despised ; until the indulgence of this humour ended in an indiscriminate ridicule of all that failed to commend

---

[1] *Scaunce-laid,* uneven.          [2] *Iwreene,* displayed.
[3] The poem is entitled "On Happinesse ;" but throughout the word *selynesse* is substituted for it.

itself to his acceptance. In his satires and much else of his modern verse, as well as his prose, it is easy to detect the models that he imitated ; and sometimes, in the latter, the sources from whence he borrowed without scruple. In those hasty productions, the cuckoo note re-echoes the tone and sentiment of the age, in social manners, in politics, and in religion.

From that happy day when his sacred Majesty's restoration was proclaimed to its delighted citizens, Bristol has held dissenters in most orthodox disfavour ; and the masters of Colston's charity had, as their paramount duty, to see that its Bluecoat boys were trained up in the same creed. " Antipathy to dissent," says Colston's admiring biographer, "was his most vulnerable point, which, once touched, his serenity forsook him, and he stood no longer exempt from the weakness of human nature."[1] A letter to his trustees refers with horror to the " scandal" their chaplain had given rise to, apparently by recording his vote, at a general election in the neighbouring county, for a dissenter ; and declines all further intercourse with him, as " no sound son of the Church, but rather inclined to, and a favourer of fanaticism." Mr. Colston's later trustees have proved more faithful to their duty ; and in Chatterton's days they found occasion for their most urgent zeal.

In the earlier part of the eighteenth century, the city of Bristol was one of the chosen fields of labour in the cause of vital religion, both of Whitfield and the Wesleys ; and the reflex of the agitation they excited is discernible in the " Apostate Will," written when Chatterton was eleven years old, and long regarded as his first effort in verse. But the antagonism to religion in every form, which so largely pervaded English society then, had been openly avowed by him before the close of 1769 ; and numerous passages in the productions of that period—including the discarded or fugitive trifles which have been preserved with so little regard to his good name,—give painful evidence of it. Among the

---

[1] Tovey's Colston, p. 79.

Chatterton MSS. in the British Museum is the rude draft of one book, or division of an unfinished satire, styled " Journal 6th," dated Sept. 30th, 1769 ; and immediately following it, on the same sheet, are two other fragmentary pieces, without title, the latter of which pictures " the mighty Whitfield " preaching :

> " Tearing, sweating, bawling, thumping,
>   Oblique lightning in his eyes."

If quoted now, it might possibly recall to some readers the " Holy Fair," and other equally witty and profane satires, of one who, ten years before this, was born to like poverty on the banks of the Ayr.   But enough has been produced to illustrate this melancholy phase of noble gifts perverted to such a purpose.   Let it suffice —while remembering that Chatterton was still little more than a boy, whose childhood had known no " saint-like father's" care,—that he merely re-echoed the prejudices of an age in which even Cowper disguised the evangelist's name " beneath well-sounding Greek." [1]   When, moreover, we reflect on the mental crisis through which Coleridge and Southey passed, ere they won a firm foothold of faith : we can only mourn the fate of the strangely gifted boy, abandoned in his most impressible years to such companionship as Bristol then yielded ; and perishing while still blindly groping his way by the light of Reason.

The creed of Chatterton was common to that sceptical age ; and scarcely differed from that of its greatest poet, Pope.   Bolingbroke, Toland, Bayle, Voltaire, Rousseau, and Hume, had followed in succession, the teachers of a coldly speculative deism.   The intellect of the era

---

[1] " Leuconomus (beneath well-sounding Greek
     I slur the name a poet must not speak)
     Stood pilloried on infamy's high stage,
     And bore the pelting scorn of half an age ;
     The very butt of Slander, and the blot
     For every dart that Malice ever shot.
     The man that mentioned him at once dismissed
     All mercy from his lips, and sneered and hissed," &c.
                                        COWPER'S *Hope.*

seemed to have declared itself on the side of unbelief : when Johnson and Cowper, holding fast by faith and truth, gave to the rising generation a new and healthful bias. But this Chatterton did not live to feel. Johnson was to him but the pensioned ministerial penman; and Cowper, in 1769, had his work as a poet and a satirist to begin, when Chatterton reduced to form what he called articles of belief. Among the Chatterton MSS. in the British Museum is a small piece of foolscap paper, much frayed and soiled, apparently from having been carried in his pocket, containing :



"THE ARTICLES OF THE BELIEF OF ME, THOMAS CHATTERTON.

"That God is incomprehensible. It is not required of us to know the mysteries of the Trinity, &c. &c. &c.

"That it matters not whether a man is a Pagan, Turk, Jew, or Christian, if he acts according to the religion he professes.

"That if a man leads a good moral life, he is a Christian.

"That the stage is the best school of morality.[1]    And

"That the Church of Rome (some tricks of priestcraft excepted) is certainly the true Church.

"THOMAS CHATTERTON."



The poor negation of a creed, thus systematically set forth, would have received the subscription of thousands in that age, as an admirable substitute for the Articles of the Church, and a liberal definition of the philosophy of the day. The miserable fruits of such teaching fully accorded with their source. It becomes only too obvious that, ere long, Chatterton had learned to contemplate self-destruction as a possible means of escape from the difficulties that environed him. It was part of the freethinker's creed, not only advocated but practised in that Bristol circle in which he moved. Peter Smith, a brother



---

[1] It must not be forgotten, in judging of this item of his creed, that in the eighteenth century the stage was really esteemed to be a good school of morality by Johnson, Burke, Hannah More, and many others. Warburton was one of its zealous patrons ; and Newton,— the object of Chatterton's satirical invectives,—was the earliest and most discriminating of Garrick's critics ; and continued his regard for him after he became a bishop.

of his friend . William, on being brought to task by his father for irregular courses, according to his nephew's mode of stating it, " retired to his chamber, and set his associate an example that was but too soon to be followed."  A curious chance evidence enables us now to contradict the accompanying statement which represents Chatterton as the personal friend of Peter, and sharer in his excesses.  Among the MSS. in the British Museum is an " Elegy on Mr. William Smith," written evidently on the first news of Peter's death, under the misapprehension that his own friend was the victim.  But he has subsequently added this note, in the attorney-like fashion to which so many facts invaluable to his biographer are due : " Happily mistaken, having since heard, from good authority, it is Peter."  Peter it is obvious was not his personal friend, though, no doubt, an occasional associate.  Of the intercourse with his brother William, Mr. George Pryce has recovered a highly interesting memorial, which proves that the two friends did at times indulge in earnest interchange of thought on worthiest themes.  The question of the immortality of the soul appears to have been started ; when Chatterton produced the following lines, written impromptu in the presence of his companion :—

> " Say, O my soul, if not allowed to be
> Immortal, whence the mystery we see
> Day after day, and hour after hour,
> But to proclaim its never-ceasing power?
> If not immortal, then our thoughts of thee
> Are visions but of non-futurity.
> Why do we live to feel of pain on pain,
> If, in the midst of hope, we hope in vain ?
> Perish the thought in night's eternal shade :
> To live, then die, man was not only made.
> There's yet an awful something else remains
> Either to lessen or increase our pains.
> Whate'er it be, whate'er man's future fate,
> Nature proclaims there is another state
> Of woe, or bliss.  But who is he can tell?
> None but the good, and they that have done well.
> Oh ! may that happiness be ours, my friend !
> The little we have now will shortly end ;

> When joy and bliss more lasting will appear,
> Or all our hopes translated into fear.
> Oh ! may our portion in that world above,
> Eternal fountain of Eternal Love,
> Be crowned with peace that bids the sinner live ;
> With praise to Him who only can forgive—
> Blot out the stains and errors of our youth ;
> Whose smile is mercy, and whose word is truth."

*A pleasant memorial of companionship.*

The sentiments thus rendered into verse at the moment of their utterance preserve for us one pleasant memorial of a companionship, which might seem, thus far, akin to that enjoyed with Phillips, when the evening walks were prolonged till their return " through the darkened valley, in converse such as heavenly spirits use."  But whatever other bonds of friendship knit the two together, the congenial element of appreciative sympathy was wanting in his companion.  In the elegy written under the belief of his death Chatterton exclaims :—

> "I loved him with a brother's ardent love ;
> Beyond the love which tenderest brothers bear."

It is sufficient to show of what stuff this friend was made, whose supposed loss he thus mourned, that he survived his elegist upwards of half a century, and died in the belief that " Tom no more wrote the Rowley Poems than he did!"

*Tossing on a sea of doubt.*

It is obvious enough from the vacillating contrasts of earnest thought and crude scepticism apparent in the later writings of Chatterton, that his mind was then tossing on a sea of doubt.  In confidential moments of private intercourse he would give utterance to the devout aspirations of his better nature ; but in the companionship of such a circle as the Young Bristol of his day a well-founded religious belief was needed for the avowal of such sentiments.

*A characteristic incident.*

An incident said to have happened towards the close of his Bristol career is not inconceivable in such a circle.  One evening the question was started as to the bravery or cowardice of self-destruction, when Chatterton is affirmed to have pulled a pistol out of his breast, and, holding it to his forehead, exclaimed: "Now, if one had but the courage to pull the trigger!"  The story rests on no satisfactory authority;[1] and there seems little probability to favour the idea of his carrying fire-arms in any such fashion.  But it is not always easy to form a correct judgment on such points.  His old school-mate, Thistlethwaite, is described by Mr. Richard Smith as "a short, stocky man, who walked about the city exchange with the butt-ends of two horse-pistols peeping out of his coat pockets;"[2] and, according to the state-ment of the latter, when Chatterton was parting with him before setting out for London, after telling with confidence of his literary projects, and other schemes, he reverted to the pistol as his last resource.  Whether in earnest, or mere bravado, such an idea undoubtedly received expres-sion in those last months of Bristol life; and is thus embodied on a stray sheet, dated 1769, found among his papers after his death :—

> "Since we can die but once, what matters it
>   If rope, or garter, poison, pistol, sword,
>   Slow-wasting sickness, or the sudden burst
>   Of valve-arterial in the noble parts,
>   Curtail the miseries of human life?
>   Tho' varied is the cause, the effect's the same;
>   All to one common dissolution tends."

To companions such as those, among whom the philo-sophic teachings of that eighteenth century were thus freely avowed, I presume Mr. Barrett to refer, in the brief notice of Chatterton near the close of his "History;" where he speaks of "the bad company and principles he had adopted."[3]  Bad, indeed, they undoubtedly were; but the remark has been turned to another account by his traducers.  It is obvious, from the context, that it was to the bad principles of a free-thinker, and not of a profligate libertine, that Barrett alluded.  Of that youth-

[1] The anecdote occurs in the anonymous life attached to Chatter-ton's Works, two vols. 8vo. Grant, Cambridge, 1842, p. cxvi.  It is claimed as first recorded there, but no authority is given.

[2] Richard Smith's MSS. Bristol Library.

[3] Barrett's History, p. 646.

CHAP. XI.

*An early playmate.*

*Letter to Mr. Clayfield.*

*Mr. Barrett's narrative.*

*Characteristic letter to him.*

ful circle, the one for whom alone it possesses any interest for us now was already treading on life's brief close. Another, Richard, the brother of William and Peter Smith, and an early playmate of Chatterton, died in 1791, senior surgeon of the Bristol Infirmary, "beloved and regretted by the whole city."

The new opinions of Chatterton had probably already reached the ear of Mr. Lambert, when, one day, he found on his clerk's writing-desk,—or more probably concealed among his papers,—a letter addressed to his friend Mr. Clayfield, stating his distresses, and that on the receipt of that letter he should be no more. Mr. Lambert, in alarm, despatched the letter, not to Mr. Clayfield, but to Mr. Barrett, on whose authority the narrative rests ; and, according to his statement, he sent "immediately for Chatterton, questioned him closely upon the occasion, in a tender and friendly manner ; but forcibly urged to him the horrible crime of self-murder, however glossed over by our present libertines ; blaming the bad company and principles he had adopted. This betrayed him into some compunction, and by his tears he seemed to feel it. At the same time he acknowledged he wanted for nothing ; and denied any distress upon that account." Mr. Barrett had concealed from Chatterton his mode of acquiring the information, and the following day he received this characteristic letter :—

"SIR,—Upon recollection I don't know how Mr. Clayfield could come by his letter ; as I intended to have given him a letter, but did not. In regard to my motives for the supposed rashness, I shall observe that I keep no worse company than myself. I never drink to excess ; and have, without vanity, too much sense to be attached to the mercenary retailers of iniquity. No ! it is my pride, my damn'd, native, unconquerable pride, that plunges me into distraction. You must know that 19-20ths of my composition is pride. I must either live a slave, a servant ; have no will of my own, no sentiments of my own which I may freely declare as such ; or die ! —perplexing alternative. But it distracts me to think of it. I will endeavour to learn humility, but it cannot be here. What it will cost me on the trial Heaven knows !

"I am, your much obliged, unhappy, humble Servant,

"T. C."

The letter is merely dated " Thursday evening." Mr. Cottle gives an extract from another written to Mr. Baster about the same time, in which he curses the Muses, exclaiming: " I abominate them and their works. They are the nurses of poverty and insanity." Other influences, besides the failure of his plans for the publication of the Rowley Poems, combined to seduce Chatterton from his devotion to the Muses. At this very time Mr. Woodfall's *Public Advertiser* was making England ring with the bold invectives of Junius. In the previous December his famous "Address to the King" had seemed to set authority and power at defiance; and all newspaper writers were ambitious to emulate his daring. But the boldness of this masked assailant was surpassed by the reckless audacity of Wilkes; and the follies of the Grafton administration consummated the triumph of the demagogue. Burke was at this time the avowed leader of the Opposition; and Junius so effective an ally that the popular belief of the time regarded them as one. The Duke of Grafton cowered before the parliamentary philippics of the great orator, backed by a power beyond the reach of authority or law. A vote on one of the endless Wilkes' debates brought matters to a crisis. On the 28th January 1770, the affrighted premier resigned, and Lord North became First Lord of the Treasury.

The change is memorable in English history on many accounts. To us its present interest lies in this, that, within a month, Chatterton, to his inexpressible delight, read—and fancied all Bristol and all England reading,—in the columns of the *Middlesex Journal*, his own letter, under the signature "Decimus," addressed in the true Junius vein "To the Duke of G———n, on his resignation." A brief extract will suffice to illustrate this Bristol echo of the great *Umbra*. " Those who would know the real cause of your retreat, must trace it to the root of all authority and power : the Earl of Bute. It was the influence of this sun of state that ripened your latent genius into life. He drew your talents out of obscurity; he raised you to the pinnacle of place, and you have (as in duty bound)

CHAP. XI.<br>
*Nurses of poverty and insanity.*<br><br>
*Junius and Wilkes.*<br><br>
*A change of ministry.*<br><br>
*Echo of the great Umbra.*

been his pack-ass till your late retreat. 'Tis true, the measures which have set the nation in a flame were executed by you; but they were planned by him and his more inventive projectors. . . . The people are indeed to be pitied. They have a king (the best of kings, in the language of flattery), who never hears the truth. They petition, and are not regarded ; and if they assume a becoming spirit of freedom, it is licentiousness." Aiming still higher, on the 10th of April, he writes his letter " To the Princess of Gotham," in which he draws a parallel between the England of Charles I. and that of the present time. " Both are misled, and both by women."



It was while thus admonishing statesmen and their masters ; and intoxicated with the delight of fancied political influence : that Chatterton penned a piece of composition of a very different character, which, whether written in jest or earnest, brought his Bristol career abruptly to a close. The letter of Decimus " To the Princess of Gotham,"—or, as he more clearly indicates in a subsequent letter, " To the P—— D. of W——," *i.e.* the King's mother, Princess Dowager of Wales ;—appeared in the *Middlesex Journal* of the 17th April, 1770. In the interval between its writing and publication, as the dates show, he sat down, on Easter Eve, Saturday, April 14th, and penned " The last Will and Testament of



Thomas Chatterton of the City of Bristol," the only original document of a legal character he has left us. It has been treated by most of his biographers as a thoroughly serious one, written in desperation, and on the eve of suicide. It is no easy matter to determine in what light it should be viewed ; but its model, as a mere bit of literary workmanship, must have been manifest enough to those into whose hands it first came.



The *Town and Country Magazine* for 1769 has already been noted as a rich biographical repertory of Chatterton and his doings. By its means we recover the very subjects of his reading in those months. Here, after perusing his own pieces, he turned to the study of Wilkes, Beckford, and Junius himself; to the scandal of the month, and the news of the day.   In the April number, after D. B.'s "Kenrick, a Saxon Poem," had been read: a wood-cut on the following leaf attracted him to the "Life of a Deceased Monarch," with its anecdotes of Samuel Derrick, Esq., late Master of the Ceremonies at Bath, including this, that "our Bath King, a few days before his death, dictated and ratified his Last Will and Testament, in the name of wit, gallantry, and the Muses," after a fashion worthy of the frivolous fop.[1]   The humour of the thing took Chatterton's fancy ; and stimulated by occurrences which tended to foster the idea of a testamentary farewell to his Bristol friends and the world in general, we find him, in the following April, reproducing its fancies in a version of his own.   Possibly enough, in the mood that then possessed him, there was a serious purpose implied in his first paragraphs.   But this speedily gave way to the conceit of rivalling the Bath King in a series of satirical bequests.

Chatterton's original intention was to write in verse ; nor did he abandon this for the legally constructed prose satire, till the motives for the more earnest production had passed away.   But, as printed in Southey and Cottle's edition of his works, the will is prefaced by fifty-three lines, breaking off abruptly with a scornful reference to the indignities of a suicide's grave.   In those alone can be traced unmistakeable evidence of the purpose

---

[1] Derrick's Will altogether wants the serious element which inextricably blends with the grave jests of that of Chatterton ; and as the production of an old man, in the actual prospect of death, its jests, and still more its impure allusions, are a melancholy exhibition of human folly.   The following items, however, are clearly recognisable as the source of passages in Chatterton's Will: "To Charles J——s, Esq. all my modesty and Christian patience.   To the witty but unfortunate Lady C——r all my prudence and discretion.   To the citizens and frequenters of Bath discernment sufficient to elect another Master of the Ceremonies equal to myself.   My courage to Mr. B——ph.   My poetical genius to the New Foundling Hospital of Wit.   My ghost to the inhabitants of Cock Lane, for their sole use and emolument.   To Dr. S——l J——n, the power of laying it by the pressure of his tremendous dictionary," &c.

Снар. XI.

*The King of Bath.*

*Testamentary conceit.*

*Metrical portion of the Will.*

*Derrick's Last Will and Testament.*

usually ascribed to the whole ; and there also occurs the only allusion to his poems.  To Catcott he says :—

> "If ever obligated to thy purse,
> Rowley discharges all."



For, curiously enough, amid all the unquestionable seriousness that pervades this testamentary jest, his bequests include no reference to the only, and really valuable property, the poet did leave as an inheritance to posterity.  Dr. Gregory states that he had been "informed on good authority it was occasioned by the refusal of a gentleman, whom he had occasionally complimented in his poems, to accommodate him with a supply of money."  Clearly enough, as appears from the document itself, the gentleman in question was Mr. Burgum, though he could scarcely be described with propriety as one much complimented by Chatterton's muse.[1]  I am inclined however to regard Mrs. Edkins' version as the true one, where she says : "Lambert had little business, and of course the clerk had little to do ; but, like the dog in the manger, he would neither employ him, or let him employ himself ; and when he wrote a paper about killing himself, as worn out with vexations, she had no doubt he did it to induce Lambert—whom he represented as afraid of his own shadow,—to let him go." He had already told his mother and her he was resolved to run away, if he could not get his dismissal from a master who was continually insulting him, and making his life miserable.[2]





Yet the document has its flashes of tragic earnestness too ; reminding us that it is the jest of one, to whom the idea of self-destruction was already familiar.  His mind was in disordered strife with all its most cherished passions ; and he bitterly exclaims in the apostrophe to Catcott :—

---

[1] According to his own statement, Chatterton had at this time only two creditors : the debts amounting together to less than five pounds.

[2] Cumberland ; Dix, App. p. 312.

> "Thy friendship never could be dear to me,
> Since all I am is opposite to thee ;
> If ever obligated to thy purse,
> Rowley discharges all : my first, chief curse ;
> For had I never known the antique lore,
> I ne'er had ventured from my peaceful shore,
> To be the wreck of promises and hopes :
> A Boy of Learning, and a Bard of Tropes ;
> But happy in my humble sphere had moved,
> Untroubled, unrespected,[1] unbeloved."

Omitting the portion in verse, from which the most characteristic passages have already been quoted, the strange document is as follows :



"This is the last Will and Testament of me, Thomas Chatterton, of the City of Bristol : being sound in body, or it is the fault of my last surgeon. The soundness of my mind the Coroner and Jury are to be judges of ; desiring them to take notice, that the most perfect masters of human nature in Bristol distinguish me by the title of the Mad Genius ; therefore if I do a mad action, it is conformable to every action of my life, which all savoured of insanity.

"*Item.* If after my death, which will happen to-morrow night before eight o'clock, being the Feast of the Resurrection, the Coroner and Jury bring it in lunacy, I will and direct, that Paul Farr, Esq. and Mr. John Flower, at their joint expense, cause my body to be interred in the tomb of my fathers, and raise the monument over my body to the height of four feet five inches, placing the present flat stone on the top, and adding six tablets."



Then follow the inscriptions, in French, Latin, and English, in memory of real and imaginary ancestors, occupying three of the tablets. The fourth reads :—

"To the Memory of Thomas Chatterton. Reader, judge not ; if thou art a Christian, believe that he shall be judged by a superior power. To that power only is he now answerable."

The fifth and sixth tablets are devoted to his favourite heraldic achievements ; and then it thus proceeds :—

"And I will and direct, that if the Coroner's inquest bring it in felo-de-se, the said monument shall be, notwithstanding, erected. And if the said Paul Farr and John Flower have souls so Bristolish

---

[1] Cottle prints this *unsuspected*, and has been followed, as usual, by all subsequent editors.

as to refuse this my Bequest, they will transmit a copy of my Will to the Society for supporting the Bill of Rights, whom I hereby empower to build the same monument according to the aforesaid directions. And if they, the said Paul Farr and John Flower, should build the said monument, I will and direct that the second edition of my Kew Gardens shall be dedicated to them in the following Dedication :—To Paul Farr and John Flower, Esqs. this book is most humbly dedicated by the Author's Ghost.

"*Item.* I give and bequeath all my vigour and fire of youth to Mr. George Catcott, being sensible he is most in want of it.

"*Item.* From the same charitable motive, I give and bequeath unto the Reverend Mr. Camplin, senior, all my humility. To Mr. Burgum all my prosody and grammar, likewise one moiety of my modesty; the other moiety to any young lady who can prove without blushing that she wants that valuable commodity. To Bristol all my spirit and disinterestedness: parcels of goods unknown on her quay since the days of Canyng and Rowley! 'Tis true a charitable gentleman, one Mr. Colston, smuggled a considerable quantity of it, but it being proved he was a Papist, the Worshipful Society of Aldermen endeavoured to throttle him with the Oath of Allegiance. I leave also all my religion to Dr. Cutts Barton, Dean of Bristol, hereby empowering the sub-sacrist to strike him on the head when he goes to sleep in church. My powers of utterance I give to the Reverend Mr. Broughton, hoping he will employ them to a better purpose than reading lectures on the immortality of the soul. I leave the Reverend Mr. Catcott some little of my free-thinking, that he may put on the spectacles of Reason, and see how vilely he is duped in believing the Scriptures literally. I wish he and his brother would know how far I am their real enemy; but I have an unlucky way of railing, and when the strong fit of satyre is upon me, spare neither friend nor foe. This is my excuse for



what I have said of them elsewhere. I leave Mr. Clayfield the sincerest thanks my gratitude can give; and I will and direct that whatever any person may think the pleasure of reading my works worth, they immediately pay their own valuation to him, since it is then become a lawful debt to me, and to him as my executor in this case.

"I leave my moderation to the politicians on both sides the question. I leave my generosity to our present Right Worshipful Mayor, Thomas Harris, Esq. I give my abstinence to the Company at the Sheriff's annual feast, in general, more particularly to the Alderman.

"*Item.* I give and bequeath to Mr. Mat. Mease a mourning ring with this motto, "Alas poor Chatterton!" provided he pays for it himself. *Item.* I leave the young ladies all the letters they have had from me, assuring them they need be under no apprehensions from the appearance of my Ghost, for I die for none of them. *Item.* I leave all my debts, in the whole not Five pounds, to the payment of the charitable and generous Chamber of Bristol, on penalty, if

CHAP. XI.

refused, to hinder every member from ever eating a good dinner, by appearing in the form of a Bailiff. If, in defiance of this terrible spectre, they obstinately persist in refusing to discharge my debts, let my two creditors apply to the supporters of the Bill of Rights.

"*Item.* I leave my mother and sister to the protection of my friends, if I have any.

"Executed in the presence of Omniscience, this 14th of April, 1770.

"T. CHATTERTON.

"*Codicil.* It is my pleasure that Mr. Cocking and Miss Farley print this my Will the first Saturday after my death.

"T. C."

*Grave endorsement.*

Such is Chatterton's will, to which is added the endorsement : "All this wrote between 11 and 2 o'clock, Saturday, in the utmost distress of mind, April 14." Yet, in spite of the unmistakeable earnestness of some passages, no one can study the grim satire, and believe that it was composed, as a whole, in the utmost distress of mind. No stranger document was ever penned at such an age. It is a grave jest, which, but for the terrible reality of its author's violent death within a few months, could suggest to no reader that it was written with any serious intention.

*State of the original MSS.*

The original manuscript, as now preserved in the Library of the Bristol Philosophical Institution, has been separated into detached leaves, trimmed, and mounted in a blank folio volume ; so that the sequence of the pages can now only be inferred from the context. The mode of editing pursued by Mr. Cottle lends no aid on this point; and his text is vitiated by some important errors and omissions. The postscript, or endorsement, quoted above, is at the top of the second page, as now arranged, the other side being blank ; and refers, I think, exclusively to the verse : with which alone it harmonises. Beginning in scornful irony, the bitterness of its abrupt close might well be written "in the utmost distress of mind," as he alludes to the indignities of a suicide's grave, and exclaims :—

> "Poor superstitious mortals ! wreak your hate
> Upon my cold remains——"

R 2

CHAP. XI.

*Barrett's good advice.*

*" Decimus" to supplant Rowley.*

*A prudent retailer of advice.*

Barrett, it is obvious, from allusions in this poetical fragment, had been advising the imprudent satirist to abjure the follies of verse; leave the Worshipful Mr. Harris and other civic dignitaries alone; abandon the public journals, where " Decimus " was proving himself a second Junius : and stick to his scrivener's desk. Some creditor,—his tailor not improbably,—who had trusted him to the amount of two or three pounds at most, was pressing him for payment of his little bill; and Rowley, once his unfailing solace, had been abandoned for the time, and pronounced, with all the bitterness of a lover's hate, his " first, chief curse !" His plans for emerging from obscure poverty, with the aid of his ideal Mæcenas, Horace Walpole, had utterly failed; but, could he only be his own master, " Decimus " was, in his present humour, no unwelcome supplanter of Rowley. But this only rendered his menial position in Lambert's service all the more intolerable to one who already fancied himself an object of interest or fear to statesmen ; and saw no end to the glorious vistas opening to his view, could he but break the hated chain.

Mr. Barrett tells us that when he tendered his friendly counsels to Chatterton, and questioned him in reference to the distresses about which he wrote in the letter for Mr. Clayfield, " he acknowledged he wanted for nothing." The statement—recorded by Barrett nineteen years after his death,—meant no more than that it was useless to make that prudent retailer of advice the confidant of his troubles. The counsel was judicious enough, no doubt ; but the historian and antiquarian luminary of Bristol should have been able to discern that it was something more than a mere common attorney's apprentice he was advising. There. was no consolation for Chatterton. at any rate, in such advice ; and so, while rendering him thanks which, by their very sincerity, prove the earnestness of his feelings at the moment, he persisted in his deadly purpose.

But, of the detached leaves as now arranged in the blank folio, and as printed consecutively by Mr. Cottle, there follows, immediately after the brief endorsement, a postscript which ought obviously to intervene between the verse and the satirical testamentary document. Chatterton had been denouncing Burgum in bitterest irony, as lavish enough with his patronising criticism, but much too prudent to fulfil his promised loan without security. But now he writes :—

"NOTA BENE.—In a dispute concerning the character of David, it was argued that he must be a holy man from the strain of piety that breathes through his whole works. Being of a contrary opinion, and knowing that a great-genius can affect every thing;[1] endeavouring in the foregoing poems to represent an enthusiastic Methodist, intended to send it to Romaine, and impose it upon the infatuated world as a reality ; but, thanks to Mr. Burgum's generosity, I am now employed in matters of more importance.

"SATURDAY, *April* 14, '70."

"The foregoing poems" were, no doubt, entered in the same copybook, but they have not been preserved. Here, however, a complete revulsion of feeling is manifest. The bitter taunts on Burgum's prudence are replaced by hearty thanks for his generosity; and then it was, as I conceive, that, under the reflex influence of previous passion, he relieved his mind by the composition of a satirical will, after the model of "The late King of Bath," written, not as a legal document on professional foolscap, but in just such another copybook as that in which the De Bergham Pedigree was engrossed. Dr. Gregory, who regarded the Will as seriously indicating Chatterton's "design of committing suicide on the following day, namely Easter Sunday," says he had repeatedly intimated to the servants his intention of putting an end to his own life. Mr. Lambert's mother listened to such reported threats with terror; but she was unable to persuade her son that they meant anything serious, till he found upon his desk the copybook containing the Will: purposely left there perhaps, to meet his eye. It is noticeable, at any rate, that it contains no allusion to himself. But overlooking alike its satirical

---

[1] Cottle prints this "*can effect anything*."

humour and irony, he regarded it only as a desperate suicide's last farewell to the world. If Mrs. Edkins' interpretation be the right one, Chatterton had accomplished his purpose. The indentures which bound him to the attorney were forthwith cancelled, and within six days thereafter he was writing his first London letter to his mother.

*Literary work of the year.*

The volume of the *Town and Country Magazine* for 1769 shows that, to the very end of that year, his labours were purely literary. Rowley still reigned supreme; and he only turned to politics, and enlisted as a free lance in the bitter party strife of that period of excitement, when his successive efforts to find a patron or publisher for his antique poems had failed. But from the beginning of 1769 he had been in frequent correspondence with London booksellers and printers. His contributions, both in prose and verse, found ready acceptance: however meagre the pecuniary returns may have been; and, as Thistlethwaite tells Dean Milles: "The printers finding him of advantage to them in their publications, were by no means sparing of their praises and compliments;

*Liberal promises.*

adding thereto the most liberal promises of assistance and employment, should he choose to make London the place of his residence." Here, then, was a splendid opening for the emancipated apprentice.

*Talks of going to London.*

Mrs. Chatterton and Mrs. Edkins listened in grief to him when he talked of going to London; but when they became urgent, he replied: "What am I to do? Would you have me stay here and starve?" Then he reverted with high hope to the comforts in store for his mother and sister, when fortune should crown his endeavours. Thistlethwaite records an apocryphal story of his telling him that his first attempt was to be in literature; but failing that, he would turn Methodist preacher, devise a new sect, and trust to the credulity of mankind! But this was no more than some passing jest, to repel the importunities of an officious acquaintance, who, according to his own account, "anxious for his welfare, interrogated him as to the object of his views and expectations;

and what mode of life he intended to pursue on his arrival at London." Views and expectations !—it would have been difficult indeed to reduce to sober prose the expectations that then flitted before the eager-hearted boy, just emancipated from a hated thraldom. London was before him, and he knew no fear. He only longed to reach that goal of his aspirations ; to be " in among the throngs of men," and begin for himself the battle of life. So his friends and acquaintances made him up a purse. Burgum, the Catcotts, and other victims of his satirical licence, forgot their wrongs, we will hope, and contributed each his guinea. Barrett, who is our authority for the fact, no doubt spared a guinea for the boy to whom he owed the chief materials for his future volume, and all his chances for fame.

What the gift altogether amounted to, we can but guess. Dr. Maitland, with a case to make out against Chatterton, is very liberal in his interpretation of the amount :—a much larger sum than was expended on the road to London :—more money in pocket than he had ever had in his life.[1] Professor Masson, taking a more probable estimate of Bristol liberality, under all the circumstances, conceives of Chatterton " elated with the prospect of invading London with a pecuniary force of five guineas."[2] Elated undoubtedly he was, whatever his present resources may have been : and so, provided with funds, more or less ; with a light heart, and a bundle of manuscripts of rare worth, on which his fame—and, as he still fondly hoped, his fortune,—was to be founded ; the boy bade farewell to mother and sister, to St. Mary Redcliffe, and all the cherished associations of the city of his birth, and set forth, at the age of seventeen, to play his brief part as a man of letters in the great metropolis.

[1] Maitland, p. 35.
[2] Masson's Essays, p. 232.

# CHAPTER XII.

## LONDON.



THE adventurous boy who entered London on the 25th of April, 1770, confident of winning a foremost place in the republic of letters, had not, so far as appears, ever before been further than a holiday's ramble beyond the bounds of his native city. His actual funds consisted of the surplus of the purse provided for him by his Bristol friends; his resources lay in his pen and fertile brain; and on these, and the promises of the booksellers, rested hopes which for the time being flattered him with the assured realization of his brightest dreams. He reached London about five in the evening, made his way to Mr. Walmsley's, a plasterer in Shoreditch, where a relative, Mrs. Ballance, lodged; hunted up sundry aunts and cousins whom he found well, and ready to welcome him; and, what was still more practical, either that evening, or early next forenoon, waited on the most reliable of his literary connexions. This done, he sat down before his first day in London was over, and wrote his mother a graphic account of the journey.

"Here I am," he writes, "safe and in high spirits:" and then follow incidents of the stage coach and its company; a snowy night on Marlborough Downs, and a bright morning which tempted him to mount the coach-box for the remainder of the day: all matters of liveliest interest to the poor mother. What follows more concerns us now. "Got into London about five o'clock in the evening; called upon Mr. Edmunds, Mr. Fell, Mr. Hamilton, and Mr. Dodsley. Great encouragement from them; 'all approved of my design; shall soon be settled;" and then follows the proud message to Mr. Lambert already quoted, asking such a recommendation as he merited.



Chatterton's connexions with the London press were of some standing: but his contributions had hitherto, for the most part, been made, like the earlier ones to *Felix Farley's Journal*, with no thought of other reward than the pride of authorship. In March 1770, only a few weeks before leaving Bristol, he transmitted the first instalment of his "Kew Gardens" to the editor of the *Middlesex Journal*, with this note: "Mr. Edmunds will send the author, Thomas Chatterton, twenty of the journals in which the above poem—which I shall continue,—shall appear, by the machine, if he thinks proper to put it in. The money shall be paid to his orders." The first political letters were probably offered on similar terms; though payment for the author's copies would no doubt be declined by a judicious editor. The way was thus opened for the literary adventurer; but relations between him and the publishers had now to be established on a very different footing. Mr. Edmunds alone of London publishers knew that the great Decimus of his journal, and rival of Woodfall's Junius, was Mr. Thomas Chatterton of Bristol. The first sight of the youthful demagogue must have taken him somewhat aback, one would think. It did not, however, prevent the publication of further Decimus philippics, and other contributions from the same pen. Mr. Fell was editor and printer of the *Freeholders' Magazine*, another political miscellany of the day, strong for Wilkes and liberty; and therefore quite in Chatterton's present line. As to Hamilton, of the *Town and Country Magazine;* and Dodsley, of the *Annual Register:* he had already, as we know, been in correspondence with them both; and, to the former at least, was known as one of his most industrious contributors. It is not unworthy of note that all four are named to his mother without word of explanation. His plans had evidently been talked over in

*First
London
ramble.*

*Sources of
informa-
tion.*

*First host
and hostess.*

*Uses of poet-
folks.*

the little home circle, and he was only assuring her now that they were in a fair way of successful realization.

Mr. Hamilton was to be found close by the haunt of Cave and Dr. Johnson, at St. John's Gate, Clerkenwell; while Mr. Dodsley's establishment lay far to the west of Temple Bar. We can thus follow the young stranger in his first eager exploration of the London of an hundred years ago : from Shoreditch, through the crowded city, to St. Paul's, and Paternoster Row, in search of Mr. Fell; by Smithfield to Clerkenwell and old St. John's Gate; then to Mr. Edmunds, in Shoe Lane, Holborn; and so westward, past Charing Cross, to the great publisher's house in Pall Mall. The ramble was a long one, full of interest, in the freshness of its novelty, to the Bristol boy; and with "great encouragement," as yet, from all.

Partly by means of the information derived from Chatterton's own letters, and still more through the persevering researches of Sir Herbert Croft, opportunely prosecuted within a few years after his death : we can realize with considerable minuteness the circumstances attendant on his settlement in London. His first host and hostess, Mr. and Mrs. Walmsley, were on the whole favourably impressed with the lad : notwithstanding certain habits incident to his literary labours, not likely to prove acceptable to any tidy housekeeper. Mr. Walmsley was struck with "something manly and pleasing about him;" and added, that "he did not dislike the wenches." As for Mrs. Walmsley, "she never saw any harm of him, he never *mislisted* her," as she phrased it, "but was always very civil, whenever they met in the house by accident. He would never suffer the room in which he used to read and write to be swept; because, he said, poets hated brooms. She told him she did not know anything poet-folks were good for, but to sit in a dirty cap and gown, in a garret, and at last be starved :"—the traditions of Grub Street having by this time penetrated eastward to Shoreditch. She also stated that during the whole period Chatterton lodged with her he never, but once, stayed out after the family hours. Then "he did not come home all night, and had been, she heard, poeting a song about the streets :"—a report which his relative, Mrs. Ballance, corrected; as she ascertained that he lodged that night at one of the aunts or cousins already referred to.[1]

Mrs. Walmsley had a nephew and niece, to whom reference has already been made. The former, a young man about twenty-four years of age,[2] shared his bed with the stranger, and was rather put out, as we have already seen, by some of the odd ways of this, the first poet he had ever encountered. Yet he also said that, "notwithstanding his pride and haughtiness, it was impossible to help liking him." The niece, a young woman nearly ten years his senior, somewhat resented the lad's saucy ways; and declared that, "for her part, she always took him more for a mad boy than anything else." Yet she also was impressed, in spite of herself, with the countenance and bearing of the youth, and said that, "but for his face, and her knowledge of his age, she should never have thought him a boy, he was so manly, and so much himself." His own relative, Mrs. Ballance, was even more puzzled what to make of him than Miss Walmsley. From Chatterton's efforts, ere long, to obtain some interest in her behalf at the Trinity House, she appears to have been the widow of a seaman, originally, we may presume, from the port of Bristol. She knew her relative, Mrs. Chatterton, to have been left, like herself, in a very humble way; and no doubt, when written to, was ready to do what little was in her power for the widow's son. But, instead of the poor lad she had expected, she found a youth "proud as Lucifer. He very soon quarrelled with her for calling him 'Cousin Tommy,' and asked her

---

[1] Croft, p. 215.

[2] The relative ages of Chatterton and his companions is of importance in correctly estimating their statements regarding him. Professor Masson speaks of the nephew as a boy of fourteen. But Sir H. Croft, writing in 1779, says: "Their nephew and niece; the latter about as old as Chatterton would be now, the former three years younger." The nephew, therefore, must have been about twenty-four, and the niece twenty-seven.



*A London room-mate.*

*Manly self-possession.*

*Proud as Lucifer.*

if she ever heard of a poet's being called Tommy? But she assured him that she knew nothing of poets, and only wished he would not set up for a gentleman. Upon her recommending him to get into some office, when he had been in town two or three weeks, he stormed about the room like a madman, and frightened her not a little by telling her that he hoped, with the blessing of God, very soon to be sent prisoner to the Tower : which would make his fortune." The two took their meals together ; though not in the most social manner, for he would eat no meat, drank only water : and scared the poor woman, in the midst of her well-meant advices, by declaring "he



should settle the nation before he had done ! How could she think that her poor Cousin Tommy was so great a man as she now finds he was? His mother should have written word of his greatness ; and then, to be sure, she would have humoured the gentleman accordingly."



Chatterton was busy in those days on letters to the *Middlesex Journal, Freeholders' Magazine,* &c., "settling the nation." The return, in the form of pride, and the flattering notoriety so acceptable to the literary neophyte, was ample. In actual money it must have been small indeed. Fell, a needy adventurer on the verge of bankruptcy, was only too happy to find a novice eager to contribute clever political essays on the chance of future pay. But literary work was no longer, as in Bristol, the pastime of leisure hours. Some more reliable patron must be found, if the profession of letters was to furnish



him with permanent bread-work. There is a piece in the *Annual Register* for 1769, in imitation of an Ode of Casimir on "The Flight of Youth," which bears the initials T. C. and was possibly sent to Dodsley while the "Ælla" MS. was under consideration. Its merits are small, nor do I find any distinct trace of Chatterton using his own initials ;[1] though the very nature of his correspondence about the mysterious "Ælla" might tempt him to assume this signature for an inferior modern piece ; and any

[1] T. C. was the signature adopted by Thomas Cary, of Bristol. From his sixteenth year Chatterton most frequently signed D. B.

accepted piece would serve as an introduction to the publisher. Chatterton accordingly presented himself before the great bibliopole as he tells his mother, and was dismissed with fair words which he estimated as full of encouragement. Could he have made the shy, retiring, but kind-hearted bookseller his friend, no better patron need have been desired. With the worth of his genuine works once known; and through him introduced to the noble band who formed the real representatives of letters in that day; how different must have been the boy's fate. The famous Turk's Head Club, founded in 1764, with Burke, Reynolds, Johnson, Goldsmith, Nugent; and by and by with Garrick, Percy, Dyer, and other London wits and celebrities among its members: had been effecting an infusion of new blood. Goldsmith,—who was giving his final polish to his " Deserted Village," preparatory to its publication, some four weeks after Chatterton's arrival in London ;—had just provoked Johnson into one of his characteristic retorts, by telling the Club that " they had travelled over each other's minds ;" and wanted new men to give zest to their meetings. Fancy the boy transferred from his Catcotts, Barretts, and Burgums, to such society as this ; and interchanging saucy wit, brilliant satire, and grave, earnest thought, with intellectual equals who could estimate his true worth :

> " And greet with smiles the young-eyed Poesy,
> All deftly mask'd as hoar Antiquity."

And what was to prevent it ? No social inequality ; and as for the intellectual patent of nobility : it was Coleridge who thus in fancy conceived of himself with Lloyd, Southey, and Wordsworth gathering round the boy " at sober eve," to listen to his " stately song."

But Chatterton had made a false start with Mr. Dodsley, and whatever encouraging words he might say to the self-introduced visitor, his present aims as an author were not in the great publisher's line. No real good, indeed, temporary or otherwise, was to be derived from his Decimus letters, and other dealings with Edmunds, Fell, and the political adventurers of the London press. It was as the True Thomas, the genuine Rowley, that his place must be won, if at all, among men of letters. Yet it is probable that the literary treasures he possessed were not even hinted at, in his visit to Mr. Dodsley. He was dazzled, for the time, with the empty noise and glare of Junius letters and Churchill satires ; and dreamt, to the no small alarm of Mrs. Ballance, of being sent ere long to the Tower, and so becoming as famous as Wilkes himself.



There was no lack of energy or self-reliance about the youth, in his first efforts in this novel career. He went straight to his point, like one to whom London, and all the arts of its literary guild, had been long familiar ; and, in the wild whirl of that new life, the war of parties had in it a fascination well calculated to banish for a time the antique muse. There was much, moreover, in the character of the period, to tempt an ardent young writer into the political arena, for it was one of the most memorable crises in the history of periodical literature.



The accession of George III. to his grandfather's throne, in 1760, reawakened the war of parties with all its old bitterness, and with a coarseness of vituperation on a par with the worst days of the Restoration. The popular prejudices against the Scot, to which Johnson lent all the weight of his intense one-sidedness, acquired a concentrated bitterness, when John Stuart, Earl of Bute, became the royal favourite, and Smollett led the van in defence of his administration. Within the ten years preceding Chatterton's arrival in London the newspaper press had successfully asserted, under the strangest auspices, its legitimate influence in popular government. The *Rambler, Idler, Adventurer*, and other light literary serials which followed on the model of Steele and Addison's famous essays, had been superseded by Smollett's



*Briton*, Wilkes' unscrupulous *North Briton*, and the still more famous letters of Junius. Churchill, a profligate churchman, had allied himself to the notorious demagogue ; and the pungency of their shameless wit and audacity proved more than a match for royal favour. But with a Scottish Peer for the butt of their scurrilous vituperation, and a Scottish journalist as his ally, the temptation to enlist the prejudices of race and nationality in the strife were irresistible : and so Churchill produced the bitterest of his satires : " The Prophecy of Famine ; a Scots Pastoral," replete with profane humour and prejudice ; and dedicated it to Wilkes. As for the *North Briton*, it had come to a violent end with the famous No. 45, seven years before Chatterton's arrival in London ; but the arrest of Wilkes, and the question of general search-warrants, which grew out of the prosecutions of its publisher, protracted the strife till long after his brief London career was at an end.

The smouldering fires of this combustible embroglio had suddenly blazed up, with no little smoke and heat, at the very time when Chatterton started as a literary adventurer. Wilkes, popular candidate, and, as far as majority of votes could make him, member for Middlesex, had been expelled the House of Commons, condemned to pay a fine of £1,000, and undergo a protracted imprisonment. On the 17th of April,—in that very Easter week when Chatterton had his Will in hand,— his term of imprisonment came to an end ; and the patriot hero of the mob emerged from the King's Bench to enjoy an ovation such as has not often greeted the noblest and best. " Wilkes and Liberty " was the motto of the day. " Violation of the right of election," of " The Bill of Rights " itself, and much else, were involved in the wrongs of the demagogue. So his fine was more than paid by popular subscription ; public dinners throughout England celebrated his release ; while already in far-away Scotland he was commemorated in very different fashion. For, curiously enough, on every Fifth of November, when protestant English boys are kindling their bonfires for Guy Fawkes, those of presbyterian Scotland take advantage of the occasion to make an *auto-da-fé* of Johnny Wilkes !

While still in Bristol, and busy with Saxon heraldry

CHAP. XII.

*Churchill's satires.*

*Wilkes expelled the House of Commons.*

*" Wilkes and Liberty."*

Chap. XII.

*A London Alderman.*

and Rowley poems, Chatterton had read in the first number of the *Town and Country Magazine* an article on the power and dignity of a London Alderman, illustrated by a full-length portrait of Alderman Wilkes in his official robes. For the citizens had testified their sympathy for that suffering patriot, while still in gaol, by conferring on him this distinguished honour; and the article treats accordingly of "the abolition of general warrants; the seizure of private papers; and the liberty of the press, that great bulwark of our rights and properties:" telling the reader that, if such things "be dear to Englishmen, or valuable to posterity, John Wilkes, Esq. will be held in that estimation by his countrymen to the latest period of time." All this, and much more of the like kind, Chatterton read and pondered, while still busy on his own literary projects, in his last year in Lambert's office.

*The demagogue's career.*

Some legal technicalities had enabled the Court of Aldermen to set aside the election of Wilkes by the Ward of Farringdon Without, but he was re-elected unanimously; and by the time Chatterton reached London, he had been sworn in to the dignified office; in due time to be Sheriff; Lord Mayor; and when, as he himself styled it, he was "a fire burned out," to retire at last into the lucrative office of City Chamberlain. Barely a month later, Lord Mayor Beckford — also engraved at full length in the same volume,—bearded Majesty itself in an extempore speech in St. James's Palace, still readable on his monument in Guildhall: and so the young Bristol literateur, with his Decimus fulminations in progress, found ferment enough to stimulate his excitable brain.

*Rewards of a literary patriot.*

But it was one thing for Decimus to write his letters in the leisure intervals of office work, and enjoy the delight of receiving from London his copy of the *Middlesex,* or other journal, in which they were given forth to the world; and quite another thing for Chatterton to pay his London board on the profits of such patriotic outbursts. So ere long he gave his sister the results of his experience. . Essay writing, as he told her, had the advantage of being sure of constant pay ; but " Essays on the patriotic side fetch no more than what the copy is sold for. As the patriots themselves are searching for a place, they have no gratuities to spare. So says one of the beggars, in a temporary alteration of mine, in the ' Jovial Crew :'

' A patriot was my occupation,
  It got me a name, but no pelf,
Till, starved for the good of the nation,
  I begged for the good of myself.
      Fal, lal, &c.

' I told them if 'twas not for me,
  Their freedoms would all go to pot ;
I promised to set them all free,
  But never a farthing I got.
      Fal, lal, &c.'

On the other hand, unpopular essays "—that is papers on the side of the Government,—" will not even be accepted ; and you must pay to have them printed ; but then you seldom lose by it. Courtiers are so sensible of their deficiency in merit, that they generally reward all who know how to daub them with the appearance of it."

The caricature is not greatly overdrawn. Enormous sums were yearly expended in subsidising such literary adventurers, and organizing a guerilla service on behalf of the ministry of the day. Brief as was the London career of Chatterton : his letters, and the productions of his pen, alike in prose and verse, betray abundant traces of this transitional period in the history of literary patronage, when the awards of the Crown to the most distinguished men of letters were regarded as bribes to tempt them from their true vocation, rather than recognitions of their intellectual worth. Home, the author of " Douglas," was one of the literary partisans pensioned for such services by the Scottish favourite. Smollett won his reward, not as the poet and novelist, but as the political pamphleteer ; and Johnson — who also owed his pension to Bute,—was accredited with earning it

S

*Pensioned
Johnson.*

*Patronage
of Mac-
pherson.*

*Prejudices
and passions
of the day.*

by political subserviency; as in Chatterton's "Kew Gardens:"

> " When Bute, the ministry and people's head,
> With royal favour pension'd Johnson dead :
> His works in undeserved oblivion sunk,
> Were read no longer, and the man was drunk.
> Some blockhead, ever envious of his fame,
> Massacred Shakespear in the doctor's name. . . .
> And universal cat-calls testified
> How mourn'd the critics when the genius died.
> But now, though strange the facts to deists seem,
> His ghost is risen in a vernal theme,
> And emulation maddened all the Row
> To catch the strains which from a spectre flow ;
> And print the reasons of a bard deceased,
> Who once gave all the town a weekly feast.
> As beer, to every drinking purpose dead,
> Is to a wondrous metamorphose led,
> And opened to the action of the winds
> In vinegar a resurrection finds :
> His genius dead, and decently interred,
> The clamorous noise of duns sonorous heard,
> Scour'd into life, assumed the heavy pen,
> And saw existence for an hour again ;
> Scattered his thoughts spontaneous from his brain,
> And proved we had no reason to complain."

One evidence, however, peculiarly appropriate to our present subject, shows that Lord Bute could appreciate purely literary claims ; for it was under his patronage that Macpherson had published the poems of Ossian only a few years before. But, as the young satirist ironically exclaims in the same satire :

> "Alas ! I was not born beyond the Tweed."

It is amusing thus to trace the reflex of the prejudices and passions of that excited period, in the satires of the Bristol boy : a zeal for Chatham, that can forgive even the crime of his coronet ; a contempt for Grafton, that cannot be appeased by his resignation ; and a dislike of the Scot as intense as if the southern bank of the Tweed, instead of that of the Severn, had witnessed his

birth and training.  His " Resignation," a spirited piece
of satirical invective, furnishes the following picture of
the Scottish favourite :

*Picture of
the Scottish
favourite.*

> " Far in the North, amid whose dreary hills
> None hear the pleasant murmuring sound of rills ;
> Where no soft gale in dying raptures blows,
> Or aught which bears the look of verdure grows,
> Save where the north wind cuts the solemn yew
> And russet rushes drink the noxious dew ;
> Dank exhalations drawn from stagnant moors,
> The morning dress of Caledonia's shores.
> Upon a bleak and solitary plain,
> Exposed to every storm of wind and rain,
> A humble cottage rear'd its lowly head. . . .
> Here lived a laird the ruler of his clan,
> Whose fame thro' every northern mountain ran.
> Great was his learning, for he long had been
> A student at the town of Aberdeen ;
> Professor of all languages at once,
> To him some reckoned Chappellow[1] a dunce.
> With happy fluency he learned to speak
> Syriac or Latin, Arabic or Greek ;
> Not any tongue in which Oxonians sing
> When they rejoice, or blubber, with the King,
> To him appeared unknown. . . . . . .
> 'Tis true his rent roll just maintained his state,
> But some in spite of poverty are great.
> Though famine sunk her impress on his face,
> Still you might there his haughty temper trace ;
> Descended from a catalogue of kings,
> Whose warlike arts Macpherson sweetly sings,
> He bore the majesty of monarchs past,
> Like a tall pine rent with the winter's blast,
> Whose spreading trunk and withered branches show
> How glorious once the lordly tree might grow.
>
>       .         .         .         .
>
> Fired by Ambition he resolved to roam
> Far from the famine of his native home ;
> To seek the warmer climate of the south,
> And at one banquet feast his eyes and mouth.
> As from the hills the land of promise rose,
> A secret transport in his bosom glows,

*A royal line.*

---

[1] This learned Professor of Arabic at Cambridge, celebrated for
his knowledge of Oriental languages, died in 1768.

> A joy prophetic, until then unknown,
> Assured him all he viewed would be his own.
>
> .　　　.　　　.　　　.　　　.
>
> He reached the great Metropolis at last.
> Here fate beheld him as he trudged the street,
> Bare was his buttocks and unshod his feet ;
> A lengthening train of boys displayed him great,
> He seem'd already minister of state.
> The Carlton Sybil saw his graceful mien
> And straight forgot her hopes of being Queen."

Then follows a cleverly drawn picture of the revolution wrought by the great Thane, when he at length attained to power. "Plenty smiled in Scotland's barren land ;" Merit hastened southward to receive its reward,

> " And Genius having ranged beyond the Tweed
> Sat brooding upon bards who could not read."

One more brief extract will suffice to illustrate the vigour with which the young satirist could wield his pen as the political partisan :

> " When Grafton shook oppression's iron rod,
> Like Egypt's lice, the instrument of God ;
> When Camden, driven from his office, saw
> The last weak efforts of expiring law ;
> When Bute, the regulator of the state,
> Preferr'd the vicious, to supplant the great ;
> When rank corruption thro' all orders ran,
> And infamy united Sawney's clan ;
> When every office was with rogues disgraced,
> And the Scotch dialect became the taste——
> Could Beaufort with such creatures stay behind ?
> No ! Beaufort was a Briton, and resigned."

Much longer extracts of equal vigour and pungency might be made. Yet this poem only exists in the first rough unfinished draft, preserved among other rescued papers, in the British Museum, with all the blanks, erasures, and illegible lines, as it was originally dashed off and thrown aside. Such a writer, it might be supposed, was worth enlisting on one side or the other, when literary partisans were in such requisition. He had naturally taken the popular side ; believed in all the current scandals about the Court and its favourites ; and so employed the old weapons he had used so recklessly against the ecclesiastical and civic dignitaries of Bristol, in assailing the supposed betrayers of the nation's liberties.

There is surely something very noteworthy in the versatility thus manifested at so early an age. The boy, whose natural tastes had made of him the old-world poet and recluse, passes to London, and steps into the front rank of partisan combatants, with all the ease of a veteran politician. It is the same in every department of prose and verse. Chameleon-like, he catches the satiric vein of Churchill ; the envenomed prejudice of Wilkes ; and the lofty-toned, yet narrow, bitterness of Junius. He assumes, not unsuccessfully, the rough vigour of Smollett ; apes at times the rythmical niceties and the antithesis of Pope, or the polished grace of Gray and Collins ; or, in the guise of a Saxon monk, rivals the Gaelic Ossian, in his heroic affectations. But, all the while, this versatile mocking-bird had his own genuine song, in virtue of which those imitative echoes of contemporaries have still a value for us.

Confident in such varied resources ; and by no means scrupulous as to the mode of employing them : the sanguine youth flattered himself with dreams of imaginary triumphs and abundant recompense. The essays and poems already penned ; and all the possible essays, poems, and literary achievements of every kind, projected, or deemed achievable by him : were coined into actual wealth by his facile imagination ; and he hastened to make his mother and sister sharers of his fortune. The boastful extravagance of his home letters would at times be sufficiently amusing, as a real Alnascar's dream, could we forget the tragic bitterness of the awakening. He was drawing on his imagination ; but only, he fancied, as the heir of an unrealised fortune is free to pledge what is already his own. And amid all the bombastic foibles of the self-reliant youth there is ever the genuine element

CHAP. XII.

*The popular side.*

*Wonderful versatility.*

*Confident and unscrupulous.*

*A real Alnascar's dream.*

of domestic affection, anticipating the rays of a promised dawn, that those whose poverty he had shared might partake of its sunshine. Yet with all this, it is not easy to determine how much is the realization of sanguine fancy, and how much the mere romancing of the boastful youth, bent on impressing his provincial friends with an imposing idea of his achievements. Before he had been a fortnight in London he addressed a second letter to his mother, in which he tells her : " I am settled, and in such a settlement as I would desire. I get four guineas a month by one magazine ; shall engage to write a History of England and other pieces, which will more than double that sum. Occasional essays for the daily papers would more than support me. What a glorious prospect ! Mr. Wilkes knew me by my writings, since I first corresponded with the booksellers here. I shall visit him next week, and by his interest will insure Mrs. Ballance the Trinity House. He affirmed that what Mr. Fell had of mine could not be the writings of a youth ; and expressed a desire to know the author. By the means of another bookseller I shall be introduced to Townsend and Sawbridge,"—two of Wilkes's Liberal colleagues in the aldermanic office. He then adds, " I am quite familiar at the Chapter Coffee-house, and know all the geniuses there ;" and so Mr. Cary, Mr. Kator, and other literary correspondents are instructed to address letters for him to this City haunt of authors and booksellers.

Wilkes knew him by his writings !—had indeed expressed a desire to know their author ! Possibly enough the young literateur made his way into the presence of the great demagogue—then playing the roll of popular patriot to all England; introduced himself as the veritable Decimus of the *Middlesex Journal*, and was graciously dismissed with the flattering lie. Or perhaps it was Mr. Fell, who palmed off the story on his inexperienced correspondent, along with some vague promise of four guineas a month for contributions to the *Freeholders' Magazine ;* for Mr. Fell is one of the neediest of adventurers, who in another week has to be reported by Chatterton as safe in the debtors' wing of the King's Bench ; and was therefore likely enough to be liberal in fine words. Mr. Edmunds, also, of the *Middlesex Journal,* is by the same date in Newgate, under fine of the House of Lords, on political grounds ; so that the boy was not so far wrong, after all, in thinking that if he handled his pen to good purpose, he might land some day in the Tower, or its equivalent.

Meanwhile Chatterton has an eye to his friends. His interest with Mr. Wilkes he relies on for Mrs. Ballance ; but should that great man fail him, there are higher influences within reach, as he indicates in his next letter. " Intended waiting on the Duke of Bedford, relative to the Trinity House ; but his Grace is dangerously ill." He also encloses a letter to his friend Cary, with messages for sundry other literary Bristolians of his old circle. They are to read the *Freeholders' Magazine;* and anything they have for publication, they are to address to him, to be left at the Chapter Coffee-house, " and it shall most certainly appear in some periodical." Before the close of the month, he dates a letter to his sister from Tom's Coffee-house in the Strand, another favourite resort of men of letters in Johnson's time ; and writes, according to his own account, amid the noisy hum of their talk on politics and public business. He is more sanguine and boastful than ever ; has engaged to live with a gentleman, the brother of a Lord,—only a Scotch one however,—who has extensive bookselling schemes in view; is about to write a voluminous history of London, and much else. In fact if money flowed in upon him as fast as honours, he would give his sister a portion of £5,000.

There is an amusing air of self-importance in all this romancing, which, like so much else of what is good as well as evil in Chatterton, requires us to keep in mind his age, and utter inexperience of the world in which he now moved with so confident a bearing. He next proceeds to put his sister in possession of the public news, which has a personal interest for her. " You have doubt-

CHAP. XII.

*An editor in Newgate.*

*Has an eye to his friends.*

*Tom's Coffee-house.*

*Amusing air of self-importance.*

less heard," he writes, "of the Lord Mayor's remonstrating and addressing the King; but it will be a piece of news to inform you that I have been with the Lord Mayor on the occasion. Having addressed an essay to his Lordship, it was very well received; perhaps better than it deserved; and I waited on his Lordship, to have his approbation, to address a second letter to him, on the subject of the remonstrance and its reception. His Lordship received me as politely as a citizen could; and warmly invited me to call on him again. The rest is a secret. But the devil of the matter is, there is no money to be got on this side of the question. Interest is on the other side. But he is a poor author who cannot write on both sides. I believe I may be introduced—and if not,



I'll introduce myself,—to a ruling power in the Court party." He has been little more than a month in London; and already is learning how precarious are the rewards of such literary taskwork. The thought has crossed him in some moment of despondency of escaping all this feverish drudgery by "a step to sea;" and he lets slip the hint: "I might have a recommendation to Sir George Colebrook, an East India director, as qualified



for an office no ways despicable; but I shall not take a step to the sea, whilst I can continue on land." So he turns aside to Mr. Wensley, some seafaring cousin, as it would seem, whose ship, "the *Levant* man-of-war," he had already mentioned in a former letter as at Portsmouth; and who is now at Woolwich receiving his pay.



In his second letter to his mother, Chatterton draws a sufficiently disparaging contrast between London, as already revealed to him in a ten days' sojourn, and the "mean and despicable" Bristol of his life-long experience, and then proceeds: "The poverty of authors is a common observation, but not always a true one. No author can be poor who understands the arts of booksellers. Without this necessary knowledge the greatest genius may starve; and with it the greatest dunce live in splendour;" —prophetic words! But he fancied himself master of this literary craft, so needful even to genius; and ere long embodied his experience in his " Art of Puffing by a Bookseller's Journeyman:" a slight satirical piece, in which its reputed author deals in sufficiently disparaging terms with one of his most gifted contemporaries :—

> " The trading wits endeavour to attain,
> Like booksellers, the world's first idol—gain.
> For this they puff the heavy Goldsmith's line,
> And hail his sentiment, though trite, divine ;
> For this the patriotic bard complains,
> And Bingley binds poor liberty in chains ;
> For this was every reader's faith deceived,
> And Edmunds swore what nobody believed ;
> For this the wits in close disguises fight,
> For this the varying politicians write ;
> For this each month new magazines are sold,
> With dulness filled and transcripts of the old.
> The *Town and Country* struck a lucky hit,
> Was novel, sentimental, full of wit ;
> Aping her walk the same success to find,
> The *Court and City* hobbles far behind.
> Sons of Apollo, learn : merit's no more
> Than a good frontispiece to grace the door.
> The author who invents a title well,
> Will always find his covered dulness sell ;
> Flexney and every bookseller will buy ;
> Bound in neat calf, the work will never die."

The trick of new magazines " filled with transcripts of the old " was notorious among the literary hacks of that eighteenth century. When Goldsmith collected his essays into a volume, he thus humorously reclaimed his pilfered ideas : " If there be a pride in multiplied editions, I have seen some of my labours sixteen times reprinted, and claimed by different parents as their own." Nor did Chatterton, himself, scruple to resort to the same process when hard pressed. But, with every deduction on account of such borrowed transcripts : in mere quantity, the amount of literary work he accomplished is as remarkable as the diversity of its character.

Chatterton tells his sister, before the end of May, of his essay addressed to the patriotic Lord Mayor; and of a second letter on his Lordship's uncourtly remonstrance, about which its author hints a mysterious secrecy. The history of this performance is fortunately preserved by Walpole in one of the Appendices to his " Narrative." Chatterton was at this time attaining all the success that a patriot writer could desire. The Lord Mayor had actually agreed that his forthcoming letter should be publicly addressed to him. Bingley, printer and proprietor of the *Political Register*, and also of the revived *North Briton*, had undertaken its publication. He might fairly consider himself second to none among the political free-lances on the popular side ; and though unhappily there was nothing to be got by it in the way of direct money payment, his prospects justified the tone of



exultation which his letter betrays. He assumed a fresh *nom de plume;* and as *Probus* his first Beckford letter appeared early in the following month, in the *Political Register*. The second was written, and accepted by Bingley ; and Chatterton only waited its appearance to present himself once more before the Lord Mayor, and claim the reward of his able championship : when, on the 21st of June, London was startled with the news of Beckford's sudden death.

The letter which was to signalise Chatterton's triumph by its appearance in the *North Briton* had become so



much waste paper. All his fine air-built castles had toppled down ; and, as Mrs. Ballance told Sir Herbert Croft, " when Beckford died, he was perfectly frantic, and out of his mind ; and said that he was ruined." But he recovered his equanimity ; and, years after his own death, among sundry manuscripts examined by Walpole in the hands of a private collector, was one which



is thus described by him : " *A Letter to the Lord Mayor Beckford*, signed Probus ; dated May 26, 1770. This is a violent abuse of Government for rejecting the remonstrance, and begins thus : ' When the endeavours of a spirited people to free themselves from an unsupportable slavery.'"

On the back of this essay, which is directed to Cary, is this characteristic endorsement :—

"Accepted by Bingley, set for, and thrown out of the *North Briton*, 21st June, on account of the Lord Mayor's death.



|  | £ s. d. | £ s. d. |
|---|---|---|
| Lost by his death on this Essay . . . . |  | 1 11 6 |
| Gained in Elegies . . . . . . . . | 2 2 0 |  |
| „ Essays . . . . . . . . | 3 3 0 |  |
|  |  | 5 5 0 |
| Am glad he is dead by . . . . . . . | | £3 13 6." |

One at least of the Elegies written on this occasion is preserved. It extends to twenty-eight stanzas, and was published in a quarto pamphlet by Mr. Kearsley of Fleet Street. Its tone is worthy of the grief that found such ready consolation; but a stanza or two may be aptly quoted here :—



"He knew when flatterers besiege a throne
    Truth seldom reaches to a monarch's ear ;
Knew if oppressed a loyal people groan,
    'Tis not the courtier's interest he should hear.

"Hence, honest to his prince, his manly tongue
    The public wrong and loyalty conveyed,
While titled tremblers, every nerve unstrung,
    Looked all around, confounded and dismayed ;

"Looked all around, astonish'd to behold—
    Trained up to flattery from their early youth—
An artless, fearless citizen unfold
    To royal ears a mortifying truth."

And so another patron had failed; and political writing was altogether proving a very thankless task. An ironical letter of his addressed to Lord North, which appeared in the *Freeholders' Magazine* for August, is shown by Dr. Maitland to have been mainly borrowed from a long-forgotten periodical, entitled *Common Sense*, published upwards of ten years before he was born.[1] But he would appear to have put in practice his maxim that "he is a poor author who cannot write on both sides," if Walpole be right in ascribing to him an unpublished letter to Lord North, under the signature of "The Moderator," dated May 26, 1770, and de-



[1] Maitland, p. 57.

Chap. XII.

*A venal
young
politician.*

*Trials of a
literary
adventurer.*

*Harry
Wildfire
and Mr.
Britannicus.*

scribed by him as "an encomium on the administration for rejecting the Lord Mayor Beckford's remonstrance." If so, the date is the same as that on which the venal young politician addressed to the Mayor the letter which was in the hands of Bingley's compositors when its author was driven frantic by his Lordship's death. Another of his unpublished *Decimus* letters, "To Lord Mansfield," as seen by Walpole in MS., being penned in no such courtly style, had many of its paragraphs cancelled, with the marginal note, "Prosecution will lye upon this."

It was hard to have his literary handicraft returned once and again on his hands in this untoward fashion. Until matters came to such a crisis in the political world, Chatterton doubtless reckoned for a time with reasonable confidence on an income from the productions of his versatile pen ; and even when the crash came he was loth to abandon the exciting arena of party strife. Beckford was still Mayor when, with a dignity becoming his new importance, he addressed his mother as " Dear Madam," dating from the King's Bench, where he had been hunting up his debtor, Mr. Fell, and getting paid seemingly by an introduction to the new proprietors of the *Freeholders' Magazine;* and so he flatters himself he will be "bettered by this accident ;"—have at least a chance of pay for work done : for it is to be feared that there has been little forthcoming as yet for a large amount of political essay work.

We have a glimpse, I suspect,—autobiographic of a sort,—of some of the experiences that were already beginning to open his eyes, in Harry Wildfire's account of his dealings with Mr. Britannicus, the publisher, when that "Sad Dog," as a last resort, turns author. "As I did not doubt my invention," he says, "and had vanity enough for the character, I sat down to invoke the Muses. The first fruits of my pen were a political essay and a piece of poetry. The first I carried to a patriotic bookseller, who is, in his own opinion, of much consequence to the cause of liberty ; and the poetry was left with another of the same tribe, who made bold to make it a means of puffing his magazine, but refused any gratuity.  Mr. Britannicus, at first imagining the piece was not to be paid for, was lavish of his praises, and I might depend upon it, it should do honour to his flaming patriotic paper; but when he was told that I expected some recompense, he assumed an air of criticism, and begged my pardon.  He did not know that circumstance; and really he did not think it good language or sound reasoning.  I was not discouraged by the objections and criticisms of the bookselling tribe; and as I know the art of Curlism pretty well, I make a tolerable hand of it.  But, Mr. Printer, the late prosecution against the booksellers having frightened them all out of their patriotism, I am necessitated either to write for the entertainment of the public or in defence of the ministry.  As I have some little remains of conscience, the latter is not very agreeable."  Harry Wildfire is, in truth, only repeating what Chatterton had already written to his friend Cary: "The printers of the daily publications are all frightened out of their patriotism, and will take nothing unless 'tis moderate or ministerial.  I have not had five patriotic essays this fortnight. All must be ministerial or entertaining."

Lord North, in his unsteady, vacillating way, had been stimulated into active measures of coercion by the joint influence of Lord Mayor Beckford's uncourtly remonstrance, and one of the most rancorous of the Junius letters, assailing the whole policy of the administration, and backing up the ireful and insulted city.  Both events belong to Chatterton's first month in London, and formed acts in the stirring drama in which he fancied himself ere long no insignificant actor.  Events, indeed, crowded on him with exciting celerity.  The *Middlesex Journal* of the 22d May contains the letter of Decimus "To the Prime Minister," which closes in this magniloquent style: "You, my Lord, how mean and servile soever your department is, may be of some use in averting the impending storm.  Fly to the Council with your

CHAP. XII.

*Lavish of praise.*

*The art of Curlism.*

*Lord North's measure of coercion.*

face whitened with fear. Tell them that justice is at the
door, and the axe will do its office. Tell them, while the
spirit of English freedom exists, vengeance has also an
existence; and when Britons are denied justice from the
powers who have the trust of their rights, the constitution
hath given them a power to do themselves justice." This
letter appeared on the 22d; the famous City remonstrance
belongs to the following day; the letter of Junius to the
28th; and by the 1st of June the law-officers of the
Crown had the publishers under prosecution. So the
chances of the patriot-politician were at an end for the
present; and Chatterton had to return to his older
vocation as a poet, or try his hand at tales and literary
essays.



Numerous fugitive pieces of Chatterton no doubt
remain undiscovered in the ephemeral periodicals of this
time. He adopted various signatures, and no less varied
styles and subjects, according to the nature of the publica-



tion. He names in different letters the *Freeholders'*, the
*Town and Country*, the *Court and City*, *The London*, *The
Christian*, and *The Gospel* Magazines; *The Political
Register*, *The London Museum*, *The Middlesex*, and *The
Foreign* Journals: as periodicals to which he was a con-
tributor; and we know, besides those, of *The Lady's
Magazine*, *The Annual Register*, and the *North Briton*.
In the *Town and Country Magazine* his "Hunter of
Oddities" ran through a series of eleven slight but humorous articles. His "Polite Advertiser" and "Memoirs
of a Sad Dog,"—in which the Baron of Otranto figures,—
were contributed to the same magazine. Some of his poems
appear in it also under the signature Asaphides, to which
he drew attention in a letter to his relative, Mr. Stephens;
and "Cutholf," one of his latest compositions,—a professed
translation of an ancient Saxon poem,—was contributed
to Robinson's *Lady's Magazine* in the same name. There



is no volume of the *Christian Magazine* for 1770 in the
British Museum. A few years earlier it was under the
editorship of the notorious Dr. Dodd, and received contributions from Goldsmith when still a literary adventurer

struggling for bread. But the *Gospel Magazine* for that and earlier years exists, and rewards the search for traces of the last fugitive pieces of Chatterton. In the volume for 1766, when the Bluecoat boy was sending contributions to Felix Farley's *Bristol Journal,* a poem entitled "The Retreat" appears with the initials T. C., possibly by Chatterton, though nothing but the signature would suggest such authorship. It is of inferior merit, and unlike any of his known early productions.[1] But, in the volume for 1770, one piece at least is clearly recognisable as his. In May he tells his sister, "They publish the *Gospel Magazine* here. For a whim I write in it." Then, or at a later date, he tried his hand once more on the old subject of Happiness, for which experience lent him even less aid. There is a hollow ring about the piece, in painful contrast to his earlier and more earnest religious musings. "The following lines," it is stated, "were found written on a blank leaf in ' Lucas's Enquiry after Happiness.' " They bear the favourite initials, D. B., and aptly enough set forth his own experience in the pursuit :—

> "Tho' happiness be each man's darling aim,
> Yet folly too, too often plays the game;
> To that one centre all our wishes tend,
> We fly the means but still pursue the end.
> No wonder then we find our hopes were vain;
> The wretch who shuns his cure must still complain.
> In labyrinths of crooked error lost,
> Or on life's sea with raging tempest tost,
> We by no compass steer, but blindly stray,
> And, knowing we are wrong, ne'er ask the way."[2]

Before the "Enquiry after Happiness," of which these formed the opening lines, made its appearance in the

---

[1] Chatterton was then in his fourteenth year, and may have used his own initials. But they most frequently mark the productions of his friend Thomas Cary; and were probably on that account avoided by him. After leaving Colston's Hospital his most common signature was D. B. His African Eclogues in the *London Magazine* are simply signed C. In the October number of the *Town and Country Magazine* following his death (1770, p. 551) his friend contributed an Elegy to the memory of Chatterton with the signature T. C.

[2] Gospel Magazine, Nov. 1770, p. 600.

*Gospel Magazine* for November, life's fitful fever, and all its vain pursuits, were at an end. For a time the fascination of political essay-writing had seemed to harmonise with the excitement of his new career, and reconciled him to the disappointment of his fondly cherished poetic dreams. But that proved even more illusory; so he turned to his old art, though in a new form, and aspired to popular favour as a writer of modern verse. It is easily seen, however, that he is catering for others' tastes, instead of yielding to his own inspiration; and the results are for the most part feeble and insipid.

This change in Chatterton's literary avocations had possibly something to do with his quitting his Shoreditch lodgings. The letter to his friend Cary, in which he tells of the scare of the patriotic publishers, also directs his attention to two efforts in an entirely new line, the second of which, his "Death of Nicou," was "coming out to-morrow," in the June number of the *London Magazine:* issued, according to the practice of eighteenth century publishers, on the last day of the month. Patrons and the public alike slighted the genuine creations of his muse. Rowley as yet found even less favour in London than in Bristol; and if his pen was to win him bread, he must cater for the taste of his masters. So taking the Oriental Eclogues of Collins for his model, he set to work on a series of African Eclogues, already started in the beginning of the year, with equal ignorance of the geography and natural history of the region thus selected. The choice indeed was made apparently for no other reason than that Asia was already appropriated in Collins' pastorals. His second Eclogue, "Nerva and Mored,"—dated from Shoreditch on the 2d of May,—was published in the *London Magazine* of that month. In the succeeding number "The Death of Nicou" appears with the name of his new quarters, "Brook Street, Holborn, June 12th." He was as sanguine of the new venture as of that which it superseded, and in a fit of characteristic self-complacency tells his friend, "I am surprised you took no notice of the last

*London.* In that, and the magazine coming out to-morrow, are the only two pieces I have the vanity to call poetry." The verdict, like that of most other poets on their own works, is one in which no modern critic is likely to concur.

But he has other news for Cary. He is now engaged on some lyrical pieces, which leads him to discuss the merits of rival Bristol organists, already contrasted in his "Kew Gardens." He draws his illustrations of the genius of his favourite musician from the noble symmetry and beauty of Redcliffe Church; and then, apropos to this, he says: "A song of mine is a great favourite with the town on account of the fulness of the music. It has much of Mr. Allan's"—his favourite organist's—"manner in the airs. You will see that and twenty more in print after the season is over. I yesterday heard several airs of my burletta sung to the harpsicord, &c., and will venture to pronounce, from the excellence of the music, that it will take with the town."

Of the songs thus heralded, we know a little more from other sources. In an earlier letter to his mother, he had already told her, in sequel to Mr. Edmunds' prosecution: "Last week, being in the pit of Drury Lane Theatre, I contracted an immediate acquaintance with a young gentleman in Cheapside, partner in a music-shop, the greatest in the City. Hearing I could write, he desired me to write a few songs for him. This I did the same night, and conveyed them to him the next morning. These he showed to a doctor in music, and I am invited to treat with this doctor, on the footing of a composer, for Ranelagh and the Gardens. Bravo, hey boys, up we go! Besides the advantage of visiting these expensive places gratis: my vanity will be fed with the sight of my name in copper-plate; and my sister will receive a bundle of printed songs, the words by her brother." The single night's work of "a few songs" suggests rather hasty productions of the muse; though he probably had not slept in the interval between the two interviews with his new acquaintance. But it was a mere

*CHAP. XII.*

*The rival organists.*

*A London introduc- tion.*

*A single night's work*

T

change of literary task-work.  The poet was writing not for fame but for bread ; and his pen was no less prolific in this new line.  We know of an oratorio, written apparently for Dr. Arnold ; his burlettas, for Mr. Henslow, or Mr. Atterbury of the Marylebone Gardens ; songs for Ranelagh Gardens ; and " The Dowager," an unfinished tragedy : some of which are by no means devoid of merit.  Along with great lyrical power, he had undoubted dramatic talent, which with fair opportunities might have achieved considerable success in the minor drama.



Among other characteristic tastes, Chatterton had a fine ear for music.  His operatic verse is varied and harmonious, and his burlettas, though slight, display a dramatic action fully equal to the occasion.  The "Woman of Spirit" has already been referred to, with its satirical fling at Horatio Trefoil and his brother antiquaries.  "The



Revenge," with less dramatic vigour, is excellently suited for its purpose ; and, if the musical composer did his work equally well, had a fair chance of popularity with the frequenters of the Marylebone Gardens.  The jealous Queen of Olympus has a quarrel with Jupiter on account of the favour he shows for Maia.  Cupid and Bacchus encounter one another, and set forth the rival influences of love and wine.  The whole is a broad farcical burlesque, in which Juno figures as an arrant scold ; Jupiter as a faithless and somewhat hen-pecked husband ; and



Bacchus as the roystering, jovial debauchee.  The piece is in two acts, running through twelve scenes of varied rhythm, adapted for recitative, solo, duet, and chorus. To quote largely from it, divorced from its musical complement, would do little justice to the author.  But Dr. Maitland, assuming that it is not Chatterton's work, admits it to be "capital;" in fact so superior to the ordinary run of such productions, as to satisfy him that it could not be his.[1]  It is indeed far above the average of such musical burlesques, and wonderful for the evidence it yields of the versatility of his prolific pen.  A

----

[1] Maitland, 45.  The original MS. in Chatterton's own handwriting has been recovered.

brief extract or two will suffice to illustrate its character. Cupid has been playing the eavesdropper, and reveals to Juno an assignation of her truant lord :—

"JUNO.  When?  Where?  Nay, prithee now unfold it.

CUPID. Gad, so I will ; for, faith, I cannot hold it.
His mighty godship, in a fiery flurry,
Met me just now,—confusion to his hurry !
I stopt his way forsooth, and, with a thwack,
He laid a thunderbolt across my back.
Bless me ! I feel it now,—my short-ribs ache yet ;
I vow'd revenge, and now, by Styx, I'll take it.
Miss Maia, in her chamber, after nine,
Receives the Thunderer, in his robes divine.
I undermined it all ; see, here's the letter ;
Could Dukes spell worse, whose tutors spell no better ?
You know false-spelling now is much the fashion——"

In a subsequent scene Bacchus enters, bowl in hand, reeling under the influence of his deep potations, and sings in varying cadence :—

" *Air*—If Jove should pretend that he governs the skies,
I swear by this liquor his Thundership lies ;
A slave to his bottle, he governs by wine,
And all must confess he's a servant of mine.

*Air changes*—Rosy, sparkling, powerful wine,
All the joys of life are thine.
Search the drinking world around,
Bacchus everywhere sits crowned ;
Whilst we lift the flowing bowl,
Unregarded thunders roll.

*Air changes*—Since man, as says each bearded sage,
Is but a piece of clay,
Whose mystic moisture, lost by age,
To dust it falls away ;
'Tis orthodox, beyond a doubt,
That drought will only fret it ;
To make the brittle stuff hold out
Is thus to drink and wet it.

*Recitative*—Ah ! Master Cupid, 'slife I did not s' ye !
'Tis excellent champagne, and so here's t' ye :
Come, drink, my boy——

T 2

CHAP. XII.
*An
Olympian
eaves-
dropper.*

*Bacchus and
his bowl.*

CHAP. XII.

A flash of earnestness.

Quarrel of Cupid and Bacchus.

Too tardy production of the burletta.

CUPID. Hence, monster, hence!  I scorn thy flowing bowl;
   It prostitutes the sense, degenerates the soul."

Here spoke the poet, with a flash of earnestness, almost out of keeping with Dan Cupid, on whom Bacchus retorts the charge :—

" He plays with ethics like a bell and coral."

The dialogue proceeds, in greatly varied measure, adapted to recitative and airs, till Cupid transfixes the drunken god with his arrow: on which Bacchus throws the contents of the bowl in his face, and runs off.  After the plot has set all its Olympian characters at cross-purposes, harmony is at last restored ; and Bacchus and Cupid, turning to the audience, pay, in song, their duty to the fair and gay, closing thus :—

"BACCHUS. For you the vine's delicious fruit
   Shall on the lofty mountains shoot;
   And every wine to Bacchus dear
   Shall sparkle in perfection here.

CUPID. For you shall Handel's lofty flight
   Clash on the listening ear of night ;
   And the soft, melting, sinking lay
   In gentle accents die away ;
   And not a whisper shall appear,
   Which modesty would blush to hear."

This spirited burletta there can be little doubt Chatterton did not live to see produced, with all the charms of music and scenery.  His letter to Cary is undated ; but it appears to have been written in the end of June, when the *London Museum* was on the eve of publication, with his second African Eclogue, "The Death of Nicou." He had then heard several airs of his burletta sung ; and his head was so full of music, that much of his letter is taken up with a discussion of it, and its Bristol professors. The original receipt, attached to the last chorus of the burletta, was accidentally recovered in 1824.  It is dated July 6th, 1770,—only seven weeks before the fatal close,

—and shows that he received five guineas for his labours.[1]
Three years later, Mr. Upcott, one of the librarians of
the London Institution, picked up, among the waste
paper on the counter of a City cheesemonger, the original
manuscript, in Chatterton's handwriting, written in a common school copybook, as was his wont; and with some
additional songs, after the receipt to Mr. Atterbury.[2]  It
had been given by the latter to Mr. Egerton, for the
purpose of printing; and after its issue from his press
in 1795, the MS. was reported to have been lost at the
printing-office: where it no doubt lay, till transferred
with other waste copy to the cheesemonger's use.[3]

The remuneration for the burletta was liberal in comparison with most of Chatterton's pecuniary returns: and
probably the largest sum he ever received for any literary
production.  His sister recovered a pocket-book after
his death, in which, among other entries of moneys received, Mr. Hamilton is credited with payment of ten
shillings and sixpence for sixteen songs; or somewhat
less than eightpence each.  Of those, and probably
many other ephemeral productions, we have no trace.
Walpole describes among the manuscripts seen by him:
"The Flight; addressed to a great man; Lord B——e,"
—no doubt a political satire on the Scottish favourite.  It
extended to forty stanzas of six lines each; and had been
rejected by the *Political Register* because of its length.
A second satire dealt with Mr. Alexander Catcott and
his book on the Deluge; and no doubt others have
perished, or can no longer be traced in the periodicals
to which they were contributed.

From all this we can form some idea of the amount
and variety of literary work accomplished by a youth of
seventeen, during four months' sojourn amid the distract-
ing novelties and temptations of London.  Much of it
was mere task-work; but indications are not wanting to

[1] Gent. Mag. vol. xcv. Part I. p. 99.
[2] Ibid. vol. xcvii. Part II. p. 355.
[3] J. H.  List of publications relating to Chatterton, p. 537.
Cottle.

Chap. XII.

*Recovery of
the MS.*

*Liberal
remunera-
tion.*

*Ephemeral
productions
lost.*

*Amount and
variety of
work.*

show that even then, amid all the exactions which necessity imposed on him, the old inspiration revived; and he lived and wrote once more as the poet-monk of an elder and nobler time. The resources of his brain seemed inexhaustible. But such mental strain, followed as it was by disappointment, and utter failure even in the poor return for which so much of it had been undertaken, may amply account for the despondency which ended in despair.

# CHAPTER XIII.

## THE LAST HOPE.



BRISTOL is not so inferior to London, as are most of the hasty productions of Chatterton's pen during his brief sojourn there to the true Rowley Poems. He carried the manuscripts of these with him; but could Thomas Rowley, priest and poet, live in that intoxicating fever of politics, strife, and dissipation, amid which there seemed even less hope of an appreciative audience than on the banks of the Avon? This at least seems certain, that, at a very early period after he reached London, he meditated the resumption of his antique art. When little more than a fortnight from home, we find him specially naming "the MS. glossary, composed of one small book, annexed to a larger," as most needful among his missing volumes. Again, some two weeks later, on the 30th May, he writes his sister: "The manuscript glossary I mentioned in my last must not be omitted." No doubt, therefore, he not only cherished the dream of his youth, but even then contemplated perpetuating the old reveries of Redcliffe Hill in his new lodging, at Shoreditch, or elsewhere.



The last, seemingly, of all his Rowley Poems in point of date, and the fitting close to the whole, is his "Balade of Charitie." Some ten weeks after his arrival in London it was forwarded to Mr. Hamilton, of the *Town and Country Magazine*, where his "Elinoure and Juga" had already appeared. According to his first editor, the note which accompanied it bore the date: "*Bristol*, July 4th, 1770;" so that he was still guarding the secret of his

CHAP. XIII.

*Its appropriate tone and sentiment.*

antique muse with even more than his old precautions. The tone and sentiment of this fine ballad are so appropriate to a date which brings us within little more than a month of the last sad scene of all, that it seems as though it foreshadowed the ending. But a month is an important item in the brief life of Chatterton, and a large portion of his whole London career. Dating professedly. from Bristol on the 4th, we may presume that the packet was not actually delivered till the 6th of July: which brings us to the very day on which he signed the receipt for his well-earned five guineas, the price of his burletta. Never, perhaps, was he in better spirits. The prosecutions of the press had driven him back to verse, and here was a substantial return.

*Generous remembrance of home.*

There is indeed touching evidence that this was the only remuneration Chatterton received on such a scale as really to seem to leave him a surplus in hand. He had meditated from the first making the dear ones at home sharers in his earliest good fortune. Before he had been three weeks in London, we find him telling his mother: "Thorne shall not be forgot, when I remit the small trifles to you." In his letter from Tom's Coffee-house, on the last day of the month, replete with high anticipations, he tells his sister: "Assure yourself every month shall end to your advantage. I will send you two silks this summer, and expect, in answer to this, what colours you prefer. My mother shall not be forgotten;" and as he closes with the usual greetings to mother and grandmother, he adds: "Sincerely and without ceremony, wishing them both happy. When it is in my power to make them so, it shall be so."

*Boastful extravagance.*

The letter, in which this occurs, is the same in which he recounts his interview with the Lord Mayor, and much else. Amid its boastful extravagance, we might be tempted to fancy such promises mere empty talk. May passes over; June succeeds, and draws to a close; his sister, as we discover from one of his own letters, fails not to inform him of her choice of colour for the silks: but still there is no word of the promised gifts. But on the 6th of July he signs the receipt for "five pounds, five shillings, being in full for all the manuscripts contained in this book:" viz. his burletta "Revenge;" with sundry additional songs. The 7th is proudly and happily spent in purchasing and packing the long-promised "trifles;" and on the 8th he thus writes:—

"DEAR MOTHER,—I send you in the box six cups and saucers, with two basons for my sister. If a china teapot and creampot is, in your opinion, necessary, I will send them; but I am informed they are unfashionable, and that the red china, which you are provided with, is more in use. A cargo of patterns for yourself, with a snuff-box, right French, and very curious in my opinion.

"Two fans—the silver one is more grave than the other, which would suit my sister best. But that I leave to you both.

"Some British herb snuff, in the box; be careful how you open it. (This I omit lest it injure the other matters.)

"Some British herb tobacco for my grandmother. Some trifles for Thorne. Be assured, whenever I have the power, my will won't be wanting to testify that I remember you.

"Yours,

"*July 8th*, 1770.                    "T. CHATTERTON.

"N.B.—I shall forestall your intended journey and pop down upon you at Christmas. I could have wished you had sent my red pocket-book, as 'tis very material.

"I bought two very curious twisted pipes for my grandmother: but both breaking, I was afraid to buy others, lest they should break in the box; and, being loose, injure the china. Have you heard anything further of the clearance?

"Direct for me at Mrs. Angel's, Sack-Maker, Brooke Street, Holborn."

Three days later his sister also gets a letter, with loving tokens of remembrance, and abundant indications that the all-important matter of silks is not forgotten, though still beyond the present means of the sanguine boy. He is a little astonished at the choice his sister has made: not that "purple and gold" is beyond his expected wealth, but it is scarcely elegant or genteel! "I went into the shop," he says, "to buy it; but it is the most disagreeable colour I ever saw—dead, lifeless, and inelegant. Purple and pink, or lemon and pink, are more genteel and lively. Your answer in this affair will oblige me." A few days later, he tells her:

CHAP. XIII.

*Expending his first surplus.*

*Promised Christmas visit.*

*Purple and gold.*

" I am now about an oratorio, which, when finished, will purchase you a gown.  You may be certain of seeing me before the 1st January 1771.  My mother may expect more patterns : " that is, for her millinery and dressmaking. He had already enclosed " a cargo of patterns " for her when the box of presents was made up ; but with the expected pay for communications already in Hamilton's hands, almost enough to fill the next number of the *Town and Country Magazine*, he sees his way to still more liberal gifts.  So after a brief paragraph in his most jubilant style, he adds : " You will have a longer letter from me soon, and more to the purpose."  Pay day, as he trusted, was at hand.  With the end of the month would come the means of fulfilling such promises, and accomplishing much else.  So that we see, whatever momentary fit of despondency may have prompted the " Balade of Charitie," it is by no means to be regarded as the last plaint of failing hope.



There appears to have been an autograph copy of the ballad in Mr. Barrett's hands, either left behind, or else transmitted to him from London,—which, at first thought, seems unlikely.  But communications, as we shall see, did pass between them after Chatterton left Bristol, and he had his own reasons for conciliating the antiquary, and reminding him of the excellency of charity.  Certain at any rate it is that the text in Southey's edition is " printed from a single sheet in Chatterton's handwriting, com-municated by Mr. Barrett, who received it from Chatter-ton : " whether personally, or transmitted from London, to complete the intending historian's set of the Rowley antiques, and keep the way open for future favours.



It is not, therefore, indispensable that we should reject the idea that Rowley did become a Londoner at last. It was a grand thing for the proud, self-confident youth to congratulate ambassadors, countenance and flatter the Lord Mayor, dictate to the Prime Minister, and lecture Royalty itself.  For a time it actually seemed to him as though the wheels of state moved with an accelerated speed under the impetus of his exertions.  So, to the no small wonder of Mrs. Ballance, he quarrelled with her for calling him "Cousin Tommy," and nearly frightened the poor woman out of her wits by his extravagant procedure. She might be a fit enough object for the patronage of the young poet, once his fortune was made; but he had not left Bristol, and his quarters in Mr. Lambert's, with a share of the footboy's attic, to be addressed in such terms: or, indeed, to prosecute his work in a room shared with the Shoreditch plasterer's nephew. So, as Mrs. Walmsley told Sir Herbert Croft, his stay at her house was limited to nine weeks, or rather less, as appears from the date of his second Eclogue. He parted with her on good terms, but assigned no reason for quitting his lodging. His bedfellow had noted that "almost every morning the floor was covered with pieces of paper not so big as sixpences, into which he had torn what he had been writing before he came to bed;" and when he finally quitted, he left the room littered with, what Mrs. Walmsley called, the remains of his poetings.

On the 12th of June, if not earlier, Chatterton found himself for the first time absolutely alone, in new quarters, and a more convenient locality for all his resorts of business or pleasure. Brooke Street, Holborn, lies on the western verge of the City proper; and the house of Mrs. Angel, sack or dressmaker, in which he now secured lodgings, still stands unchanged, as when he occupied one of its rooms. It has been identified with the aid of the books for collecting the poor-rates for 1772, as No. 39, on the west side of the street.[1] There, in a room looking towards the street, we find him, on the 19th, telling his sister some of the first experiences of his

---

[1] Tradition professed to identify the house as No. 4; and this is duly notified accordingly in Mr. Peter Cunningham's carefully edited "Handbook of London." An impudent forgery of a "Report of the Coroner's Inquest" (*Notes and Queries*, vii. 138), shifted it to No. 17; with this good result, that Mr. W. Moy Thomas, in proving its spuriousness, produced the contemporary evidence of the actual house where Mrs. Angel's taxes were collected (*Athenæum*, Dec. 5th, 1857).

new outlook, in very familiar fashion :
cold.  The relation of my manner of ca
you more pleasure than the circumsta
wrote very late Sunday night (or rather i
morning), I thought to have gone to be
night : when, being half-undressed, I he
voice singing Miss Hill's favourite bedl
humdrum of the voice so struck me,
obliged to listen a long while before
words, I found the similitude in the so
ing her with pleasure drawl for about
jumped into a brisker tune, and hobl
famous song in which poor Jack Fowle
satirized.  'I put my hand into a busl
finger to the bone ;' 'I saw a ship :
thought the sweetest flowers to find ;
flowery expressions, were twanged with
bray.  I now ran to the window and t
resolved to be satisfied whether or not
tical Miss Hill *in propriâ personâ.*"  B
be only a drunken ballad-singer singin
A huxter selling stale mackerel joins i:
before the listener's curiosity is satisfie
horrible wheezing in the throat."



The picture is not a very refined c
us the young poet writing far on into
was his wont : busy, it may be, in the
of the flimsy pieces already noted ; c
delights of new-found solitude, taking
in that antique past, in which, as a po
from early childhood.  For this remova
has brought with it a change of no



As a Bluecoat boy Chatterton slept
shared their common room with the
ward.  As Mr. Lambert's apprentice
between the kitchen and the attic h
footboy.  At Mr. Walmsley's, in like
room-mate in the plasterer's nephew,
not a little by his long night-watches

proceedings. . Now, for the first time, he enjoyed the delights of solitude; could withdraw into those inner chambers of imagery where all the petty wranglings of that eighteenth century disappeared; was with the builders of Redcliffe Church, or the choice cotery of the Rudde House: and elevated, earnest thoughts held mastery of his soul. Nor is the "Excelente Balade of Charitie" unworthy to have been the first-fruits of such a time. There we do know that the grey dawn found him busy with the poet's pen; and there, with none to remind him that the body has claims, and night is her fitting time for rest, he would work on untiringly into a new day.

Chatterton did not wear his heart on his sleeve. We have seen him on more than one occasion hide his mortification under the bravest outside show. Walpole makes shipwreck of the hopes of half a lifetime; and he writes of it to his relative Mr. Stephens, as of a tilt between two literary knight-errants, of which, perchance, the best was yet to come. Lord Mayor Beckford dies, and with him perish expectations of honour and fortune. To his poor relation, Mrs. Ballance, he betrayed his feelings at the moment, frantically declaring he was ruined. But the serio-comic balance-sheet of debit and credit, already given, in which he finds himself "glad he is dead by 3*l.* 13*s.* 6*d.*" of net profit, was his mode of showing Cary and other Bristol friends how indifferent he could be to such a trick of fortune. It would not, therefore, conflict in any degree with the gay spirits manifested in his letters written in the beginning of July, with their talk of china, silver fans, and purple and gold silks: to find traces of the shadow of defeated hopes already clouding his solitary musings, as he transcribes from imaginary parchments of the olden time his "Excelente Balade of Charitie." Slightly modernised and elucidated with the help of his own glossary, it reads as follows :—

CHAP. XIII.

*The delights of solitude.*

*Concealment of his feelings.*

*Shadows of defeated hopes.*

# AN EXCELENTE BALADE OF CHARITIE.

AS WROTEN BIE THE GODE PRIESTE THOMAS ROWLEIE, 1464.

In virgyne[1] the sweltrie sun 'gan sheen,
  And hot upon the meads did cast his ray :
The apple rudded from its paley green,
  And the mole pear did bend the leafy spray ;
  The pied chelandry[2] sung the livelong day ;
'Twas now the pride, the manhood of the year,
And eke the ground was dight in its most deft aumere.[3]

The sun was gleaming in the mid of day,
  Dead still the air, and eke the welkin blue,
When from the sea arose in drear array
  A heap of clouds of sable, sullen hue,
  The which full fast unto the woodland drew,
Hiltring at once the sunè's festive face,
And the black tempest swelled and gathered up apace.



Beneath a holm, fast by a pathway side,
  Which did unto Saint Godwin's convent lead,
A hapless pilgrim moaning did abide ;
  Poor in his view, ungentle in his weed,
  Long bretful[4] of the miseries of need :
Where from the hailstone could the almer fly ?
He had no housen there, nor any convent nigh.

Look in his gloomed face, his sprite there scan,
  How woe-begone, how withered, sapless, dead !
Haste to thy church-glebe house,[5] ashrewed man ;
  Haste to thy kist, thy only dortour[6] bed.
  Cold as the clay which will gree on thy head
Is charity and love among high elves ;
Knightès and barons live for pleasure and themselves.



The gathered storm is ripe ; the big drops fall ;
  The forswat[7] meadows smethe, and drink the rain ;
The coming ghastness doth the cattle 'pal,
  And the full flocks are driving o'er the plain ;
  Dash'd from the clouds the waters float again ;
The welkin opes ; the yellow levin flies ;
And the hot fiery steam in the wide lowings dies.

---

[1] *Virgyne,* the sign of Virgo.    [2] *Chelandry,* goldfinch.
[3] *Aumere,* mantle.    [4] *Bretful,* filled.
[5] *Church-glebe house,* churchyard house, or grave.
[6] *Dortour,* dormitory, or sleeping room.  [7] *Forswat,* sunburnt.

List ! now the thunder's rattling, clanging sound
    Moves slowly on, and then embollen,[1] clangs,
Shakes the high spire, and lost, dispended, drowned,
    Still on the frighted ear of terror hangs ;
    The winds are up ; the lofty elmen swangs ;
Again the levin and the thunder pours,
And the full clouds are burst at once in stonen shours.

*The Abbot of St. Godwin's.*

Spurring his palfry o'er the watry plain,
    The Abbot of Saint Godwin's convent came ;
His chapournet[2] was drenchèd with the rain,
    And his peynct girdle met with meikle shame ;
    He backward told his bederoll[3] at the same ;
The storm increased, and he drew aside,
With the poor almes-craver, near the holm to bide.

His cope was all of Lincoln cloth so fine,
    With a gold button fasten'd near his chin ;
His autremete[4] was edged with golden twine,
    And his peaked shoon a lover's might have been ;
    Full well it showed he thoughten cost no sin ;
The trammels of his palfry pleased his sight,
For the horse-milliner his head with roses dight !

"An almes, Sir Priest !" the drooping pilgrim said ;
    "Oh! let me wait within your convent door
Till the sun shineth high above our head,
    And the loud tempest of the air is o'er ;
    Helpless and old am I, alas ! and poor ;
No house, no friend, no money in my pouch ;
All that I call my own is this my silver crouch."[5]

"Varlet," replied the Abbot, "cease your din ;
    This is no season alms and prayers to give ;
My porter never lets a beggar in ;
    None touch my rynge[6] who not in honour live."
    And now the sun with the black clouds did strive,
And shooting on the ground his glaring ray,
The Abbot spurr'd his steed, and eftsoons rode away.

*The storm returns.*

Once more the sky was black, the thunder roll'd ;
    Fast running o'er the plain a priest was seen :
Not dight full proud, nor buttoned up in gold ;
    His cope and jape were grey, and eke were clean ;
    A Limitour[7] he was of order seen ;

---

[1] *Embollen,* strengthened.    [2] *Chapournet,* hat.
[3] *Backward told his bederoll,* i.e. cursed.
[4] *Autremete,* white robe.    [5] *Crouch,* crucifix.
[6] *Rynge,* ring ; probably, door-handle.    [7] *Limitour,* begging friar.

And from the pathway side then turned he,
Where the poor almer lay beneath the holmen tree.

"An almes, Sir Priest !" the drooping pilgrim said,
  "For sweet Saint Mary and your order's sake."
The Limitour then loosen'd his pouch thread,
  And did thereout a groat of silver take ;
  The hapless pilgrim did for halline [1] shake :
"Here, take this silver, it may ease thy care ;
We are God's stewards all ; nought of our own we bear.

"But ah ! unhappy pilgrim, learn of me,
  Scarce any give a rentroll to their Lord ;
Here, take my seme-cope, [2] thou art bare, I see ;
  'Tis thine ; the saints will give me my reward."
  He left the pilgrim, and his way abord.
Virgin and holy saints who sit in glore,
Or give the mighty will, or give the good man power.



This beautiful poem, perversely disguised, according to his wont, with such professed antiques, Chatterton transmitted, through some indirect channel, to Mr. Hamilton of the *Town and Country Magazine*, and had it rejected. The act was creditable to the worldly wisdom of the editor, who was printing in his July number the first moiety of the "Memoirs of a Sad Dog," one of his "Hunter of Oddities ;" and Sir Butterfly's "Polite Advertiser :" in which the poet had aimed sufficiently low to hit the taste of magazine readers. But the market



was already overstocked with such wares. "Almost all the next *Town and Country Magazine* is mine," he writes to his sister, on the 20th July,—having then supplied its editor with materials enough, had he been disposed to use them. But, as became an able editor, he aimed at variety ; had other contributors, as well as his readers, tastes to consult ; and so withheld the larger portion of Chatterton's work, and with it the money so needful to him : issuing his pieces in later numbers, when their writer no longer solicited either space or pay.

Among the finished materials brought with him to that great world's mart, Chatterton had his "Ælla," "Godd-

---

[1] *Halline*, joy.          [2] *Seme-cope*, short under-cloak.

wyn," and " Bristowe " Tragedies ; his " Tournament,"
" Parliament of Sprytes," and other interludes ; his
" Battle of Hastings," and numerous minor poems
wrought after the same antique model : enough to make
a goodly volume of verse such as ought to have sufficed
for fame and fortune to any bard.  Possibly it was in
the hope of attracting the notice of some appreciative
patron that he attempted to secure the publication of
his " Balade."  But whatever his plans may have been,
he made no other attempt to bring them before the
world ; and only when hard-pressed by the necessities
that now gathered around him, like the lowering tempest
of his hapless pilgrim, did he offer to pawn this one,—
not for fame, but bread.

Walpole had failed him, in part at least, through his
own mismanagement ; though the portraiture was most
true :—

> " Knightes and barons live for pleasure and themselves."

Dodsley had been approached with little less tact, and
with no more success.  But could he have found some
experienced friend to stand between him and the publishers,—as Johnson did for Goldsmith, when the bailiffs
had him in hand for his landlady's arrears ;—to keep his
secret if it must be kept, yet enlist their sympathy on
behalf of his literary venture, what a different chapter in
the history of that eighteenth century we might now
have to write.  Think who the men of that generation
were from whom the award should have come.  Walpole,
as he tells us, on getting Chatterton's " impertinent "
letter, wrapped up both poems and letters, returned all
to him, and thought no more of him or them till about
a year and a half after, when, dining at the Royal
Academy, Sir Joshua Reynolds in the chair, and the
most distinguished representatives of art and letters
around him : Dr. Goldsmith attracted the attention of
the company by his account of a marvellous treasure of
ancient poems lately discovered at Bristol, and got
laughed at by Dr. Johnson for his enthusiastic belief in

CHAP. XIII.

*Treasures
of antique
verse.*

*Causes of
failure.*

*Want of an
experienced
friend.*

*The Royal
Academy
dinner.*

U

them. "I told Dr. Goldsmith," says Walpole, "that this novelty was none to me, who might, if I had pleased, have had the honour of ushering the great discovery to the learned world. But though his credulity diverted me, my mirth was soon dashed; for on asking about Chatterton, he told me he had been in London, and had destroyed himself." But though rough old Samuel Johnson was ready enough to raise the laugh at Goldsmith's credulity as to the antiquity of the poems, that was not his verdict as to their worth. When he did read them, his exclamation was: "This is the most extraordinary young man that has encountered my knowledge!"

But whatever plans Chatterton may have cherished for ultimately presenting Rowley to the world, he was right in keeping his secret,—however wrong in the modes he resorted to for accomplishing that purpose. They had been conceived in their antique form in the splendid dream of the child-poet; and could not be modernised without loss. Presented as mere imitations of writings of an imaginary monk of the fifteenth century, they would have repelled the general reader, while inviting the censorious criticism of the professed antiquary. Either they had to astonish the literary world as the strangely recovered treasures of an unknown poet of the days of the Roses,—as they ultimately did;—and so arouse criticism, controversy, and research: acquiring thereby a fictitious interest, such as actually pertains to them even now; or they had to be rewritten in, at least, the English of Spenser. But the latter idea was foreign to the whole dream of the poet's life. So when the "Balade of Charitie" was rejected, and the ways of modern literature grew ever more thorny, he bethought himself of another fancied way to fortune.

According to his foster-mother's account, Chatterton wished to have been bound to Barrett, to study medicine, and share in the congenial pastimes of the antiquarian surgeon. He would, at any rate, have found some employment for his active mind; for he read largely of Mr. Barrett's professional library, obtained from him what instruction he could be induced to impart, and ever after availed himself of all chances of increasing his little stock of knowledge. Thistlethwaite, when describing the versatility of his tastes, says: " Even physic was not without a charm to allure his imagination, and he would talk of Galen, Hippocrates, and Paracelsus, with all the confidence and familiarity of a modern empiric." In this vein he writes to his sister from London, about Mrs. Carty, the mother of one of his Bristol friends: " My physical advice is, to leech her temples plentifully ; keep her very low in diet ; as much in the dark as possible. Nor is this last prescription the advice of an old woman. Whatever hurts the eyes affects the brain ; and the particles of light, when the sun is in the summer signs, are highly prejudicial to the eyes ; and it is from this sympathetic effect that the headache is general in summer. But above all, talk to her but little, and never contradict her in anything. This may be of service. I hope it will." The advice is given with all the confidence of an experienced physician.

In Brooke Street, Holborn, within a few doors of Mrs. Angel's, was the shop of Mr. Cross, an apothecary. Chatterton made his acquaintance ere long, and frequently visited him on his way to and from his lodging. As usual, his fascinating manner won the stranger's goodwill ; and he afterwards told Mr. Warton that he found his conversation most captivating, in spite of the occasional intrusion of deistical opinions. · There was no lack of subject for talk. The stirring politics of the day ; gossip about the London periodicals ; the wider range of literature, so thoroughly at his command ; and even medicine itself, on which he would surprise the apothecary with the amount of his knowledge.

As high hopes began to fade, old ideas of turning this crude knowledge to account revived. While representing his prospects in such brilliant colours to his friends, he had evidently, from an early date, recognised the possibility of failure. He had been little more than a month in London, when, in the midst of some of his most sanguine revelations to his sister, he hinted of a possible "step to the sea." Two more months had transpired ; the brilliant prospects of the young litterateur had all faded away ; and he confessed to himself the bitter truth that he had failed. The presents sent to his mother and sister in the beginning of July, were bought on the faith of new supplies never forthcoming. The rate of remuneration for work done and published was not such as to leave much surplus ; and for much work accepted but still unpublished, no money was to be had. He had probably begun to urge payment under the pressure of ever-increasing necessities, and then the manner of his reception by the dispensers of literary patronage would undergo a marvellous change. Flattery was a cheap coin, liberally dispensed ; but when fair promises were required to be discounted, unpalatable truths would be apt to be substituted for them. And so, at length, Chatterton sits down, on the 12th of August, and pens a long and seemingly purposeless letter to Mr. George Catcott, in which rumour, gossip, art, and politics are discussed in a laboured fashion, in striking contrast to the usual spirited style of his letters. Yet even now, in the last letter he was ever to pen, his thoughts linger around St. Mary Redcliffe ; and he refers ironically to the incredible rumour that spirit and liberality enough for the completion of its long mutilated spire have at length manifested themselves among the citizens of Bristol. But the real object of the letter appears in the last paragraph : "I intend going abroad as a surgeon. Mr. Barrett has it in his power to assist me greatly, by his giving me a physical character. I hope he will ; " and then he adds : "I trouble you with a copy of an essay I intend publishing." So the letter closed, with respectful greeting. He is sending, as a conciliatory gift, some piece of literary workmanship adapted to Mr. Catcott's taste. The act suggests the possibility that the copy of the "Balade of Charitie," written on a single sheet, which long years after supplied the text for Southey's edition of the poet's works, was the propitiatory offering now forwarded to Mr. Barrett, "as wrote bie the gode prieste Thomas Rowleie." He had at any rate written to him intimating the hope to which he now clung, of obtaining an appointment as surgeon's mate on board an African trading, or probably slave ship.

In Sir Herbert Croft's strange series of letters, styled " Love and Madness," to which so much curious information about Chatterton is due, he refers to an article in the *Town and Country Magazine*, which must have met his eye ; and ignorant of this last scheme of becoming surgeon's mate to an African trader, he exclaims : " What must have been the sensations of Chatterton's feeling mind, when he read that the number of slaves brought from the coast of Africa in one year, 1768, between Cape Blanco and Rio Congo, amounted to one hundred and four thousand one hundred?  How must the genius of Rowley have fired at such a sum total of fellow-creatures made beasts of burden, only because the common Creator had made them of a different colour!"[1] In reality Chatterton had read this at most but a very few days before he wrote to Barrett.  It was published at the end of July, and by the 12th of August he is telling Mr. Catcott of the application he has made to the Bristol surgeon, and of his intention to go abroad :—rather encouraged than repelled, it seems probable, by such accounts of the flourishing condition of the African slave-trade.

The requisites that then sufficed for surgeon's mate have been described by another poet and literary adventurer of the eighteenth century.  Smollett was himself present in that capacity in 1741, at Carthagena, on board a ship of the line ; and, in his " Roderick Random," pictures some of the scenes he witnessed.[2] A very moderate training would have put Chatterton on

[1] Croft, p. 253.

[2] Oliver Goldsmith, it will be remembered, also strove to escape from an author's garret, and starvation, to an appointment as surgeon to one of the East India Company's factories on the coast of Coromandel.  The salary was 100*l.* and he was broken-hearted when the prospect failed.  But Goldsmith had studied medicine at Edinburgh ; and practised it, after a fashion, in London.

*A lover's
farewell.*

a par with many who had preceded him in the unenviable occupation; and possibly enough Mr. Barrett's testimonial might have sufficed to secure him the appointment, and so given him one more chance in the battle of life. While, therefore, this seemed still within his reach, he addressed some reproachful lines, in the high-flown, unimpassioned strain of most of his amatory verse, to Miss Bush, of Bristol, beginning thus :—

> "Before I seek the dreary shore,
>   Where Gambia's rapid billows roar,
>     And foaming pour along;
>   To you I urge the plaintive strain,
>   And though a lover sings in vain,
>     Yet you shall hear the song."

*His African
Eclogue.*

The earliest of Chatterton's Brooke Street productions was one of his African Eclogues; but there is nothing in it to show that his thoughts were then seaward toward "the regions of the sun." But a single month had brought with it bitter experiences. His position strongly recalls that of Burns, when in a like hopeless condition,— and with far more cause for self-reproach,—he published his first volume of poems with the object, mainly, of raising funds to carry him beyond the Atlantic. A clerkship on a Jamaica plantation was the Scottish poet's outlook; and with this in view, he wrote, as he believed, the last song he should ever compose on his native soil :—

> "The gloomy night is gathering fast."

The Ayrshire peasant was in his twenty-eighth year; his passage had already been taken for the West Indies : when a collected edition of his poems raised him from humble obscurity to a social equality with the noblest in the land, and changed the whole course of his life. The Bristol boy was but seventeen when the gloomy

*No friendly
hand nigh.*

night gathered around him; but no friendly hand was nigh to publish, ere too late, the abundant evidence of his versatile genius.

Barrett refused the needful certificate on which all Chatterton's hopes of appointment as a surgeon's mate rested; and assuredly no one will censure him for that act. But the refusal, made in full consciousness of his destitution, was accompanied by no other proffered aid. His callousness is far more criminal than that of Walpole; but his excuse is to be found in the dreary stupidity of his volume of "Antiquities and History," which proves his incapacity to appreciate the boy, or snatch from him the thinly disguised secret of his antique muse. The only trace of any recognition of his rare qualities by Barrett is preserved in the highly interesting note of Sir Herbert Croft that he used often to send for him while still a Bluecoat boy, "and differ from him in opinion, on purpose to make him earnest, and to see how wonderfully his eye would strike fire, kindle, and blaze up." Yet the purblind antiquary could look into the boy's flashing eyes; spell his way through the rare inventions of his infant muse, palmed on him as the productions of an unheard-of monk; and recognise at the last no more than the idle apprentice "led astray by the false glare of a strong imagination, and flattering pride of superior understanding."

Barrett devotes the last chapter of his quarto to "a biographical account of eminent Bristol men," in which the Canynges have a large share, and Rowley is not forgotten; but of the true Rowley, of whom he could have told so much that would be invaluable now, he records only some trite lamentations over his "libertine principles" and hapless fate. Of the last despairing scheme of the boy, and his unsuccessful appeal for aid, Barrett says nothing. To him Chatterton was the mere "producer of Rowley and his poems to the world;" and so, after discussing various surmises as to his death before or after A.D. 1474, it is finally "left to the judicious and candid reader to form his own opinion concerning Rowley and Chatterton."

In his second London letter to his mother, Chatterton says: "I am under very few obligations to any person in Bristol. One, indeed, has obliged me; but, as most do, in a manner which makes his obligation no obligation."

CHAP. XIII.

*Barrett's refusal.*

*The purblind antiquary.*

*Eminent Bristol men.*

*Obligations to his patrons.*

CHAP. XIII.

Was this intended for Mr. Barrett, or was it Mr. Lambert he had in view? It was for either no unmerited return. No wonder that, in the last letter he ever wrote, he refers, in bitter irony, to a correspondent from Bristol, who has raised his admiration to the highest pitch by informing him that an appearance of spirit and generosity had crept into its niches of avarice and meanness.

# CHAPTER XIV.

## DESPAIR AND DEATH.

On the 12th of August, 1770, Chatterton penned the last piece of writing of which any distinct account has been preserved, if we except the fragments which littered the floor of the room in which he died. There is indeed a story told, in more than one form, of a still later letter received by his mother, in which he stated that, wandering a few days before in some London churchyard, he was so lost in thought that he did not perceive a newly opened grave till he fell into it. According to Mr. Dix's version, it occurred in St. Pancras Churchyard, and within three days of his death. He was accompanied by a friend, who, as he helped him out again, jestingly congratulated him on the happy resurrection of Genius; but Chatterton, taking him by the arm, replied, with a sad smile: "My dear friend, I feel the sting of a speedy dissolution. I have been at war with the grave for some time, and find it is not so easy to vanquish as I imagined. We can find an asylum from every creditor but that."[1] It is difficult to conceive of any confidential friend in London to whom Chatterton would unbosom himself in such a fashion. In all probability this apocryphal narrative is only an improved version of the more probable account Mrs. Edkins gives, of being sent for by Mrs. Chatterton the week before she heard of her son's death, when she found her in tears over a letter just received. In this he had narrated the incident of his stumbling into an open grave; but added, with characteristic humour, "it was not the quick and the dead together;"

[1] Dix's Life, p. 290.

for he found the sexton under him, and still able to pursue his work.

The letter was written about the 15th or 16th of August. Mr. Barrett, it may be presumed, had by this time sent his refusal of the needful testimonial; but possibly a lingering hope of Mr. Catcott's or other friend's interposition still kept him in suspense. The letter, no doubt, contained some desponding reflections, suggested by his desperate circumstances, to which the accident that brought his churchyard reveries to a close was apropos. Hence his mother's anxiety and tears, in spite of the sardonic jest with which the half-revealed truth was turned aside. His mind was already in that morbid state in which every trifle seems to carry an ill omen. Proud, and still ready to snatch at every illusive promise, he strove to assume a cheerful bearing, and to suggest hopes to others which no longer deceived himself. His mind had fluctuated during the weeks of July, and up to this date, through all the extremes of which it was so capable: extravagant dreams of unrealizable fortune; moody reveries, in which he would lapse, as in childhood, into a seeming stupor, and gaze blankly into the face of the questioner, as though lost to all consciousness of an external world; and passionate outbursts of feeling that found relief in tears.

Among all its millions, long since gone to their account, no more forlorn one was to be found in the vast solitudes of that old London, than the youth in whose mind hope and pride were now battling with despair. In his last letter to Mr. George Catcott, this melancholy avowal occurs: "Heaven send you the comforts of Christianity. I request them not, for I am no Christian." Terrible words at any moment, but how terrible now! Amid the wreck of all his hopes in this life, he looked beyond it into the dreary void of infidelity. He owned, indeed, a God; but he had no reliance on his divine fatherhood. With a faculty of veneration, rare in his day, and with sensibilities intensely acute, vibrating responsive to every tender emotion, his soul yielded no response of faith in that Divine One, himself made perfect through suffering, that he might be the succourer of the afflicted. A stubborn, haughty pride was his only stay, nor did it wholly fail him in the terrible ordeal.

Chatterton had now occupied his lodgings in Brooke Street fully eleven weeks. So late as the 20th of July, when he wrote the last letter his sister was ever to receive from him, there is no doubt that his hopes were still high. The next number of the *Town and Country Magazine*, due on the last of the month, was to appear, as he fancied, nearly filled with his accepted articles; and he might reasonably anticipate payment for that amount of work, and an ample commission for more. But with the new month came the overthrow of all such hopes. The larger portion of his literary labours, if not absolutely rejected, was at any rate thrown aside for some indefinite future. His chief market was glutted. No pay, apparently, was forthcoming for what had actually been published; and Mr. Hamilton had doubtless told him,—in terms wonderfully different from the first gracious reception of his Bristol correspondent,—that he need not trouble himself to call again for months to come.

The notes, endorsements, and letters of Chatterton partake somewhat of the business-like method which he, no doubt, acquired in Lambert's office; and, among other information due to this source, we possess one important memorandum of pecuniary receipts. The pocket-book of her brother, which Mrs. Newton recovered and presented to Mr. Joseph Cottle, contained this jotting of receipts during his first month in London:—

| | | | £ | s. | d. |
|---|---|---|---|---|---|
| "Received to May 23, | of Mr. Hamilton, for *Middlesex* | | 1 | 11 | 6 |
| ,, | ,, | of B—— . . . . . . . . . | 1 | 2 | 3 |
| ,, | ,, | of Fell for *The Consuliad* . . | 0 | 10 | 6 |
| ,, | ,, | of Mr. Hamilton for "Candidus" and "Foreign Journal" | 0 | 2 | 0 |
| ,, | ,, | of Mr. Fell . . . . . . . | 0 | 10 | 6 |
| ,, | ,, | *Middlesex Journal* . . . . . | 0 | 8 | 6 |
| ,, | ,, | of Mr. Hamilton for 16 songs . | 0 | 10 | 6 |
| | | | £4 | 15 | 9" |

Chap. XIV.

*His only stay.*

*Last letter to his sister.*

*Overthrow of all hopes.*

*Business-like method.*

*Jotting of receipts.*

The record unmistakeably suggests the idea that Hamilton was making a tool of the inexperienced youth. A shilling a piece for two articles; eightpence each or rather less for sixteen songs; and no pecuniary acknowledgment for a pile of work accepted and held in reserve! Fell's payments are scarcely more liberal; for "The Consuliad: an Heroic Poem," is a spirited satire, extending to upwards of two hundred and fifty lines. Here then are the actual receipts of the first month, while the author was yet fresh, and his productions had some charm of novelty. If they are accepted, as they probably may be, as a fair average of the whole period of Chatterton's London career, it is easy to guess his condition when the last guinea of his Bristol purse had vanished; and he began to dun his fair-spoken patrons for fulfilment of promises, or payment for work already furnished.



The abstemious habits of his earlier days were retained by Chatterton unchanged during his short London career. He drank only water, and rarely touched animal food. He frequented the theatres and pleasure gardens of the metropolis; but as a professional man, and for the most part, it may be presumed, gratuitously. These were indeed the most promising professional resorts.



He pleads such legitimate occupation of his time in excuse for unwritten letters; telling his mother: "What with writing for publications, and going to places of public diversion, which is as absolutely necessary to me as food, I find but little time to write to you." The most profitable of all his literary labours, and that which supplied him with means for gratifying his generous designs for his mother and sister, was his "Marylebone Burletta." Immediately on receipt of its well-earned five guineas, the sanguine boy wrote his mother: "I shall forestall your intended journey; and pop down on you at Christmas."



There is no trace of the squandering of funds in any form of dissipation. Mrs. Walmsley, who had no special reason to uphold his character; and Mrs. Ballance, to whom "his flights and vagaries" were anything but a cause of respect : concurred in testifying to his conformity to the regular family hours, during the period of his lodging at Shoreditch. His new landlady, Mrs. Angel, noted in like manner his abstemious habits. He was reserved, yet social and kindly in his ways, leaving on the mind the impression of one superior to the rank in which he moved. Mrs. Wolfe, the wife of a barber in Brooke Street, spoke of his proud and haughty spirit, and added that he appeared both to her and Mrs. Angel as if born for something great.

One expensive taste, however, he did indulge in. The social importance of dress had been a source of trouble and irritation in Bristol; and he early congratulated himself that in London it was a mere matter of taste. Yet there also he found ere long that a man was apt to be judged by his outward appearance. Oliver Goldsmith had already figured in his famous plum-coloured coat, and was running up new bills with Mr. Filby, for velvets, silks, and lace. It was an age in which the tailor had a much larger share in the making of the man than he has now ; and so Chatterton tells his sister, before May is at an end : "I employ my money now in fitting myself fashionably, and getting into good company. This last article always brings me in good interest."

Still meditating fresh gifts for home, we find him, on the 20th of July, anticipating the profits of his unfinished oratorio as a means of gratifying his sister in the same important matter of dress. He is still sanguine, in spite of disappointments ; but his funds are now running very low, and he must await the publication of the magazines, and the anticipated payment for accepted articles. But here also the inexperienced youth was reckoning on fallacious data. The outlay is indisputable ; but the source of income rapidly fails.

With the utmost abstemiousness and moderation in all ways, it is not difficult to understand how Chatterton's slender finances must have well-nigh come to an end, when with the commencement of another month he

CHAP. XIV.

*Uniform testimony to his regularity.*

*Social importance of dress.*

*The tailor makes the man.*

*Fresh gifts for home.*

*Slender finances failing.*

learned that he was bankrupt not only in money, but in hope.  Yet let it not be overlooked that there was a sense of honour in the pride of the unhappy youth, which upheld him in the resolve to be under no pecuniary obligation to strangers.  Dr. Maitland refers, in his usual harsh style, to Chatterton's acceptance of the purse raised for him by his Bristol friends : "without any reluctance or sense of humiliation."  The unflinching pride with which he refused all proffered charity at the last, ought to have protected his memory from such a sneer.



The inquiries pursued by Warton, while they placed beyond doubt the utter destitution of the boy, showed him to the last proudly resenting every offer of friendly help.  The gift of his old Bristol acquaintances was no more than he had a right to, and could be accepted without any sense of humiliation ; or received as a loan to be repaid with interest ere long.  But it was otherwise with those among whom he had so recently come as a stranger.  The opportunities of frequent intercourse with



Mr. Cross, the Brooke Street apothecary, were welcome ; but, as he informed Mr. Warton, every proffer of aid was rejected, however delicately concealed under a hospitable guise.  He gladly availed himself of the society and conversation of his new acquaintance, but he would accept of no hospitalities that could minister to his necessities.  Mr. Cross speedily discerned in the look of his visitor evidence of the want to which he was reduced; and repeatedly pressed him to dine or sup with him, but in vain.  One evening, however, his importunity—aided it may be by the sore necessities of his visitor,—did



prevail.  Chatterton was induced to join the supper-table and partake of a barrel of oysters, when he was observed to eat voraciously.[1]  Mrs. Angel had also looked with wonder and compassion on her strange, proud lodger, who, while enduring the utmost privations, haughtily repelled every proffered alleviation.  After his death, she told her neighbour, Mrs. Wolfe, that, "as she knew he had not eaten anything for two or three days, she

---

[1] Warton's Inquiry, p. 107.

begged he would take some dinner with her on the 24th of August; but he was offended at her expressions, which seemed to hint that he was in want, and assured her—though his looks showed him to be three-parts starved,—that he was not hungry."[1]

How he struggled against fate, or what wrongs he endured, can now only be surmised. He was resolute, courageous, and not easily daunted. At Mr. Walmsley's he used frequently to say that he had many writings by him which would produce a great deal of money if they were printed. To this it was once or twice observed that they lay in a small compass, for he had not much luggage. But he said that he had them nevertheless. The whole Rowley manuscripts would indeed make little show as a traveller's baggage. But he had other purposes for these than to use them for the mere necessities of the moment. The return expected from them was of a different kind. " When he talked of writing something which should procure him money to get some clothes, to paper the room in which he lodged, and to send some more things to his sister, mother, and grandmother: he was asked why he did not enable himself to do all this by means of these writings, which were 'worth their weight in gold.' His answer was that they were not written with a design to buy old clothes, or to paper rooms; and that if the world did not behave well, it should never see a line of them."[2] Every indication we can recover serves to prove that he maintained this proud resolution to the last ; and that last had now come.

On Friday, the 24th of August, 1770,. Chatterton retired to his room in Brooke Street, carrying with him the means of self-destruction,—arsenic or opium, according to different accounts ;—and there he was found the following morning, with limbs and features distorted as after convulsions : a ghastly corpse. As all earthly hope waned the unhappy boy had turned stoically to the philosophic creed of that eighteenth century, that death is an eternal sleep ; yet also, not calmly, but maddened

*Chap.* XIV.

*Mrs. Angel's aid rejected.*

*Struggle against fate.*

*The Rowley treasure.*

*Worth its weight in gold.*

*Last scene of all.*

[1] Croft, p. 219.    [2] Ibid. p. 234.

*Taint of hereditary insanity.*

*The lyre unstrung.*

*Lost poems.*

*Tragedy of "The Apostate."*

with the despairing sense of failure, and of wrong, he destroyed the works on which he had rested all his hopes of fame.   What indeed was fame to him now?

Southey ascertained that Chatterton's sister had been confined for a time in an asylum for the insane; and remarks: "His mighty mind brought with it into the world a taint of hereditary insanity, which explains the act of suicide; and divests it of its fearful guilt."   Alas! it may be so.   This only is certain, that the boy's career had terminated abruptly, in the saddest of all possible forms of life's close.   The precious little bundle of MSS. he had estimated so highly was never recovered.   His latest productions, torn into fragments, littered the floor where he lay.   "His daring hand unstrung the lyre," and with its last effort strove to efface every memory of its notes. His works, when at length collected for publication, were derived mainly from copies in Mr. Catcott's and Mr. Barrett's hands.   Of the tragedy of "Goddwyn," only two scenes are preserved; though there seems good reason to believe that the prologue was not written till he had completed the whole.   Other poems spoken of by him have either wholly perished, or mere fragments survive in evidence of the worth of what is lost.   "I wrote my 'Justice of Peace,'" says Rowley, in his "Memoirs of Sir William Canynge," "which Master Canynge advised me secret to keep, which I did."   Judging from the mention of nearly all his chief works in the correspondence ascribed to the imaginary priest of St. John's, it is probable that "The Justice of Peace" is one of the missing poems; its secret only too well kept.   Another poem entitled "The Apostate: a Tragedy," of which a small portion fell into Mr. Barrett's hands, had for its subject the apostatizing of its hero from the Christian to the Jewish faith.   Its loss is great, on account of the light it might have thrown on the earlier phases of his own mind in reference to the momentous questions of religious belief, which received from him at last so fatal a negative.

The little bundle of manuscripts, including probably

poems not even known to us by name, was either deposited in some place from whence it was never recovered, or was purposely destroyed. The last act of their author undoubtedly was to tear in pieces whatever manuscripts remained in his possession ; and no one dreamt of attempting to piece together the fragments which strewed his room, when it was broken open after his death.

Thus perished by his own hand, in an obscure lodging in London, among strangers, and in absolute want, a youth assuredly without his equal—if his age is borne in remembrance,—in that eighteenth century. Uncomprehended, misjudged, and maligned : he seemed to pass away like the brief glance of the meteor, which flashes from darkness into a deeper gloom. Oblivion gathered around him and his works, with an obscuration which his own final acts had striven to render complete. But his name could not be so blotted out from the records of his age ; though it was reserved for others to do it the justice which was then denied. His own generation stood too near him to recognise his greatness; and though poets have since rendered fitting tribute to his powers, yet only now, after a century of confused and blundering controversies, do we clearly discern how wonderful was the genius that wrapped itself in such quaint disguise to tempt the credulity of that faithless age.

CHAP. XIV.

*Destruction of last MSS.*

*Perishing by his own hand.*

*Oblivion claims the victory.*

# CHAPTER XV

.THE POET'S MONUMENT.



THE death of Chatterton excited but a passing notice even in Bristol, beyond the sorrowful little circle in the home he had so recently left. The London periodicals of that month of August, 1770, have been repeatedly ransacked, but in vain, for any recognition of the fact, that a youth of high promise had perished there, the victim of want. The caterers for news had not brought their craft to the perfection of the modern press; but many a trivial incident figures in the publications of the month in which the event occurred, unheeded then, but so notable to us now. Hamilton's *Town and Country Magazine* came out a week later, with its columns filled in part by three of Chatterton's contributions, the meagerest remuneration for which might have rescued their author from despair; but its editor had his own reasons for leaving out of its "Domestic Intelligence" an occurrence in which he had so much personal interest. Sylvanus Urban by and by found much to say about both the ancient and the modern Rowley; but the event passed unnoted in the "Historical Chronicle" of the *Gentleman's Magazine* for August 1770. The name of "Old Rowley" does indeed occur in that very number, in a "New Baby Ballad," full of political allusions to Parson Horne, Wilkes, Paoli, &c., but a foot-note explains it as "a nick-name of King Charles."[1] It had then no other recognised literary significance. On the 22d of August is chronicled the appearance of a Junius letter,

[1] Gent. Mag. vol. xl. p. 385.

"written with the usual spirit of the admired author."
The 24th,—the fatal day,—only yields for it the robbery
by a highwayman, at the foot of Highgate Hill, of the
postboy carrying the Chester mail.

The death of Chatterton, it is obvious, attracted no
attention beyond the immediate neighbourhood of Brooke
Street. An inquest was, indeed, held on the body; but
it appears to have passed off as a very ordinary affair.
All that could, by and by, be learned, was that a youth
had " swallowed arsenic in water, on the 24th of August,
and died in consequence thereof the next day." There
was no friend at hand to claim the body; and it has been
assumed, though without any distinct evidence, that it
was buried as that of a deliberate suicide's, without any
religious rites. It was, at any rate, placed in a mere
shell, and deposited in the common pit prepared for
paupers, in the neighbouring burying-ground of Shoe
Lane workhouse, in the parish of St. Andrew's, Holborn,
in which Brooke Street is situated; and of which, moreover, by a strange coincidence, Dr. Broughton, Vicar of
St. Mary Redcliffe, was also rector.[1] Delay appears
to have taken place in the interment, probably in the
hope that some of his relatives might appear. The
register of burials contains this entry under the date
August 28th, 1770, "William Chatterton, Brooke Street,"
to which has been subsequently added, "the Poet."[2]
The addition is, no doubt, correct, notwithstanding the
error in the Christian name. It adds one more proof
that his remains were coldly consigned by strangers to a
pauper's grave.

When, some nine years afterwards, interest had revived
in the memory of Chatterton; and controversy waxed
fierce over the disputed authenticity of Rowley and the
Bristol poems: the coroner was appealed to. But,
according to Sir Herbert Croft's account, he had no
minutes of the melancholy business; and was unable,
after so long an interval, to recall any of the circum-

[1] *Vide* inscription on tablet in Redcliffe Church, *ante*, p. 193.
[2] Goodwin's Churches of London: St. Andrew's, Holborn.

X 2

stances to his memory. The witnesses, as appears by his memorandum, were Frederick Angel, Mary Foster, and William Hamsley: none of whom he had been able to find out.[1] This is absolutely all that is known of the inquest. In 1853, however, the Rev. Dr. Maitland, after long fretting over the "imposture" of Chatterton, resolved on a new protest against the idea of his authorship of Rowley's Poems, which "he had long believed to be a popular delusion."[2] So he started with an inquiry in " Notes and Queries," as to certain discrepancies in the account of the means by which Chatterton's death was effected. To his "great surprise and satisfaction this brought forth a report of the coroner's inquest from Mr. Gutch." The coroner had told Sir Herbert Croft, more than seventy years before, that no minutes existed, beyond his mere memorandum of the witnesses' names. Yet meagre as this was, it contradicts the report so surprisingly brought to light, without even a pretence of authentication. The date is said to be *Friday*, 27th August, 1770, whereas the 27th fell that year on a Monday. The witnesses, with one exception, differ from those named by the coroner ; and the process of making up the whole from old materials is obvious to any student of Chatterton's memorials. Yet this new Rowleyan, having exhausted his unbelief on Chatterton's "literary imposture," accepted the hoax as eagerly as did Mr. Burgum his famous Norman pedigree ; and his " Essay" is garnished throughout with confirmations derived from the silly imposture. It furnishes one more illustration of the amazing credulity of a scepticism still on the look-out for the "undisfigured old Rowley" of the days of Henry VI. and Edward IV.[3]

[1] Croft, p. 221. Gent. Mag. N.S. x. p. 133. Notes and Queries, second series, vol. iv. p. 24.

[2] Chatterton : an Essay, p. 9.

[3] The document was in the handwriting of Mr. Dix ; and passed from his possession to that of Mr. Gutch, who communicated it to " Notes and Queries," vii. p. 138. As Mr. Dix had it in possession when writing Chatterton's Life, yet did not even refer to it, the inference is legitimate that he regarded it as spurious. For its

But another disclosure of the present century, to which a keener interest attaches, has been the subject of much faith and more scepticism. It is impossible to think, without a shuddering sense of wrongful indignity, of the remains of the poet huddled into a pauper's grave; and then, after brief lease of the workhouse burial-ground, carted off with its nameless dead, when it was converted into a site for Farringdon Market. But when, in 1837, Mr. Dix undertook to write a life of the poet, he appended to it notes collected long before by George Cumberland, Esq., a man of reputed literary tastes. These have already been repeatedly referred to; and from them it appears that Sir Robert Wilmot first communicated to him the report "that Chatterton lay buried in Redcliffe Churchyard, and that he believed it was a fact from the manner in which it had been communicated to him." Pursuing his inquiries farther, Mr. Cumberland discovered Sir R. Wilmot's informant, Mrs. Stockwell, an old pupil of Mrs. Chatterton, who had resided with her till nearly twenty years of age. In her belief, as well as in that of others with whom he conversed, the body of Chatterton was recovered, through the intervention of a relative in London, forwarded by waggon to Bristol, and there secretly interred, by his uncle, Richard Phillips, in Redcliffe Churchyard.

The statements are minute and circumstantial. Mrs. Chatterton is affirmed to have often expressed her happiness at the thought that her son lay buried with his kin. Fresh inquiry added only such second-hand information as rendered the probability of the reinterment conceivable enough. The old sexton was just the man to do it for his favourite nephew, and to conceal it when done. His daughter, Mrs. Stephens, said he was very reserved on all occasions; and it was by no means likely he

history, *vide* "Notes and Queries," second series, iii. 362. For arguments based on it *vide* ibid. p. 54; Maitland, pp. 6, 51, 64, 68, 82, 104, where the argument frequently depends on the genuineness of this obvious fiction. It was burned some years since, with more valuable MSS. in the possession of Mr. T. Kerslake, of Bristol.

would have mentioned the interment, if he had done it secretly; "but she thinks he would not have refused the hazardous office, being much attached to Chatterton, and friendly with his mother." Since Mr. Cumberland's notes were published, they have been corroborated by a letter of Mr. Joseph Cottle, in which he thus gives Mrs. Edkins' version of it :—"Mrs. Chatterton was passionately fond of her darling and only son, Thomas; and when she heard that he had destroyed himself, she immediately wrote to a relation of hers,—the poet's uncle, then residing in London,—a carpenter, urging him to send down his body in a coffin or box. The box was accordingly sent down to Bristol; and when I called on my friend Mrs. Chatterton to condole with her, she as a great secret took me up stairs and showed me the box; and, removing the lid, I saw the poor boy, whilst his mother sobbed in silence." Afterwards she was told that he had been secretly buried, by night, in Redcliffe Churchyard; and Mrs. Chatterton said, " she had managed it very well, so that none but the sexton and his assistant knew anything about it."[1] Mr. Cottle adds that the evidence appeared to him sufficient to satisfy all reasonable minds.

This reputed rescue of the poet's remains, and their reinterment in his own favourite haunt on Redcliffe Hill, has been challenged by more than one writer, with proofs of discrepancies in the narrative, and impossibilities in the affirmed transaction.[2] Some of the arguments against it are sufficiently fallacious. Mr. Richard Smith considers it quite apocryphal because they "neglected to mark the spot, or write a notice in the newspapers of the day;" whereas the evidence of secrecy is the strongest argument in its favour. Dr. Broughton, the vicar, had personal as well as professional reasons for excluding Chatterton's remains from Redcliffe Churchyard; and so strongly were the latter

---

[1] Pryce's Memorials of Canynge, p. 294.
[2] *Vide* Notes and Queries, second series, vol. iv. pp. 23, 54, 92, for both sides of the question.

inherited by his successors, that a subsequent vicar refused even to admit a memorial of him within the precincts of the church, which is itself his truest monument. But then, what shall we say to the argument of an over-zealous believer, whose faith removes mountains by setting forth how unlikely it is "that Barrett would have allowed the youth to whom he was so attached, and who had so materially added to his stock of antiquities of Bristol, to have remained in that loathsome pit, if money and influence could have rescued him from it?" It reads as a fine bit of irony; but there is no doubt "Bristoliensis" means it seriously; and, indeed, accompanies it with arguments better worthy of consideration.

In reality, the cost to the poor mother of the recovery and reinterment of the body is the greatest impediment to belief. Otherwise her desire to accomplish it cannot be doubted; and in most other respects facilities were not wanting. A long family line of sextons may be supposed to have attached peculiar importance to the interment of their dead. The London uncle, stimulated by such hereditary feelings, and turning his own carpentering craft to account, would not find his share of the task beyond his means. With a friendly carrier cooperating, the greatest obstacle would be surmounted; and at Bristol the old Redcliffe sexton wanted no more than an assurance of secrecy, to undertake the most critical part of the work. Let us then be content to leave for the poet a possible grave. Assuredly his remains no longer lie in the horrible pit of the Shoe Lane workhouse. It is pleasant to think of their finding a resting-place in Redcliffe Churchyard, among his kin, and amid scenes on which his imaginative genius and keen poetic sympathies have conferred so wide an interest. If it be another Chatterton romance, it is the most innocent of all. Let us give it what credit we can.

> "'Tis little; but it looks in truth
>   As if the quiet bones were blest
>   Among familiar names to rest,
> And in the places of his youth."

Chap. XV.<br><br>Transmitted ecclesiastical prejudices.<br><br>Chief impediment to belief.<br><br>A possible grave for the poet.

Chatterton is fitly spoken of as a boy. He was only seventeen years and nine months old at his death; and the recollections of Mrs. Newton, Mrs. Edkins, and others who had been familiar with him under his mother's roof, all refer to him as one in whom the tender susceptibilities, as well as the impulsiveness of youth, were manifest to the last. The best of his numerous productions, both in prose and verse, betray no immaturity; yet he was writing spirited verses at ten, and produced some of the finest of his antiques before he was sixteen years of age. Nor must his age be forgotten when referring to his errors and shortcomings. At the age when



this boy's career terminated, in unbelief and despair, what intellectual development, or well-defined creed, is ordinarily looked for? Enthusiastic biographers have tried to make of Shakespeare himself an attorney's clerk at that age, with troubles enough of his own, in the way of deer-stealing and love-making; but his "Venus and Adonis," the "first heir of his invention," belongs to later years. Even Milton has not escaped the prejudiced record of juvenile follies at the same stage; and



another Christian poet, Cowper, the contemporary of Chatterton,—from whose life the saddest parallel might be drawn,—was already eighteen, when he and the future Lord Chancellor Thurlow met as fellow-clerks in the same law office, and employed their time "from morning till night, in giggling and making giggle." How insignificant would the record of follies, doubts, or unbeliefs, of their seventeenth years appear to us now! But the poet whose career we have traced to its abrupt close, crowded into these immature years all its triumphs and its failures; and though it did end in the saddest of all possible closes of life's battle, we shall learn to deal more tenderly with its follies, when a just estimate has been formed of what he achieved.



The appearance of Chatterton corresponded with the maturity of his intellect. He had a proud yet frank bearing, and a manly presence beyond his years. He was naturally self-reliant, spirited, and possessed of a keen sense of humour; though liable to fits of abstraction, in which he seemed moody and unsocial, when in reality he was unconscious of all that transpired around him. But in spite of the free licence which he gave to his satirical powers, he is described, by all who were familiar with him, as of a serious yet engaging manner, with something about him which prepossessed even a stranger in his favour. The Shoreditch plasterer, whose bed he shared for a time, declared that "it was impossible to help liking him." Brief as was his residence in his latest lodging, he had awakened a kindly interest on his behalf both in the mind of Mrs. Angel, and in that of the neighbouring apothecary. There was obviously a fascination in his address, and in his fine expressive countenance, which won the favour of nearly every one with whom he was brought into contact; and even disarmed their resentment when it had been roused by the assaults of his satirical pen.

His expressive face, in which matured intellectual vigour blended with the contour of childhood, was a fitting subject for the highest art of portraiture. But no distinct account has been preserved of his features as a whole; and no authentic portrait of him is known. In 1784, a rustic monument was erected to his memory, on the property of Philip Thichnesse, Esq., near Bath, and decorated with his profile sculptured in relief; which seems to imply some existing likeness.[1] Mrs. Edkins mentioned to Mr. George Cumberland a picture her son had seen which was painted by Wheatly, possibly during his brief residence in London. But if so, no trace of it seems now to be known. Mr. Dix was deceived into engraving for the frontispiece of his biography of the poet, a portrait in the possession of a Bristol collector, on the back of which the name of Chatterton had been written in mere jest. This has since been recognised as a likeness executed by Morris, a Bristol portrait painter, of his own son.[2] Southey is indeed said to have traced

----

[1] Gent. Mag. vol. liv. part i. p. 231.
[2] Notes and Queries, second series, vol. iii. p. 53.

CHAP. XV.

*Engaging manner and address.*

*Reputed portraits.*

*A spurious likeness.*

CHAP. XV.

*Gains-
borough's
Bristol boy.*

in it a resemblance to the poet's sister ; but there is no doubt, if any such exists, it is purely accidental.

Chatterton is affirmed to have sat to Gainsborough ; and the portrait, with his long flowing hair, and child-like face, is spoken of as a masterpiece.[1] The date of this supposed portrait, if executed at all, must have been between 1768, when the painter removed for a time to Bath, and that of Chatterton's leaving Bristol. It is supposed to represent him wearing the garb of Colston's Hospital ; though the colour is green, instead of blue. "The hair falls very much over the forehead, and reaches at the side to the shoulders. The face is looking sideways, and three parts of it can be seen." The date is, of course, subsequent to Chatterton's leaving the Bluecoat School. But the "genius-loving painter," as his biographer has styled him, if tempted to paint the Bristol boy, might prefer to represent him in his quaint charity-school dress. No allusion, however, in Chatterton's letters or poems refers to the painting of his portrait ; though, in

*Alcock the
miniature
painter.*

1769, he celebrated the powers of Mr. Alcock's pencil as a miniature painter :—

> "He paints the passions of mankind,
> And in the face displays the mind,
> Charming the heart and eye."

*Descriptive
portraiture.*

It is to be feared that no authentic portrait of Chatterton exists ; and even the accounts furnished as to his appearance, only partially aid us in realizing an idea of the manly, handsome boy, with his flashing, hawk-like eye, through which even the Bristol pewterer thought he could see his soul. His forehead one fancies must have been high ; though hidden, perhaps, as in the supposed Gainsborough portrait, with long, flowing hair. His mouth, like that of his father, was large. But the brilliancy of his eyes seems to have diverted attention from every other feature ; and they have been repeatedly noted for the way in which they appeared to kindle in sympathy with his earnest utterances. Mr. Edward

---

[1] E. S. Felcher, Notes and Queries, second series, vol. iii. p. 492.

Gardner, who only knew him during his last three months in Bristol, specially recalled "the philosophic gravity of his countenance, and the keen lightning of his eye." Mr. Capel, on the contrary, resided as an apprentice, in the same house where Lambert's office was, and saw Chatterton daily. His advances had been repelled at times with the flashing glances of the poet ; and the terms in which he speaks of his pride and visible contempt for others show there was little friendship between them. But he also remarks : "Upon his being irritated or otherwise greatly affected, there was a light in his eyes which seemed very remarkable."[1] He had frequently heard this referred to by others ; and Mr. George Catcott speaks of it as one who had often quailed before such glances, or been spell-bound, like Coleridge's wedding guest by the "glittering eye" of the Ancient Mariner. He said he could never look at it long enough to see what sort of an eye it was; but it seemed to be a kind of hawk's eye. You could see his soul through it. Mr. Barrett, as Sir Herbert Croft states, took particular notice of his eyes, from the nature of his profession ; and did venture to look long enough to see what they were. "He never saw such. One was still more remarkable than the other. You might see the fire roll at the bottom of them, as you sometimes do in a black eye, but never in grey ones, which his were ;" and then he added, as already noted, how wonderfully his eye would strike fire, kindle, and blaze up, when in earnest discussion. The Rev. C. V. Le Grice has also noted the peculiarity that one eye was brighter than the other ; so much so, indeed, as to appear larger, when flashing— or glittering as he describes it,—when under strong excitement.[2] It has been already noted that, in his "Battle of Hastings," he ascribes to Adhelm's lovely bride his own "featly sparkling, grey eye." The Rev. Mr. Le Grice when describing those of his sister, Mrs. Newton, says, "her eyes were fine grey eyes, which an admirer would call blue."[3]

[1] Bryant's Obs. p. 525.    [2] Gent. Mag. vol. x. N.S. p. 133.
[3] Notes and Queries, second series, vol. iv. p. 93.

CHAP. XV.

*Keen lightning of his eye.*

*Catcott and Barrett's descriptions.*

*Peculiar character of his eyes.*

Both the antique and modern prose and verse of Chatterton have been turned to account here for biographical purposes; and enough has been quoted in previous pages to enable the reader to form some just estimate of his powers. Perhaps the clearest evidence of his high poetic gift is to be found in the comparisons instituted between him and other poets. By reason of his very excellence he .has been tried by the highest standards, without thought of his immaturity. Grave critics are found testing the Rowley Poems by Chaucer, or matching them with Cowley and Prior ; and even finding in the acknowledged satires of a boy of sixteen " more of the luxuriance, fluency, and negligence of Dryden, than of the terseness and refinement of Pope." One of the



strongest evidences of his self-originating power is, in reality, to be found in the contrast which his verse presents to that of his .own day. In an age when the seductive charm of Pope's polished numbers captivated public taste, Chatterton struck a new chord ; and evolved principles of harmony which suggest comparison with Elizabethan poets, rather than with those of Anne's Augustan era. But he was no imitator. Amid all the assumption of antique thought, the reader perceives everywhere that he had looked on Nature for himself ; and could discern in her, alike in her calm beauty, and in her stormiest moods, secrets hidden from the common eye.



He had, moreover, patriotic sympathies as intense as Burns himself. His Goddwyn, Harold, Ælla, and Rycharde ; his Hastings, Bristowe, or Ruddeborne : are all lit up with the same passionate fire, to which some of his finest outbursts of feeling were due ; and which was still more replete with promise for the future.



Few English readers know what a rich vein of romance and true poetry lies concealed in the Rowley Poems. In their affectation of a fifteenth-century English in language and orthography, they are almost as completely beyond the reach of the ordinary reader as if they were actually secured under the six locks of Maistre Canynge's coffer : more so, perhaps, than the vigorous and graphic tales of the Canterbury pilgrimage, in one of those older editions of Chaucer, alone accessible to Chatterton. For his affected archaism is overstrained and inconsistent, and could deceive no competent critic now. In this respect there is some room for comparison with Spenser, who not only retained the obsolete language of Chaucer, but took the fullest licence of selection or adaptation of modern and antique phraseology, and of old inflectional forms, according to the exigencies of his rhymes. To a great extent the antique phraseology must have become natural to Chatterton whenever he reverted to the heroic age of his muse, and the inspiration of Rowley animated his pen. But many instances occur, where the difficulties both of rhyme and measure have been evaded by a licence in the forms of language such as Spenser dared not venture upon; or even an actual coining of words fully as much due to the exigencies of rhythm, as to the assigned age of the verse. Then it was that the glossary came into vogue; and this makes it impossible wholly to modernize Rowley, without the sacrifice of cadences, alliterations, and other rhythmical niceties, on which, in part, the musical charm of the verse depends.

It is easy to perceive how Chatterton not only thought more naturally, when, under the influence of a high poetic fervour, the modern world was shut out from his view; but that he moved with greater ease in the language ascribed to the antique period. Hence, whenever the strong impulses of poetic inspiration possessed him, he reverted to that world of his fancy's creation, and thought and wrote in a pure idealism worthy of the fit audience of poets, artists, and patrons of letters, with which his imagination had peopled the old Rudde House of Bristowe in the days of Edward IV.

The poems thus produced have been amply illustrated in previous chapters. They abound in passages as worthy of a place among the select beauties of English poetry as many of the most popular extracts from Coleridge, Scott, or Byron; and constitute a unique chapter in the literature of that eighteenth century. Pope belongs alto-

CHAP. XV.

*Contem-
porary poets.*

gether to the first half of the century, and died eight years before the birth of Chatterton ; but Gray, Akenside, Churchill, Goldsmith, and Cowper, were all his contemporaries. Collins died when Chatterton was in his fifth year; Burns was not born till his eighth. In that little group of true poets, who, each with distinct individuality of his own, succeeded to the place which the imitators of Pope failed to occupy, Chatterton takes an honourable place ; while contributing the charm of mystery to his share in the literature of the period which intervenes between the age of Queen Anne and the wonderful outburst of genius pertaining to the era of the French Revolution. .

*Vain
speculations.*

It is vain to speculate on what so proud, impetuous, ungovernable a spirit, involved in such moral perplexities, might have accomplished in mature years. Yet this cannot be overlooked, that though it is easy to detect inequalities and imperfections enough in the best of his antique poems ; lines of meagre thought ; stanzas eked out with redundant epithets ; and, still more, characters individualised with only a boy's knowledge of the springs of human action : still the productions, as a whole, are not irregular flashes of premature genius. They form parts of one consistent whole, the unity of which is never sacrificed. This is no characteristic of untimely precocity. It is only the immaturity natural to summer's early fruit, needing but time for its ripening. Warton,—no mean critic,—exclaims : " Chatterton was a prodigy of genius, and would have proved the first of English poets, had he reached a mature age." Without going to this extreme, it may be legitimately affirmed of him that, with the evidences of a rare poetic power such as is without a parallel at his age, his works prove a capacity for further development to which it is impossible to fix a limit.

*Imma-
turities
natural to
youth.*

The pleasure derived from the intense poetic spirit with which the verse of Keats is inspired is ever mingled with the regretful thought that we possess only the creations of his immature genius. We compare such early blossom with the well-ripened fruit, and reflect how little would remain of all that Milton, Dryden, or even Pope,

*Early
blossom.*

accomplished, had their years been limited to the term accorded to Burns, Shelley, or Byron. Yet even Keats attained his twenty-fifth year, Byron his thirty-seventh, and Burns his thirty-eighth; while Chatterton was but seventeen when he perished despairingly, with no belief in a future of life, or of fame.

As an Author, his fate has been altogether unique. Seven years after his death, the Rowley Poems were collected and published; and a second and more complete edition followed a few years later. The first was issued under the care of Thomas Tyrwhitt, the amiable and accomplished editor of Chaucer, who denied the existence of Rowley, and the antiquity of the poems. The second appeared under the auspices of Jeremiah Milles, D.D. Dean of Exeter, and President of the Society of Antiquaries of London, who laboriously asserted their antiquity, and the genuineness of their reputed author. Forthwith critics and antiquaries marshalled on either side, and the Rowley controversy expanded into a library of tracts, pamphlets, and volumes : with Bryant, Mathias, Glynne, Symmons, Henley, &c., stoutly holding their ground in defence of the antiquity of the poems; while the Wartons, Malone, Stephens, Jamieson, Gough, Mason, and a long array of anti-Rowleyans, ridiculed, in fiercest terms, the credulity of their opponents. But amid all this prolonged strife, the real author suffered more detraction from his allies, than from the credulous champions of the monk he had created. His death, unheeded in the world of letters, involved the home of his childhood in trouble as well as sorrow. A venerable citizen of Bristol recalls for me early reminiscences of conversations with an aged female relative of his own, who resided near Mrs. Chatterton, and appears to have been on friendly terms with her. She had spoken to him of having seen the poet's mother, on receiving the intelligence of his death, weep bitterly; and frequently afterwards bring out copy-books and other juvenile papers, and bedew them with her tears. But when the Rowleyan warfare was at its height, such memorials of her boy became objects of suspicion and fear. Mercenary collectors gleaned from them treasures, to be turned ere long to account for their own profit; and curious pilgrims invaded her privacy, and alarmed the widow and her daughter by their assumptions and suspicions. After the utter neglect of the treasures of the Redcliffe muniment-room for upwards of forty years, its custodians suddenly awoke to the belief that they had been despoiled of something precious. The strife over the poet's literary remains caused no small stir among those parochial authorities within whose bounds his life had been passed unheeded in their production. Legal demand was made for restitution of the manuscripts, as documents removed from the church by his father before he was born. Any



scraps of old papers or parchments that remained were given up by the affrighted widow; and amongst others, the book containing a few leaves inscribed with entries relating to church matters, from which Mr. Pryce has reproduced the last fly-leaf, with its evidence of Chatterton's juvenile attempts at the mastery of an antique caligraphy suited to the times of his imaginary Rowley.[1] "A gentleman who saw these two women last year," writes Sir Herbert Croft, in 1779, "declares that he will not be sure they might not easily have been made to believe that injured justice demanded their lives at Tyburn, for being the mother and sister of him who was suspected to have *forged* the poems of Rowley. Such terror had the humanity of certain curious inquirers impressed upon their minds."[2]



Neither those who accredited Chatterton with the recovery of valuable antiques, nor their opponents who affirmed the wonderful creations to be his own, appear to have bethought themselves of the bereaved mother, excepting for the gratification of their own curiosity. Twenty years after the poet's death a correspondent of the *Gentleman's Magazine* draws a mournful picture of the little household: the widow, under the infirmities of

[1] Memorials of the Canynge Family, p. 297.
[2] Croft, p. 156.

age, reduced to indigence, and in great suffering from cancer in her breast, yet bearing all with Christian fortitude; the sister, Mrs. Newton,—then also a widow, —struggling unsuccessfully to carry on the school; and her little orphan daughter completing the sad family group.[1]

The writer dates from Oxford, towards the close of 1790. But long before that another Oxford man, the Rev. Dr. Fry, head of St. John's College there, made his way to Bristol, the very year of Chatterton's death, bent on hunting up the discoverer or author of certain wonderful antiques that had fallen into his hands. Much has been said of what might have happened had Dr. Fry reached Bristol in time. It may be that the head of St. John's College would have appreciated the genius of the boy, and stood his friend, in spite of waywardnesses and self-assertions such as Oxford dons are least tolerant of. All we do know is that the poor mother, after years of suffering, died at last, in 1791, in poverty and neglect.

At the very close of the century, the poet Southey, and his friend Joseph Cottle,—themselves natives of Bristol,—prepared an edition of Chatterton's works, to be published by subscription, for behoof of his sister, whose sight was then beginning to fail.[2] Hitherto, as Southey says in the preface, they "had been published only for the emolument of strangers, who procured them by gift or purchase from the author himself, or pilfered them from his family." The subscription proved a failure; but Messrs. Longman and Rees entered into friendly arrangements with Southey, and he was able to report, in 1804, that Mrs. Newton lived to receive 184*l*. 15*s*. from the profits, which supported her in the decline of life, when, as she expressed it, she would otherwise have wanted bread.[3] Ultimately Mary Ann Newton, the poet's niece, received, it is said, about 600*l*., the fruits of the generous exertions of a brother poet, and of others

CHAP. XV.

A sad family group.

The head of St. John's College.

Southey and Cottle's efforts.

Opportune help to Mrs. Newton.

---

[1] Gent. Mag. vol. lx. part ii. p. 988.
[2] Southey's Letter, Gent. Mag. vol. lxx. part i. p. 226.
[3] Gent. Mag. vol. lxxiv. part ii. p. 723.

Y

CHAP. XV.

*Hannah More's kindness.*

*Interesting recollections.*

*Bristol's memorial of the poet.*

anxious to make some tardy requital to the Chatterton family.

Miss Hannah More, who had shown kindness to the widow for her son's sake, continued it to her granddaughter, after the death of Mrs. Newton; and she resided for some time under her roof at Barleywood, not, as has been said, as a servant, but as a friend. But she also died, in 1807, at the age of twenty-four, leaving the larger portion of the money to her paternal relatives, the Newtons, then resident at the Little Minories, London; but bequeathing 100*l.* to a young man, a manufacturer in Bristol, to whom she was about to be married. More than half a century afterwards Mr. George Pryce derived from him some interesting recollections of her conversations with him. Among these, perhaps the most noteworthy is that of Mrs. Newton telling her that, on the arrival of the news of Chatterton's death, their mother became so distressed that she burnt lapfuls of his papers, in order to remove whatever might recall to her the bitter remembrance of her loss.[1] The incident seems to conflict with the recollections of another contemporary, already referred to, of her deriving a melancholy pleasure from pondering over such relics of her gifted son.[2] But Mrs. Newton's reference was probably to the later period, described by Sir Herbert Croft, when parochial authorities were demanding restitution of lost parchments, and the terrified widow might well destroy what she was learning to regard as criminal forgeries of the boy.

After repeated efforts, a sum of money was at length raised, in 1840, sufficient to erect, in Bristol, a memorial of its boy-poet. It was the desire of those with whom it originated to place the monument within the Church of St. Mary Redcliffe, as its most appropriate site. But it was only after a prolonged struggle that one was yielded for it in the churchyard. Time had soothed many local asperities, and healed the wounds of personal vanity. But prejudices, secular and ecclesiastical, had still to be

[1] Notes and Queries, second edition, vol. iv. p. 93.
[2] Dix, App. p. 303.

overcome ; and there is perhaps poetical justice, and a certain fitness of things, in the perpetuation, on the very monument of the boy, of the antagonism between the vicars of St. Mary Redcliffe and the heir of line of its hereditary sextons. The friendly hand of a Bristol clergyman had supplied a metrical inscription, closing with the couplet :

> "He lived a mystery—died ; Here, reader, pause :
> Let God be judge, and mercy plead the cause."

But "the quality of mercy" meted out to Chatterton was still unchanged. The appeal proved ineffective seventy years after his death ; and before the design could obtain the needful ecclesiastical approval, it included, as an indispensable feature, the appropriation of its most prominent panel, facing Redcliffe Street, to a passage dictated by the vicar, from Young's "Night Thoughts," beginning :—

> "Know all ; know, infidels : unapt to know ;
> 'Tis immortality your nature solves," &c.[1]

Without the perpetration of this offence against good taste and feeling, no site would be allowed for the monument of the boy to whom St. Mary Redcliffe owes a world-wide fame. The admirers of the poet accepted the hard condition. It only required them to supplement it with the vicar's name, and convert it into a fitter monument of his own intolerance. Good men might hesitate about the erection of any monument ; but they could have no doubt that a memorial of the dead should not be converted into a tasteless insult. It was all the more objectionable, since the better taste of those by whom the monument was erected had already led them to select the brief, but appropriate words supplied by the

---

[1] Young's "Night's Thoughts," Night VII. nine lines. The monument has five sides. The various inscriptions engraved on them originally are given at length in Pryce's "Canynges Family," p. 296.

poet's own pen; which only need the dates of his birth and death to make the inscription complete:—

"TO THE MEMORY OF

### THOMAS CHATTERTON.

Reader! judge not.  If thou art a Christian, believe that he shall be judged by a Superior Power.  To that Power only is he now answerable."

*The poet's own epitaph.*

After evading or overcoming many difficulties, the poet's monument was at length erected, in 1840, on the north side of Redcliffe Church, between the tower and the muniment-room, so intimately associated with the romantic dream of his life.  But ere long the restoration of the north porch, of which the muniment-room forms a part, furnished an excuse for its removal; and only after long delay, and renewed difficulties, has it been rebuilt on another site.  No inscription has yet been placed on it; and as a new vicar now exercises authority, it may be presumed that better taste will be allowed to prevail in refilling the panels of the restored monument.

*Removal of the monument.*

It was scarcely needed for the poet.  His works are a more durable memorial even than the venerable edifice he had already appropriated as a monument, by titles beyond the challenge of any ecclesiastical consistory.  But it was due to the city in which the boy had achieved such triumphs of genius, amid poverty, and every impediment that an unbelieving generation could interpose, to make such reparation to itself, if not to him.  And so the monument, which in seeming jest he willed and directed to be executed, has at length been reared within the consecrated precincts of St. Mary Redcliffe; and Bristol now mingles somewhat of pride with the conflicting emotions with which it recalls the name of Chatterton.

*The poet's true memorial.*

# INDEX.

**THE END.**

LONDON : R. CLAY, SONS, AND TAYLOR, PRINTERS.

*November, 1869.*
16, BEDFORD STREET, COVENT GARDEN, LONDON.

# MACMILLAN AND CO.'S
## List of Publications.

**ABBOTT.—***A Shakespearian Grammar.*
An attempt to Illustrate some of the Differences between Elizabethan and Modern English. By E. A. ABBOTT, M.A. Head Master of the City of London School. *Second Edition.* Extra fcap. 8vo. 2*s.* 6*d.*

*Æschyli Eumenides.*
The Greek Text with English Notes, and an Introduction. By BERNARD DRAKE, M.A. 8vo. 3*s.* 6*d.*

**AIRY.—***Works by* G. B. AIRY, M.A. LL.D. D.C.L. *Astronomer Royal, &c.*

*Treatise on the Algebraical and Numerical Theory of Errors of Observations and the Combination of Observations.*
Crown 8vo. 6*s.* 6*d.*

*Popular Astronomy.*
A Series of Lectures delivered at Ipswich. *Sixth Edition.* 18mo. cloth, 4*s.* 6*d.* With Illustrations. Uniform with MACMILLAN'S SCHOOL CLASS BOOKS.

*An Elementary Treatise on Partial Differential Equations.*
With Stereoscopic Cards of Diagrams. Crown 8vo. 5*s.* 6*d.*

*On the Undulatory Theory of Optics.*
Designed for the use of Students in the University. Crown 8vo. 6*s.* 6*d.*

*On Sound and Atmospheric Vibrations,*
With the Mathematical Elements of Music. Designed for the use of Students of the Universities. Crown 8vo. 9*s.*

*Algebraical Exercises.*
Progressively arranged by Rev. C. A. JONES, M.A. and C. H. CHEYNE, M.A. Mathematical Masters in Westminster School. 18mo. 2*s.* 6*d.*

*Alice's Adventures in Wonderland.*
By LEWIS CARROLL. With Forty-two Illustrations by TENNIEL. 18th Thousand. Crown 8vo. cloth. 6*s.*

*A German Translation of the same.*
With TENNIEL's Illustrations. Crown 8vo. gilt. 6*s.*

*A French Translation of the same.*
With TENNIEL's Illustrations. Crown 8vo. gilt. 6*s.*

A

**ALLINGHAM.**—*Laurence Bloomfield in Ireland; or, The New Landlord.*
*Cheaper Issue*, with New Preface. By WILLIAM ALLINGHAM. Fcap. 8vo. 4s. 6d.

**ANSTED.**—*The Great Stone Book of Nature.*
By DAVID THOMAS ANSTED, M.A. F.R.S. F.G.S. Fcap. 8vo. 5s.

**ANSTIE.**—*Stimulants and Narcotics, their Mutual Relations.*
With Special Researches on the Action of Alcohol, Æther, and Chloroform on the Vital Organism. By FRANCIS E. ANSTIE, M.D. M.R.C.P. 8vo. 14s.

*Neuralgia, and Diseases which resemble it.*
8vo. [In the Press.

*Aristotle on Fallacies; or, the Sophistici Elenchi.*
With a Translation and Notes by EDWARD POSTE, M.A. 8vo. 8s. 6d.

**ARNOLD.**—*Works by* MATTHEW ARNOLD.
*The Complete Poetical Works.*
Vol. I.—*Narrative and Elegiac Poems.*
Vol. II.—*Dramatic and Lyric Poems.*
Extra fcap. 8vo. Price 6s. each.
*New Poems. Second Edition.*
Extra fcap. 8vo. 6s. 6d.
*A French Eton; or, Middle-Class Education and the State.*
Fcap. 8vo. 2s. 6d.
*Essays in Criticism.*
*New Edition*, with Additions. Extra fcap. 8vo. 6s.
*Schools and Universities on the Continent.*
8vo. 10s. 6d.

**BAKER.**—*Works by* SIR SAMUEL W. BAKER, M.A. F.R.G.S.
*The Nile Tributaries of Abyssinia, and the Sword Hunters of the Hamran Arabs.*
With Portraits, Maps, and Illustrations. *Third Edition.* 8vo. 21s.

*The Albert N'yanza Great Basin of the Nile, and Exploration of the Nile Sources. New and cheaper Edition.*
With Portraits, Maps, and Illustrations. Two Vols. crown 8vo. 16s.

*Cast up by the Sea; or, The Adventures of Ned Grey.*
With Illustrations by HUARD. *Second Edition.* Crown 8vo. Cloth gilt. 7s. 6d.

**BARNES.**—*Poems of Rural Life in Common English.*
By the Rev. W. BARNES, Author of "Poems of Rural Life in the Dorset Dialect." Fcap. 8vo. 6*s.*

**BARWELL.**—*Guide in the Sick Room.*
By RICHARD BARWELL, F.R.C.S. Extra fcap. 8vo. 3*s.* 6*d.*

**BATES AND LOCKYER.**—*A Class-Book of Geography. Adapted to the recent programme of the Royal Geographical Society.*
By H. W. BATES, Assistant Secretary to the Society, and J. N. LOCKYER, F.R.S. [In the Press.

**BAXTER.**—*Works by* R. DUDLEY BAXTER, M.A.
*National Income.*
With Coloured Diagram. 8vo. 3*s.* 6*d.*
*The Taxation of the United Kingdom. Its Amount, its Distribution, and Pressure.*
8vo. 4*s.* 6*d.*

**BAYMA.**—*Elements of Molecular Mechanics.*
By JOSEPH BAYMA, S. J. 8vo. 10*s.* 6*d.*

**BEASLEY.**—*An Elementary Treatise on Plane Trigonometry.*
With a Numerous Collection of Examples. By R. D. BEASLEY, M.A. *Second Edition.* Crown 8vo. 3*s.* 6*d.*

**BELL.**—*Romances and Minor Poems.*
By HENRY GLASSFORD BELL. Fcap. 8vo. 6*s.*

**BERNARD.**—*The Progress of Doctrine in the New Testament.*
In Eight Lectures preached before the University of Oxford. By THOMAS DEHANY BERNARD, M.A. *Second Edition.* 8vo. 8*s.* 6*d.*

**BERNARD.**—*Four Lectures on Subjects connected with Diplomacy.*
By MOUNTAGUE BERNARD, M.A., Chichele Professor of International Law and Diplomacy, Oxford. 8vo. 9*s.*

**BERNARD (ST.).**—*The Life and Times of St. Bernard, Abbot of Clairvaux.*
By J. C. MORISON, M.A. *New Edition.* Crown 8vo. 7*s.* 6*d.*

**BESANT.**—*Studies in Early French Poetry.*
By WALTER BESANT, M.A. Crown 8vo. 8*s.* 6*d.*

**BINNEY.**—*Sermons preached in the King's Weigh House Chapel, 1829–1869.*
By THOMAS BINNEY. *New and Cheaper Edition,* containing the "Farewell Sermon." Extra fcap. 8vo. 4*s.* 6*d.*

A 2

BIRKS.—*Works by* THOMAS RAWSON BIRKS, M.A.

*The Difficulties of Belief in connexion with the Creation and the Fall.*
Crown 8vo.  4s. 6d.

*On Matter and Ether ; or, the Secret Laws of Physical Change.*
Crown 8vo.  5s. 6d.

BLAKE.—*The Life of William Blake, the Artist.*
By ALEXANDER GILCHRIST.  With numerous Illustrations from Blake's Designs, and Fac-similes of his Studies of the "Book of Job."  Two Vols.  Medium 8vo.  32s.

*Blanche Lisle, and other Poems.*
By CECIL HOME.  Fcap. 8vo.  4s. 6d.

BOOLE.—*Works by the late* GEORGE BOOLE, F.R.S.  *Professor of Mathematics in the Queen's University, Ireland, &c.*

*A Treatise on Differential Equations.*
*New Edition.*  Edited by I. TODHUNTER, M.A. F.R.S.  Crown 8vo.  14s.

*Treatise on Differential Equations.*
Supplementary Volume.  Crown 8vo.  8s. 6d.

*A Treatise on the Calculus of Finite Differences.*
Crown 8vo.  10s. 6d.

BRADSHAW.—*An Attempt to ascertain the state of Chaucer's Works, as they were Left at his Death,*
With some Notices of their Subsequent History.  By HENRY BRADSHAW, of King's College, and the University Library, Cambridge.                                [In the Press.

BRIGHT.—*Speeches on Questions of Public Policy.*
By the Right Honourable JOHN BRIGHT, M.P.  Edited by PROFESSOR THOROLD ROGERS.  *Second Edition.*  2 vols. 8vo.  25s.  With Portrait.
Author's Popular Edition.  Extra fcap. 8vo.  3s. 6d.

BRIMLEY.—*Essays by the late* GEORGE BRIMLEY, M.A.
Edited by W. G. CLARK, M.A.  With Portrait.  *Cheaper Edition.*  Fcap. 8vo.  3s. 6d.

BROOK SMITH.—*Arithmetic in Theory and Practice.*
For Advanced Pupils.  Part First.  By J. BROOK SMITH, M.A.  Crown 8vo.  3s. 6d.

BRYCE.—*The Holy Roman Empire.*
By JAMES BRYCE, B.C.L. Fellow of Oriel College, Oxford. *A New Edition, revised and enlarged.* Crown 8vo. [In the Press.

BUCKNILL.—*The Mad Folk of Shakespeare.*
Psychological Lectures by J. C. BUCKNILL, M.D. F.R.S. Second Edition. Crown 8vo. 6*s.* 6*d.*

BULLOCK.—*Works by* W. H. BULLOCK.
*Polish Experiences during the Insurrection of* 1863-4.
Crown 8vo. With Map. 8*s.* 6*d.*

*Across Mexico in* 1864-5.
With Coloured Map and Illustrations. Crown 8vo. 10*s.* 6*d.*

BURGON.—*A Treatise on the Pastoral Office.*
Addressed chiefly to Candidates for Holy Orders, or to those who have recently undertaken the cure of souls. By the Rev. JOHN W. BURGON, M.A. 8vo. 12*s.*

BURNS.—*Globe Edition.*
*The Poems, Letters, and Songs.*
Being the Complete Works of Robert Burns. Edited, with Biographical Memoir, by ALEXANDER SMITH. Globe 8vo. 3*s.* 6*d.*

BUTLER (ARCHER).—*Works by the Rev.* WILLIAM ARCHER BUTLER, M.A. *late Professor of Moral Philosophy in the University of Dublin.*
*Sermons, Doctrinal and Practical.*
Edited, with a Memoir of the Author's Life, by THOMAS WOODWARD, M.A. Dean of Down. With Portrait. *Eighth and Cheaper Edition.* 8vo. 8*s.*

*A Second Series of Sermons.*
Edited by J. A. JEREMIE, D.D. Regius Professor of Divinity at Cambridge. *Fifth and Cheaper Edition.* 8vo. 7*s.*

*History of Ancient Philosophy.*
Edited by WM. H. THOMPSON, M.A. Master of Trinity College, Cambridge. Two Vols. 8vo. 1*l.* 5*s.*

*Letters on Romanism, in reply to Dr. Newman's Essay on Development.*
Edited by the Dean of Down. *Second Edition,* revised by Archdeacon HARDWICK. 8vo. 10*s.* 6*d.*

BUTLER (MONTAGU).—*Sermons preached in the Chapel of Harrow School.*
By H. MONTAGU BUTLER, Head Master. Crown 8vo. 7*s.* 6*d.*
———— Second Series. Crown 8vo. 7*s.* 6*d.*

BUTLER (GEORGE).—*Works by the Rev.* GEORGE BUTLER.
*Family Prayers.*
> Crown 8vo. 5s.

*Sermons preached in Cheltenham College Chapel.*
> Crown 8vo. 7s. 6d.

CAIRNES.—*The Slave Power; its Character, Career, and Probable Designs.*
> Being an Attempt to Explain the Real Issues Involved in the American Contest. By J. E. CAIRNES, M.A. *Second Edition.* 8vo. 10s. 6d.

CALDERWOOD.—*Philosophy of the Infinite.*
> A Treatise on Man's Knowledge of the Infinite Being, in answer to Sir W. Hamilton and Dr. Mansel. By the Rev. HENRY CALDERWOOD, M.A. Professor of Moral Philosophy at Edinburgh. *Second Edition.* 8vo. 14s.

*Cambridge Senate-House Problems and Riders, with Solutions.*
> 1848—1851.—*Problems.*
>> By FERRERS and JACKSON. 8vo. 15s. 6d.
>
> 1848—1851.—*Riders.*
>> By JAMESON. 8vo. 7s. 6d.
>
> 1854.—*Problems and Riders.*
>> By WALTON and MACKENZIE, M.A. 8vo. 10s. 6d.
>
> 1857.—*Problems and Riders.*
>> By CAMPION and WALTON. 8vo. 8s. 6d.
>
> 1860.—*Problems and Riders.*
>> By WATSON and ROUTH. Crown 8vo. 7s. 6d.
>
> 1864.—*Problems and Riders.*
>> By WALTON and WILKINSON. 8vo. 10s. 6d.

*Cambridge Lent Sermons.—*
> Sermons preached during Lent, 1864, in Great St. Mary's Church, Cambridge. By the BISHOP of OXFORD, Rev. H. P. LIDDON, T. L. CLAUGHTON, J. R. WOODFORD, Dr. GOULBURN, J. W. BURGON, T. T. CARTER, Dr. PUSEY, DEAN HOOK, W. J. BUTLER, DEAN GOODWIN. Crown 8vo. 7s. 6d.

*Cambridge Course of Elementary Natural Philosophy, for the Degree of B.A.*
> Originally compiled by J. C. SNOWBALL, M.A., late Fellow of St. John's College. *Fifth Edition,* revised and enlarged, and adapted for the Middle-Class Examinations by THOMAS LUND, B.D. Crown 8vo. 5s.

*Cambridge and Dublin Mathematical Journal.*
> The Complete Work, in Nine Vols. 8vo. Cloth. 7*l.* 4*s.* Only a few copies remain on hand.

*Cambridge Union Society's Inaugural Proceedings.*
> Fcap. 8vo. 3*s.*

*Cambridge Characteristics in the Seventeenth Century.*
> By JAMES BASS MULLINGER, B.A. Crown 8vo. 4*s.* 6*d.*

CAMPBELL.—*Works by* JOHN M'LEOD CAMPBELL.
> *Thoughts on Revelation, with Special Reference to the Present Time.*
>> Crown 8vo. 5*s.*
>
> *The Nature of the Atonement, and its Relation to Remission of Sins and Eternal Life.*
>> Third Edition. With an Introduction and Notes. 8vo. 10*s.* 6*d.*
>
> *Christ the Bread of Life.*
>> An attempt to give a profitable direction to the present occupation of thought with Romanism. *Second Edition.* Greatly enlarged. Crown 8vo. 4*s.* 6*d.*

CANDLER.—*Help to Arithmetic, designed for the Use of Schools.*
> By H. CANDLER, M.A. Mathematical Master at Uppingham. Fcap. 8vo. 2*s.* 6*d.*

CARTER.—*King's College Chapel : Notes on its History and present condition.*
> By T. J. P. CARTER, M.A. Fellow of King's College, Cambridge. With Photographs. 8vo. 5*s.*

*Catullus.*
> Edited by R. ELLIS. 18mo. 3*s.* 6*d.*

CHALLIS.—*Creation in Plan and in Progress :*
> Being an Essay on the First Chapter of Genesis. By the Rev. JAMES CHALLIS, M.A. F.R.S. F.R.A.S. Crown 8vo. 3*s.* 6*d.*

CHATTERTON.—*Leonore; a Tale.*
> By GEORGIANA LADY CHATTERTON. *A New Edition.* Beautifully printed on thick toned paper. Crown 8vo. with Frontispiece and Vignette Title engraved by JEENS. 7*s.* 6*d.*

CHEYNE.—*Works by* C. H. H. CHEYNE, B.A.
> *An Elementary Treatise on the Planetary Theory.*
>> With a Collection of Problems. Crown 8vo. 6*s.* 6*d.*
>
> *The Earth's Motion of Rotation (including the Theory of Precession and Nutation).*
>> Crown 8vo. 3*s.* 6*d.*

CHEYNE.—*Notes and Criticisms on the Hebrew Text of Isaiah.*
By the Rev. T. K. CHEYNE, M.A. Fellow of Balliol College, Oxford. 8vo. 2s. 6d.

*Choice Notes on the Four Gospels, drawn from Old and New Sources.*
Crown 8vo. 4s. 6d. each Vol. (St. Matthew and St. Mark in One Vol. price 9s.)

CHRISTIE (J. R.).—*Elementary Test Questions in Pure and Mixed Mathematics.*
Crown 8vo. 8s. 6d.

*Church Congress (Authorized Report of) held at Wolverhampton in October, 1867.*
8vo. 3s. 6d.

CHURCH.—*Sermons preached before the University of Oxford.*
By R. W. CHURCH, M.A. late Fellow of Oriel College, Rector of Whatley. Crown 8vo. 4s. 6d. *Second Edition.*

CICERO.—*The Second Philippic Oration.*
With an Introduction and Notes, translated from KARL HALM. Edited, with Corrections and Additions, by JOHN E. B. MAYOR, M.A. *Third Edition.* Fcap. 8vo. 5s.

CLARK.—*Four Sermons preached in the Chapel of Trinity College, Cambridge.*
By W. G. CLARK, M.A. Fcap. 8vo. 2s. 6d.

AY.—*The Prison Chaplain.*
A Memoir of the Rev. JOHN CLAY, B.D. late Chaplain of the Preston Gaol. With Selections from his Reports and Correspondence, and a Sketch of Prison Discipline in England. By his Son, the Rev. W. L. CLAY, M.A. 8vo. 15s.

*The Power of the Keys.*
Sermons preached in Coventry. By the Rev. W. L. CLAY, M.A. Fcap. 8vo. 3s. 6d.

*Clemency Franklyn.*
By the author of "Janet's Home." Crown 8vo. 6s.

*Clergyman's Self-Examination concerning the Apostles' Creed.*
Extra fcap. 8vo. 1s. 6d.

CLOUGH.—*The Poems of Arthur Hugh Clough,*
sometime Fellow of Oriel College, Oxford. With a Memoir by F. T. PALGRAVE. *Second Edition.* Fcap. 8vo. 6s.

CLOUGH.—*The Poems and Prose Remains of Arthur Hugh Clough.*
> Edited by his Wife. With a Selection from his Letters, and a Memoir. 2 vols. Crown 8vo. 21s.

COLENSO.—*Works by the Right Rev. J. W. COLENSO, D.D. Bishop of Natal.*

*The Colony of Natal.*
> A Journal of Visitation. With a Map and Illustrations. Fcap. 8vo. 5s.

*Village Sermons.*
> Second Edition. Fcap. 8vo. 2s. 6d.

*Companion to the Holy Communion,*
> Containing the Service and Select Readings from the writings of Professor MAURICE. *Common paper,* 1s.

*Connells of Castle Connell.*
> By JANET GORDON. Two Vols. Crown 8vo. 21s.

COOPER.—*Athenae Cantabrigienses.*
> By CHARLES HENRY COOPER, F.S.A. and THOMPSON COOPER, F.S.A. Vol. I. 8vo. 1500—85, 18s. Vol. II. 1586—1609, 18s.

COPE.—*An Introduction to Aristotle's Rhetoric.*
> With Analysis, Notes, and Appendices. By E. M. COPE, Senior Fellow and Tutor of Trinity College, Cambridge. 8vo. 14s.

COTTON.—*Works by the late GEORGE EDWARD LYNCH COTTON, D.D. Bishop of Calcutta.*

*Sermons and Addresses delivered in Marlborough College during Six Years.*
> Crown 8vo. 10s. 6d.

*Sermons, chiefly connected with Public Events of 1854.*
> Fcap. 8vo. 3s.

*Sermons preached to English Congregations in India.*
> Crown 8vo. 7s. 6d.

*Expository Sermons on the Epistles for the Sundays of the Christian Year.*
> Two Vols. Crown 8vo. 15s.

COX.—*Recollections of Oxford.*
> By G. V. Cox, M.A. late Esquire Bedel and Coroner in the University of Oxford. Crown 8vo. 10s. 6d.

CURE.—*The Seven Words of Christ on the Cross.*
Sermons preached at St. George's, Bloomsbury.   By the Rev. E.
CAPEL CURE, M.A.   Fcap. 8vo. 3s. 6d.

DALTON.—*Arithmetical Examples progressively arranged ;
together with Miscellaneous Exercises and Examination
Papers.*
By the Rev. T. DALTON, M.A.   Assistant Master at Eton
College.  18mo.   2s 6d.

DANTE.—*Dante's Comedy, The Hell.*
Translated by W. M. ROSSETTI.   Fcap. 8vo. cloth. 5s.

DAVIES.—*Works by the Rev. J. LLEWELYN DAVIES, M.A.
Rector of Christ Church, St. Marylebone, &c.*

*Sermons on the Manifestation of the Son of God.*
With a Preface addressed to Laymen on the present position of
the Clergy of the Church of England ; and an Appendix, on the
Testimony of Scripture and the Church as to the Possibility
of Pardon in the Future State.  Fcap. 8vo.   6s. 6d.

*The Work of Christ ; or, the World Reconciled to God.*
With a Preface on the Atonement Controversy.  Fcap. 8vo.  6s.

*Baptism, Confirmation, and the Lord's Supper.*
As interpreted by their outward signs.   Three Expository
Addresses for Parochial Use.  Fcap. 8vo.  Limp cloth.  1s. 6d.

*Morality according to the Sacrament of the Lord's Supper.*
Crown 8vo.  3s. 6d.

*The Epistles of St. Paul to the Ephesians, the Colossians,
and Philemon.*
With Introductions and Notes, and an Essay on the Traces of
Foreign Elements in the Theology of these Epistles.  8vo. 7s. 6d.

*The Gospel and Modern Life.*
Sermons on some of the Difficulties of the Present Day.   With
a Preface on a Recent Phase of Deism.  Extra fcap. 8vo.  6s.

DAWSON.—*Acadian Geology, the Geological Structure,
Organic Remains, and Mineral Resources of Nova
Scotia, New Brunswick, and Prince Edward Island.*
By J. W. DAWSON, LL.D. F.R.S. F.G.S. *Second Edition,*
revised and enlarged, with Geological Maps and Illustrations.
8vo.  18s.

DAY.—*Properties of Conic Sections proved Geometrically.*
By the Rev. H. G. DAY, M.A. Head-Master of Sedbergh Grammar School. Crown 8vo. 3*s*. 6*d*.

*Days of Old ; Stories from Old English History.*
By the Author of "Ruth and her Friends." *New Edition,* 18mo. cloth, gilt leaves. 3*s*. 6*d*.

DELAMOTTE.—*A Beginner's Drawing Book.*
By PHILIP H. DELAMOTTE, F.S.A. Professor of Drawing in King's College and School, London. Progressively arranged. With upwards of Fifty Plates. Stiff Covers, crown 8vo. 2*s*. 6*d*.

*Demosthenes, De Corona.*
The Greek Text with English Notes. By B. DRAKE, M.A. *Third Edition,* to which is prefixed ÆSCHINES AGAINST CTESIPHON, with English Notes. Fcap 8vo. 5*s*.

DE TEISSIER.—*Works by* G. F. DE TEISSIER, B.D.
*Village Sermons.*
Crown 8vo. 9*s*.
*Second Series.*
Crown 8vo. 8*s*. 6*d*.
*The House of Prayer ; or, a Practical Exposition of the Order for Morning and Evening Prayer in the Church of England.*
18mo. extra cloth. 4*s*. 6*d*.

DE VERE.—*The Infant Bridal, and other Poems.*
By AUBREY DE VERE. Fcap. 8vo. 7*s*. 6*d*.

DILKE.—*Greater Britain.*
A Record of Travel in English-speaking Countries during 1866-7. (America, Australia, India.) By Sir CHARLES WENTWORTH DILKE, M.P. *Fourth and Cheaper Edition.* Crown 8vo. 6*s*.

DODGSON.—*Elementary Treatise on Determinants.*
By C. L. DODGSON, M.A. 4to. 10*s*. 6*d*.

DONALDSON.—*A Critical History of Christian Literature and Doctrine, from the Death of the Apostles to the Nicene Council.*
By JAMES DONALDSON, LL.D. Three Vols. 8vo. cloth. 31*s*.

DOYLE.—*Works by Sir* FRANCIS HASTINGS DOYLE, *Professor of Poetry in the University of Oxford.*
*The Return of the Guards, and other Poems.*
Fcap. 8vo. 7*s*.
*Lectures on Poetry.*
Delivered before the University of Oxford in 1868. Crown 8vo. 3*s*. 6*d*.

**DREW.**—*Works by W. H. DREW, M.A.*

*A Geometrical Treatise on Conic Sections.*
Fourth Edition. Crown 8vo. 4s. 6d.

*Solutions to Problems contained in Drew's Treatise on Conic Sections.*
Crown 8vo. 4s. 6d.

**DÜRER (ALBRECHT).**—*The History of the Life of Albrecht Dürer of Nürnberg, with a Translation of his Letters and Journal, and some Account of his Works.*
By Mrs. CHARLES HEATON. With Thirty Photographic and Autotype Illustrations. Royal 8vo. 31s. 6d.

*Early Egyptian History for the Young.*
With Descriptions of the Tombs and Monuments. *New Edition,* with Frontispiece. Fcap. 8vo. 5s.

**EASTWOOD.**—*The Bible Word Book.*
A Glossary of Old English Bible Words. By J. EASTWOOD, M.A. of St. John's College, and W. ALDIS WRIGHT, M.A. Trinity College, Cambridge. 18mo. 5s. 6d. Uniform with Macmillan's School Class Books.

*Ecce Homo.*
A Survey of the Life and Work of Jesus Christ. 23d Thousand. Crown 8vo. 6s.

*Echoes of Many Voices from Many Lands.*
By A. F. 18mo. cloth, extra gilt. 3s. 6d.

**EDGAR.**—*Note Book on Practical Solid Geometry, containing Problems with Help for Solution.*
By J. H. EDGAR, M.A. Lecturer on Mechanical Drawing in the Royal School of Mines, London. 4to. 2s.

**ELAM.**—*A Physician's Problems.*
By CHARLES ELAM, M.D. M.R.C.P. Contents : Natural Heritage—On Degenerations in Man—On Moral and Criminal Epidemics—Body *v.* Mind—Illusions and Hallucinations—On Somnambulism—Reverie and Abstraction. Crown 8vo. 9s.

**ELLICE.**—*English Idylls.*
By JANE ELLICE. Fcap. 8vo. cloth. 6s.

**ELLIOTT.**—*Life of Henry Venn Elliott, of Brighton.*
By JOSIAH BATEMAN, M.A. Author of " Life of Daniel Wilson, Bishop of Calcutta," &c. With Portrait, engraved by JEENS. Crown 8vo. 8s. 6d.

**ERLE.**—*The Law relating to Trade Unions.*
By Sir WILLIAM ERLE, formerly Chief Justice in the Common Pleas. Crown 8vo. 3s. 6d.

*Essays on Church Policy.*
Edited by the Rev. W. L. CLAY, M.A. Incumbent of Rainhill, Lancashire. 8vo. 9s.

*Essays on a Liberal Education.*
By Various Writers. Edited by the Rev. F. W. FARRAR, M.A. F.R.S. &c. *Second Edition.* 8vo. 10s. 6d.

**EVANS.**—*Brother Fabian's Manuscript, and other Poems.*
By SEBASTIAN EVANS. Fcap. 8vo. cloth. 6s.

**FARRAR.**—*The Fall of Man, and other Sermons.*
By the Rev. F. W. FARRAR, M.A. late Fellow of Trinity College, Cambridge. Fcap, 8vo. 6s.

**FAWCETT.**—*Works by* HENRY FAWCETT, M.P.

*The Economic Position of the British Labourer.*
Extra fcap. 8vo. 5s.

*Manual of Political Economy.*
*Second Edition.* Crown 8vo. 12s.

*Fellowship : Letters addressed to my Sister Mourners.*
Fcap. 8vo. cloth gilt. 3s. 6d.

**FERRERS.**—*A Treatise on Trilinear Co-ordinates, the Method of Reciprocal Polars, and the Theory of Projections.*
By the Rev. N. M. FERRERS, M.A. *Second Edition.* Crown 8vo. 6s. 6d.

**FLETCHER.**—*Thoughts from a Girl's Life.*
By LUCY FLETCHER. *Second Edition.* Fcap. 8vo. 4s. 6d.

**FORBES.**—*Life of Edward Forbes, F.R.S.*
By GEORGE WILSON, M.D. F.R.S.E., and ARCHIBALD GEIKIE, F.R.S. 8vo. with Portrait. 14s.

**FORBES.**—*The Voice of God in the Psalms.*
By GRANVILLE FORBES, Rector of Broughton. Crown 8vo. 6s. 6d.

**FOX.**—*On the Diagnosis and Treatment of the Varieties of Dyspepsia, considered in Relation to the Pathological Origin of the different Forms of Indigestion.*
By WILSON FOX, M.D. Lond. F.R.C.P. Holme Professor of Clinical Medicine at University College, London, and Physician to University College Hospital. *Second Edition.* Demy 8vo. 7s. 6d.

FOX.—*On the Artificial Production of Tubercle in the Lower Animals.*
>4to. 5s. 6d.

FREELAND.—*The Fountain of Youth.*
>Translated from the Danish of Frederick Paludan Müller. By HUMPHREY WILLIAM FREELAND, late M.P. for Chichester. With Illustrations designed by Walter Allen. Crown 8vo. 6s.

FREEMAN.—*History of Federal Government from the Foundation of the Achaian League to the Disruption of the United States.*
>By EDWARD A. FREEMAN, M.A. Vol. I. General Introduction. —History of the Greek Federations. 8vo. 21s.

*Old English History for Children.*
>With Five Coloured Maps. Extra fcap. 8vo. 6s.

FRENCH.—*Shakspeareana Genealogica.*
>PART I.—Identification of the Dramatis Personæ in the Historical Plays, from King John to King Henry VIII.: Notes on Characters in Macbeth and Hamlet: Persons and Places belonging to Warwickshire alluded to. PART II.—The Shakspeare and Arden Families and their Connections, with Tables of Descent. By GEORGE RUSSELL FRENCH. 8vo. 15s.

FROST.—*The First Three Sections of Newton's Principia.*
>With Notes and Problems in Illustration of the Subject. By PERCIVAL FROST, M.A. *Second Edition.* 8vo. 10s. 6d.

FROST AND WOLSTENHOLME.—*A Treatise on Solid Geometry.*
>By the Rev. PERCIVAL FROST, M.A. and the Rev. J. WOLSTENHOLME, M.A. 8vo. 18s.

*The Sicilian Expedition.*
>Being Books VI. and VII. of Thucydides, with Notes. By the Rev. P. FROST, M.A. *New Edition.* Fcap. 8vo. 5s.

FURNIVALL.—*Le Morte Arthur.*
>Edited from the Harleian M.S. 2252, in the British Museum. By F. J. FURNIVALL, M.A. With Essay by the late HERBERT COLERIDGE. Fcap. 8vo. 7s. 6d.

GALTON.—*Works by* FRANCIS GALTON, F.R.S.

*Meteorographica, or Methods of Mapping the Weather.*
>Illustrated by upwards of 600 Printed Lithographed Diagrams. By FRANCIS GALTON, F.R.S. 4to. 9s.

*Hereditary Genius, its Laws and Consequences.*
>With numerous illustrative Examples. [In the Press.

**GARNETT.**—*Idylls and Epigrams.*
Chiefly from the Greek Anthology. By RICHARD GARNETT. Fcap. 8vo. 2s. 6d.

**GEIKIE.**—*Works by* ARCHIBALD GEIKIE, F.R.S. *Director of the Geological Survey of Scotland.*

*Story of a Boulder; or, Gleanings by a Field Geologist.*
Illustrated with Woodcuts. Crown 8vo. 5s.

*Scenery of Scotland, viewed in connexion with its Physical Geology.*
With Illustrations and a New Geological Map. Crown 8vo. 10s. 6d.

*Elementary Lessons in Physical Geology.* [In the Press.

**GIFFORD.**—*The Glory of God in Man.*
By E. H. GIFFORD, D.D. Fcap. 8vo. 3s. 6d.

**GLADSTONE.**—*Juventus Mundi: Gods and Men of the Greek Heroic Age.*
With Map of the outer Geography of the Odyssey. By the Right Hon. W. E. GLADSTONE, M.P. Crown 8vo. 10s. 6d.

*Globe Editions :*

*The Complete Works of William Shakespeare.*
Edited by W. G. CLARK and W. ALDIS WRIGHT. Ninety-first Thousand. Globe 8vo. 3s. 6d.

*Morte DArthur.*
SIR THOMAS MALORY's Book of KING ARTHUR and of his noble KNIGHTS of the ROUND TABLE. The Edition of Caxton, revised for Modern use. With an Introduction by SIR EDWARD STRACHEY, Bart. Globe 8vo. 3s. 6d. *Second Edition.*

*The Poetical Works of Sir Walter Scott.*
With Biographical and Critical Essay by F. T. PALGRAVE.

*The Poetical Works and Letters of Robert Burns.*
Edited, with Life and Glossarial Index, by ALEXANDER SMITH. Globe 8vo. 3s. 6d.

*The Adventures of Robinson Crusoe.*
Edited, from the Original Editions, with Introduction, by HENRY KINGSLEY. Globe 8vo. 3s. 6d.

*Goldsmith's Miscellaneous Works.*
With Biographical Essay by PROF. MASSON. Globe 8vo. 3s. 6d.

*Globe Editions:*

*Alexander Pope's Poetical Works.*
Edited, with Memoir and Notes, by PROFESSOR WARD.  Globe
8vo.  3*s.* 6*d.*

*Spenser's Complete Works.*
Edited by R. MORRIS.  With Memoir by J. W. HALES, M.A.
Globe 8vo.  3*s.* 6*d.*
Other Standard Works are in the Press.

*Globe Atlas of Europe.*
Uniform in Size with MACMILLAN'S GLOBE SERIES.  Containing
Forty-Eight Coloured Maps on the same scale, Plans of London
and Paris, and a Copious Index.  Strongly bound in half morocco,
with flexible back, 9*s.*

GODFRAY.—*An Elementary Treatise on the Lunar Theory.*
With a brief Sketch of the Problem up to the time of Newton.  By
HUGH GODFRAY, M.A. *Second Edition revised.* Crown 8vo. 5*s.* 6*d.*

*A Treatise on Astronomy, for the Use of Colleges
and Schools.*
By HUGH GODFRAY, M.A.  8vo.  12*s.* 6*d.*

*Golden Treasury Series :*
Uniformly printed in 18mo. with Vignette Titles by Sir NOEL
PATON, T. WOOLNER, W. HOLMAN HUNT, J. E. MILLAIS,
ARTHUR HUGHES, &c.  Engraved on Steel by JEENS.  Bound
in extra cloth, 4*s.* 6*d.*

*The Golden Treasury of the Best Songs and Lyrical
Poems in the English Language.*
Selected and arranged, with Notes, by FRANCIS TURNER PAL-
GRAVE.

*The Children's Garland from the Best Poets.*
Selected and arranged by COVENTRY PATMORE.

*The Book of Praise.*
From the Best English Hymn Writers.  Selected and arranged
by Sir ROUNDELL PALMER.  *A New and Enlarged Edition.*

*The Fairy Book: the Best Popular Fairy Stories.*
Selected and rendered anew by the Author of "John Halifax,
Gentleman."

*The Ballad Book.*
A Selection of the choicest British Ballads.  Edited by WILLIAM
ALLINGHAM.

*The Jest Book.*
The choicest Anecdotes and Sayings.  Selected and arranged by
MARK LEMON.

November, 1869.

16, Bedford Street, Covent Garden, London.

# MACMILLAN AND CO.'S
## List of Publications.

ABBOTT.—*A Shakespearian Grammar.*

An attempt to Illustrate some of the Differences between Elizabethan and Modern English. By E. A. ABBOTT, M.A. Head Master of the City of London School. *Second Edition.* Extra fcap. 8vo. 2*s.* 6*d.*

*Æschyli Eumenides.*

The Greek Text with English Notes, and an Introduction. By BERNARD DRAKE, M.A. 8vo. 3*s.* 6*d.*

AIRY.—*Works by* G. B. AIRY, M.A. LL.D. D.C.L. *Astronomer Royal, &c.*

*Treatise on the Algebraical and Numerical Theory of Errors of Observations and the Combination of Observations.*

Crown 8vo. 6*s.* 6*d.*

*Popular Astronomy.*

A Series of Lectures delivered at Ipswich. *Sixth Edition.* 18mo. cloth, 4*s.* 6*d.* With Illustrations. Uniform with MACMILLAN'S SCHOOL CLASS BOOKS.

*An Elementary Treatise on Partial Differential Equations.*

With Stereoscopic Cards of Diagrams. Crown 8vo. 5*s.* 6*d.*

*On the Undulatory Theory of Optics.*

Designed for the use of Students in the University. Crown 8vo. 6*s.* 6*d.*

*On Sound and Atmospheric Vibrations,*

With the Mathematical Elements of Music. Designed for the use of Students of the Universities. Crown 8vo. 9*s.*

*Algebraical Exercises.*

Progressively arranged by Rev. C. A. JONES, M.A. and C. H. CHEYNE, M.A. Mathematical Masters in Westminster School. 18mo. 2*s.* 6*d.*

*Alice's Adventures in Wonderland.*

By LEWIS CARROLL. With Forty-two Illustrations by TENNIEL. 18th Thousand. Crown 8vo. cloth. 6*s.*

*A German Translation of the same.*

With TENNIEL's Illustrations. Crown 8vo. gilt. 6*s.*

*A French Translation of the same.*

With TENNIEL's Illustrations. Crown 8vo. gilt. 6*s.*

A

15,000 11.69.

**ALLINGHAM.**—*Laurence Bloomfield in Ireland; or, The New Landlord.*
*Cheaper Issue*, with New Preface. By WILLIAM ALLINGHAM. Fcap. 8vo. 4s. 6d.

**ANSTED.**—*The Great Stone Book of Nature.*
By DAVID THOMAS ANSTED, M.A. F.R.S. F.G.S. Fcap. 8vo. 5s.

**ANSTIE.**—*Stimulants and Narcotics, their Mutual Relations.*
With Special Researches on the Action of Alcohol, Æther, and Chloroform on the Vital Organism. By FRANCIS E. ANSTIE, M.D. M.R.C.P. 8vo. 14s.

*Neuralgia, and Diseases which resemble it.*
8vo. [In the Press.

*Aristotle on Fallacies; or, the Sophistici Elenchi.*
With a Translation and Notes by EDWARD POSTE, M.A. 8vo. 8s. 6d.

**ARNOLD.**—*Works by* MATTHEW ARNOLD.
*The Complete Poetical Works.*
Vol. I.—*Narrative and Elegiac Poems.*
Vol. II.—*Dramatic and Lyric Poems.*
Extra fcap. 8vo. Price 6s. each.
*New Poems. Second Edition.*
Extra fcap. 8vo. 6s. 6d.
*A French Eton; or, Middle-Class Education and the State.*
Fcap. 8vo. 2s. 6d.
*Essays in Criticism.*
*New Edition*, with Additions. Extra fcap. 8vo. 6s.
*Schools and Universities on the Continent.*
8vo. 10s. 6d.

**BAKER.**—*Works by* SIR SAMUEL W. BAKER, M.A. F.R.G.S.
*The Nile Tributaries of Abyssinia, and the Sword Hunters of the Hamran Arabs.*
With Portraits, Maps, and Illustrations. *Third Edition.* 8vo. 21s.
*The Albert N'yanza Great Basin of the Nile, and Exploration of the Nile Sources. New and cheaper Edition.*
With Portraits, Maps, and Illustrations. Two Vols. crown 8vo. 16s.
*Cast up by the Sea; or, The Adventures of Ned Grey.*
With Illustrations by HUARD. *Second Edition.* Crown 8vo. Cloth gilt. 7s. 6d.

BARNES.—*Poems of Rural Life in Common English.*
By the Rev. W. BARNES, Author of "Poems of Rural Life in the Dorset Dialect." Fcap. 8vo. 6*s.*

BARWELL.—*Guide in the Sick Room.*
By RICHARD BARWELL, F.R.C.S. Extra fcap. 8vo. 3*s.* 6*d.*

BATES AND LOCKYER.—*A Class-Book of Geography. Adapted to the recent programme of the Royal Geographical Society.*
By H. W. BATES, Assistant Secretary to the Society, and J. N. LOCKYER, F.R.S. [In the Press.

BAXTER.—*Works by* R. DUDLEY BAXTER, M.A.
*National Income.*
With Coloured Diagram. 8vo. 3*s.* 6*d.*

*The Taxation of the United Kingdom. Its Amount, its Distribution, and Pressure.*
8vo. 4*s.* 6*d.*

BAYMA.—*Elements of Molecular Mechanics.*
By JOSEPH BAYMA, S. J. 8vo. 10*s.* 6*d.*

BEASLEY.—*An Elementary Treatise on Plane Trigonometry.*
With a Numerous Collection of Examples. By R. D. BEASLEY, M.A. *Second Edition.* Crown 8vo. 3*s.* 6*d.*

BELL.—*Romances and Minor Poems.*
By HENRY GLASSFORD BELL. Fcap. 8vo. 6*s.*

BERNARD.—*The Progress of Doctrine in the New Testament.*
In Eight Lectures preached before the University of Oxford. By THOMAS DEHANY BERNARD, M.A. *Second Edition.* 8vo. 8*s.* 6*d.*

BERNARD.—*Four Lectures on Subjects connected with Diplomacy.*
By MOUNTAGUE BERNARD, M.A., Chichele Professor of International Law and Diplomacy, Oxford. 8vo. 9*s.*

BERNARD (ST.).—*The Life and Times of St. Bernard, Abbot of Clairvaux.*
By J. C. MORISON, M.A. *New Edition.* Crown 8vo. 7*s.* 6*d.*

BESANT.—*Studies in Early French Poetry.*
By WALTER BESANT, M.A. Crown 8vo. 8*s.* 6*d.*

BINNEY.—*Sermons preached in the King's Weigh House Chapel, 1829–1869.*
By THOMAS BINNEY. *New and Cheaper Edition,* containing the "Farewell Sermon." Extra fcap. 8vo. 4*s.* 6*d.*

**BIRKS.**—*Works by* THOMAS RAWSON BIRKS, M.A.

*The Difficulties of Belief in connexion with the Creation and the Fall.*
Crown 8vo. 4s. 6d.

*On Matter and Ether; or, the Secret Laws of Physical Change.*
Crown 8vo. 5s. 6d.

**BLAKE.**—*The Life of William Blake, the Artist.*
By ALEXANDER GILCHRIST. With numerous Illustrations from Blake's Designs, and Fac-similes of his Studies of the "Book of Job." Two Vols. Medium 8vo. 32s.

*Blanche Lisle, and other Poems.*
By CECIL HOME. Fcap. 8vo. 4s. 6d.

**BOOLE.**—*Works by the late* GEORGE BOOLE, F.R.S. *Professor of Mathematics in the Queen's University, Ireland, &c.*

*A Treatise on Differential Equations.*
*New Edition.* Edited by I. TODHUNTER, M.A. F.R.S. Crown 8vo. 14s.

*Treatise on Differential Equations.*
Supplementary Volume. Crown 8vo. 8s. 6d.

*A Treatise on the Calculus of Finite Differences.*
Crown 8vo. 10s. 6d.

**BRADSHAW.**—*An Attempt to ascertain the state of Chaucer's Works, as they were Left at his Death,*
With some Notices of their Subsequent History. By HENRY BRADSHAW, of King's College, and the University Library, Cambridge.　　　　　　　　　　　[In the Press.

**BRIGHT.**—*Speeches on Questions of Public Policy.*
By the Right Honourable JOHN BRIGHT, M.P. Edited by PROFESSOR THOROLD ROGERS. *Second Edition.* 2 vols. 8vo. 25s. With Portrait.
Author's Popular Edition. Extra fcap. 8vo. 3s. 6d.

**BRIMLEY.**—*Essays by the late* GEORGE BRIMLEY, M.A.
Edited by W. G. CLARK, M.A. With Portrait. *Cheaper Edition.* Fcap. 8vo. 3s. 6d.

**BROOK SMITH.**—*Arithmetic in Theory and Practice.*
For Advanced Pupils. Part First. By J. BROOK SMITH, M.A. Crown 8vo. 3s. 6d.

**BRYCE.**—*The Holy Roman Empire.*
> By JAMES BRYCE, B.C.L. Fellow of Oriel College, Oxford. *A New Edition, revised and enlarged.* Crown 8vo. [In the Press.

**BUCKNILL.**—*The Mad Folk of Shakespeare.*
> Psychological Lectures by J. C. BUCKNILL, M.D. F.R.S. Second Edition. Crown 8vo. 6*s.* 6*d.*

**BULLOCK.**—*Works by* W. H. BULLOCK.
*Polish Experiences during the Insurrection of 1863-4.*
> Crown 8vo. With Map. 8*s.* 6*d.*

*Across Mexico in 1864-5.*
> With Coloured Map and Illustrations. Crown 8vo. 10*s.* 6*d.*

**BURGON.**—*A Treatise on the Pastoral Office.*
> Addressed chiefly to Candidates for Holy Orders, or to those who have recently undertaken the cure of souls. By the Rev. JOHN W. BURGON, M.A. 8vo. 12*s.*

**BURNS.**—*Globe Edition.*
*The Poems, Letters, and Songs.*
> Being the Complete Works of Robert Burns. Edited, with Biographical Memoir, by ALEXANDER SMITH. Globe 8vo. 3*s.* 6*d.*

**BUTLER (ARCHER).**—*Works by the Rev.* WILLIAM ARCHER BUTLER, M.A. *late Professor of Moral Philosophy in the University of Dublin.*

*Sermons, Doctrinal and Practical.*
> Edited, with a Memoir of the Author's Life, by THOMAS WOOD-WARD, M.A. Dean of Down. With Portrait. *Eighth and Cheaper Edition.* 8vo. 8*s.*

*A Second Series of Sermons.*
> Edited by J. A. JEREMIE, D.D. Regius Professor of Divinity at Cambridge. *Fifth and Cheaper Edition.* 8vo. 7*s.*

*History of Ancient Philosophy.*
> Edited by WM. H. THOMPSON, M.A. Master of Trinity College, Cambridge. Two Vols. 8vo. 1*l.* 5*s.*

*Letters on Romanism, in reply to Dr. Newman's Essay on Development.*
> Edited by the Dean of Down. *Second Edition,* revised by Archdeacon HARDWICK. 8vo. 10*s.* 6*d.*

**BUTLER (MONTAGU).**—*Sermons preached in the Chapel of Harrow School.*
> By H. MONTAGU BUTLER, Head Master. Crown 8vo. 7*s.* 6*d.*
> ———— Second Series. Crown 8vo. 7*s.* 6*d.*

BUTLER (GEORGE).—*Works by the Rev.* GEORGE BUTLER.

*Family Prayers.*
Crown 8vo. 5s.

*Sermons preached in Cheltenham College Chapel.*
Crown 8vo. 7s. 6d.

CAIRNES.—*The Slave Power; its Character, Career, and Probable Designs.*
Being an Attempt to Explain the Real Issues Involved in the American Contest. By J. E. CAIRNES, M.A. *Second Edition.* 8vo. 10s. 6d.

CALDERWOOD.—*Philosophy of the Infinite.*
A Treatise on Man's Knowledge of the Infinite Being, in answer to Sir W. Hamilton and Dr. Mansel. By the Rev. HENRY CALDERWOOD, M.A. Professor of Moral Philosophy at Edinburgh. *Second Edition.* 8vo. 14s.

*Cambridge Senate-House Problems and Riders, with Solutions.*

1848—1851.—*Problems.*
By FERRERS and JACKSON. 8vo. 15s. 6d.

1848—1851.—*Riders.*
By JAMESON. 8vo. 7s. 6d.

1854.—*Problems and Riders.*
By WALTON and MACKENZIE, M.A. 8vo. 10s. 6d.

1857.—*Problems and Riders.*
By CAMPION and WALTON. 8vo. 8s. 6d.

1860.—*Problems and Riders.*
By WATSON and ROUTH. Crown 8vo. 7s. 6d.

1864.—*Problems and Riders.*
By WALTON and WILKINSON. 8vo. 10s. 6d.

*Cambridge Lent Sermons.—*
Sermons preached during Lent, 1864, in Great St. Mary's Church, Cambridge. By the BISHOP OF OXFORD, Rev. H. P. LIDDON, T. L. CLAUGHTON, J. R. WOODFORD, Dr. GOULBURN, J. W. BURGON, T. T. CARTER, Dr. PUSEY, DEAN HOOK, W. J. BUTLER, DEAN GOODWIN. Crown 8vo. 7s. 6d.

*Cambridge Course of Elementary Natural Philosophy, for the Degree of B.A.*
Originally compiled by J. C. SNOWBALL, M.A., late Fellow of St. John's College. *Fifth Edition,* revised and enlarged, and adapted for the Middle-Class Examinations by THOMAS LUND, B.D. Crown 8vo. 5s.

*Cambridge and Dublin Mathematical Journal.*
> The *Complete Work*, in Nine Vols. 8vo. Cloth. 7*l.* 4*s.* Only a few copies remain on hand.

*Cambridge Union Society's Inaugural Proceedings.*
> Fcap. 8vo. 3*s.*

*Cambridge Characteristics in the Seventeenth Century.*
> By JAMES BASS MULLINGER, B.A. Crown 8vo. 4*s.* 6*d.*

CAMPBELL.—*Works by* JOHN M'LEOD CAMPBELL.
> *Thoughts on Revelation, with Special Reference to the Present Time.*
>> Crown 8vo. 5*s.*
>
> *The Nature of the Atonement, and its Relation to Remission of Sins and Eternal Life.*
>> *Third Edition.* With an Introduction and Notes. 8vo. 10*s.* 6*d.*
>
> *Christ the Bread of Life.*
>> An attempt to give a profitable direction to the present occupation of thought with Romanism. *Second Edition.* Greatly enlarged. Crown 8vo. 4*s.* 6*d.*

CANDLER.—*Help to Arithmetic, designed for the Use of Schools.*
> By H. CANDLER, M.A. Mathematical Master at Uppingham. Fcap. 8vo. 2*s.* 6*d.*

CARTER.—*King's College Chapel: Notes on its History and present condition.*
> By T. J. P. CARTER, M.A. Fellow of King's College, Cambridge. With Photographs. 8vo. 5*s.*

*Catullus.*
> Edited by R. ELLIS. 18mo. 3*s.* 6*d.*

CHALLIS.—*Creation in Plan and in Progress:*
> Being an Essay on the First Chapter of Genesis. By the Rev. JAMES CHALLIS, M.A. F.R.S. F.R.A.S. Crown 8vo. 3*s.* 6*d.*

CHATTERTON.—*Leonore; a Tale.*
> By GEORGIANA LADY CHATTERTON. *A New Edition.* Beautifully printed on thick toned paper. Crown 8vo. with Frontispiece and Vignette Title engraved by JEENS. 7*s.* 6*d.*

CHEYNE.—*Works by* C. H. H. CHEYNE, B.A.
> *An Elementary Treatise on the Planetary Theory.*
>> With a Collection of Problems. Crown 8vo. 6*s.* 6*d.*
>
> *The Earth's Motion of Rotation (including the Theory of Precession and Nutation).*
>> Crown 8vo. 3*s.* 6*d.*

**CHEYNE.**—*Notes and Criticisms on the Hebrew Text of Isaiah.*
By the Rev. T. K. CHEYNE, M.A. Fellow of Balliol College, Oxford. 8vo. 2s. 6d.

*Choice Notes on the Four Gospels, drawn from Old and New Sources.*
Crown 8vo. 4s. 6d. each Vol. (St. Matthew and St. Mark in One Vol. price 9s.)

**CHRISTIE (J. R.).**—*Elementary Test Questions in Pure and Mixed Mathematics.*
Crown 8vo. 8s. 6d.

*Church Congress (Authorized Report of) held at Wolverhampton in October, 1867.*
8vo. 3s. 6d.

**CHURCH.**—*Sermons preached before the University of Oxford.*
By R. W. CHURCH, M.A. late Fellow of Oriel College, Rector of Whatley. Crown 8vo. 4s. 6d. *Second Edition.*

**CICERO.**—*The Second Philippic Oration.*
With an Introduction and Notes, translated from KARL HALM. Edited, with Corrections and Additions, by JOHN E. B. MAYOR, M.A. *Third Edition.* Fcap. 8vo. 5s.

**CLARK.**—*Four Sermons preached in the Chapel of Trinity College, Cambridge.*
By W. G. CLARK, M.A. Fcap. 8vo. 2s. 6d.

AY.—*The Prison Chaplain.*
A Memoir of the Rev. JOHN CLAY, B.D. late Chaplain of the Preston Gaol. With Selections from his Reports and Correspondence, and a Sketch of Prison Discipline in England. By his Son, the Rev. W. L. CLAY, M.A. 8vo. 15s.

*The Power of the Keys.*
Sermons preached in Coventry. By the Rev. W. L. CLAY, M.A. Fcap. 8vo. 3s. 6d.

*Clemency Franklyn.*
By the author of "Janet's Home." Crown 8vo. 6s.

*Clergyman's Self-Examination concerning the Apostles' Creed.*
Extra fcap. 8vo. 1s. 6d.

**CLOUGH.**—*The Poems of Arthur Hugh Clough,*
sometime Fellow of Oriel College, Oxford. With a Memoir by F. T. PALGRAVE. *Second Edition.* Fcap. 8vo. 6s.

CLOUGH.—*The Poems and Prose Remains of Arthur Hugh Clough.*
Edited by his Wife. With a Selection from his Letters, and a Memoir. 2 vols. Crown 8vo. 21s.

COLENSO.—*Works by the Right Rev. J. W. COLENSO, D.D. Bishop of Natal.*

*The Colony of Natal.*
A Journal of Visitation. With a Map and Illustrations. Fcap. 8vo. 5s.

*Village Sermons.*
Second Edition. Fcap. 8vo. 2s. 6d.

*Companion to the Holy Communion,*
Containing the Service and Select Readings from the writings of Professor MAURICE. *Common paper,* 1s.

*Connells of Castle Connell.*
By JANET GORDON. Two Vols. Crown 8vo. 21s.

COOPER.—*Athenae Cantabrigienses.*
By CHARLES HENRY COOPER, F.S.A. and THOMPSON COOPER, F.S.A. Vol. I. 8vo. 1500—85, 18s. Vol. II. 1586—1609, 18s.

COPE.—*An Introduction to Aristotle's Rhetoric.*
With Analysis, Notes, and Appendices. By E. M. COPE, Senior Fellow and Tutor of Trinity College, Cambridge. 8vo. 14s.

COTTON.—*Works by the late* GEORGE EDWARD LYNCH COTTON, D.D. *Bishop of Calcutta.*

*Sermons and Addresses delivered in Marlborough College during Six Years.*
Crown 8vo. 10s. 6d.

*Sermons, chiefly connected with Public Events of 1854.*
Fcap. 8vo. 3s.

*Sermons preached to English Congregations in India.*
Crown 8vo. 7s. 6d.

*Expository Sermons on the Epistles for the Sundays of the Christian Year.*
Two Vols. Crown 8vo. 15s.

COX.—*Recollections of Oxford.*
By G. V. COX, M.A. late Esquire Bedel and Coroner in the University of Oxford. Crown 8vo. 10s. 6d.

**CURE.**—*The Seven Words of Christ on the Cross.*
Sermons preached at St. George's, Bloomsbury. By the Rev. E. CAPEL CURE, M.A. Fcap. 8vo. 3s. 6d.

**DALTON.**—*Arithmetical Examples progressively arranged; together with Miscellaneous Exercises and Examination Papers.*
By the Rev. T. DALTON, M.A. Assistant Master at Eton College. 18mo. 2s 6d.

**DANTE.**—*Dante's Comedy, The Hell.*
Translated by W. M. ROSSETTI. Fcap. 8vo. cloth. 5s.

**DAVIES.**—*Works by the Rev. J. LLEWELYN DAVIES, M.A. Rector of Christ Church, St. Marylebone, &c.*

*Sermons on the Manifestation of the Son of God.*
With a Preface addressed to Laymen on the present position of the Clergy of the Church of England; and an Appendix, on the Testimony of Scripture and the Church as to the Possibility of Pardon in the Future State. Fcap. 8vo. 6s. 6d.

*The Work of Christ; or, the World Reconciled to God.*
With a Preface on the Atonement Controversy. Fcap. 8vo. 6s.

*Baptism, Confirmation, and the Lord's Supper.*
As interpreted by their outward signs. Three Expository Addresses for Parochial Use. Fcap. 8vo. Limp cloth. 1s. 6d.

*Morality according to the Sacrament of the Lord's Supper.*
Crown 8vo. 3s. 6d.

*The Epistles of St. Paul to the Ephesians, the Colossians, and Philemon.*
With Introductions and Notes, and an Essay on the Traces of Foreign Elements in the Theology of these Epistles. 8vo. 7s. 6d.

*The Gospel and Modern Life.*
Sermons on some of the Difficulties of the Present Day. With a Preface on a Recent Phase of Deism. Extra fcap. 8vo. 6s.

**DAWSON.**—*Acadian Geology, the Geological Structure, Organic Remains, and Mineral Resources of Nova Scotia, New Brunswick, and Prince Edward Island.*
By J. W. DAWSON, LL.D. F.R.S. F.G.S. *Second Edition,* revised and enlarged, with Geological Maps and Illustrations. 8vo. 18s.

DAY.—*Properties of Conic Sections proved Geometrically.*
By the Rev. H. G. DAY, M.A. Head-Master of Sedbergh Grammar School. Crown 8vo. 3*s.* 6*d.*

*Days of Old ; Stories from Old English History.*
By the Author of "Ruth and her Friends." *New Edition,* 18mo. cloth, gilt leaves. 3*s.* 6*d.*

DELAMOTTE.—*A Beginner's Drawing Book.*
By PHILIP H. DELAMOTTE, F.S.A. Professor of Drawing in King's College and School, London. Progressively arranged. With upwards of Fifty Plates. Stiff Covers, crown 8vo. 2*s.* 6*d.*

*Demosthenes, De Corona.*
The Greek Text with English Notes. By B. DRAKE, M.A. *Third Edition,* to which is prefixed ÆSCHINES AGAINST CTESIPHON, with English Notes. Fcap 8vo. 5*s.*

DE TEISSIER.—*Works by* G. F. DE TEISSIER, B.D.
*Village Sermons.*
Crown 8vo. 9*s.*
*Second Series.*
Crown 8vo. 8*s.* 6*d.*
*The House of Prayer; or, a Practical Exposition of the Order for Morning and Evening Prayer in the Church of England.*
18mo. extra cloth. 4*s.* 6*d.*

DE VERE.—*The Infant Bridal, and other Poems.*
By AUBREY DE VERE. Fcap. 8vo. 7*s.* 6*d.*

DILKE.—*Greater Britain.*
A Record of Travel in English-speaking Countries during 1866–7. (America, Australia, India.) By Sir CHARLES WENTWORTH DILKE, M.P. *Fourth and Cheaper Edition.* Crown 8vo. 6*s.*

DODGSON.—*Elementary Treatise on Determinants.*
By C. L. DODGSON, M.A. 4to. 10*s.* 6*d.*

DONALDSON.—*A Critical History of Christian Literature and Doctrine, from the Death of the Apostles to the Nicene Council.*
By JAMES DONALDSON, LL.D. Three Vols. 8vo. cloth. 31*s.*

DOYLE.—*Works by Sir* FRANCIS HASTINGS DOYLE, *Professor of Poetry in the University of Oxford.*
*The Return of the Guards, and other Poems.*
Fcap. 8vo. 7*s.*
*Lectures on Poetry.*
Delivered before the University of Oxford in 1868. Crown 8vo. 3*s.* 6*d.*

DREW.—*Works by* W. H. DREW, M.A.

*A Geometrical Treatise on Conic Sections.*
Fourth Edition.   Crown 8vo.   4s. 6d.

*Solutions to Problems contained in Drew's Treatise on Conic Sections.*
Crown 8vo.   4s. 6d.

DÜRER (ALBRECHT).—*The History of the Life of Albrecht Dürer of Nürnberg, with a Translation of his Letters and Journal, and some Account of his Works.*
By Mrs. CHARLES HEATON.   With Thirty Photographic and Autotype Illustrations.   Royal 8vo. 31s. 6d.

*Early Egyptian History for the Young.*
With Descriptions of the Tombs and Monuments.   *New Edition,* with Frontispiece.   Fcap. 8vo.   5s.

EASTWOOD.—*The Bible Word Book.*
A Glossary of Old English Bible Words.   By J. EASTWOOD, M.A. of St. John's College, and W. ALDIS WRIGHT, M.A. Trinity College, Cambridge.   18mo.   5s. 6d.   Uniform with Macmillan's School Class Books.

*Ecce Homo.*
A Survey of the Life and Work of Jesus Christ.   23d Thousand. Crown 8vo.   6s.

*Echoes of Many Voices from Many Lands.*
By A. F.   18mo. cloth, extra gilt.   3s. 6d.

EDGAR.—*Note Book on Practical Solid Geometry, containing Problems with Help for Solution.*
By J. H. EDGAR, M.A. Lecturer on Mechanical Drawing in the Royal School of Mines, London.   4to.   2s.

ELAM.—*A Physician's Problems.*
By CHARLES ELAM, M.D. M.R.C.P.   Contents : Natural Heritage—On Degenerations in Man—On Moral and Criminal Epidemics—Body v. Mind—Illusions and Hallucinations—On Somnambulism—Reverie and Abstraction.   Crown 8vo.   9s.

ELLICE.—*English Idylls.*
By JANE ELLICE.   Fcap. 8vo. cloth.   6s.

ELLIOTT.—*Life of Henry Venn Elliott, of Brighton.*
By JOSIAH BATEMAN, M.A. Author of "Life of Daniel Wilson, Bishop of Calcutta," &c.   With Portrait, engraved by JEENS. Crown 8vo.   8s. 6d.

ERLE.—*The Law relating to Trade Unions.*
> By Sir WILLIAM ERLE, formerly Chief Justice in the Common Pleas. Crown 8vo. 3s. 6d.

*Essays on Church Policy.*
> Edited by the Rev. W. L. CLAY, M.A. Incumbent of Rainhill, Lancashire. 8vo. 9s.

*Essays on a Liberal Education.*
> By Various Writers. Edited by the Rev. F. W. FARRAR, M.A. F.R.S. &c. *Second Edition.* 8vo. 10s. 6d.

EVANS.—*Brother Fabian's Manuscript, and other Poems.*
> By SEBASTIAN EVANS. Fcap. 8vo. cloth. 6s.

FARRAR.—*The Fall of Man, and other Sermons.*
> By the Rev. F. W. FARRAR, M.A. late Fellow of Trinity College, Cambridge. Fcap, 8vo. 6s.

FAWCETT.—*Works by* HENRY FAWCETT, M.P.

*The Economic Position of the British Labourer.*
> Extra fcap. 8vo. 5s.

*Manual of Political Economy.*
> *Second Edition.* Crown 8vo. 12s.

*Fellowship : Letters addressed to my Sister Mourners.*
> Fcap. 8vo. cloth gilt. 3s. 6d.

FERRERS.—*A Treatise on Trilinear Co-ordinates, the Method of Reciprocal Polars, and the Theory of Projections.*
> By the Rev. N. M. FERRERS, M.A. *Second Edition.* Crown 8vo. 6s. 6d.

FLETCHER.—*Thoughts from a Girl's Life.*
> By LUCY FLETCHER. *Second Edition.* Fcap. 8vo. 4s. 6d.

FORBES.—*Life of Edward Forbes, F.R.S.*
> By GEORGE WILSON, M.D. F.R.S.E., and ARCHIBALD GEIKIE, F.R.S. 8vo. with Portrait. 14s.

FORBES.—*The Voice of God in the Psalms.*
> By GRANVILLE FORBES, Rector of Broughton. Crown 8vo. 6s. 6d.

FOX.—*On the Diagnosis and Treatment of the Varieties of Dyspepsia, considered in Relation to the Pathological Origin of the different Forms of Indigestion.*
> By WILSON FOX, M.D. Lond. F.R.C.P. Holme Professor of Clinical Medicine at University College, London, and Physician to University College Hospital. *Second Edition.* Demy 8vo. 7s. 6d.

Fox.—*On the Artificial Production of Tubercle in the Lower Animals.*
4to. 5s. 6d.

Freeland.—*The Fountain of Youth.*
Translated from the Danish of Frederick Paludan Müller. By Humphrey William Freeland, late M.P. for Chichester. With Illustrations designed by Walter Allen. Crown 8vo. 6s.

Freeman.—*History of Federal Government from the Foundation of the Achaian League to the Disruption of the United States.*
By Edward A. Freeman, M.A. Vol. I. General Introduction. —History of the Greek Federations. 8vo. 21s.

*Old English History for Children.*
With Five Coloured Maps. Extra fcap. 8vo. 6s.

French.—*Shakspeareana Genealogica.*
Part I.—Identification of the Dramatis Personæ in the Historical Plays, from King John to King Henry VIII.: Notes on Characters in Macbeth and Hamlet: Persons and Places belonging to Warwickshire alluded to. Part II.—The Shakspeare and Arden Families and their Connections, with Tables of Descent. By George Russell French. 8vo. 15s.

Frost.—*The First Three Sections of Newton's Principia.*
With Notes and Problems in Illustration of the Subject. By Percival Frost, M.A. *Second Edition.* 8vo. 10s. 6d.

Frost and Wolstenholme.—*A Treatise on Solid Geometry.*
By the Rev. Percival Frost, M.A. and the Rev. J. Wolstenholme, M.A. 8vo. 18s.

*The Sicilian Expedition.*
Being Books VI. and VII. of Thucydides, with Notes. By the Rev. P. Frost, M.A. *New Edition.* Fcap. 8vo. 5s.

Furnivall.—*Le Morte Arthur.*
Edited from the Harleian M.S. 2252, in the British Museum. By F. J. Furnivall, M.A. With Essay by the late Herbert Coleridge. Fcap. 8vo. 7s. 6d.

Galton.—*Works by* Francis Galton, F.R.S.

*Meteorographica, or Methods of Mapping the Weather.*
Illustrated by upwards of 600 Printed Lithographed Diagrams. By Francis Galton, F.R.S. 4to. 9s.

*Hereditary Genius, its Laws and Consequences.*
With numerous illustrative Examples. [In the Press.

**GARNETT.**—*Idylls and Epigrams.*
Chiefly from the Greek Anthology. By RICHARD GARNETT. Fcap. 8vo. 2s. 6d.

**GEIKIE.**—*Works by* ARCHIBALD GEIKIE, F.R.S. *Director of the Geological Survey of Scotland.*

*Story of a Boulder; or, Gleanings by a Field Geologist.*
Illustrated with Woodcuts. Crown 8vo. 5s.

*Scenery of Scotland, viewed in connexion with its Physical Geology.*
With Illustrations and a New Geological Map. Crown 8vo. 10s. 6d.

*Elementary Lessons in Physical Geology.* [In the Press.

**GIFFORD.**—*The Glory of God in Man.*
By E. H. GIFFORD, D.D. Fcap. 8vo. 3s. 6d.

**GLADSTONE.**—*Juventus Mundi: Gods and Men of the Greek Heroic Age.*
With Map of the outer Geography of the Odyssey. By the Right Hon. W. E. GLADSTONE, M.P. Crown 8vo. 10s. 6d.

*Globe Editions ;*

*The Complete Works of William Shakespeare.*
Edited by W. G. CLARK and W. ALDIS WRIGHT. Ninety-first Thousand. Globe 8vo. 3s. 6d.

*Morte DArthur.*
SIR THOMAS MALORY's Book of KING ARTHUR and of his noble KNIGHTS of the ROUND TABLE. The Edition of Caxton, revised for Modern use. With an Introduction by SIR EDWARD STRACHEY, Bart. Globe 8vo. 3s. 6d. *Second Edition.*

*The Poetical Works of Sir Walter Scott.*
With Biographical and Critical Essay by F. T. PALGRAVE.

*The Poetical Works and Letters of Robert Burns.*
Edited, with Life and Glossarial Index, by ALEXANDER SMITH. Globe 8vo. 3s. 6d.

*The Adventures of Robinson Crusoe.*
Edited, from the Original Editions, with Introduction, by HENRY KINGSLEY. Globe 8vo. 3s. 6d.

*Goldsmith's Miscellaneous Works.*
With Biographical Essay by PROF. MASSON. Globe 8vo. 3s. 6d.

*Globe Editions:*

*Alexander Pope's Poetical Works.*
Edited, with Memoir and Notes, by PROFESSOR WARD. Globe
8vo. 3*s.* 6*d.*

*Spenser's Complete Works.*
Edited by R. MORRIS. With Memoir by J. W. HALES, M.A.
Globe 8vo. 3*s.* 6*d.*
Other Standard Works are in the Press.

*Globe Atlas of Europe.*
Uniform in Size with MACMILLAN'S GLOBE SERIES. Containing
Forty-Eight Coloured Maps on the same scale, Plans of London
and Paris, and a Copious Index. Strongly bound in half morocco,
with flexible back, 9*s.*

GODFRAY.—*An Elementary Treatise on the Lunar Theory.*
With a brief Sketch of the Problem up to the time of Newton. By
HUGH GODFRAY, M.A. *Second Edition revised.* Crown 8vo. 5*s.* 6*d.*

*A Treatise on Astronomy, for the Use of Colleges
and Schools.*
By HUGH GODFRAY, M.A. 8vo. 12*s.* 6*d.*

*Golden Treasury Series :*
Uniformly printed in 18mo. with Vignette Titles by Sir NOEL
PATON, T. WOOLNER, W. HOLMAN HUNT, J. E. MILLAIS,
ARTHUR HUGHES, &c. Engraved on Steel by JEENS. Bound
in extra cloth, 4*s.* 6*d.*

*The Golden Treasury of the Best Songs and Lyrical
Poems in the English Language.*
Selected and arranged, with Notes, by FRANCIS TURNER PAL-
GRAVE.

*The Children's Garland from the Best Poets.*
Selected and arranged by COVENTRY PATMORE.

*The Book of Praise.*
From the Best English Hymn Writers. Selected and arranged
by Sir ROUNDELL PALMER. *A New and Enlarged Edition.*

*The Fairy Book: the Best Popular Fairy Stories.*
Selected and rendered anew by the Author of "John Halifax,
Gentleman."

*The Ballad Book.*
A Selection of the choicest British Ballads. Edited by WILLIAM
ALLINGHAM.

*The Jest Book.*
The choicest Anecdotes and Sayings. Selected and arranged by
MARK LEMON.

MULLINGER.—*Cambridge Characteristics in the Seventeenth Century.*
By J. B. MULLINGER, B.A. Crown 8vo. 4s. 6d.

MURPHY.—*Habit and Intelligence, in their connexion with the Laws of Matter and Force.*
A Series of Scientific Essays. By JOSEPH JOHN MURPHY. Two vols. 8vo. 16s.

MYERS.—*St. Paul.*
A Poem. By F. W. H. MYERS. *Second Edition.* Extra fcap. 8vo. 2s. 6d.

MYERS.—*The Puritans.*
A Poem. By ERNEST MYERS. Extra fcap. 8vo. 2s. 6d.

NETTLESHIP.—*Essays on Robert Browning's Poetry.*
By JOHN T. NETTLESHIP. Extra fcap. 8vo. 6s. 6d.

*New Landlord, The.*
Translated from the Hungarian of MAURICE JOKAI by A. J. PATTERSON. Two vols. crown 8vo. 21s.

NOEL.—*Beatrice, and other Poems.*
By the Hon. RODEN NOEL. Fcap. 8vo. 6s.

*Northern Circuit.*
Brief Notes of Travel in Sweden, Finland, and Russia. With a Frontispiece. Crown 8vo. 5s.

NORTON.—*The Lady of La Garaye.*
By the Hon. Mrs. NORTON. With Vignette and Frontispiece. *Sixth Edition.* Fcap. 8vo. 4s. 6d.

O'BRIEN.—*Works by* JAMES THOMAS O'BRIEN, *D.D. Bishop of Ossory.*

*An Attempt to Explain and Establish the Doctrine of Justification by Faith only.*
*Third Edition.* 8vo. 12s.

*Charge delivered at the Visitation in 1863.*
*Second Edition.* 8vo. 2s.

*Old Sir Douglas.*
By the Hon. Mrs. NORTON. *Cheap Edition.* Crown 8vo. 6s.

*Oldbury.*
By MISS A. KEARY, Author of "Janet's Home." Three vols. crown 8vo. £1 11s. 6d.

OLIPHANT.—*Agnes Hopetoun's Schools and Holidays.*
By Mrs. OLIPHANT. Royal 16mo. gilt leaves. 3s. 6d.

OLIVER.—*Lessons in Elementary Botany.*
With nearly 200 Illustrations. By DANIEL OLIVER, F.R.S. F.L.S. 18mo. *Second Edition.* 4s. 6d.

**OPPEN.**—*French Reader,*
> For the Use of Colleges and Schools. By EDWARD A. OPPEN. Fcap. 8vo. 4*s.* 6*d.*

**ORWELL.**—*The Bishop's Walk and the Bishop's Times.*
> Poems on the Days of Archbishop Leighton and the Scottish Covenant. By ORWELL. Fcap. 8vo. 5*s.*

*Our Year.*
> A Child's Book, in Prose and Verse. By the Author of "John Halifax, Gentleman." Illustrated by CLARENCE DOBELL. Royal 16mo. 3*s.* 6*d.*

*Oxford Spectator (The).*
> Reprinted. Extra fcap. 8vo. 3*s.* 6*d.*

**PALGRAVE.**—*History of Normandy and of England.*
> By Sir FRANCIS PALGRAVE. Completing the History to the Death of William Rufus. Vols. I. to IV. 8vo. each 21*s.*

**PALGRAVE.**—*A Narrative of a Year's Journey through Central and Eastern Arabia, 1862-3.*
> By WILLIAM GIFFORD PALGRAVE (late of the Eighth Regiment Bombay N.I.) *Fifth and Cheaper Edition.* With Map, Plans, and Portrait of Author, engraved on Steel by JEENS. Crown 8vo. 7*s.* 6*d.*

**PALGRAVE.**—*Works by* FRANCIS TURNER PALGRAVE, M.A. *late Fellow of Exeter College, Oxford.*

*The Five Days' Entertainments at Wentworth Grange.*
> A Book for Children. With Illustrations by ARTHUR HUGHES, and Engraved Title-page by JEENS. Small 4to. cloth extra. 9*s.*

*The Golden Treasury of the best Songs and Lyrical Poems in the English Language.*
> Selected and arranged, with Notes, by FRANCIS TURNER PALGRAVE. 18mo. cloth extra. 4*s.* 6*d.*

*Essays on Art.*
> Mulready—Dyce—Holman Hunt—Herbert—Poetry, Prose, and Sensationalism in Art—Sculpture in England—The Albert Cross, &c. Extra fcap. 8vo. 6*s.*

*Sonnets and Songs.*
> By WILLIAM SHAKESPEARE. Edited by F. T. PALGRAVE. GEM EDITION. With Vignette Title by JEENS. 3*s.* 6*d.*

*Original Hymns.*
> Second Edition, enlarged. 18mo. 1*s.* 6*d.*

**PALGRAVE.**—*The House of Commons.*
> Illustrations of its History and Practice. Lectures delivered at Reigate, Dec. 1868. By REGINALD F. D. PALGRAVE. With Notes and Index. Crown 8vo. 4*s.* 6*d.*

PALMER.—*The Book of Praise:*
>From the Best English Hymn Writers. Selected and arranged by SIR ROUNDELL PALMER. With Vignette by WOOLNER. 18mo. *4s. 6d. Large Type Edition*, demy 8vo. 10*s. 6d.*

*A Hymnal.*
>Chiefly from the BOOK OF PRAISE. In various sizes.
>A.—In royal 32mo. cloth limp. *6d.*
>B.—Small 18mo. larger type, cloth limp. 1*s.*
>C.—Same Edition, fine paper, cloth. 1*s. 6d.*
>An Edition with Music, Selected, Harmonized, and Composed by JOHN HULLAH. Square 18mo. 3*s. 6d.*

PARKES.—*Australian Views of England.*
>Eleven Letters written during the years 1861 and 1862. By HENRY PARKES, late Colonial Secretary of New South Wales. Crown 8vo. 3*s. 6d.*

PARKINSON.—*Works by* S. PARKINSON, B.D.

*A Treatise on Elementary Mechanics.*
>For the Use of the Junior Classes at the University and the Higher Classes in Schools. With a Collection of Examples. *Fourth Edition, revised.* Crown 8vo. 9*s. 6d.*

*A Treatise on Optics.*
>*Second Edition, revised.* Crown 8vo. 10*s. 6d.*

PATMORE.—*Works by* COVENTRY PATMORE.

*The Angel in the House.*
>Book I. The Betrothal.—Book II. The Espousals.—Book III. Faithful for Ever. With Tamerton Church Tower. Two vols. fcap. 8vo. 12*s.*
>*** A New and Cheap Edition, in one vol. fcap. 8vo. beautifully printed on toned paper, price 2*s. 6d.*

*The Victories of Love.*
>Fcap. 8vo. 4*s. 6d.*

PENROSE.—*On a Method of Predicting by Graphical Construction, Occultations of Stars by the Moon and Solar Eclipses for any given place.*
>Together with more Rigorous Methods for the accurate Calculation of Longitude. By F. C. PENROSE, F.R.A.S. With Charts, Tables, &c. 4to. 12*s.*

*Phantasmagoria and other Poems.*
>By LEWIS CARROLL, Author of "Alice's Adventures in Wonderland." Fcap. 8vo. gilt edges. 6*s.*

PHEAR.—*Elementary Hydrostatics.*
>By J. B. PHEAR, M.A. *Third Edition.* Crown 8vo. 5*s. 6d.*

PHILLIMORE.—*Private Law among the Romans.*
>From the Pandects. By JOHN GEORGE PHILLIMORE, Q.C. 8vo. 16*s.*

*Philology.*

The Journal of Sacred and Classical Philology.  Four Vols. 8vo. 12*s*. 6*d*. each.

The Journal of Philology. New Series. Edited by W. G. CLARK, M.A. JOHN E. B. MAYOR, M.A. and W. ALDIS WRIGHT, M.A. Nos. I. II. and III.  8vo.  4*s*. 6*d*. each.  (Half-yearly.)

PLATO.—*The Republic of Plato.*

Translated into English, with Notes.  By Two Fellows of Trinity College, Cambridge (J. Ll. Davies, M.A. and D. J. Vaughan, M.A.).  With Vignette Portraits of Plato and Socrates engraved by JEENS from an Antique Gem. (Golden Treasury Series) *New Edition*, 18mo. 4*s*. 6*d*.

*Platonic Dialogues, The,*

For English Readers.  By the late W. WHEWELL, D.D. F.R.S. Master of Trinity College, Cambridge.  Vol. I. *Second Edition*, containing *The Socratic Dialogues*, fcap. 8vo. 7*s*. 6*d*. ; Vol. II. containing *The Anti-Sophist Dialogues*, 6*s*. 6*d*. ; Vol. III. containing *The Republic*, 7*s*. 6*d*.

PLAUTUS.—*The Mostellaria.*

With Notes, Prolegomena, and Excursus.  By the late PROFESSOR RAMSAY.  Edited by G. G. RAMSAY, M.A.  8vo. 14*s*.

*Plea for a New English Version of the Scriptures.*

By a Licentiate of the Church of Scotland.  8vo.  6*s*.

POPE.—*The Poetical Works of Alexander Pope.*

Edited, with Notes and Introductory Memoir, by PROFESSOR WARD.  Globe Series.  Globe 8vo.  3*s*. 6*d*.

POTTER.—*A Voice from the Church in Australia :*

Sermons preached in Melbourne.  By the Rev. ROBERT POTTER, M.A.  Extra fcap. 8vo.  4*s*. 6*d*.

POTTS.—*Hints towards Latin Prose Composition.*

By A. W. POTTS, M.A. Head Master of the Fettes School, Edinburgh.  Extra fcap. 8vo.  2*s*. 6*d*.

*Practitioner (The), a Monthly Journal of Therapeutics.*

Edited by FRANCIS E. ANSTIE, M.D. 8vo.  Price 1*s*. 6*d*. Vols. I. and II.  8vo. cloth.  10*s*. 6*d*. each.

PRATT.—*Treatise on Attractions, La Place's Functions, and the Figure of the Earth.*

By J. H. PRATT, M.A. *Third Edition*.  Crown 8vo.  6*s*. 6*d*.

PRESCOTT.—*The Threefold Cord.*

Sermons preached before the University of Cambridge.  By J. E. PRESCOTT, B.D.  Fcap. 8vo. 3*s*. 6*d*.

PRESCOTT.—*Strong Drink and Tobacco Smoke ; the Structure, Growth, and Uses of Malt, Hops, Yeast, and Tobacco.*

By HENRY P. PRESCOTT, F.L.S.  With 167 Original Illustrations, engraved on Steel.  8vo.  7*s*. 6*d*.

**PROCTER.**—*A History of the Book of Common Prayer :*
With a Rationale of its Offices. *Eighth Edition, revised and enlarged.* Crown 8vo. 10s. 6d.

**PROCTER AND MACLEAR.**—*An Elementary Introduction to the Book of Common Prayer.*
*Third Edition,* Re-arranged, and Supplemented by an Explanation of the Morning and Evening Prayer and the Litany. By F. PROCTER, M.A. and G. F. MACLEAR, B.D. 18mo. 2s. 6d.

*Psalms of David chronologically arranged.*
An Amended Version, with Historical Introductions and Explanatory Notes. By FOUR FRIENDS. Crown 8vo. 10s. 6d.

**PUCKLE.**—*An Elementary Treatise on Conic Sections and Algebraic Geometry, with numerous Examples and Hints for their Solution,*
Especially designed for the Use of Beginners. By G. HALE PUCKLE, M.A. Head Master of Windermere College. *Third Edition, enlarged.* Crown 8vo. 7s. 6d.

**PULLEN.**—*The Psalter and Canticles, Pointed for Chanting,*
With Marks of Expression, and a List of Appropriate Chants. By the Rev. HENRY PULLEN, M.A. 8vo. 5s.

**RALEGH.**—*The Life of Sir Walter Ralegh, based upon Contemporary Documents.*
By EDWARD EDWARDS. Together with his LETTERS, now first Collected. With Portrait. Two Vols. 8vo. 32s.

**RAMSAY.**—*The Catechiser's Manual ;*
Or, the Church Catechism Illustrated and Explained, for the Use of Clergymen, Schoolmasters, and Teachers. By ARTHUR RAMSAY, M.A. *Second Edition.* 18mo. 1s. 6d.

**RAWLINSON.**—*Elementary Statics.*
By G. RAWLINSON, M.A. Edited by EDWARD STURGES, M.A. Crown 8vo. 4s. 6d.

*Rays of Sunlight for Dark Days.*
A Book of Selections for the Suffering. With a Preface by C. J. VAUGHAN, D.D. 18mo. *New Edition.* 3s. 6d. Morocco, old style, 7s. 6d.

*Reform.*—*Essays on Reform.*
By the Hon. G. C. BRODRICK, R. H. HUTTON, LORD HOUGHTON, A. V. DICEY, LESLIE STEPHEN, J. B. KINNEAR, B. CRACROFT, C. H. PEARSON, GOLDWIN SMITH, JAMES BRYCE, A. L. RUTSON, and Sir GEO. YOUNG. 8vo. 10s. 6d.

*Questions for a Reformed Parliament.*
By F. H. HILL, GODFREY LUSHINGTON, MEREDITH TOWNSEND, W. L. NEWMAN, C. S. PARKER, J. B. KINNEAR, G. HOOPER, F. HARRISON, Rev. J. E. T. ROGERS, J. M. LUDLOW, and LLOYD JONES. 8vo. 10s. 6d.

REYNOLDS.—*A System of Medicine. Vol. I.*

Edited by J. RUSSELL REYNOLDS, M.D. F.R.C.P. London. PART I. GENERAL DISEASES, or Affections of the Whole System. § I.—Those determined by agents operating from without, such as the exanthemata, malarial diseases, and their allies. § II.—Those determined by conditions existing within the body, such as Gout, Rheumatism, Rickets, &c. PART II. LOCAL DISEASES, or Affections of particular Systems. § I.— Diseases of the Skin. 8vo. 25*s.*

*A System of Medicine. Vol. II.*

PART II. § I.—Diseases of the Nervous System. A. General Nervous Diseases. B. Partial Diseases of the Nervous System. 1. Diseases of the Head. 2. Diseases of the Spinal Column. 3. Diseases of the Nerves. § II.—Diseases of the Digestive System. A. Diseases of the Stomach. 8vo. 25*s.*

*A System of Medicine. Vol III.*                     [In the Press.

REYNOLDS.—*Notes of the Christian Life.*

A Selection of Sermons by HENRY ROBERT REYNOLDS, B.A. President of Cheshunt College, and Fellow of University College, London. Crown 8vo. 7*s.* 6*d.*

REYNOLDS.—*Modern Methods in Elementary Geometry.*

By E. M. REYNOLDS, M.A. Mathematical Master in Clifton College. Crown 8vo. 3*s.* 6*d.*

*Ridicula Rediviva.*

Being old Nursery Rhymes. Illustrated in Colours by J. E. ROGERS. With Illuminated Cover. Imp. 4to. 9*s.*

ROBERTS.—*Discussions on the Gospels.*

By the Rev. ALEXANDER ROBERTS, D.D. *Second Edition, revised and enlarged.* 8vo. 16*s.*

ROBERTSON.—*Pastoral Counsels.*

By the late JOHN ROBERTSON, D.D. of Glasgow Cathedral. New Edition. With Preface by the Author of "Recreations of a Country Parson." Extra fcap. 8vo. 6*s.*

*Robinson Crusoe.*

Edited after the Original Editions, with Introduction, by HENRY KINGSLEY. Globe Series. Globe 8vo. 3*s.* 6*d.*

ROBINSON.—*Diary, Reminiscences, and Correspondence of Henry Crabb Robinson, Barrister at Law, F.S.A.*

Selected and Edited by Dr. T. SADLER. Three vols. 8vo. With Portrait. 36*s.*

ROBY.—*A Latin Grammar for the Higher Classes in Grammar Schools, based on the "Elementary Latin Grammar."*

By H. J. ROBY, M.A.                     [In the Press.

ROBY.—*Story of a Household, and other Poems.*
By MARY K. ROBY. Fcap. 8vo. 5s.

ROGERS.—*Historical Gleanings.*
A Series of Sketches by J. E. THOROLD ROGERS. Contents: Montagu—Walpole—Adam Smith—Cobbett. Crown 8vo. 4s. 6d.

ROMANIS.—*Sermons preached at St. Mary's, Reading.*
By WILLIAM ROMANIS, M.A. *First Series.* Fcap. 8vo. 6s. Also, *Second Series.* 6s.

ROSCOE.—*Works by* PROFESSOR ROSCOE, F.R.S.
*Lessons in Elementary Chemistry, Inorganic and Organic.*
Thirteenth Thousand. 18mo. 4s. 6d.
*The Spectrum Analysis.*
A Series of Lectures delivered in 1868. With Four Appendices. Largely illustrated with Engravings, Maps, and Chromolithographs of the Spectra of the Chemical Elements and Heavenly Bodies. Medium 8vo. Cloth extra, gilt top, 21s.

ROSSETTI.—*Works by* CHRISTINA ROSSETTI.
*Goblin Market, and other Poems.*
With Two Designs by D. G. ROSSETTI. *Second Edition.* Fcap. 8vo. 5s.
*The Prince's Progress, and other Poems.*
With Two Designs by D. G. ROSSETTI. Fcap. 8vo. 6s.

ROSSETTI.—*Works by* WILLIAM MICHAEL ROSSETTI.
*Dante's Comedy, The Hell.*
Translated into Literal Blank Verse. Fcap. 8vo. 5s.
*Fine Art, chiefly Contemporary.*
Crown 8vo. 10s. 6d.

ROUTH.—*Treatise on Dynamics of Rigid Bodies.*
With Numerous Examples. By E. J. ROUTH, M.A. *New Edition.* Crown 8vo. 14s.

ROWSELL.—*Works by* T. J. ROWSELL, M.A.
*The English Universities and the English Poor.*
Sermons preached before the University of Cambridge. Fcap. 8vo. 2s.
*Man's Labour and God's Harvest.*
Sermons preached before the University of Cambridge in Lent, 1861. Fcap. 8vo. 3s.

RUFFINI.—*Vincenzo ; or, Sunken Rocks.*
By JOHN RUFFINI. Three vols. crown 8vo. 31s. 6d.

*Ruth and her Friends.*
A Story for Girls. With a Frontispiece. *Fourth Edition.* Royal 16mo. 3s. 6d.

Scott.—*The Poetical Works of Sir Walter Scott.*
Edited, with Biographical and Critical Memoir, by Francis Turner Palgrave. Globe Series. Globe 8vo. 3s. 6d.

Scott.—*Discourses.*
By A. J. Scott, M.A. late Professor of Logic in Owens College, Manchester. Crown 8vo. 7s. 6d.

*Scouring of the White Horse.*
Or, the Long Vacation Ramble of a London Clerk. By the Author of "Tom Brown's School Days." Illustrated by Doyle. *Eighth Thousand.* Imp. 16mo. 8s. 6d.

Seaton.—*A Hand-Book of Vaccination.*
By Edward C. Seaton, M.D. Medical Inspector to the Privy Council. Extra fcap. 8vo. 8s. 6d.

Selkirk.—*Guide to the Cricket Ground.*
By G. H. Selkirk. With Woodcuts. Extra Fcap. 8vo. 3s. 6d.

Selwyn.—*The Work of Christ in the World.*
By G. A. Selwyn, D.D. Bishop of Lichfield. *Third Edition.* Crown 8vo. 2s.

Shakespeare.—*The Works of William Shakespeare. Cambridge Edition.*
Edited by Wm. George Clark, M.A. and W. Aldis Wright, M.A. Nine Vols. 8vo. cloth. 4l. 14s. 6d.

*Shakespeare. Globe Edition.*
Edited by W. G. Clark and W. A. Wright. *91st Thousand.* Globe 8vo. 3s. 6d.

*Shakespeare's Tempest.*
With Glossarial and Explanatory Notes. By the Rev. J. M. Jephson. 18mo. 1s. 6d.

Shairp.—*Kilmahoe, and other Poems.*
By J. Campbell Shairp. Fcap. 8vo. 5s.

Shirley.—*Elijah; Four University Sermons.*
I. Samaria. II. Carmel. III. Kishon. IV. Horeb. By W. W. Shirley, D.D. Fcap. 8vo. 2s. 6d.

Simpson.—*An Epitome of the History of the Christian Church.*
By William Simpson, M.A. *Fourth Edition.* Fcap. 8vo. 3s. 6d.

Smith.—*Works by* Alexander Smith.
*A Life Drama, and other Poems.*
Fcap. 8vo. 2s. 6d.
*City Poems.*
Fcap. 8vo. 5s.
*Edwin of Deira.*
*Second Edition.* Fcap. 8vo. 5s.

Smith.—*Poems by* Catherine Barnard Smith.
Fcap. 8vo. 5*s*.

Smith.—*Works by* Goldwin Smith.

*A Letter to a Whig Member of the Southern Independence Association.*
Extra fcap. 8vo. 2*s*.

*Three English Statesmen ; Pym, Cromwell, and Pitt.*
A Course of Lectures on the Political History of England.
Extra fcap. 8vo. *New and Cheaper Edition.* 5*s*.

Smith.—*Works by* Barnard Smith, M.A. *Rector of Glaston, Rutland, &c.*

*Arithmetic and Algebra.*
Tenth Edition. Crown 8vo. 10*s*. 6*d*.

*Arithmetic for the Use of Schools.*
Ninth Edition. Crown 8vo. 4*s*. 6*d*.

*A Key to the Arithmetic for Schools.*
Seventh Edition. Crown 8vo. 8*s*. 6*d*.

*Exercises in Arithmetic.*
With Answers. Cr. 8vo. limp cloth, 2*s*. 6*d*. Or sold separately
as follows :—Part I. 1*s*. Part II. 1*s*. Answers, 6*d*.

*School Class Book of Arithmetic.*
18mo. 3*s*. Or sold separately, Parts I. and II. 10*d*. each.
Part III. 1*s*.

*Keys to School Class Book of Arithmetic.*
Complete in One Volume, 18mo. 6*s*. 6*d*. ; or Parts I. II. and III.
2*s*. 6*d*. each.

*Shilling Book of Arithmetic for National and Elementary Schools.*
18mo. cloth. Or separately, Part I. 2*d*. ; II. 3*d*. ; III. 7*d*.

*Answers to the Shilling Book of Arithmetic.*
18mo. 6*d*.

*Key to the Shilling Book of Arithmetic.*
18mo. 4*s*. 6*d*.

*Examination Papers in Arithmetic.*
In Four Parts. 18mo. 1*s*. 6*d*. With Answers, 1*s*. 9*d*.

*Key to Examination Papers in Arithmetic.*
18mo. 4*s*. 6*d*.

Smith.—*Hymns of Christ and the Christian Life.*
By the Rev. Walter C. Smith, M.A. Fcap. 8vo. 6*s*.

SMITH.—*Works by* W. S. SMITH, M.A. *Principal of St. Aidan's College, Birkenhead.*

*Obstacles to Missionary Success among the Heathen.*
The Maitland Prize Essay for 1867. Crown 8vo. 3*s.* 6*d.*

*Christian Faith.*
Sermons preached before the University of Cambridge. Fcap. 8vo. 3*s.* 6*d.*

SMITH.—*Works by* J. H. SMITH, M.A. *Gonville and Caius College, Cambridge.*

*A Treatise on Elementary Statics.*
Second Edition. Royal 8vo. 5*s.* 6*d.*

*A Treatise on Elementary Trigonometry.*
Royal 8vo. 5*s.*

*A Treatise on Elementary Hydrostatics.*
Royal 8vo. 4*s.* 6*d.*

*A Treatise on Elementary Algebra.*
For the use of Colleges and Schools. Crown 8vo. 6*s.* 6*d.*

SNOWBALL.—*The Elements of Plane and Spherical Trigonometry.*
By J. C. SNOWBALL, M.A. *Tenth Edition.* Crown 8vo. 7*s.* 6*d.*

*Social Duties considered with Reference to the Organization of Effort in Works of Benevolence and Public Utility.*
By a MAN OF BUSINESS. Fcap. 8vo. 4*s.* 6*d.*

SPENCER.—*Elements of Qualitative Chemical Analysis.*
By W. H. SPENCER, B.A. 4to. 10*s.* 6*d.*

*Spenser's Complete Works.*
Globe Edition. Edited by R. MORRIS, with Memoir by J. W. HALES. Globe 8vo. 3*s.* 6*d.*

*Spring Songs.*
By a WEST HIGHLANDER. With a Vignette Illustration by GOURLAY STEELE. Fcap. 8vo. 1*s.* 6*d.*

STEPHEN.—*General View of the Criminal Law of England.*
By J. FITZ-JAMES STEPHEN. 8vo. 18*s.*

STEWART AND LOCKYER.—*The Sun.*
By BALFOUR STEWART, F.R.S. and J. NORMAN LOCKYER, F.R.S. [*Preparing.*

STRATFORD DE REDCLIFFE.—*Shadows of the Past, in Verse.*
By VISCOUNT STRATFORD DE REDCLIFFE. Crown 8vo. 10*s.* 6*d.*

STRICKLAND.—*On Cottage Construction and Design.*
>By C. W. STRICKLAND. With Specifications and Plans. 8vo.
7*s*. 6*d*.

*Sunday Library for Household Reading. Illustrated.*
>Monthly Parts, 1*s*. ; Quarterly Vols. 4*s*. Gilt edges, 4*s*. 6*d*.
>Vol. I.—The Pupils of St. John the Divine, by the Author of
"The Heir of Redclyffe."
>Vol. II.—The Hermits, by PROFESSOR KINGSLEY.
>Vol. III.—Seekers after God, by the Rev. F. W. FARRAR.
>Vol. IV.—England's Antiphon, by GEORGE MACDONALD, LL.D.
>Vol. V.—Great Christians of France, St. Louis and Calvin.
By M. GUIZOT.
>Vol. VI.—Christian Singers of Germany, by CATHERINE
WINKWORTH, Translator and Compiler of "Lyra Germanica."
>Vol. VII.—Apostles of Mediæval Europe, by the Rev. G. F.
MACLEAR, B.D.
>Vol. VIII.—Alfred the Great, by THOMAS HUGHES, M.P.
>>[In December.

*Sunday Library for* 1868.
>4 Vols. Limp cloth, red Edges, in ornamental Box. Price 21*s*.

SWAINSON.—*Works by* C. A. SWAINSON, D.D.

*A Handbook to Butler's Analogy.*
>Crown 8vo. 1*s*. 6*d*.

*The Creeds of the Church in their Relations to Holy Scripture and the Conscience of the Christian.*
>8vo. cloth. 9*s*.

*The Authority of the New Testament,*
>And other Lectures, delivered before the University of Cambridge. 8vo. cloth. 12*s*.

TACITUS.—*The History of Tacitus translated into English.*
>By A. J. CHURCH, M.A. and W. J. BRODRIBB, M.A. With a
Map and Notes. 8vo. 10*s*. 6*d*.

*The Agricola and Germany.*
>By the same Translators. With Map and Notes. Fcap. 8vo. 2*s*.6*d*.

*The Agricola and Germania.*
>A Revised Text. With English Notes and Maps. By A. J. CHURCH,
M.A. and W. J. BRODRIBB. Fcap. 8vo. 3*s*. 6*d*.
>The *Agricola* and *Germania* may be had separately, price 2*s*. each.

TAIT AND STEELE.—*A Treatise on Dynamics.*
>With numerous Examples. By P. G. TAIT and W. J. STEELE.
*Second Edition.* Crown 8vo. 10*s*. 6*d*.

TAYLOR.—*Words and Places ;*
Or, Etymological Illustrations of History, Ethnology, and Geography. By the Rev. ISAAC TAYLOR. *Second Edition.* Crown 8vo. 12s. 6d.

TAYLOR.—*The Restoration of Belief.*
*New and Revised Edition.* By ISAAC TAYLOR, Esq. Crown 8vo. 8s. 6d.

TAYLOR (C.).—*Geometrical Conics.*
By C. TAYLOR, B.A. Crown 8vo. 7s. 6d.

TEBAY.—*Elementary Mensuration for Schools,*
With numerous Examples. By SEPTIMUS TEBAY, B.A. Head Master of Queen Elizabeth's Grammar School, Rivington. Extra fcap. 8vo. 3s. 6d.

TEMPLE.—*Sermons preached in the Chapel of Rugby School.*
By F. TEMPLE, D.D. Head Master. *New and Cheaper Edition.* Crown 8vo. 7s. 6d.

THORNTON.—*On Labour; its Wrongful Claims and Rightful Dues, Actual Present and Possible Future.*
By W. T. THORNTON, Author of "A Plea for Peasant Proprietors." 8vo. 14s.

THORPE.—*Diplomatarium Anglicum Ævi Saxonici.*
A Collection of English Charters, from the Reign of King Æthelberht of Kent, A.D. DC.V. to that of William the Conqueror. With a Translation of the Anglo-Saxon. By BENJAMIN THORPE, Member of the Royal Academy of Sciences, Munich. 8vo. cloth. 21s.

THRING.—*Works by* EDWARD THRING, M.A. *Head Master of Uppingham.*

*A Construing Book.*
Fcap. 8vo. 2s. 6d.

*A Latin Gradual.*
A First Latin Construing Book for Beginners. 18mo. 2s. 6d.

*The Elements of Grammar taught in English.*
*Fourth Edition.* 18mo. 2s.

*The Child's Grammar.*
*A New Edition.* 18mo. 1s.

*Sermons delivered at Uppingham School.*
Crown 8vo. 5s.

*School Songs.*
With the Music arranged for Four Voices. Edited by the Rev. EDWARD THRING, M.A. and H. RICCIUS. Small folio. 7s. 6d.

THRING.—*Education and School.*
Second Edition. Crown 8vo. 6s.
*A Manual of Mood Constructions.*
Extra fcap. 8vo. 1s. 6d.

THRUPP.—*Works by the Rev. J. F. THRUPP.*

*The Song of Songs.*
A New Translation, with a Commentary and an Introduction. Crown 8vo. 7s. 6d.

*Introduction to the Study and Use of the Psalms.*
Two Vols. 8vo. 21s.

*Psalms and Hymns for Public Worship.*
Selected and Edited by the Rev. J. F. THRUPP, M.A. 18mo. 2s. Common paper, 1s. 4d.

*The Burden of Human Sin as borne by Christ.*
Three Sermons preached before the University of Cambridge in Lent, 1865. Crown 8vo. 3s. 6d.

THUCYDIDES.—*The Sicilian Expedition :*
Being Books VI. and VII. of Thucydides, with Notes. By the Rev. PERCIVAL FROST, M.A. Fcap. 8vo. 5s.

TOCQUEVILLE.—*Memoir, Letters, and Remains of Alexis de Tocqueville.*
Translated from the French by the Translator of "Napoleon's Correspondence with King Joseph." With numerous Additions. Two vols. Crown 8vo. 21s.

TODD.—*The Books of the Vaudois.*
The Waldensian Manuscripts preserved in the Library of Trinity College, Dublin, with an Appendix by JAMES HENTHORN TODD, D.D. Crown 8vo. cloth. 6s.

TODHUNTER.—*Works by* ISAAC TODHUNTER, M.A. F.R.S.

*Euclid for Colleges and Schools.*
New Edition. 18mo. 3s. 6d.

*Algebra for Beginners.*
With numerous Examples. *New Edition.* 18mo. 2s. 6d.

*Key to Algebra for Beginners.*
Crown 8vo. 6s. 6d.

*Mechanics for Beginners.*
With numerous Examples. 18mo. 4s. 6d.

*Trigonometry for Beginners.*
With numerous Examples. *Second Edition.* 18mo. 2s. 6d.

TODHUNTER.—*Mensuration for Beginners.*
With numerous examples. 18mo. 2*s.* 6*d.*

*A Treatise on the Differential Calculus.*
With numerous Examples. *Fourth Edition.* Crown 8vo. 10*s.* 6*d.*

*A Treatise on the Integral Calculus.*
With numerous Examples. *Third Edition.* Crown 8vo. 10*s.* 6*d.*

*A Treatise on Analytical Statics.*
*Third Edition.* Crown 8vo. 10*s.* 6*d.*

*A Treatise on Conic Sections.*
*Fourth Edition.* Crown 8vo. 7*s.* 6*d.*

*Algebra for the Use of Colleges and Schools.*
*Fourth Edition.* Crown 8vo. 7*s.* 6*d.*

*Plane Trigonometry for Colleges and Schools.*
*Third Edition.* Crown 8vo. 5*s.*

*A Treatise on Spherical Trigonometry for the Use of Colleges and Schools.*
*Second Edition.* Crown 8vo. 4*s.* 6*d.*

*Critical History of the Progress of the Calculus of Variations during the Nineteenth Century.*
8vo. 12*s.*

*Examples of Analytical Geometry of Three Dimensions.*
*Second Edition.* Crown 8vo. 4*s.*

*A Treatise on the Theory of Equations.*
*Second Edition.* Crown 8vo. 7*s.* 6*d.*

*Mathematical Theory of Probability.*
8vo. 18*s.*

*Tom Brown's School Days.*
By an OLD BOY. Fcap. 8vo. 5*s.*
Golden Treasury Edition, 4*s.* 6*d.*
PEOPLE'S EDITION, 2*s.*
Illustrated Edition. By A. HUGHES and SYDNEY HALL. Square. 12*s.*

*Tom Brown at Oxford.*
By the Author of "Tom Brown's School Days." *New Edition.* Crown 8vo. 6*s.*

*Tracts for Priests and People.* (*By various Writers.*)
THE FIRST SERIES, Crown 8vo. 8*s.*
THE SECOND SERIES, Crown 8vo. 8*s.*
The whole Series of Fifteen Tracts may be had separately, price One Shilling each.

**TRENCH.**—*Works by* R. CHENEVIX TRENCH, D.D. *Archbishop of Dublin.*

*Notes on the Parables of Our Lord.*
Tenth Edition. 8vo. 12s.

*Notes on the Miracles of Our Lord.*
Eighth Edition. 8vo. 12s.

*Synonyms of the New Testament.*
New Edition. One vol. 8vo. cloth. 10s. 6d.

*On the Study of Words.*
Thirteenth Edition. Enlarged and Revised. Fcap. 8vo. 4s. 6d.

*English Past and Present.*
Sixth Edition. Enlarged and Revised. Fcap. 8vo. 4s. 6d.

*Proverbs and their Lessons.*
Sixth Edition. Enlarged. Fcap. 8vo. 3s. 6d.

*Select Glossary of English Words used formerly in Senses different from the present.*
Third Edition. Fcap. 8vo. 4s.

*On some Deficiencies in our English Dictionaries.*
Second Edition. 8vo. 3s.

*Sermons preached in Westminster Abbey.*
Second Edition. 8vo. 10s. 6d.

*The Fitness of Holy Scripture for Unfolding the Spiritual Life of Man :*
Christ the Desire of all Nations; or, the Unconscious Prophecies of Heathendom. Hulsean Lectures. Fcap. 8vo. *Fourth Edition.* 5s.

*On the Authorized Version of the New Testament.*
Second Edition. 8vo. 7s.

*Justin Martyr, and other Poems.*
Fifth Edition. Fcap. 8vo. 6s.

*Gustavus Adolphus.—Social Aspects of the Thirty Years' War.*
Fcap. 8vo. 2s. 6d.

*Poems.*
Collected and arranged anew. Fcap. 8vo. 7s. 6d.

*Poems from Eastern Sources, Genoveva and other Poems.*
Second Edition. Fcap. 8vo. 5s. 6d.

*Elegiac Poems.*
Third Edition. Fcap. 8vo. 2s. 6d.

TRENCH (R. CHENEVIX)—*Calderon's Life's a Dream :*
The Great Theatre of the World. With an Essay on his Life and
Genius. Fcap. 8vo. 4*s.* 6*d.*

*Remains of the late Mrs. Richard Trench.*
Being Selections from her Journals, Letters, and other Papers.
*New and Cheaper Issue.* With Portrait. 8vo. 6*s.*

*Commentary on the Epistles to the Seven Churches in Asia.*
*Third Edition, revised.* 8vo. 8*s.* 6*d.*

*Sacred Latin Poetry.*
Chiefly Lyrical. Selected and arranged for Use. *Second Edition*
Corrected and Improved. Fcap. 8vo. 7*s.*

*Studies in the Gospels.*
*Second Edition.* 8vo. 10*s.* 6*d.*

*The Sermon on the Mount.*
An Exposition drawn from the writings of St. Augustine, with
an Essay on his merits as an Interpreter of Holy Scripture
*Third Edition.* Enlarged. 8vo. 10*s.* 6*d.*

*Shipwrecks of Faith :*
Three Sermons preached before the University of Cambridge in
May, 1867. Fcap. 8vo. 2*s.* 6*d.*

*A Household Book of English Poetry.*
Selected and Arranged with Notes. By the ARCHBISHOP OF
DUBLIN. Extra fcap. 8vo. 5*s.* 6*d.*

TRENCH (Rev. FRANCIS).—*Brief Notes on the Greek of
the New Testament (for English Readers).*
Crown 8vo. cloth. 6*s.*

TRENCH (CAPTAIN F.).—*The Russo-Indian Question Histo-
rically, Strategically, and Politically Considered.*
With a Sketch of Central Asiatic Politics. By Captain F.
TRENCH, F.R.G.S. 20th Hussars. With Map. Crown 8vo. 7*s.* 6*d*

TREVELYAN.—*Works by* G. O. TREVELYAN, M.P.

*The Competition Wallah.*
*New Edition.* Crown 8vo. 6*s.*

*Cawnpore,*
Illustrated with Plan. *Second Edition.* Crown 8vo. 6*s.*

TUDOR.—*The Decalogue viewed as the Christian's Law.*
With Special Reference to the Questions and Wants of the Times.
By the Rev. RICH. TUDOR, B.A. Crown 8vo. 10*s.* 6*d.*

TULLOCH.—*The Christ of the Gospels and the Christ of Modern Criticism.*
> Lectures on M. RENAN's "Vie de Jésus." By JOHN TULLOCH, D.D. Principal of the College of St. Mary, in the University of St. Andrew. Extra fcap. 8vo. 4s. 6d.

TURNER.—*Sonnets.*
> By the Rev. CHARLES TENNYSON TURNER. Dedicated to his Brother, the Poet Laureate. Fcap. 8vo. 4s. 6d.

*Small Tableaux.*
> By the Rev. C. TURNER. Fcap. 8vo. 4s. 6d.

*Twelve Parables of Our Lord.*
> Illustrated in Colours from Sketches taken in the East by McENIRY, with Frontispiece from a Picture by JOHN JELLICOE, and Illuminated Texts and Borders. Royal 4to. in Ornamental Binding. 42s.

TYRWHITT.—*The Schooling of Life.*
> By R. ST. JOHN TYRWHITT, M.A. Vicar of St. Mary Magdalen, Oxford. Fcap. 8vo. 3s. 6d.

*Vacation Tourists;*
> And Notes of Travel in 1861. Edited by F. GALTON, F.R.S. With Ten Maps illustrating the Routes. 8vo. 14s.

*Vacation Tourists;*
> And Notes of Travel in 1862 and 1863. Edited by FRANCIS GALTON, F.R.S. 8vo. 16s.

VANDERVELL AND WITHAM.—*A System of Figure Skating.*
> Being the Theory and Practice of the Art as developed in England, with a Glance at its Origin and History. By H. E. VANDERVELL and T. M. WITHAM, Members of the London Skating Club. Extra fcap. 8vo. 6s.

VAUGHAN.—*Works by* CHARLES J. VAUGHAN, D.D. *Master of the Temple.*

*Notes for Lectures on Confirmation.*
> With suitable Prayers. *Seventh Edition.* Fcap. 8vo. 1s. 6d.

*Lectures on the Epistle to the Philippians.*
> *Second Edition.* Crown 8vo. 7s. 6d.

*Lectures on the Revelation of St. John.*
> *Third Edition.* Two vols. [In the Press.

*Epiphany, Lent, and Easter.*
> A Selection of Expository Sermons. *Third Edition.* Crown 8vo. 10s. 6d.

**VAUGHAN (CHARLES J.).—*The Book and the Life*,**
And other Sermons, preached before the University of Cambridge. *New Edition.* Fcap. 8vo. 4*s.* 6*d.*

***Memorials of Harrow Sundays.***
A Selection of Sermons preached in Harrow School Chapel. With a View of the Chapel. *Fourth Edition.* Crown 8vo. 10*s.* 6*d.*

***St. Paul's Epistle to the Romans.***
The Greek Text with English Notes. *New Edition in the Press.*

***Twelve Discourses on Subjects connected with the Liturgy and Worship of the Church of England.***
Fcap. 8vo. 6*s.*

***Lessons of Life and Godliness.***
A Selection of Sermons preached in the Parish Church of Doncaster. *Third Edition.* Fcap. 8vo. 4*s.* 6*d.*

***Words from the Gospels.***
A Second Selection of Sermons preached in the Parish Church of Doncaster. *Second Edition.* Fcap. 8vo. 4*s.* 6*d.*

***The Epistles of St. Paul.***
For English Readers. Part I. containing the First Epistle to the Thessalonians. *Second Edition.* 8vo. 1*s.* 6*d.* Each Epistle will be published separately.

***Lessons of the Cross and Passion.***
Six Lectures delivered in Hereford Cathedral during the Week before Easter 1869. Fcap. 8vo. 2*s.* 6*d.*

***The Church of the First Days.***
Series I. The Church of Jerusalem. *Second Edition.*
   „ II. The Church of the Gentiles. *Second Edition.*
   „ III. The Church of the World. *Second Edition.*
Fcap. 8vo. cloth. 4*s.* 6*d.* each.

***Life's Work and God's Discipline.***
Three Sermons. Fcap. 8vo. cloth. 2*s.* 6*d.*

***The Wholesome Words of Jesus Christ.***
Four Sermons preached before the University of Cambridge in November, 1866. Fcap. 8vo. cloth. 3*s.* 6*d.* *Second Edition.*

***Foes of Faith.***
Sermons preached before the University of Cambridge in November, 1868. Fcap. 8vo. 3*s.* 6*d.*

VAUGHAN.—*Works by* DAVID J. VAUGHAN, M.A. *Vicar of St. Martin's, Leicester.*

*Sermons preached in St. John's Church, Leicester,*
During the Years 1855 and 1856. Crown 8vo. 5*s.* 6*d.*

*Sermons on the Resurrection.*
With a Preface. Fcap. 8vo. 3*s.*

*Three Sermons on the Atonement.*
1*s.* 6*d.*

*Sermons on Sacrifice and Propitiation.*
2*s.* 6*d.*

*Christian Evidences and the Bible.*
*New Edition.* Revised and enlarged. Fcap. 8vo. cloth. 5*s.* 6*d.*

VAUGHAN.—*Memoir of Robert A. Vaughan,*
Author of "Hours with the Mystics." By ROBERT VAUGHAN, D.D. *Second Edition.* Revised and enlarged. Extra fcap. 8vo. 5*s.*

VENN.—*The Logic of Chance.*
An Essay on the Foundations and Province of the Theory of Probability, with special reference to its application to Moral and Social Science. By the Rev. J. VENN, M.A. Fcap. 8vo. 7*s.* 6*d.*

*Village Sermons.*
By a NORTHAMPTONSHIRE RECTOR. With a Preface on the Inspiration of Holy Scripture. Crown 8vo. 6*s.*

*Vittoria Colonna.—Life and Poems.*
By MRS. HENRY ROSCOE. Crown 8vo. 9*s.*

*Volunteer's Scrap Book.*
By the Author of "The Cambridge Scrap Book." Crown 4to. 7*s.* 6*d.*

WAGNER.—*Memoir of the Rev. George Wagner,*
late of St. Stephen's, Brighton. By J. N. SIMPKINSON, M.A. *Third and Cheaper Edition.* 5*s.*

WALLACE.—*The Malay Archipelago: The Land of the Orang Utan and the Bird of Paradise.*
A Narrative of Travel. With Studies of Man and Nature. By ALFRED RUSSEL WALLACE. With Maps and Illustrations. *Second Edition.* Two Vols. crown 8vo. 24*s.*

WARD.—*The House of Austria in the Thirty Years' War.*
Two Lectures. With Illustrative Notes. By A. W. WARD, M.A. Professor of History in Owens College, Manchester. Extra Fcap. 8vo. 2*s.* 6*d.*

WARREN.—*An Essay on Greek Federal Coinage.*
By the Hon. J. LEICESTER WARREN, M.A.   8vo.   2s. 6d.

WEBSTER.—*Works by* AUGUSTA WEBSTER.
*Dramatic Studies.*
Extra fcap. 8vo.   5s.
*A Woman Sold,*
And other Poems.  Crown 8vo. 7s. 6d.
*Prometheus Bound, of Æschylus,*
Literally Translated into English Verse.  Extra fcap. 8vo.  3s. 6d.
*Medea of Euripides,*
Literally Translated into English Verse.  Extra fcap. 8vo.  3s. 6d.

WESTCOTT.—*Works by* BROOKE FOSS WESTCOTT. B.D.
*Canon of Peterborough.*
*A General Survey of the History of the Canon of the New Testament during the First Four Centuries.*
*Third Edition, revised.*                          [In the Press.
*Characteristics of the Gospel Miracles.*
Sermons preached before the University of Cambridge.  *With Notes.*  Crown 8vo.  4s. 6d.
*Introduction to the Study of the Four Gospels.*
*Third Edition.*  Crown 8vo.  10s. 6d.
*The Gospel of the Resurrection.*
Thoughts on its Relation to Reason and History.  *New Edition.*  Fcap. 8vo.  4s. 6d.
*The Bible in the Church.*
A Popular Account of the Collection and Reception of the Holy Scriptures in the Christian Churches.  *Second Edition.*  18mo.  4s. 6d.
*A General View of the History of the English Bible.*
Crown 8vo.  10s. 6d.
*The Christian Life, Manifold and One.*
Six Sermons preached in Peterborough Cathedral.  Crown 8vo.  2s. 6d.

*Westminster Plays.*
Lusus Alteri Westmonasterienses, Sive Prologi et Epilogi ad Fabulas in Sti Petri Collegio : actas qui Exstabant collecti et justa quoad licuit annorum serie ordinati, quibus accedit Declamationum quæ vocantur et Epigrammatum Delectus.  Curantibus J. MURE, A.M., H. BULL, A.M., C. B. SCOTT, B.D. 8vo.  12s. 6d.
IDEM.—Pars Secunda, 1820—1865.  Quibus accedit Epigrammatum Delectus.  8vo.  15s.

WILKINS.—*The Light of the World.*
>An Essay by A. S. WILKINS, M.A. Professor of Latin in Owens College, Manchester. Crown 8vo. 3*s.* 6*d.*

WILSON.—*Works by* GEORGE WILSON, M.D.
>*Counsels of an Invalid.*
>>Letters on Religious Subjects. With Vignette Portrait. Fcap. 8vo. 4*s.* 6*d.*

>*Religio Chemici.*
>>With a Vignette beautifully engraved after a Design by Sir NOEL PATON. Crown 8vo. 8*s.* 6*d.*

WILSON (GEORGE).—*The Five Gateways of Knowledge.*
>New Edition. Fcap. 8vo. 2*s.* 6*d.* Or in Paper Covers, 1*s.*

>*The Progress of the Telegraph.*
>>Fcap. 8vo. 1*s.*

WILSON.—*An English, Hebrew, and Chaldee Lexicon and Concordance.*
>By WILLIAM WILSON, D.D. Canon of Winchester. *Second Edition.* 4to. 25*s.*

WILSON.—*Memoir of George Wilson, M.D. F.R.S.E.*
>Regius Professor of Technology in the University of Edinburgh. By HIS SISTER. *New Edition.* Crown 8vo. 6*s.*

WILSON.—*A Treatise on Dynamics.*
>By W. P. WILSON, M.A. 8vo. 9*s.* 6*d.*

WILSON.—*Works by* DANIEL WILSON, LL.D.
>*Prehistoric Annals of Scotland.*
>>New Edition. With numerous Illustrations. Two Vols. demy 8vo. 36*s.*

>*Prehistoric Man.*
>>New Edition. Revised and partly re-written, with numerous Illustrations. One vol. 8vo. 21*s.*

WILSON.—*Elementary Geometry.*
>Angles, Parallels, Triangles, Equivalent Figures, the Circle, and Proportion. By J. M. WILSON, M.A. Fellow of St. John's College, Cambridge, and Mathematical Master at Rugby. *Second Edition.* Extra fcap. 8vo. 3*s.* 6*d.*
>PART II.—The Circle and Proportion. Extra fcap. 8vo. 2*s.* 6*d.*

WINSLOW.—*Force and Nature. Attraction and Repulsion.*
>The Radical Principles of Energy graphically discussed in their Relations to Physical and Morphological Development. By C. F. WINSLOW, M.D. 8vo. 14*s.*

WOLLASTON.—*Lyra Devoniensis.*
> By T. V. WOLLASTON, M.A. Fcap. 8vo. 3s. 6d.

WOLSELEY.—*The Soldier's Pocket Book for Field Service.*
> By Colonel G. J. WOLSELEY, Deputy Quartermaster-General in Canada. 16mo. roan. 5s.

WOLSTENHOLME.—*A Book of Mathematical Problems.*
> Crown 8vo. 8s. 6d.

*Woman's Culture and Woman's Work.*
> A Series of Essays, by FRANCES POWER COBBE, C. PEARSON, JESSIE BOUCHERETT, SOPHIA JEX-BLAKE, Rev. G. BUTLER, ELIZABETH WOLSTENHOLME, JAMES STUART, M.A. *Fellow of Trinity College, Cambridge,* HERBERT MOZLEY, *Barrister-at-Law,* J. BOYD-KINNEAR, *Barrister-at-Law,* and JULIA WEDGWOOD. Edited by JOSEPHINE E. BUTLER. 8vo. 10s. 6d.

WOODFORD.—*Christian Sanctity.*
> By JAMES RUSSELL WOODFORD, M.A. Fcap. 8vo. cloth. 3s.

WOODWARD.—*Works by the Rev.* HENRY WOODWARD, *edited by his Son,* THOMAS WOODWARD, *M.A. Dean of Down.*

*Essays, Thoughts and Reflections, and Letters.*
> *Fifth Edition.* Crown 8vo. 10s. 6d.

*The Shunammite.*
> *Second Edition.* Crown 8vo. 10s. 6d.

*Sermons.*
> *Fifth Edition.* Crown 8vo. 10s. 6d.

WOOLLEY.—*Lectures delivered in Australia.*
> By the late JOHN WOOLLEY, D.C.L. Crown 8vo. 8s. 6d.

WOOLNER.—*My Beautiful Lady.*
> By THOMAS WOOLNER. With a Vignette by ARTHUR HUGHES. *Third Edition.* Fcap. 8vo. 5s.

*Words from the Poets.*
> Selected by the Editor of " Rays of Sunlight." With a Vignette and Frontispiece. 18mo. Extra cloth gilt. 2s. 6d. *Cheaper Edition,* 18mo. limp. 1s.

*Worship (The) of God and Fellowship among Men.*
> Sermons on Public Worship. By PROFESSOR MAURICE, and Others. Fcap. 8vo. 3s. 6d.

WORSLEY.—*Christian Drift of Cambridge Work.*
> Eight Lectures. By T. WORSLEY, D.D. Master of Downing College, Cambridge. Crown 8vo. cloth. 6s.

**WRIGHT.**—*Works by* J. WRIGHT, M.A.

*Hellenica;*
Or, a History of Greece in Greek, as related by Diodorus and Thucydides, being a First Greek Reading Book, with Explanatory Notes Critical and Historical. *Third Edition,* WITH A VOCABULARY. 12mo. 3*s.* 6*d.*

*The Seven Kings of Rome.*
An Easy Narrative, abridged from the First Book of Livy by the omission of difficult passages, being a First Latin Reading Book, with Grammatical Notes. Fcap. 8vo. 3*s.*

*A Vocabulary and Exercises on the " Seven Kings of Rome."*
Fcap. 8vo. 2*s.* 6*d.*

*** The Vocabulary and Exercises may also be had bound up with "The Seven Kings of Rome." Price 5*s.*

*A Help to Latin Grammar;*
Or, the Form and Use of Words in Latin, with Progressive Exercises. Crown 8vo. 4*s.* 6*d.*

*David, King of Israel.*
Readings for the Young. With Six Illustrations. Royal 16mo. cloth, gilt. 3*s.* 6*d.*

**WURTZ.**—*A History of Chemical Theory from the Age of Lavoisier down to the present Time.*
Translated by HENRY WATTS, F.R.S. Crown 8vo. 6*s.*

**YOUMANS.**—*Modern Culture,*
Its True Aims and Requirements. A Series of Addresses and Arguments on the Claims of Scientific Education. Edited by EDWARD L. YOUMANS, M.D. Crown 8vo. 8*s.* 6*d.*